An Honest Man

Also by Ben Fergusson

The Spring of Kasper Meier
The Other Hoffmann Sister

BEN FERGUSSON

An Honest Man

Little, Brown

LITTLE, BROWN

First published in Great Britain in 2019 by Little, Brown

3 5 7 9 10 8 6 4 2

A CIP catalogue record for this book
is available from the British Library.

HB ISBN 978-1-4087-0892-7
C format 978-1-4087-0893-4

Typeset in Caslon by M Rules
Printed and bound in Great Britain by
Clays Ltd, Elcograf S.p.A

Papers used by Little, Brown are from well-managed forests
and other responsible sources.

Little, Brown
An imprint of
Little, Brown Book Group
Carmelite House
50 Victoria Embankment
London EC4Y 0DZ

An Hachette UK Company
www.hachette.co.uk

www.littlebrown.co.uk

For Mum, Dad, Sam and Katie-Jane

The Athenians watched askance as Diogenes wandered about the city in broad daylight with a lit lamp in his hand. When he was asked by the gawping crowd what he was doing, he replied, 'Why, I am looking for an honest man.'

One

When I was still a geology student it terrified me, shucking open a chunk of mud-black shale to find a single fossilised ginkgo leaf. It was the idea of it falling onto the soft silt of a Pangaean river, sinking, compacting and finding its way into my hands 270 million years later. All that time compressed in hot darkness – it made me claustrophobic. But now it consoles me. When I have to listen to someone clipping their nails on the U-Bahn or watch shouting demagogues on TV dressed in ill-fitting suits, I think of molten rock, ice and pressure, that our short time on earth will go the way of the ginkgo leaf – a few flat impressions in a split black rock.

The Berlin Wall too is a trace now, a faint line of cobbles at Potsdamer Platz, a toothy wall of rusted rebars along Bernauer Straße marking the brief division, one of any number of divisions in the city and, viewed from a distance, the least important. For centuries the river was the deadly barrier, when the first Berliners and their cattle were sporadically swept from the shallow ford after a hard winter and a warm spring brought torrents heaving down the valley from the Lusatian Highlands.

From the geologist's point of view, the greatest division is the oldest and most enduring: the great glacial valley that

Berlin fills, a valley carved out, not by the glacier itself, but by the meltwater that poured from it as it retreated north. In life as it is lived, though, perspective is lost to us. Most Berliners feel the valley's sides only unconsciously when they haven't turned the pedals of their Dutch bikes for a few minutes, descending from Prenzlauer Berg, Schöneberg or Kreuzberg – mountains all – into the valley bottom below.

Even in that final summer of 1989, when West Berlin was still the lopsided half-city of my childhood and the Wall still a 155-kilometre physical reality, it was only a trace to me. I sometimes caught sight of its graffitied face lurking at the end of a street like a fugitive, but it was no more striking than the shoes and handbags in glass vitrines on Kurfürstendamm; the punks at Kotbusser Tor asleep on benches, stinking of leather and vodka; the scrubbed concrete buildings of Ernst-Reuter-Platz topped with endless luminous letters – AEG, Osram, Leiser, Telefunken, Scharlachberg – and the circular signs of Bayer and Mercedes turning incessantly, like coins spun on their edges.

I remember clearly the dense heat of the dining hall at the Berlin British School where I did my A-level exams, my grey polyester trousers damp and pinching. I remember the packet of Polos peeled open on the graffitied ply of the exam desk, and the smell of the school hall: plimsolls, Dettol and savoury mince. I remember waiting in the underpass by Berlin Zoo Station by a Beate Uhse sex shop, avoiding the glances of prostitutes and tramps while my friend Stefan earnestly bought his first pornographic VHS tape (which he later binned in a pique of feminist solidarity). I remember the tallies with the Wildlife Trust, the silver fish skin of the goggle-eyed sunbleaks that my friends and I counted in red buckets at Riemeisterfenn, the grey herons we counted at Grunewaldsee and the bog rosemary we counted at Hundekehlefenn, crushing the pink bulbs between our pink fingers as the morning sun bleached the alders and turned the silver bark of the birches the pinky orange of melon flesh.

And I remember Prinzenbad public baths, three huge outdoor pools and two meadows in the centre of Kreuzberg, a sparkling mass of white and red tile, blue water and pale bodies in bright spandex, where I met Oz and where the last traces of my childhood were washed away.

Two

As he swam past, Stefan's bone-white arm lifted out of the water, revealing his face, goggled, shaved, his air-blowing lips a soft pink ring. I was sitting with Petra and my girlfriend Maike by the low tiled wall that ran the pool's 50-metre length, draped with colourful towels drying in the sun. I could hear the tinny sound of The Motels coming from a cassette I'd made Maike. Through the Walkman's plastic window, I could see 'New Songs for M' written in Tippex next to a lumpen blob, an ugly attempt at a flower that I'd obliterated because it'd looked childish.

Maike stared down at a school copy of *The Count of Monte Cristo* striated with another student's pencilled underlinings. She took so much pleasure in reading that her only prerequisite for a book was that it be long; if it was less than five hundred pages she wasn't interested. So she consumed Stephen King and Rosamunde Pilcher as voraciously as she did Victor Hugo, Thomas Mann and Günter Grass. She squinted against the sun, her height visible in the folded leg that she clung to like a rock, her chin resting on her knee. Her damp hair, long, brown and unfashionably straight, hung around her shoulders, the tips adorned with water droplets like glass beads.

Petra lay on her front with her bikini top undone. Her ashy bob was tied into a ponytail and was dry, because she never swam at the pool – she just tanned. She wore large white-framed sunglasses and flicked through *Brigitte*, snorting derisively at the fashion spreads. It was always hard to tell if this glibness of hers was genuine. It certainly didn't square with her academic successes; although Maike was always the cleverest, it was Petra who worked the hardest. She'd got the second-best *Abitur* grades – German A levels – in her school, and the Head of Biology at the University of Hohenheim had called her personally when he received her application.

'Listen to this,' Petra said, slapping my leg, as she began to read out my horoscope. Stefan passed again. The lifeguard blew his whistle at the rippling shadow of two boys who'd bombed into the water, and I saw a man emerging from the pool, water pouring from his brown back and red trunks.

The man rubbed his face and turned, and the water falling from his body shattered and steamed on the terra-cotta tiles. The trees behind him retained the bright green of early summer and his face, as he slicked back his black hair, was fixed in an expression of doubtful, open-mouthed concentration.

He was hairier than me, an attractive flurry across his chest and on his stomach, in his armpits as he lifted his arms to squeeze the water from his hair. A gold chain, very fine, shimmered like fish scales near his throat, and on his wrist he wore a digital watch, gold too, the link-strap brilliant with sunshine. His fingers parted and I looked down at the novel between my legs, white as tripe, and the amber hairs peeping out from the ancient elastic of my black trunks.

I knew him, or at least I'd seen him before, parked on our street, near the corner of Schiller Straße. He was there on

5

the last day I cycled to school, sitting in a 1970s moss-green Mercedes 240D. One wrist rested on the black plastic steering wheel, the hand limp like Michelangelo's Adam, with a cigarette between index and middle finger. The other hand was at his mouth, the nail of his middle finger touching the gap between his front teeth.

I might've forgotten about him, had he not still been there when I cycled home. His window was rolled down; I picked up a trace of cigarette smoke and tinny jazz music. And though I was cycling too fast to see what he was reading, I could tell from the pastel-coloured cloth that it was a hardback book without its dust jacket.

He reappeared once or twice a week, but he never noticed me; though the colour of the books changed, he never once looked up from them when I cycled past. When I saw him at the edge of the pool, though, our eyes met.

Perhaps the familiarity of Prinzenbad and my friends meant that I seemed in that moment completely comfortable with myself, and perhaps the novel between my legs made me look more adult and worldly than I felt. Because there were plenty of clues to my unworldliness. He might have noticed the biscuit-brown towel I sat on, stiff from a thousand washes, or my name in red thread on a white fabric label that had come loose on one side. He might have noticed that the book, a battered copy of *Midnight's Children*, still with its plastic cover and yellow Dewey Decimal sticker, had been stolen from the school library. He might have noticed my hand-sewn towelling swimming bag, with the face of Fungus the Bogeyman sewn onto it.

I looked back down at the book, embarrassed we'd made eye contact, sweat breaking out across my back as his wet feet slapped towards me on the red tiles. I read the same line over and over again, staring at the yellowed pages warped by my damp hands. When his shadow blotted out the sun for a moment, I turned back a page, as if looking for something, and I inhaled very gently, trying to catch the smell of him, but I only got the chlorine on my body, in the pool, everywhere.

I put my back on the cool tile of the low wall and watched his figure recede as he made his way to the changing rooms. I felt anxious and inexplicably nostalgic, as if I was missing a feeling that I'd never felt.

'Well?' said Petra, staring back at me.

'What?' I said.

'You weren't even listening, were you?'

'I was. You said Venus is in ascendance. And in August I need to be brave about my career,' I said, repeating the last thing she'd read out from my horoscope.

'You need to be brave about reading that here with all these Turks,' Petra said, nodding at my book. 'That's what you need to be brave about.'

'Why?'

'Iran. Khomeini. Fatwa. Salman Rushdie.'

'Have you had a stroke?'

'The writer,' said Petra, sitting up and tying her bikini top back on, briefly flashing the soft sides of her breasts, tanned to caramel and sparkling with sweat.

I looked at the name on the cover. I hadn't yet got a taste for the news; it still felt like something people's parents were interested in, and there was no internet yet to flash a constant stream of breaking stories. Back then, if you didn't read a newspaper or watch the evening news, you remained blissfully clueless about the world beyond your apartment. 'Is he dead?' I said.

7

'He's not dead. They're just trying to kill him, because it's offensive to Islam.'

'This?' I said, holding up the book.

'No.' Petra frowned. 'What's that banned Salman Rushdie book?' she asked Maike, pulling off the headphones of her Walkman, so that they fell onto her bare legs with a tinny clatter.

'Hey!' Maike said.

'What's that Salman Rushdie book that's banned?' Petra said again.

'I don't know. Didn't Khomeini just die? Isn't he off the hook?'

'*Satanic Verses*,' said Stefan, out of the pool, towelling himself down efficiently. Stefan's skin was also pale, but his forearms and calves showed the tan lines of his T-shirt and shorts, the colour ending abruptly on his thighs and upper arms, like long brown socks and evening gloves.

'Shift over,' he said to Maike. She lay down next to me and put a cool hand on my sun-hot leg.

Stefan lay down too and put his arm over his eyes, revealing a sprig of armpit hair, so black it was almost blue. I became very aware of the physicality of my friends and my sweating body in between.

Maike took a damp strand of her hair and absently brushed it across her chin like a paintbrush. Though old friends, she and I had only been dating for a year, losing our mutual virginities early in the morning in a tent on the North Sea coast, the olive air filled with the smell of waxed canvas, unwashed hair and seawater. Although I'd applied to English universities, we'd already worked out a schedule for our continuing relationship and liked to pick out places we might live after graduation on the world map taped to the back of my bedroom door.

There is a picture of the two of us that I have on the shelf in my office at university. It's fun, because my more perceptive students spot who it is; the first years have to read her book *Wetlands: Sustainability, Construction and Structural Change* in 'Introduction to Physical Geography'. In the picture, which has that grainy softness so instantly nostalgic in the digital age, Maike and I are in Grunewald sitting on a fallen tree trunk and we're both smiling with our eyes closed. Petra must have taken it, because I'm holding Katja, her sheepdog, on a lead. I'm wearing a large black T-shirt with an Adidas logo, white shorts, white socks and trainers, my auburn hair cut relatively short, but unstyled, a puffed, unselfconscious cap. Maike is wearing walking boots, jean shorts high on her waist and a white T-shirt with pale pink stripes. Her long hair pours off her shoulders in smooth brown strips like a river delta.

I remember liking my T-shirt and being aware that Adidas was an acceptable brand to be wearing, but I had no idea how these things made me look. Except for Petra, we all dressed carelessly, spending the money from our weekend and holiday jobs on four-season sleeping bags, microscopes, bright waterproofs and cards for the state library.

This is the last photograph I have of myself in which I look like this. After Oz, my poses close up, as if I'm trying to cover myself. I find it hard to find any photo of me up until my wedding day in which my arms are not crossed, my hand is not holding my throat or covering my mouth as if I'm trying to stop myself speaking.

It's the same for Maike. That summer changed her too, and in every other picture I have of her – including the striking author photo on the back of *Wetlands* – she has flicked her long hair to the right shoulder, tipped her head, removed

9

her glasses. I miss the artless, eyes-closed grin of the girl on the log.

'I read *Satanic Verses*,' Stefan said. 'It's really weird.' Stefan had little interest in literature, but a lot of interest in politics – he was a vegetarian and a member of The Greens. The only books he read were either notoriously difficult – *The Magic Mountain, Thus Spoke Zarathustra* – or, like *The Satanic Verses* and his favourite book, *Laughter in the Dark*, in some way connected to scandal.

'This is quite weird,' I said, lifting up the book.

'Suits you, Ralfi,' he said and yawned.

The boys that had bombed into the pool ran past us spraying our hot skin with water. Petra sat up and shouted, 'You vicious little cunts.' The boys froze and bowed their heads sorrowfully; the younger burst into tears. 'Oh fuck,' Petra muttered, when the swimmers who were lined up against the wall turned to us. 'I didn't think they'd care.'

We laughed to protect her from outside scorn. And this might have been my lasting memory of summer 1989. Even that moment I might have forgotten, recalling only my A levels and the Wall if people asked what that year had meant to me. But of course, in the end, 1989 meant neither of those things. It just meant Oz, and espionage – how grand that word sounds now – and I suppose my family and the terrible things we did.

Three

We queued for chips and Coke before we showered, the ceiling of the tiled pool café filled with bright inflatable animals and floats, the counter lined with bread-roll halves beneath scrambled egg, sliced egg, ham and salami, a soggy pretzel letter on each. We drank and smoked in our swimming things, our bare backs sticking to the white plastic chairs, picking unhurriedly at the chips covered in both ketchup and mayonnaise – *Pommes rot-weiß*. We were in no rush, we had nowhere to go. We'd all finished school four weeks earlier and were enjoying the impossibly long summer before university, blissfully ignorant of what our studies would involve and how they would change us.

Stefan, Petra and Maike had gone to school together and Stefan was the son of my mother's best friend, Beate, and had thus been my assigned playmate since birth. As a group, our friendship had been cemented in North Hessen when we were eleven and twelve at *Wilde Kidz*, a camp for city children with a passion for nature. You might think that city kids who were into wildlife would be an accepting cast of misfits, but it was a fortnight riven with regional antagonism. It became clear that the children from Munich and Stuttgart weren't estranged from nature at all, and spent their weekends

11

climbing mountains and plucking ticks from their legs in the Black Forest. The children from Frankfurt and the Ruhr had learned to light fires with sticks in the Taunus and the kids from Bremen and Hamburg could sail.

In West Berlin's 480 square kilometres, bounded in concrete and barbed wire, the natural habitats we roamed amounted to a few small woods, some overgrown train tracks and a bog or two, a fact made clear to the other children when, in the wooded depths of the Reinhardswald, Maike asked the trek leader when we would reach the next toilet. From then on, we were ridiculed, even when Stefan corrected one of the guides, who mixed up a medlar with a crab apple. When the guide acquiesced, one of the Bavarians shouted, 'He read it in a book. He read it in a book in the library,' and the other children collapsed into laughter, as if they had imbibed all of their knowledge from the wilderness direct.

Backed into a corner, we responded in the only way we could, becoming ostentatiously condescending. Petra led the charge, pretending not to understand the Southerners and making an overweight boy from Bochum cry when she told him he smelt of poverty. Lagging behind the others, we talked for a fortnight, shared our homesickness and agreed to meet up the first weekend back to collect owl pellets in Grunewald, the forest that fills Berlin's western edge. I think we were all surprised when we all turned up.

We joined the West Berlin Wildlife Trust, knowing it would be good for future university applications – we were right – and together began what for all of us would be a life-long pursuit: counting and measuring creatures, plants and land formations. At the lakes, we counted snails, frogs, toads, diving beetles and reeds; we sat outside ruined buildings in the dusk pressing our click counters as silhouettes of bats beat out and later beat back in; we marked out sections of rare dry grass with meter sticks and counted butterfly eggs, as grasshoppers sprang to safety, like flicked rubber bands. We loved it; it made us feel useful and grown up. Though we never talked about our shared passion abstractly, it quickly became a given.

Stefan, Maike and Petra were all a year older than me. I'd been sent to the British School run by the Army in Charlottenburg, taking A levels at eighteen while they were taking their *Abitur* at nineteen. Because my English mother worked as a psychologist and was married to my German father, we were one of the few British families that stayed in the city. Although they lived in different corners of Berlin, Stefan, Petra and Maike all came from Catholic families – a relative rarity in part-Protestant, mostly heathen Berlin – and so all attended the Catholic school in a Fifties building on Winterfeldtplatz. I had always been jealous of them, palling around together while I was stuck with another classroom of friendly British children whose approaches I rejected, embittered by years of desertions.

The final straw was a boy called Jonathan, who had arrived at the British School when we were both eight and stayed for three years. He had buck teeth, laughed at my jokes and was very badly behaved. We rode around town on buses – free with our British IDs – shoplifting from distant corners of the city and breaking windows in abandoned buildings. Once we threw stones over the wall at Spandau Prison in the hope of hitting Rudolf Hess, then still clinging on to life, and were chased off by the prison guards.

Jonathan's mother was a Queen Alexandra Nurse and very patriotic, and in the few years we were friends I went with him to the Queen's Birthday Parade at the Olympic Stadium.

Once a month, his mother drove us through Checkpoint Charlie to East Berlin to buy Meissen pottery from Unter den Linden and Russian dolls from Natasha's on Karl-Marx-Straße, then took us to a restaurant to eat cheap pink meat in breadcrumbs with tinned runner beans. Because my mum's cooking was so bad, I was as delighted by these bland, salty meals as I was by the food Jonathan's mum let us order from the FRIS book, a catalogue of goods kept in British military foodstores that military families were allowed to order at cut-rate prices. Like Christmas stockings, Jonathan's mum laid out the steel FRIS box and by the afternoon it had been filled with luxuries that had eluded me until then: sliced white bread, digestive biscuits, orange squash.

But after one Christmas holiday Jonathan didn't come back to school. His parents had been posted to Sardinia and I was heartbroken. When Stefan and Beate came over for dinner that Friday Stefan told me about *Wilde Kidz* and I begged Mum to let me go. And the moment I'd formed a permanent group of German friends I clung onto them.

I didn't just idolise them because they were older than me. Stefan was socially engaged, Maike was clever, Petra was sharp-tongued and powerfully gave the impression that she didn't give a fuck what anybody thought about her. I always felt like a pigeon that had found its way into an aviary of exotics. Stefan's thin, hairless body and mop of curling locks made him look like an Italian, as did his thick black eyebrows that met in the middle; Petra had fine, sharp features and big breasts; Maike was statuesque, with long Bill Brandt legs and a nose as straight as a Greek sculpture's.

The walking, cycling, swimming and camping we did meant I was fit enough, I wasn't too short or too tall. My hair though had been carrot-red as a child, and this had led to teasing at the British School. Nothing severe but, being half German, it added to my sense of otherness.

My hair had darkened almost to brown, its redness only revealed in direct sunlight, in the freckles that covered my face and shoulders, the pale pink of my nipples and the russet hair on my legs and arms. Nevertheless, the vague sense that gingerness was akin to ugliness, that it moved me into the category of Kevin Cuddon, the boy with a purple birthmark on his face, and Nicola Dean, who had alopecia totalis and an NHS wig, meant that, in my circle of German friends, I felt grateful for their friendship and for Maike's love.

I opened a second Coke. Behind Stefan, an overweight couple were filling in a crossword, half-shaded by an orange-and-blue Fanta umbrella. The man's miniature trunks and the woman's bikini were the same shade of turquoise, the elastic cutting into skin the colour of coffee, wrinkled and shiny like used cling film.

Behind them, I thought I saw the red swimming trunks of the man from the traffic lights, but the red cloth resolved into a white-spotted neckerchief tied Madonna-like around someone's platinum-blonde hair.

'Anyone want to watch a film at mine?' Stefan said, tossing a Pez from a Garfield-headed dispenser into the air and catching it between his teeth.

'How depressing is it on a scale of one to ten?' Petra asked. 'Ten is every other film you've made us watch.'

'Don't be a twat,' said Stefan, crunching on the Pez and straightening his baseball cap, from under which his curling black hair bloomed up like smoke beneath a door.

'What is it then?' I said.

'I got a pirate copy of *Ugetsu*. It's this very cool Japanese film.'

'Is it black-and-white?' I asked.

15

'Yeah, but it's—'

We all drowned him out with our groans. Like his reading, Stefan's film consumption was fully improving. He was a collector of difficult movies, attracted to anything that had been judged important. Through various dusty out-of-the-way shops and underground film clubs, he managed to get hold of the most obscure titles, introducing us to Satyajit Ray, Jean Renoir and Yasujirō Ozu. He was the only person I knew who'd watched the whole nine hours of *Shoah*. His preference was for anything old, black-and-white and subtitled – a rarity in Germany, where most foreign films are dubbed, a practice, of course, that disgusted him.

'It's Kenji Mizoguchi! It's one of the greatest films of all time!'

'It's too hot to watch girls laying eggs and cutting people's dicks off,' said Petra. She was referring to *In the Realm of the Senses*, which Stefan had made us watch that Christmas and which had become fodder for our teasing ever since.

Stefan's face flushed red and he said, 'It's a different culture. You're just embedded in Western norms about sexuality.'

'Just because Japan's exotic to you, doesn't mean it's not sordid,' Maike said, taking off her large gold-framed glasses and wiping sweat from her brow with her forearm. 'They have really ingrained issues with prostitution; it's tax-deductible if you're a creepy old businessman. Whatever the cultural differences are, they're still people's sisters and daughters and they're still having sex for money.'

'Fuck off, Maike,' Stefan said.

Maike listened, only speaking when she had something to say, but it was always concise and accurate when it came, and thus more devastating. It happened often enough that 'Fuck

16

off, Maike' had become a phrase we used any time someone was about to argue back and we already knew our own argument wasn't going to stand.

I lay across the table with my hand out for a Pez. Stefan popped one into my palm and behind him I saw another flash of red – this time it was the man from the pool, the sun full on his back, catching the light in his wet black hair.

'You'll come, Ralfi. *Alter*, come on?'

Stefan was the sort of only child who hated being alone and made siblings of his closest friends.

'Not a chance,' I said.

'I'm showering,' said Petra. Maike stood too, but Stefan put his hands behind his head and said, 'It's thirty-two degrees. There's no point. We're all going to be soaked in sweat by the time we get home.

'Shower later,' I said encouragingly, thinking of the man in the red trunks – that I might be able to catch another glimpse of him if I went to shower alone. I didn't want to talk to him, certainly not be noticed by him, I just wanted to pick up some detail up-close: a gesture, a scar, the sound of his voice.

'Yeah, I'll shower when I get home,' Stefan said.

'No you won't, you dirtbag,' said Petra.

The man should have already showered by the time I entered the changing rooms and, if I was lucky, have been pulling his clothes on in front of his locker. But when I walked in I found him still in his red swimming trunks, furiously spinning the wheels of a combination lock.

'*Scheiße*,' he muttered to himself.

'Everything OK?' I said.

'Oh,' said the man, straightening. 'Yeah. My lock's broken or something. Or I've forgotten the code.' I'd expected him to have a Turkish accent, but he spoke accentless, idiomatic German. He laughed and said, 'I'm a fucking idiot.'

I hesitated, thinking I could get past him, leaving him to argue it out with the site manager while I watched through the crack of my cubicle door, but I said, 'Well, if it's a combination lock you could just crack it.'

'What, like crack it off?'

'No, crack the code.'

He shrugged and smiled and said, '*Mein Freund*, you've lost me.'

The word *Freund* made me feel good. Among my real friends and my family, no one called anyone else 'friend', unless they were being ironic.

'Do you want me to . . . ?' I gestured to the lock.

'Be my guest,' he said.

I put the novel under my arm, pulled on the lock and turned the wheels. It was a cheap three-number padlock with-out false gates – you just had to feel for the give as you slowly turned each wheel. It was the sort of trick we practised when we were camping – lighting fires with flints, opening beer bottles with lighters, doing owl calls with our cupped hands. I worked it anxiously, aware of his eyes on me.

'Fuck,' the man said, close enough that I could feel the damp heat of his breath on my ear. 'You reading Rushdie?'

I realised that the book was facing him, cover out. Sweat burst from my skin so quickly that the plastic-covered book squeaked and I had to clamp my arm down hard to keep hold of it as I worked the lock.

'Sorry,' I muttered.

'You're sorry?' said the man. He put his hand on the locker. I looked at it there, the bright half-moons of his neat nails and the fine black hairs on the wrist and on his fingers, between the knuckles. Over the chlorine, I could smell his fresh sweat and his breath, which was sweet, like warm milk. The first wheel clicked into place and the book slipped lower, so that I had to dig the bone of my elbow into the cover to keep it from falling.

'I don't really like it,' I said. 'I mean, I'm not sure I do.'

'Huh,' said the man. 'I thought it was amazing. You just need to get through the first hundred pages.'

The next number clicked into place and I looked at him surprised. 'You've read it?'

'I had a magical realist phase a few years back.'

'Garcia Marquez?' I said. I had just finished *One Hundred Years of Solitude* and had been dreaming of studying plant life on the banks of the Orinoco and making Humboldtian voyages in the Colombian jungle in search of rare butterflies.

He laughed. 'That's it. Grass, Marquez, Kafka. Anything a bit weird.'

'You a teacher, or something?'

'No, but my dad has a shop on Eisenacher Straße. Used to be all Turkish books and newspapers, but he let me build up this little German literature section.'

'Huh,' I said. 'You don't look like you work in a bookshop.' I blushed and tried to pick out something about him that would make what I'd said sound less offensive, but he was only wearing swimming trunks, the gold watch and the thin gold chain. There was a smile at the edge of his lips, but it changed, the mouth softening and the eyes looking at me more intently, as if he was trying to place me. The lock clicked open beneath my fingers and he broke into laughter.

'Look at that,' he said. He put his hand on my bare shoulder; his palm was dry. '*Alter*, I owe you,' he said and in his wide smile I saw the narrow gap between his two front teeth.

'It's nothing,' I said, 'Just a ...' I gestured vaguely at the locker.

He offered up his other hand and I shook it. 'Oz,' he said.

'Like the Wizard,' I said, aware of his thumb pressing onto the back of my hand.

'It's short for Osman.'

'Like the bulb.'

I was embarrassing myself again, but Oz gave me a comforting grin, which he paired with a frown and little jolt of the head. 'Hey, you don't ...? You know, I really feel like we've met, or ...'

I blushed again; out of the corner of my eye I could see the redness spreading across my chest and felt it burning the tips of my ears. 'I live at Windscheidstraße 53. You're always parked on our street.'

'Shit,' he said, releasing me and opening his locker, 'I've been busted.' For a second, as he pulled out a towel and threw it around his neck, he looked worried.

'I didn't ...' I said, 'I mean, it's just a coincidence. I didn't follow you here, or anything. I don't care what you're doing.'

He shook his head and said, 'It's fine. I know. I'm not worried.' He held the ends of his rolled towel and said, 'Your surname's not Rode, is it?'

Rode was the surname of our neighbour Tobias. 'No,' I said, 'Dörsam.'

'Oh, OK. Fine.' He relaxed. 'My dad owns a couple of flats in your building.'

'I thought he ran a bookshop.'

'He does. And a shop. And a Turkish bakery. But he also owns a few flats, here and in Frankfurt.'

'And what's this Rode done?'

'Illegally subletting. Dad thinks he's got someone else

20

renting a room in his flat and he's not declaring it. And if he is, then Dad can void his contract and either kick him out or up the rent.'

I nodded. Oz smiled and shook his head. 'You're him, aren't you?'

'I'm not,' I said, laughing. 'Honestly. But I do know him.'

'Oh fuck,' said Oz. 'He's really nice, right?'

I nodded. 'He's pretty nice.'

He laughed. 'Well, rules is rules.' He began to transfer his clothes and a battered Puma sports bag to one of the nearby changing cubicles. 'We don't own your flat, do we?' he said.

'No,' I said, watching him pick up his trainers and throw them into the cubicle. 'We own ours.'

'Fuuuck,' he said, throwing back his head with lazy drama. He stopped and put his hand back on my bare shoulder. 'What's your name?'

'Ralf,' I said.

'OK, Ralf. So if your parents own a flat then they're on the landlords' committee, and they might not be too happy about my dad spying on his tenants. And with all these tenants' protests going on at the moment, being a dick of a landlord isn't a great look if you don't want your car set on fire. And, although Dad *is* a bit of a dick, he's also my dad. So what I want to know is what can I offer you not to tell your parents or Herr Rode about this conversation?'

'Offer me?' I laughed and held up my hands. 'It's ... My lips are sealed. Honestly.'

'Really?' he said. 'How about something from the shop? You like reading, right? You can come and pick up a book? Just as a sweetener.'

'I don't need a book,' I said.

'Well,' he said, letting me go and sticking his head into

the cubicle as my shoulder cooled in the shape of his fingers. 'This is my card. The address is the address of the shop.' He produced a silver cigarette case, which he popped open and offered up. The little white cards read 'Osman Özemir, Executive, Özemir Holdings GmbH, Eisenacher Straße 62, Berlin'. I reached out to take one and *Midnight's Children* slipped from beneath my arm into a puddle of water on the red-tiled floor that had gathered at Oz's feet. I looked at them, smooth and brown, the toes short and thick, and I tried to lock them into my memory, so that that night I could imagine him putting them into my mouth.

Four

It is odd to think of how little happens on some days and how much on others; how global histories and personal histories eddy and brew like the weather, coalesce after years of calm into squalls that wash away lives and borders that had once seemed so permanent. In the year before I'd met Oz, there'd been a presidential election in the United States, the usual scattering of natural and man-made disasters, a few political scandals and surprises, but little that suggested to me, to my friends or my family the storm gathering on the horizon.

In 1989 my family – my parents and my younger brother – lived at Windscheidstraße 53, a nineteenth-century apartment block in Charlottenburg. The ornate plaster façade had been damaged during the war and covered over with flat brown render, but past the large wood-and-glass door, everything was original: the tiled hallway, the grey wood of the staircase treads, the elaborate plasterwork on the ceiling still visible beneath a thick layer of paint, the colour of chickens' eggs.

I passed the staircase and wheeled my bike through the back door into the courtyard. Like most Berlin apartment blocks, the flats were built around a central space, with larger flats, like ours, on the street side and smaller, cheaper flats in the side and back building, all looking down into this inner core. Here too, the grubby plaster walls and windows were original, except for the top-floor flat at the back, which had a gap, like a missing tooth, where a bomb blast had knocked out a single room. I often wondered about that gap; wondered if anyone had been in there asleep, the only person to be killed in the whole block. I suppose, back then, such accidents were commonplace.

I tucked my bike beneath the green-mossed bitumen roof that covered the bike racks and bins. The cracked concrete beneath my feet was covered in white pigeon droppings, also sprayed celestially across the dark ivy that carpeted the flower-bed beneath the horse chestnut. The pigeons cooed above my head, where the tree's wide leaves brushed together, cooling the air and making the light on my skin aphid green.

There was a baker on the ground floor of the front build-ing and the air smelt deliciously of bread. I could hear Herr Klee's rattling cough coming from the second floor and the agricultural chuckle of his humidifier. And I could hear some-one's awkward steps on the front staircase, which at that time of day would usually have been one of my mum's patients. But I knew it was Tobias Rode, the neighbour that Oz was watching, because he walked with a limp, and the melody of his rocking gait – slap-thud, slap-thud, slap-thud – was one of the happiest sounds of my adolescence. Tobias was a viola player with soft strawberry-blond hair who'd fled the East and arrived in our building when I was seven, and he was the first person I'd ever fallen in love with.

It hadn't felt like a revelation at the time, and the truth is it hadn't bothered me at all. I didn't feel ashamed about it, though I was aware it was something I wouldn't be able to talk about until I was very grown up, perhaps at university. It hadn't crossed my mind that I could actually do anything about it, with Tobias or anyone else.

Even after I fell in love with Maike, there didn't seem to be any reason to put an end to my imaginary affair with Tobias. I didn't see that there would be any consequences to separating these things off – it was just a trick of the imagination. At school, I would joke with the rest of the kids about the teachers who we thought were 'benders', coughing 'poofter' whenever Mr Lawson, the French teacher, turned his back on us. It didn't occur to me that this was hypocritical, even when Kevin Cuddon drew a penis on Mr Lawson's door and I took the permanent marker from his hand to add, 'Sailors get it here.' Masturbating at night, while dreaming of a soft knock at my door, the sound of Tobias's belt buckle striking the parquet as his trousers came down, the first touch of the long amber hairs on his bare chest, was just fantasy. But pouring so much youthful emotion into a part of my brain that I'd dammed up had left it in danger of bursting.

Tobias played his viola in the afternoon, and for me, who'd only ever heard the scraping of violins in the primary-school orchestra, the shuddering vibrato was intensely melancholy and beautiful. He was in his late twenties, always friendly, charmingly unselfconscious, wearing loose collarless shirts, shorts and Birkenstocks. In winter, his woollen jumpers had holes in them. And as patronising as I know it now sounds, his limp gave him a sweet vulnerability that I found delightful.

I could see the windows of his apartment from our kitchen, and as a young teenager would sit in the dark watching him read, smoke, drink coffee and listen to records. Sometimes he brought women home. They might have been friends from the orchestra, they might have been lovers. It didn't bother me either way – it made him all the more unattainable, and thus a perfect fantasy.

I'd been caught in these lovelorn stakeouts twice: once by my younger brother and once by Stefan. My brother was easily put off the scent with a punch to the shoulder, but Stefan was more suspicious. Sick with shame, I blurted out that I thought Tobias was an East German agent and that he was spying on our apartment, because Mum used to work for the British Army. I don't think Stefan ever really believed me, but the idea was captivating enough for a thirteen-year-old in Cold War West Berlin to want to play along.

My lie had a huge and unexpected benefit. For two years, whenever he came over, Stefan wanted to play spies. If he spotted that Tobias was in, Stefan turned the lights off and we watched him together. For my fourteenth birthday, Stefan gave me binoculars and a journalist's notebook, and entreated me to keep a log of Tobias's comings and goings. There were further notebooks and many nights huddled in the dark with Stefan and me watching Tobias eating black bread and pre-sliced cheese while he read the newspaper. He did many things that appeared suspicious to us – taking calls late at night, leaving the flat at strange times of the day, burning notes in his ashtray – but of course, as teenage boys, we had no idea what the lives of single, adult men looked like, and whether these were the normal comings and goings of a cultured bachelor.

As we neared sixteen, Stefan lost interest in the project. But I still had the books, and often sated my longing for Tobias when he was touring with his orchestra by leafing through the heavily imprinted biro letters describing his quotidian movements. And whenever Stefan was round and caught me looking at the apartments on the opposite side of the courtyard, I was always able to say, 'Just keeping an eye on Comrade Rode.'

Tobias limped into the sunny courtyard from the front building and smiled at me. 'Ralf!' he said.

'Hi, Tobias.' I had thought about how I was going to formulate the revelation that Tobias was being spied on by his landlord. 'You know what I found out today?' I was going to start with, enjoying his confusion as I built up to the revelation. But with my hands shoved casually into the pockets of my shorts, I was able to stroke the edge of Oz's card and recall his sweet frowning smile. I couldn't quite imagine myself actually cycling to Eisenacher Straße for the promised book, but I didn't want to betray Oz and kill off any of the blissful impossibilities that the morning had suggested. So I said, 'You don't sublet your flat, do you?'

Tobias frowned. 'No,' he said. 'Why?'

'I just read something about it. About how landlords are cracking down.'

'Oh,' he said, confused.

I smiled. This was enough, wasn't it? If something happened, I could always say I'd asked. And if he was illegally subletting, then at least I'd sown the seed that it might not be a good idea. 'Did you want to get your key?' I said. We had swapped keys after he'd come over for dinner at ours the second time, and since then we had emptied his letter box when the orchestra was touring and he had watered our plants when we were on holiday.

Baffled again, he laughed. 'My key? Ralf, what are you talking about? I feel like I've gone senile.'

'Wasn't that you coming down the front stairs?'

'Oh,' he said, and then, for the first time in six years of spying on him, I caught him in a real lie. 'No,' he said, 'I just got in.'

I was looking forward to telling Stefan about this slip-up,

not believing for a moment that Tobias really was up to anything suspicious. All those years of playing at espionage had inured me to it.

'Dear Herr Rode!' It was Frau von Hildendorf at the window of her ground-floor flat. She had been an actress in the Fifties and thickly painted her ancient face with the bright make-up of that era, missing the true lines of her wrinkled lips, eyes and jaw. Her arm, all tendon, gripped the edge of her open window frame, and she said, 'You promised me thirty minutes of your viola. You absolutely promised.'

'Can I knock in ten?'

'Of course,' the old woman said drunkenly. 'I'm expecting a visit any time soon from my friend Eve Harris. She's in town for a play, but I haven't been able to get hold of her. She might call, though. If you can bear the interruption.'

'I can bear it,' Tobias said.

He could bear it, because Eve Harris's presence had been anticipated for decades and she had never arrived.

'She should have been less in the movies in the Sixties anyway,' Frau von Hildendorf said. 'Theatre's her true talent, but the money. *Mein Gott*, the money over there.'

'Ten minutes,' Tobias repeated. He winked at me and hobbled across the courtyard to the back building. Frau von Hildendorf slammed her window shut – she had no interest in teenage boys – and I listened to Tobias slowly climbing the stairs to his apartment, wondering if he had ever seen me staring at him from the kitchen window. The thought terrified me.

Five

There were two front doors on the second-floor landing and they both belonged to us. The story went that my German great-grandparents had bought the flats after the war and knocked them through into one large apartment. When her husband died, my great-grandmother locked the adjoining door in her kitchen and rented out the rest of the flat to a very short obstetrician called Dr Geisler in order to pay off the remaining mortgage. Despite the loud and deeply private conversations that Dr Geisler had behind the door about failed episiotomies and prolapsed uteri, Oma refused to wall it up, intending, until the day she died, to annex the old rooms again once she had the money. When my parents moved into the flat a few years before I was born, Dr Geisler was already an old man, but they still heard him behind the door having brief but loving conversations with his children. By the time the same children moved him into a home, my mother had qualified as a psychotherapist, and gave up her secretarial work with the British Army, taking over Dr Geisler's rooms for her practice. The convenience of the door was suddenly a blessing.

My mother specialised in sexual disorders and relationship problems. Grandad – Mum's dad – had been a doctor in the

British Army and his final posting had been a long stint in Berlin. My mother did her A levels at the school I had just left and then worked part-time as a secretary at the military hospital during the four years she was studying psychology at the Freie Universität. She stayed on at the British hospital even after Grandad retired, because she had met my father by then. Her secretarial work kept them afloat while she completed her training and my father qualified as a pharmacist.

Learning her lesson from Dr Geisler, Mum re-arranged the flat, setting up her consulting room in his old living room and using the room behind the adjoining door in our kitchen for her waiting room. This was the only room we could clearly hear into from the kitchen, and then only if the couples were arguing in English or German. We rarely saw the patients, because they came up the front stairs and through Dr Geisler's old front door. If we did leave as they were arriving, they couldn't know from the nameplates on the doors that we were their therapist's children, because my mother practised under her maiden name, Rees.

Our flat was empty when I entered, but something felt different or smelt different; the air didn't have the right quality, that stale coolness it usually had if I arrived home before anyone else. I looked about the hall for signs of intrusion, my eyes dancing over the many remnants of the building's former grandeur: the plaster ceilings; the gently undulating parquet floor in the central hall; the gloss-painted double windows with their brass handles; the high wooden doors.

I moved silently to the kitchen. My father had put it in in the Seventies, my parents' first purchase with the money he'd made from his first job. The cupboards were varnished pine, the tiles brown-speckled cream, intermittently enclosing a sunflower in golden yellow, brown and orange. There was a large table permanently covered with a wipe-clean plastic tablecloth studded with sunflowers. There were benches either side of the table, and in the corner of the room a ceiling-high cheese plant, its bulk supported with greying twine nailed to the wall.

The large coffee-coloured fridge with long chrome handles, bought second-hand from an American family in Dahlem, was plastered with photographs and childish drawings that spilled out onto the cream walls, above which a profusion of coloured brushstrokes, red, green and blue, betrayed a plan, never enacted, to introduce a less autumnal hue into the kitchen.

I heard a sleepy knocking and realised that the adjoining door into Mum's practice was unlocked and being bounced by the breeze against the jamb. I stepped through into the alternate universe of her waiting room, with its smoked-glass coffee table piled with battered copies of *Stern*, *Geo* and *Bunte* and said:

'Mum?'

'Here,' she replied.

I found her at her desk reading from a stack of files, the first sheet held high in her hand, the others beneath her fingers on the desk. The light from the high double windows lit her cropped red hair from behind, turning it the colour of ginger-bread. Her small freckled face, with its wide olive eyes, was a parody of concentration, her eyebrows pulled together and her mouth an open O.

She was still in her work clothes, an ankle-length grey skirt high on her waist and a smooth silk top with globular pearles-cent buttons. The buttons were undone to the top of her bra, exposing the heavily freckled skin below her straight clavi-cle, and she had kicked off her leather pixie boots. It looked as if she had been distracted by her notes in the middle of

31

undressing. She was only half sitting on the chair; one leg was stretched out beside her, her slim ankle and foot resting dramatically on the smooth parquet like a dancer's.

'The door was open,' I said. She usually had patients until seven and it wasn't even six.

Mum looked up at me and her face broke into a smile. She said in English, 'My five o'clock had to move his appointment to seven-thirty.'

'Isn't that when we're eating?'

'He's having a crisis, apparently. I'll just nip off for half an hour. I've told him I can only do thirty minutes.'

Such crises were rare among her patients. Her clientele largely consisted of expats with marriage problems, which meant that they were rarely suicidal or acutely unwell.

'I thought you were going to be at Maike's for dinner,' she said.

'No. She wanted to finish her book.'

Mum's forehead folded into a wry frown and, as if joking, she said, 'She picked a book over you? That's a bit much.'

I smiled weakly. Maike and my mother had got off to a bad start when Maike, aged thirteen, had picked me up from the flat and not said hello. She stood shyly in the hallway and was found by my mother, who, once she'd pressed Maike into telling her who she was, shouted out, 'Good Lord! Ralf – it's a ghost. There's a ghost here to see you.' Maike didn't understand this sort of humour and hadn't laughed. Petra and Stefan, on the other hand, laughed like drains at my mother's jokes, so she adored them.

She straightened her papers and dropped them into one of her filing cabinets and put the key high up on the shelf by an African mask with nails for teeth and dry coconut-husk hair.

She cupped my face in her hands and kissed my forehead. 'You smell lovely. I love that you're always out. You always smell of wood smoke or swimming pools. I spent my youth lying on the carpet eating custard creams and watching *Bonanza*.'

'I don't know what any of that means,' I said, following her through to our apartment and then my parents' bedroom.

'TV show and biscuits,' she said, stripping off her shirt and hanging it over the back of the chair. I collapsed onto my parents' bed and the water-filled mattress undulated beneath me.

'Did I hear Frau von Hildendorf's dulcet tones?' she said.

'Yup. Is Eve Harris a real person?'

'Of course. She was quite famous in the Sixties. She made a few films with that French director. Like Truffaut, but with a D.'

'Druffaut?'

Mum laughed. 'Sounds like a shampoo.'

'Do you think she's really friends with her?'

'Of course not. She's been prophesying her visit for the last two decades.'

I thought about the man at the pool, about his skin, his hair and the water, which had grown impossibly sparkly in my memory. Oz, a shimmering shadow amid blinding, glittering light. I tried to picture him in some dusty shop on Eisenacher Straße in a cardigan and horn-rimmed glasses, but couldn't capture it.

'Can Turkish people be gay?' I said. Part of the ease of my divided existence was that it was so successfully segregated that I wasn't worried that such questions might arouse suspicion.

Mum laughed and said, 'Of course, Ralf. What are you talking about?'

'Some guy at the pool today – it just made me think … I don't know, because he was—'

'… flirting with you?'

'He wasn't flirting with me. And he definitely wasn't gay, now that I think about it. But it just made me wonder about it. I mean, have you ever heard of a gay Turkish person?'

'Well, he doesn't have to be gay to find you attractive, Ralf. I had a very physically expressive relationship with a girl when we were posted in Cyprus. Almost failed my O levels, I was so wild about her.'

I rolled over and pushed my face into my mother's cool pillow. 'I don't want to hear about you lezzing it up at school. That's not the same thing.'

Mum giggled. This was a common trick of hers, which added to her popularity with Stefan and Petra: playing the educated English psychologist, all charm and good manners, then dropping in a risqué remark to make everyone roar.

I uncovered my face and watched her strip off her tights. In her bra and pants, I marvelled at how lean she was. I wondered if it wasn't her manic energy that burnt up all the fat.

I turned the book over on my mother's side table to see what she was reading. It was a very thumbed copy of *The Ambassadors*, the orange spine curved and pale with linear cracks. My mother was always buying books, but forever rereading the same old classics she'd read at university.

'Is this any good?'

'Yes,' she said, pulling on a pair of white shorts. 'You've caught the sun a bit.' She flicked my nose with her forefinger.

'We were sitting outside at the pool. I should've put suncream on.'

'I bet Maike covered herself up. To keep up that unearthly white glow.' She took out her earrings and put them in a blue

34

and white Japanese bowl on her dressing table that Martin
and I liked to empty out when we were children.

'What's that supposed to mean?'

She looked at me in the mirror, behind her on the bed. 'I
meant it as a compliment.'

'Sure,' I said. 'Anyway, I'm the pale one. Thanks to all this
English skin. Why didn't I get any of the French?'

'The skin's Scottish,' she said. 'Your great-grandparents
were from Lewis.'

I picked up a watch from the floor. The face was large and
white, the hands and the casing brass, the strap fake brown
leather. Above the hands, I read 'Ruhla' and '15 jewels'. I
wrapped it around my wrist and wondered if I should ask for
a watch for Christmas.

'I'm sure Beate knows some gay Turkish people. We'll ask
her tonight.'

'Please don't,' I said, putting the watch on the bedside table.
'She'll have a worse story than you – orgies or something.'

'Beate doesn't have orgies,' she said, frowning. She put
her hands on her hips. 'Did you get your offer confirmation
from Durham?'

'They don't confirm it until my results arrive. Anyway, I'm
going to UCL and it's the same offer, so if I get enough for
Durham I'll be going to UCL anyway.'

'I'm still not sure about London.'

'It's my degree. And what's wrong with London? Auntie
Linda lives there.'

Mum stalked out of the room. I followed her to the kitchen,
where she took a head of iceberg lettuce from the fridge and
washed it under the tap. I opened the windows, though it was
hotter outside than inside, and sat at the kitchen table, lying
across it with my eyes closed, the sticky plastic tablecloth

pleasantly cool beneath my cheek. I could hear Tobias's viola trembling in Frau von Hildendorf's apartment. The air smelt of hot plaster and green leaves.

'Your Auntie Linda doesn't do anything naughty in London. You will.'

'Isn't Auntie Linda meant to be a lesbian?'

'Rumour has it. Though if she is, she's not the naughty kind.'

I often had small spats with my brother, and my mum sometimes shouted at my dad, but otherwise this conversation represented the high peak of family disagreements; real arguments were had by families who weren't happy, like Petra's, or the Drombusches on telly.

'Maybe I could change back to Berlin,' I said, voicing a thought that struck me now and again when I felt frightened about leaving Maike.

'Being bilingual is a gift, Ralf. It would be crazy not to study abroad when it's so easy for you and so hard for everyone else.' My mother aggressively spun the salad.

'I thought you hated moving abroad all the time.'

'That was different,' she said, releasing the spinner and letting it shudder to a halt. 'We moved every two years until Berlin. Every time we got settled, every time we'd made any friends, we'd set off again.'

I made a sympathetic face, though these sorts of stories always left me cold. My parents' lives before I was born were as emotionally real to me as the Tudors'.

The door opened and Dad shouted, 'We're home!' I heard Martin drop his football things on the floor and crash into the bathroom. My father came into the kitchen and gave my mother a kiss, looking like a model West German pharmacist, orderly and trustworthy. His neatly trimmed hair, otherwise unstyled, was the same pale grey as his neatly ironed trousers, his watch and his glasses. He had a thick white moustache that was so neatly bushy that it looked as if it might come away from his face when he removed his spectacles. The only other colour on his person was a striped burgundy tie that matched his socks. I found it hard to imagine that he'd had many expressive same-sex experiences as a young man in rural Hessen.

'What are you making, *Schatz?*' my father said in German, stealing a lettuce leaf and pinching her bottom. This physicality was much commented on by friends, whose parents rarely touched each other in front of them.

'It's chicken salad. I was going to make something with lentils, but I've got a patient having a crisis that I need to see at seven-thirty, so I thought this'd be easier.'

'I like chicken salad,' I said, my cheek still pressed to the table. 'But Stefan can't eat the chicken.'

'He can eat the lettuce.'

'I'm sure we can keep ourselves entertained for half an hour,' Dad said jovially. He brushed my hair with the tips of his fingers. 'Are you ill?'

'He's having an attack of teenage ennui,' Mum said.

My father put down his jacket and Filofax and picked up my limp arm, pushing two fingers into my wrist. 'It's fatal I'm afraid, Pat.' He smelt of cigarettes and Persil.

'Dead?' Mum said.

Dad nodded. 'I'm afraid so.'

'Can I have his dinner, if he's dead?' said Martin, coming into the kitchen wearing nothing but a pair of shiny white football shorts. Back then, I couldn't have told you whether I liked Martin or not. He was my brother and he was four years younger than me, which was close enough that we'd had to spend a lot of time together as kids, but too far apart

37

for us to be friends once I'd started going through puberty and wanted to be in my room reading, cleaning up fossils and masturbating.

Martin had an easy confidence that made me jealous. He seemed completely untroubled by himself. There were a few things he liked doing – football, cycling, playing computer games – and he did each in turn until he was stopped. He would lie sprawled across the sofa watching Bundesliga, then the *Sportschau*, then tennis for hours until Mum or Dad turned off the set and said, 'You can't lie around watching telly all day.' He wouldn't complain, just sloped off and played *The Legend of Zelda* on his NES until that was switched off. Then he left the flat and took his skateboard to the Tiergarten until he got hungry and came home again.

'It's chicken salad,' I said to Martin, taking my wrist back and sitting up properly. My father kissed me on the crown of my head.

'I hate chicken salad,' Martin said. 'Please don't put grapes in it.'

'It's in the recipe,' said Mum.

'You can pick them out,' said Dad. 'I'm going to change.'

The doorbell rang. 'That'll be Beate and Stefan downstairs.'

'Martin can get it,' I said, leaving the room, wanting to have a moment alone to contemplate Oz, feeling a growing excitement at having someone new to fall briefly and fictionally in love with. 'I have work to do.'

'You can't have work to do!' Martin shouted in English. 'You just left school. You've literally never had less work to do!'

Six

I sat at my desk looking at Oz's card, thrilled by it as if it was a second-class relic religiously charged with some trace of him. I tried to imagine how my bedroom would look to Oz. Childish, I thought. It was a high square box, the white ceiling lined with overpainted plaster cornicing and a central rose, from which a lamp had been badly attached, so that blue and red wires were visible between the grubby cord and the black hole. I had my parents' old bedroom curtains, rough cotton heavy with muddy green flowers. The walls were painted a dirty yellow that I'd picked with Dad when I was eight. My pillowcases and bed sheets were mismatched family cast-offs in ancient shades of brown, burnt orange and olive green, napped by thousands of rounds in the washing machine.

I'd hung up two large posters: one of Wendy James from Transvision Vamp in ripped jeans, one of an exhibition called *Art of Germany 1945–1985* that I'd bought on a school trip because I liked the colours. These posters were orbited by hundreds of pictures of avalanches, exploding volcanoes and giant beetles cut from the *National Geographic*s that were stacked up beside our toilet. The mirrors of my large wardrobe were pocked with childish stickers: rainbows, puffy Smurfs, Muppets, Hannibal from the A-Team, *Star Wars* characters and mulleted German and English footballers. The odd furry paper silhouette revealed sporadic, unsuccessful attempts at removing them. A dusty AT-AT stared longingly down at the room from the top of the wardrobe like a stray dog. I imagined Oz's house looked like those white marble-floored interiors in *Miami Vice*, with three pastel-coloured sofas, a mirrored coffee table and a potted fern.

I heard Beate and Stefan talking to my mother, shoved Oz's card into my pocket and began going through a battered box of old cassettes, so that I looked busy when Stefan came in. He knocked at the open door and said, 'Ralfi, Ralfi.'

We gave each other the Vulcan salute.

'How was the film?'

He shrugged. 'Pretty cool. Pretty dark.'

I could hear Beate's screaming laugh in the kitchen above my mum's high giggle and the pop of the first *Sekt* cork.

'Is Mum drinking?' I said. 'She's got a late client coming.'

Stefan shrugged and pointed to my box of cassettes. 'What's that?'

'I bought a load of old cassettes at the flea market. I'm taping them up to record onto them. There's an Elvis Costello special on Radio 100 at nine.' I threw down the taped-up cassette and opened another.

Stefan flicked me hard on the ear, lay down on my bed and put his white-socked feet on my red plastic desk chair.

'Was the film any good in the end?' I said.

'Yeah,' Stefan said unconvincingly. 'It was pretty creepy. There was this woman who got knocked off and then came back as a ghost. The music was very powerful and it had this kind of fuzzy *chiaroscuro*, you know?'

I shook my head. 'Not really.'

Stefan shrugged and picked up a thumbed *National*

Geographic from my bedside table. 'Fuck,' he said, turning the open page to me, a spread of red-eyed seabirds slick with oil from the *Exxon Valdez*.

I nodded sympathetically.

'Hey, listen to this,' I said, and told him about Tobias coming down the staircase and lying about it.

Stefan frowned and smiled. 'Fuck. Ralf. That's genuinely quite weird, right?'

'It is, isn't it?' I said.

Excited, he dropped the magazine and leapt off my bed. I grabbed the binoculars and we ran into Martin's room and turned the lights off. Martin was on the bed reading a comic and shouted in protest.

'Hey, shut up, *Spasti*,' Stefan said. 'It's the traitor.'

Martin had long since been brought in on the spying game, because, other than the kitchen – where our parents usually were – his was the only room that looked out onto the court-yard. Grudgingly, he climbed off the bed and joined us a half-metre from the open window, so that in the thickening dusk our faces were still shaded. 'I thought we weren't doing this any more,' he whispered as Stefan lifted the binoculars to his face.

'He's been seen in the vicinity,' said Stefan. 'Oh shit!' he whispered.

'What?' I said. He handed me the binoculars. I looked at Tobias's living room, but it was empty.

'What am I looking at? There's nothing there.'

'The bedroom.'

I shifted the binoculars, but saw only his orangey curtains.

'The gap,' Stefan said.

There was a split between the curtains, a long triangle through which I could see Tobias pulling the sheets off his bed. He left the room and my dipping, rounded gaze followed him into his kitchen, where he nervously searched the top of his fridge and then the floor. He stood and put both hands to his mouth.

'What is it?' said Martin.

I handed him the binoculars. 'Oh,' Martin said, following Tobias to the living room, where he was turning over his sofa cushions. 'So he's lost something.'

'He's casing the joint,' Stefan said, taking the binoculars back. 'Probably looking for wires. Or maybe prepping something for this guy,' he said.

'Who?' I reached for the binoculars again.

Stefan kept hold of them and pointed into the courtyard. A tall man with white hair had just entered from the side entrance to Schiller Straße. He was moving thoughtfully but purposefully past the horse chestnut tree towards the front building.

'Mum's patient,' I said.

'Looks pretty miserable,' said Martin. He did look very sad; like the world had abandoned him.

'Military,' said Stefan.

'What do you mean?'

'Look at that haircut. It's so tight.'

'It's so sad.'

'What?' said Martin. 'His hair?'

'No. Someone that powerful, some general in charge of a nuclear arsenal, with sex problems.'

'They've all got sex problems,' Stefan said. 'That's why they have to kill people. To compensate.'

'What?' said Martin. 'That doesn't make any sense.'

'Does,' was the best retort Stefan had to offer. He stalked out of the room. I followed. Distantly we heard the doorbell to Mum's practice ringing and saw Mum doing up the buttons of her work blouse again, disappearing through the door in the kitchen.

*

Mum returned as promised after half an hour, and from that moment on our Friday night ran its usual course. We ate at the big table in the kitchen, filled with red wine and my mother's tasteless chicken salad. We talked about our weeks, Martin, Stefan and I brief and businesslike, my father too. I didn't talk about Maike, because my mother would make faces, and we didn't talk about what Beate and my mother called 'Nature Club', because we were tired of the teasing. My mother would tell stories about patients, using nicknames to hide their identity – The Cryer, The Shit, The Affair – always laced with jokes, always aimed at making Beate laugh.

The only good part of the meal was the dessert, which Beate brought: something simple and delicious, some idea she had picked up from her latest lover or another homeless artist lodging on her living-room floor. Stewed red fruit with mascarpone, baked figs, a lemon tart, *clafoutis*, a paper bag of ripe peaches.

Martin picked up *Donkey Kong* and was forced by my mother to abandon it until the adults had finished their coffee. Deprived of distractions, he chatted and made jokes that made even me laugh. Once the first bottle of wine had been drunk, my mother and Beate held court as we picked at the remnants of the meal and our parents smoked.

Beate was a warm, wild woman. She was also my godmother, and I knew as a child that it would be her that adopted us if my parents died. Although I loved my parents, whenever Stefan and I sat with her – watching her working on her sculptures in the studio by her flat, drinking nettle tea and eating some supermarket-own-brand version of Hanuta, her straw-like blonde hair tied up in a topknot, her faded dungarees and forearms spattered with white plaster – I would wish that my mum and dad could be simultaneously dead and not dead, like Schrödinger's cat, so that I could have both them and Beate as my parents.

Mum had met my father and Beate at the same medical conference in West Berlin in the Sixties. They were both working at the bar. Beate was from East Berlin, but on the night of the 13th of August 1961 she had been in bed with a trumpet player from West Berlin. She woke to find the border closed and the Wall going up and that she was trapped on the right side. This would have been a triumphant story had her mother not got cancer ten years later, forcing her to re-emigrate to the East to nurse her. She escaped again after her mother died and lived with us until I was two. This traversing of the Wall back and forth earned her the nickname *Die Gämse* – the chamois – in West Berlin's artistic circles, as if she sprang over the Wall at will like a mountain goat.

Beate was more wrinkled and heavier than my mother, but had a wide expressive beauty, embodied by her large mouth, always red-lipsticked, with wicked turned-up edges, like the Joker. It was a face that, despite what I then considered her advanced age – forty-five – kept a regular stream of bohemian men in tow, one of whom was sitting with us at the table. He sported an unfashionably long beard and wore a hand-crocheted waistcoat over a yellowing cotton shirt. He was tall and he stooped when he walked, as if he were afraid of banging his head on the ceiling. I could see, beneath the greasy hair and the smell of patchouli, that his smile were very beautiful, his teeth strong and straight, and that his eyes were glacially blue. He failed to impress anyone else though; as my mother sat down with the coffee jug, she whispered, 'Ask Charles Manson if he wants cheese.'

I don't remember the man's name, because these men were never around for more than a month or two. One Irish folk singer had lasted a year, a bald masseur from Hamburg had managed only one visit. They were never formally introduced as her partners, they just appeared, joining in with varying degrees of success.

Stefan didn't see any of these men as father figures; he had made that mistake once with the folk singer. He taught Stefan to play the Irish flute and Stefan had sketched out a complex itinerary for a planned trip to Ireland they were going to take together. At Der Gammler, the bar we frequented, Stefan had even drunkenly wondered if the man could be his real father, because their hair was the same colour and the man had called him 'son'. Stefan didn't know that, in English, this could fondly refer to anyone, and I didn't enlighten him.

A week later the man was gone. Stefan never witnessed his mother splitting up with any of them. It always seemed fine, he said, until he came home to find a specific kind of silence reigning in the house. His mother would emerge from her bedroom, taking slow, cautious steps, dressed in an old silk kimono she'd bought at a flea market, emblazoned with a huge red dragon. She would be fully made up, drinking wine from a tumbler, a cigarette between her fingers. 'I'm going to learn Arabic,' she said after the Irishman. It was always that that put the final stamp on it: the announcement of a new project. 'I'm going to go to Paraguay,' 'I'm going to start meditating.' Books would be borrowed from the library, brochures collected from the travel agent's, but within a few weeks there would be a new man and the projects would be forgotten.

'Ralf,' Beate said, gripping my chin between her perfumed fingers, 'I heard you rescued some Turk at Prinzenbad.'

'What Turk?' I said. I'd briefly mentioned the lock-breaking to my friends to excuse the time it had taken me to get changed, but it was a throwaway remark and the focus had been the lock and not Oz.

'Stefan said he'd locked himself out or in or . . . '

'Oh,' I said. 'No, he'd forgotten the code for his padlock.'

'Oh, is this the queer?' my mother said in the perfect but heavily accented German she'd learned as a student. 'You didn't tell me you helped him out. No wonder he was making eyes.'

'You didn't tell me he was gay,' said Stefan, frowning.

'I didn't say he was gay.'

'You said he was gay!' my mother said.

'Did you bum a gay Turk, Ralf?' my brother threw in from the end of the table.

'No, he was just very chatty, which, I don't know, just got me thinking about whether you ever got gay Turkish people. He wasn't even camp or anything.'

This made Beate roar with laughter. 'Why wouldn't you get gay people in Turkey?'

'Look, he's blushing,' my mother cried.

'No, it's wonderful, Ralf. Ignore these boors,' said Beate. 'Why live in West Berlin if you're not going to have a few gay Turkish friends?'

'He's not my friend, he's not actually *Turkish* Turkish – he doesn't even have an accent – and he's probably not gay. It just made me think.'

'Think about bumming him?' my brother said.

I sat feeling raw as Beate told a convoluted story about Udo Kier and a lesbian woman she'd met in Marrakech. My father winked at me and then rolled his eyes to say, 'Don't worry about these two,' as I made shapes on the table with the spilled salt. The bearded man only broke in once to say, 'Andy Warhol was gay,' to which Beate replied, 'Everyone knows that, Bernd, and it's hardly relevant,' before continuing with her story. We didn't see Bernd again.

Seven

When we collected our bikes from the courtyard, Stefan mimed zipping his lips and then pointed up at Tobias's window. It was open, the lights were off, and Tobias was staring up at our kitchen window, where my parents, Beate and Martin still sat.

'Look, look, look,' Stefan whispered. 'Watch his face.'

I watched. In the dying twilight, it was a pale blue mask, his features deep, indistinct indigo marks, like an Easter Island head. With his foot, Stefan snapped his kick stand back and said loudly, 'Oi Ralf, is that your chain on the floor?'

Tobias glanced at us and then disappeared into the dark.

'Oh my God,' Stefan said in a stifled giggle as we wheeled our bikes out and set off to Der Gammler. 'Something's really going down. At what point do we call in the BND?'

I cycled alongside him and shook my head with faux amusement. 'He's probably just in love with your mum,' I said as we turned onto Kanstraße.

*

Der Gammler – The Tramp – had once been a classic Berlin *Kneipe*, and there were still a few battered locals who ignored its transformation into the owner Peter's vision of a West

48

Coast rock bar. Peter – an idealistic surfer from Sankt Peter-Ording with shoulder-length hair, who'd come to Berlin to avoid military service – thought that the bar would be patronised solely by American servicemen, but his carefully restored neon Miller Beer sign was not enough alone to attract them, particularly when they discovered he didn't sell any Miller Beer. 'It tastes like cat piss,' he said, the few times Americans did come in, and was genuinely perplexed that they wanted to drink it or expected him to serve it.

So Peter's clientele were still the same locals that had always drunk there – striped T-shirts stretched across their stomachs and white hair sprouting from their necks, ears and noses, drinking Berliner Kindl with a chaser of Korn. And us. We frequented Der Gammler because it was convenient, lying in Schöneberg, roughly equidistant from Stefan and Maike in Kreuzberg and me in Charlottenburg. Petra lived in Wannsee and so was discounted from the equation. She had the advantage at the weekends, living walking distance from most of the scant green spaces we frequented with the Wildlife Trust.

The bar's fittings mirrored those in the rest of Berlin: homely Sixties lamps, black-and-white photographs and blond wooden cladding, so that the narrow room felt like the belly of a cheap pleasure boat. There were even lace half-curtains along the window, stained tobacco yellow.

We smoked red Marlboros, drank beer, played incessantly on the Evel Knievel pinball machine, the paddles painted with large-breasted women, while working our way through Peter's record collection, placing LP after LP onto his wood-veneered Telefunken Rondo.

Peter played American bands that no one had heard of yet: R.E.M., the B-52s, Jane's Addiction, and at the end of the evening we filled the sticky floor in the bar's darkest corner and danced with whichever of the locals were drunk enough to sway along with us.

We sat around the table by the window and Stefan told Maike and Petra about Tobias and the man in the courtyard.

'You're not allowed to talk about Mum's patients!' I said.

'Hey, I never said he was a patient. That one's on you!'

'OK, OK,' said Petra, 'we never heard he was seeing Ralf's mum for his sex problems. Who is he?'

'We don't know,' I said.

'Some general,' said Stefan.

'We don't know that,' I said, hitting him on the shoulder.

Maike tried to look interested and Petra, resting her head on her hand, said languidly, 'This is a really great story.'

'Fuck off,' said Stefan.

He downed the rest of his beer, then asked us who was going to join him the next day on a protest at Kurfürstendamm.

'We're meant to be prepping for next week's marshland count with Dr Ast,' Maike said. 'I thought we were all going.'

He turned to me pleadingly. 'I'm going to the count prep with Maike,' I said.

'Me too,' said Petra.

'*Ihr Lieben*,' Stefan said, 'this one's important.'

'What's it about?' said Peter, turning chairs over and placing them on the tables so that the floor could be swept.

'The protest?' Stefan said. 'It's that strip of houses in Kreuzberg they're trying to knock down, which is, surprise, surprise, full of squats.'

'And communists?' Peter asked, grabbing a bucket to empty the ashtrays into.

'Exactly,' said Stefan. 'Communists and Greens. But also old ladies that've lived in their apartments for years, getting turfed out so some millionaires can make a few more millions. The police presence is gonna be massive. It's all gonna go over one of these days. Shot like Ohnesorg and Dutschke, man.'

'You're hardly Rudi Dutschke,' Petra said.

'The police don't care who they shoot,' said Stefan.

'When did someone last get shot?' I asked. 'And why's the protest on Ku'damm if it's about flats in Kreuzberg?'

'They don't need to shoot you, Ralf. They can just "accidentally" run you over. Like the tank man in Tiananmen Square.'

'They didn't actually run that man over,' Maike said. 'They went around him.'

'Fuck off, Maike.'

'What are you prepping?' Peter said, wiping down the bar with a greyed floorcloth. 'What is the next adventure for the Wild Bunch?' Peter thought it was very funny that we still did what he called 'nature shit'.

'We're counting sundews in Langes Luch next weekend,' Maike said enthusiastically. 'It's a section of marshland in the woods at Grunewald. Then we're mapping amphibian species in the Schöneberger Südgelände.'

'Really?' Peter said. 'Frogs and toads?'

'There are actually thirteen species of amphibians in West Berlin.'

We played up to his teasing, trying to sound as geeky as possible.

'Species like the garlic toad are highly endangered. It emits a garlicky smell when alarmed.'

'Sounds like it should be highly endangered. Sounds gross.'

We had a last beer while Peter swept and Petra and Stefan played table football. I sat with Maike stroking the soft skin beneath her arm as she leaned her head against the slimily polyurethaned wood panelling behind her. Like all people who are genuinely wonderful, it was almost impossible to define the exact nature of Maike's greatness. She was clever and attractive, though her owlish glasses and height meant that she avoided much of the attention that Petra attracted from strangers. She could be funny, she was often kind, but there was something more fundamental. She was completely herself. I was constantly second-guessing what people wanted from me, always aware that there were many thoughts and feelings I was necessarily burying. Petra put on a front much harder than her soft under-belly. Stefan was endlessly picking up the tics and mannerisms of people he admired. But Maike was always Maike, thoughtful and reliable, genuinely listening when you spoke to her and gen-uinely interested in what you had to say. Still now, when I talk to mutual friends, they often cite a moment of realisation or insight that stemmed from a long conversation with Maike. I put this to her years later when we were both adults, married to other people with our own children, and she listed all of the ways in which she too was just pretending. But I wasn't convinced. She is still the most genuine human being I've ever met.

'How's your mum?' I said to her.

Without lifting her head, she looked up at me, then her eyes saddened and dropped to my chest. 'Same,' she said.

Maike's mother had cancer. She'd been ill for almost ten years, and in Maike's family these things weren't talked about explicitly. The drugs left her exhausted, and a few times a year she disappeared for another operation or blast of radiation. She had stopped cooking when she first fell ill, so Maike's elder sister Sandra had taken over until Maike turned twelve, at which point Sandra got her first boyfriend and Maike was expected to fend for herself.

Maike's father worked nights for the BVG – Berlin Public

Transport – and was asleep on the sofa during the day with the curtains closed. Her mother took his place in the evenings, watching television and smoking. This constant parental presence meant that I had only been to Maike's flat once, hoping to surprise her by picking her up on the way to Grunewald for a Wildlife Trust count. It hadn't occurred to me that she would live in a tower block, until I parked my bike in front of it and searched for her surname on the huge panel of buttons. When I pressed their bell, a feathery voice answered: 'Yes?'

'It's Ralf. I've come to pick up Maike.'

There was an electronic crackle and whine and the magnetic door lock clunked open.

I'd never been in an apartment block with a lift before and I stared about the aluminium box, covered in graffiti – mostly swear words, breasts and penises in black marker – that added a solvent note to the urine-scented air. Walking down the fluorescent-tube-lit corridor, past the faded rose pink of the flat doors that I'd only seen in films like *We Children from Bahnhof Zoo*, I felt lonely and afraid. It seemed so bare and inhuman. But I also wanted to be the sort of person who didn't care where people lived. I had to fight it, though, because I did care. I wished that Maike lived somewhere else, in a house or in a flat like mine.

Maike met me at the door red-faced, trying to pull on her raincoat.

'I thought I'd surprise you,' I said.

'Yeah,' she said.

She pulled the door shut.

'Could I use the loo?'

She stared down at her hand on the door handle and said, 'OK. But be quiet. Dad's asleep.'

She opened the door again and pointed to the bathroom. I crept across the landing, which smelt of cigarette smoke and acrid cleaning products, and looked towards the dark living room, where a split of white light in the curtains outlined a man on the sofa and what looked like a woman's legs in slippers and thick tights. In the bathroom, I peed sitting down, afraid of making a sound, and looked about at the brown tiles that reached up to the ceiling and the avocado bathroom suite, dated but so clean it looked bewilderingly new. I could hear snoring and the deep hush of the municipal plumbing.

'I wanted to meet your parents,' I said, when we were outside.

'You'll meet them,' Maike said, pushing her hands into her pockets.

Someone tried to open the locked door of the bar and Peter waved them away. '*Zu!*' he shouted, 'Closed! *Fermé!*'

'What about you?' Maike asked.

'Me?' I said. 'I'm OK.'

'You always are.' She smiled. Even when I was banal, she made me feel good about it. 'You're not really worried about Stefan talking about your mum's patient, are you? She's not going to get into trouble, is she?'

I shook my head. 'Stefan was just getting overexcited. He shouldn't've said anything.' I recalled the man's stooping walk. It made me sad to think of someone who was meant to fight, who was meant to be brave, having problems with sex or with intimacy, especially because – to my eighteen-year-old eyes – he was so ancient. 'Mum keeps asking about university,' I said.

Maike stretched out her long legs, laying them over my lap. She rubbed her hands together and smiled tiredly.

'Just go to London.'

I frowned. 'What if it overwhelms me?'

She pressed her fingers against my cheeks. 'Why is it overwhelming, sweet Ralfi?'

'It's big,' I said, pushing her hands away. 'And who am I going to be there?'

'Who are you here?'

'A ginger Englishman. A would-be geologist.'

'And there?'

'They'll all be geologists and geographers. And they'll all be more English than me. I'll be the weird German.'

'You'll still be ginger.'

'London'll be full of gingers.'

Maike laughed and took my hands. 'None of them will be as sweet as you though.'

'It's only you that thinks I'm sweet.'

'And your mum.'

'And my mum.'

We filtered out of Peter's and said our goodbyes. It was almost two in the morning, dark, but still hot enough that we were comfortable in our T-shirts. Petra and Stefan left me and Maike to a lengthy goodbye of kissing and almost parting, until she broke from me and walked off to unlock her bike, her hands pushed into the pockets of her shorts, her head lolling happily.

She mounted her bike and said, 'I'll pick you up at six thirty, yeah?'

'Wow,' I said. 'That's going to be, like, four hours' sleep.'

'I can just go with Petra. Honestly.'

'No, I want to come. Pick me up on the way, OK?'

She nodded and smiled and cycled off.

'I love you!' I shouted.

She raised her arms in a mime of celebration and I laughed.

55

When the red light of her bike was out of view, I climbed onto mine and rode home, feeling guilty about lying about my four hours' sleep, because I was planning on getting up in three and cycling to Eisenacher Straße.

Eight

The next morning, my body still heavy with sleep, I cycled over Winterfeldtplatz, where the metal frames were being clamped together for the market. A few vans had already arrived, and men in jeans and T-shirts were shouting to each other, emptying boxes of oranges, salad and flowers, and clattering open the green metal legs of folding tables. A middle-aged Turkish man in a bloodied white butcher's coat carried a giant skewer of muslin-wrapped doner kebab meat on his shoulder, the size and shape of a wasps' nest.

I crossed the road by the red-brick church and the Catholic school that Maike, Petra and Stefan had attended, and cycled down Eisenacher Straße, carefully reading the shop names. A woman passed with a shih-tzu on a lead and stared at me disapprovingly. Then I saw the sign, and my heart thumped in my ears. It was half in German half in Turkish: 'Özemir's: Turkish and German Newspapers, Books and Magazines'.

I locked my bike onto a lamppost and walked tentatively to the front of the little store, staring up at the hand-painted sign, peeling red on white, and smiled at the thought of the fantasy Oz I had gone there to shape in my mind, him standing at the door, inviting me in. It hadn't occurred to me that it was unusual for the shutters to be up this early in the morning, so I put my face to the glass and made binoculars of my hands to stare into the dim reaches of the room behind, savouring a new, completely authentic setting for my fantasies.

I recalled his voice and went over the mental snapshots of his body that I'd saved up at the pool. I knew that, for a few days at least, and certainly that night, he would replace Tobias in a convoluted set of repeated tableaux. Most would be sexual – him inviting me into the changing cubicle at Prinzenbad to peel off his red trunks, the skin of his belly cold against my lips – but many would be deeply sentimental – us hand in hand in the woods, his leg pushing up against mine in the cinema, us sharing a tent on the beach on the North Sea coast, his bare foot sliding through the open side of my sleeping bag.

The walls of the shop were filled with paperback books stacked haphazardly, and in the centre of the room was a low table, covered in German magazines – *Der Spiegel*, *Stern* and *Brigitte* – mixed in with *Zaman* and *Hürriyet*. Dotted about on the thin grey carpet tiles were piles of newspapers bound tightly together with electric blue twine.

The back of the shop was darker, but I could make out the counter and there, as the blood left my face, I saw Oz. He was standing on a chair behind the counter, reaching up to a dead lightbulb above his head. He looked over at the window lazily then, recognising me, he smiled and abandoned the job, clambering down off the chair.

'I didn't realise you were here,' I shouted through the glass. 'I just recognised the sign.'

He fumbled about for a key and pointed at his ears to indicate he hadn't heard me. I heard his muffled, 'Wait, wait. I'm coming.' He tripped on a pile of newspapers and laughed, pointing at himself. 'Clumsy!' he shouted.

'I should really go,' I said.

He pulled the door open. 'You're here.'

I caught the lemony scent of him, but it was immediately overwhelmed by the shop's musty breath, of old paper, pipe tobacco, cold cooking fat and dry spices.

'I was out late with friends until like five and I was on my way home,' I lied.

'Coming down Eisenacher to get to Charlottenburg?'

'We go to a bar nearby. I was wandering around before I headed home.'

'And you just happened to come by the shop?'

I don't think I have ever felt shame more intensely in my life. It kept coming at me in waves, washing coldly through me, assaulting me in its white heat as Oz stood in front of me smiling sweetly. I had often felt it for a flash, when Tobias's eyes had travelled up to our apartment windows as I watched him from the dark room, when my aunt had tried the door to her bathroom as I snooped through her medicine cabinet, but these disasters had always been avoided or easily excused. This, though, was irreparable. But I tried my best, stuttering, 'I remembered Eisenacher Straße ... Because you gave me your card. I was just passing and—'

'Of course!' he said. 'I bought off your silence with literature!' He laughed, and held the door open. 'Please. Please. Come in.'

'Oh, no. No, honestly. I should get home.' My T-shirt clung to my back. 'That's not why ... I didn't know you'd be here. I didn't mean for you to open up.'

'Please come in,' he said. 'I always have to be here early for the newspaper delivery. I'm meant to reorder books for the two hours until we open up, but it takes ten minutes. There's nothing to do. Honestly. You'll be doing me a massive favour.'

I gripped my head and squinted down the street. I could hear the distant whine of the U-Bahn train at Eisenacher Straße Station and I thought about running. He would think I was being ridiculous, but then I would be gone and if I ran hard enough I might be able to drown out the sound of him calling after me.

'You can have some tea,' he said. 'Genuine Turkish tea from a genuine Turk.'

'OK,' I said, capitulating, 'but just for five minutes.'

*

I could hear the kettle boiling and the clinking of glass from the back room. I wandered around the shop with my hands in my pockets, my mouth still tasting of toothpaste, and looked at the Turkish magazines with beautiful dark-haired men and women in heavily retouched, soft-focused photographs. I felt lightheaded from the abating shock. On the front pages of the newspapers there were pictures of Protestant hostages being held by an armed gang in Mindanao in the Philippines and a congressman from Texas who'd died in a plane crash in Ethiopia.

Der Spiegel had a picture of refugees from East Germany with the headline 'Will East Germany Implode? Mass Exodus from Honecker's Socialism'. Since the Helsinki Accords, it had become easier to apply to leave the GDR, and more and more East Berliners were appearing tearfully on Platform B of Friedrichstraße Station. There were also sporadic bursts of refugees escaping through other Eastern Bloc countries. But these were things we saw on TV. West Berlin was not awash with East German refugees and we were used to dismissing this sort of apocalyptic sentiment. We'd been hearing it for years.

The counter was like the counter of any Turkish corner shop: plastic racks filled with gum, chocolate bars and lighters. I picked up a cigarette that Oz had been smoking – an unfiltered Gitane – and I touched the damp end where his mouth had been. 'You stupid fucking cunt,' I said to myself, watching my trembling fingers. I was going to have to cycle to Grunewald with Maike in an hour having had next to no sleep and having to lie about why.

Behind the counter there was a shelf of cigarettes and in the corner nearest the door, where the morning sun misted the dusty glass gold, was Oz's German book section, with a smattering of classics and well-received contemporary novels. I smiled, because I had read so many. It looked like my bookshelf at home.

'What's your name again?' Oz shouted from the back room.

'Ralf!'

'I'm Oz,' he called.

'I remember,' I said, but felt instantly that it was the wrong thing to say.

'Not many famous Ralfs,' he said. His voice was suddenly in the room and I turned to find him standing in the doorway with a tray, holding a steaming metal teapot and two small glasses.

'No. That's why Mum picked it. She said it was for me to make famous.'

'That sounds like a lot of pressure.' He put the tray down on the counter top. 'Are you going to be famous, then?'

I shook my head. 'I'm going to study geology.'

'And become a teacher?'

'Probably do research.'

'Ralf Regenbogen.'

'Pardon?'

'He's a famous Ralf. Footballer. Plays for Rot-Weiss-Essen. Used to be at Schalke.'

I nodded. 'I'm not into football enough to know all the names. I just watch a bit of Bundesliga with my brother and the national stuff when it's on.'

Oz smiled and let out a little laughing puff of air as if I'd said something clever.

'So you work here?' I said.

He was wearing an ochre-and-blue lumberjack shirt, rolled up to the elbows. He poured out two glasses of honey-coloured tea and the shape of his hands, the strength in his bare lower arms, brushed with fine black hairs, and the delicacy of the gesture elicited in me a surge of desire so strong it felt like nausea. I grabbed the glass he offered me and took a quick sip; it burnt my tongue and the bottom of my lip. 'It's hot,' I said, putting it back on the tray.

'It'll cool down quickly,' he said, sucking the last out of his cigarette and putting it out in a full ashtray. We watched each other for a second too long.

'I need to finish this,' he said. He looked at the light above him and clicked at the switch behind the counter to show me. 'My uncle leaves me all the broken and burnt out things to sort out.' He picked up a fresh bulb and climbed onto an old office chair covered in red leatherette, its rips fixed with silver duct tape, standing up unsteadily as it rattled beneath him.

'Is that a good idea?' I said.

'It'll be fine.'

He raised himself up like an acrobat at the top of a human pyramid, slowly reaching to the ceiling to unscrew the bulb, revealing his bare stomach and the soft dark hair crowding around his belly button.

'Can you hold this,' he said, slowly passing down the old bulb.

I took it and the chair wobbled.

'*Scheiße!*' I said, thinking he was going to fall off, but he put his hand on the top of my head to steady himself.

He laughed and said, 'Fuck! Almost. Hold the chair, will you.'

I held it, as he stretched up again, my face by his bared belly. I could smell his skin, his cheap shower gel and the faint scent of laundry detergent in his underpants.

'Try it before I get down,' he said and kept his fingers pressed into my skull as I turned and tried the light switch. The bulb flashed brightly above his head and he held out his hands like a magician. 'Ta da!'

He came down off the chair slowly, moving his hand to my shoulder, his thumb pushed up against my neck, until his feet were back on the ground.

'I thought you were going to fall,' I said.

'Oh, I never fall.' His hand was still on my shoulder. He moved forward and I thought he was going to kiss me, so I automatically pulled away, hitting my elbow painfully on the edge of the counter.

'Hey!' he said. 'I was just ...'

'I know,' I said, escaping around the counter, seeing that he had been reaching past me to pick up the old light bulb, which he now tossed across the room, where it landed precisely in a stuffed bin in the corner. 'I'm hungover, and jumpy. Jumpy, jumpy, jumpy,' I said, bouncing up and down on the spot.

He looked confused.

'Sorry,' I said, 'I'm not being very funny.'

'Why do you need to be funny?'

'People like funny people.'

'You don't have to funny to be liked.'

'OK, Dr Freud.' I was embarrassing myself and I felt ashamed. 'Bet you're sorry you asked me to come now.'

'I'm not sorry.'

'Why did you ask me?' I said it as if he was at fault. I felt hot and angry. Because he shouldn't've talked to me at the pool and he shouldn't've invited me to his bookshop. It was weird.

'Ralf,' Oz said. 'I asked you ...' I flushed red, my face burned, because I thought he was going to say 'because I like you' and I was terrified and excited, but he said, '... because of Tobias Rode.'

The heat fell away. It was about his father's flats.

'Tobias can't be subletting,' I said, trying to sound indifferent. Oz had folded his arms and one hand had found its way to his chin. I stared at the tender pinkness of his nails. 'His flat's not big enough and we can see into every room, except the bathroom and the bedroom. If he was subletting to someone I'd've seen something.'

He was concentrating very hard on my face.

'Ralf, did you talk to him or your mum about what I said to you? About my dad's flat and the subletting?'

I shook my head.

'That's good. That's really good. Because I think you've probably realised this is about more than just flats.'

I felt the good schoolboy's pleasure at having done something right, but this was quickly overwhelmed by a sense of the world peeling away around me.

'I don't know what this is about at all,' I said.

'You're British–West German – that's right, isn't it? So West Berlin must be very important to you. For your family it's everything, when you think about it.'

In the dusky back of the airless shop, his eyes were the colour of turning leaves.

'No, I don't think about it,' I said, uncomfortable about being coerced, but also telling the truth: I really didn't think about it at all.

He tipped his head and tried a different tack. 'If you can see into that much of his flat, you must also notice things. Notice if he has visitors. Or does anything odd.'

I thought of the notebooks I had filled with Tobias's movements. But I couldn't give him up, whatever this man thought he'd done. Not Tobias.

'He's just a viola player,' I said.

'We're all more than our jobs,' said Oz. 'We're all lots of complicated things, sometimes contradictory things. Even good people, people we like, can do things that we don't like or that we know are wrong. And then it's our job to decide what's important. A friendly neighbour or our country.'

'Our country?' I said. 'What are you talking about?'

Oz softened instantly. 'I'm sorry, Ralf. I'm going in too hard.' He laughed to himself.

'Is something going to happen to Tobias?'

He held up his hands as if surrendering. 'Listen, I've just been asked to keep an eye on him. No one's getting into any trouble – the opposite. This is about doing something good for your country. For both of your countries.'

'What, are you a spy or something?' I said, laughing nervously.

He shook his head. 'Nothing as grand as that.'

'But you're working for the government?'

He picked up his glass, knocked back his tea and, not taking his eyes off me, held it up offering me more.

I shook my head. This wasn't a conversation with a friendly bookseller, this wasn't a new acquaintance I could desire from afar. Every word I uttered in his presence had grown heavy and dangerous.

I put down my glass and walked to the door. He dodged around the stacked papers, pulling the door open a crack and then holding it. 'What were you actually doing here at five in the morning?'

'I was out with friends at a bar.'

'The ones from the pool?'

'Yup. And ... '

'Your girlfriend? The tall one?'

'Yes,' I said, 'but ... '

'But what?'

'There isn't a "but". She is my girlfriend.'

'But ... what, you don't have sex with each other?'

I looked up at him, genuinely shocked.

'I'm sorry,' he said. 'I just got the sense that ... I don't know what I thought. Sorry.'

I nodded slowly. 'Yes,' I said, 'we have sex.'

He looked down at my feet, as if I'd wounded him, then pulled the door wide open. The sun on his face highlighted the dark freckles that peppered his cheeks.

'I'm sorry about coming,' I said. 'I really didn't think you'd be here. I don't know how to explain it. I'm sorry. I feel like I've completely got the wrong end of the stick.'

'No, no,' he said. 'I'm glad you came.'

I smiled weakly and stepped down onto the pavement.

'Ralf,' he said, squinting at me.

I turned back.

'Your neighbour, Tobias – if he does ever do anything suspicious, or if you just want to talk, you know where I am.'

'Yes,' I muttered.

I ran to my bike as he shouted, 'You didn't pick a book!' from the door.

I cycled off, not turning, pounding so hard on the pedals that my thighs were shaking when I climbed up to our apartment. Maike was already there sitting on the stairs in front of our door waiting for me. She was asleep, slumped against the cold chipped-plaster wall, her rucksack tipped over, her red thermos half rolled out. One long, bare leg was stretched out down the stairs, ending in thick bark-coloured socks and her battered walking boots. Sunlight filled with golden dust fell across it and lit the golden hairs above her tanned knees. I knelt on the steps below her and kissed her calf. She woke, inhaling deeply, her head swinging to life.

'I love you,' I said.

She smiled wearily and said, 'I know.'

Nine

That final summer was hot and humid from June through to September. Berlin sits at the centre of the Northern European Plain scraped flat by the Weichselian, Saale and Elster glaciations, and the weather migrates slowly over it in heavy masses, enveloping the city for days on end. No one waits out the weather in Berlin. When rain comes, it comes for days, when snow falls, it lies on the ground for months, when the heat comes, it stays, immune to rain, clouds, wind, stoically stripping Berliners of their clothes and sending them out to the lakes and into the parks, desperate to escape the humid air if only for the briefest moment. And when the thunderstorms come, they don't clear the air, but throw down water like water thrown on the stones of a sauna, making the air impossibly damp and hot.

So a week after the bookshop, my T-shirt was already damp when I unlocked my bike and wheeled it into the hall to find Tobias standing in front of his open mailbox. I wiped my forehead with my arm, and watched him lean on his good leg and retrieve a battered envelope.

I had only seen him one other time since Stefan and I had caught him staring up at our kitchen window. He had been sitting in his narrow kitchen eating bright orange soup, staring.

I desperately hoped that he would do nothing to confirm the vague suspicions that Oz had hinted at. But how could I not wonder what the meaning of the bowl was, of the spoon, of the curtainless kitchen window. Was someone watching him? Was he watching someone else? Was the cactus on the windowsill a message? Was the John Coltrane album on his living-room floor a message? Were his white socks discarded by the fridge a message?

At his mailbox, Tobias touched the handwriting on the envelope and smiled tenderly. I considered the soft, milky curve of his neck that sloped down into his ancient T-shirt. I studied the way his straight hair stopped dead, the beautiful skin below unencumbered by the curling fluff that covered the back of my father's neck. It was impossible to believe that he was endangering anyone.

Tobias ripped the envelope open. His head tipped and, aware that I was about to come into his field of vision, I opened my mouth to call out, 'Something nice?' But he took a watch out of the envelope. A watch with a white face and a brown strap, and before I could consciously connect the watch with the one on the floor of my mother's bedroom I reacted physically, my skin heating then cooling, my knees giving way, so that I had to lean onto my bike, making the tyres squeak on the tiled floor.

Tobias turned. His smile faltered, but he managed to lift it and to cry out, 'Ralf!' in his blustery, joyous way.

He saw me staring at the watch, so he held it up and said, 'I thought I'd lost it on the U-Bahn but someone must have sent it back.'

This lie enraged me and, in an unpleasantly high and trembling voice, I said, 'How did they know it was yours?'

'I called them. The BVG.'

69

'I didn't know they posted things like that back.'

'I know,' Tobias said. 'Neither did I. It's wonderful.'

I wheeled my bike closer, my eyes fixed on the watch held between his thumb and forefinger, hoping not to read 'Ruhla', hoping not to read '15 jewels'. But I did read them, and for a second, in that oppressive heat, I was terrified I was going to throw up.

'Sometimes people surprise you,' Tobias said.

'Yes.'

'Well, see you later.'

I stood propped up on my bike, hearing him limp across the courtyard and go up the back stairs to his apartment. I stared for a while at a crack in the glass of the heavy wooden doors to the block. It reflected the white of the sun and drew it across the vista of the street beyond. People passed by.

I felt stupid. Stupid about reading Tobias's actions through the childish spy games that Stefan and that Oz had played with me. But, more painful than that, stupid for thinking that, in its happiness, our family was special. Now I'd been shown that the tragedies of my friends' families were the tragedies of my own. It was a deadening realisation and I was overwhelmed with disgust for my mother.

Dazed, I cycled west to Grunewald to meet my friends. Between traffic lights I pumped at the pedals and rehearsed terrible confrontations with her, dramatically telling my father and Martin at the dinner table that Mum had been fucking our neighbour, leaving the flat and never returning. But when I stopped at a junction, when I listened to the ticking of the traffic lights and watched crowds of heat-tired workers and exhausted mothers with their children crossing in front of me, I also imagined pretending I'd seen nothing and avoiding my mother for long enough that I didn't feel sick about it and that it didn't hurt at all. Perhaps I could send a letter to her work, I thought. A warning from a 'friend', saying they knew all about it and that it had to stop.

When I finally reached Grunewald forest to find my friends dappled in sunlight, smoking in front of their bikes beneath a canopy of softly rustling beech leaves, I thought numbly that I couldn't say a thing. So used to burying any problematic emotions, I realised that I didn't even know how to express what had happened, nor how I felt about it.

'You all right?' Petra said. 'You look a fucking fright.'

'Fine,' I heard myself saying.

I was silent and shivery as we trudged down to the bog at Langes Luch. Maike held my hand and said quietly, 'You sure you're all right?'

'Fine,' I said again and smiled at her, through leagues of unexpressed emotion. She squeezed my hand.

Maike was no narcissist. She loved to be with her friends, but rarely talked about herself unless pressed. She wanted to hear what you had to say, but never probed you for information the way Petra did. Maike just listened. All the intimacy she required was physical. She wanted time with me, she wanted affection, she wanted sex. But she didn't want to talk about how she felt. That was why we'd sought each other out, I suppose. It was this blissful distance, this smiling agreement to stand side by side in love, but to be allowed to be lost in one's own thoughts and talk about the things that made sense: insects and plants and glacial landscapes.

At Langes Luch, the heat felt tropical. The strip of boggy moorland linking Grunewald Lake with Krumme Lanke had once been a lake itself, but as the water was pumped out of the Havel to sate thirsty Berliners at the beginning of the twentieth century, it left behind a sea of sedge-peat bog with a thin channel of water dribbling down the middle, that in turn had become a haven for wildlife.

The project leader from the Wildlife Trust was a dentist called Dr Ast. Balding, with a chubby shaved face and always dressed in shorts and a colourful Gore-tex jacket, there was something toddler-like about him. He handed out clipboards and pens, making jokes, calling us by our first names, but expecting us to use the formal '*Sie*' in return and to always use his doctor's title.

He led us slowly through the centre of the bog. We wore shorts, T-shirts and wellies, our bare legs spattered with mud black as discarded tea leaves. It was early morning, already hot, and the ground smelt primeval; it felt like the beginning of the world.

Mist rose between silhouettes of rotting logs and the early morning sun lit the sticky beads arrayed around the heads of the carnivorous sundews that we were counting. As we moved our meter sticks and scribbled on blue-lined journalists' pads with orange biros, mosquitoes screamed near our ears and bit our legs and winged beetles rose up as black and shiny as molten tarmac, thrumming high into the air. I kept thinking about Tobias, his blue mask in the dark staring up at my laughing mother in our bright apartment, watching her the way I had so often watched him. It must have been his watch he was searching for, I realised, when he was tearing his apartment apart.

There were sixteen other volunteers on the count, paired up, their colourful T-shirts dotted about the bog. I was counting with Stefan, and Petra was with Maike. They were far off, near the little canal edge, and intermittently I could hear Petra's sharp cackle and Maike's giggle. They made an odd couple, Maike so tall, the pale sun catching the gold of her huge glasses, and Petra, small, fair and busty.

'You look awful,' Stefan said. 'You sure you're all right?'

I felt light-headed and cotton-mouthed, my fingers were tingling and the humidity made me feel breathless. 'I'm fine,' I said, suffused with relief and disappointment that I had denied my friends three times.

'Maike?' Stefan said.

I shook my head.

'Sex trouble?'

I laughed and shook my head again.

'Had sex with Petra again after we left Der Gammler the other night.'

'*Ach was!*' I said. 'Fuck.'

Stefan and Petra had slept with each other a few times. There was a week we spent walking the flats at Wadden Sea when they briefly became a couple. They walked side by side over the mirrored sand reflecting the setting sun, its image peppered with sandworm piles. Maike and I felt nervous, watching the dynamics of the group re-form around us. But the condom broke on the last night and Stefan and Petra argued about abortion – she for, he against, and defending his right to have a say on 'whether his child lived or died'. There was no pregnancy, but the distance that had opened up between them at the first taste of discord was too great to bridge, and they broke up on the long coach journey home.

I knew everything about Stefan's sex life; he volunteered it earnestly as if it was educational for me, and in some ways it had been. He had slept with three girls: Karen Holt, a schoolfriend none of us liked who he'd dated for a year, an American he'd met on a school trip to Amsterdam, and a thirty-year-old friend of his mother's called Jasmine, exotically pronounced 'Yazmina' in German. He told me where they had sex, described exactly what they did, what their breasts

73

were like, the precise consistency of their pubic hair. He considered himself an enlightened lover, and lectured me on the location of the G spot and the importance of foreplay and the female orgasm.

Once while he was dating Karen I called on him at the moment they were heading to the bedroom. I tried to leave, but he told me not to be such a prude and made me wait for him in the living room. I was there for forty minutes, leafing through battered copies of *Die Tageszeitung*, trying to ignore the intermittent gasps from the next-door room. Afterwards, I had to endure an excruciating round of coffee with them both red-faced, Karen a little dazed as Stefan talked about the Taoist concept of the joining of the essences.

I made a few jokes as Stefan talked about his latest encounter with Petra, but didn't ask for more details on the sex itself – I never did. I already had a vague sense of a time when he would know I was also capable of falling in love with men, and I didn't want him to look back at these conversations and remember me grilling him for details.

'Were her parents in?' I asked.

He shook his head. 'They're never in. They're in Mallorca or Menorca. They're always somewhere, little Nazi pigs.'

'Are they?' I said, thinking of her mother as I'd last seen her in a brightly patterned peach silk jumpsuit, crying with laughter as Stefan re-enacted a Loriot sketch for her.

'Her dad is. Definitely. A little capitalist pig for sure. It's more or less the same.'

'Is it?' Usually I ignored Stefan's political pronouncements, but I was tired and upset about Mum and Tobias. What was I going to do? It was impossible. I had a stomach ache and wanted to lie down in the bog and close my eyes.

'You know,' Stefan said, 'I was round there once and he was

treating me like some sort of son-in-law in waiting. We all took a stroll around Wannsee in the sunshine and went past this school in some big villa and he pointed through the railings and said "Final Solution". Just like that: "Final Solution".'

'Final Solution?'

'Yeah,' said Stefan. 'It's where they decided on the Final Solution. In some massive house by the lake. Like a couple of streets away, and he just points at it and says, "Final Solution," like he's telling me that some film star lives there.'

'Doesn't mean he's a Nazi,' I said.

'Why are you trying to defend him?'

'I'm not,' I said. 'I'm just saying it doesn't mean he's a Nazi.'

'You know I read up on it. There's this historian, Joseph Wulf, who spent years trying to get that house turned into a Holocaust memorial, but the pigs in the government wouldn't let him do it. Just ignored him. And he was like, there are all these old Nazis working for companies, swanning around as MPs and bank managers, and fucking, I don't know . . . people working at banks.'

I laughed.

'Ralf, this is serious.'

'Sorry,' I said.

'And they just ignored him. And you know what he did in the end?' He waited wide-eyed.

'I don't know,' I said.

'Killed himself. Threw himself off his balcony, because he knew there was no hope for Germany.'

'Fuck,' I said. 'Well, that was a really depressing story.'

'Why are you being so glib?' Stefan said. 'I'm talking about the fucking Holocaust.'

'Sorry,' I said. 'I'm sorry, I'm just tired.'

We carried on the count in silence until Stefan urgently

gripped my shoulder and pointed. A fly had landed on the outstretched leaves of a sundew. It floundered among the sappy fronds, intermittently releasing a warm, plaintive buzz, until the plant's gluey beads stuck its wings down. As the fly pulled frantically, the leaf kinked at the end, rose up and curled tentacle-like over its prey.

'Sorry little bugger,' Stefan said.

'I hate flies,' I said, feeling nauseous.

When we reached Maike and Petra at the canal's edge, Stefan hung back so that I would end up standing between him and Petra. Maike said, 'Look,' and with her boot gently lifted what looked like the sedge-filled edge of the water. 'It's floating.'

'The sedge has seeded in the sphagnum moss,' said Petra. 'It's a little floating ecosystem.'

We all smiled and I was happy for a moment, but then I thought about my mother and Tobias, his body imagined in detail over many secret nights in my room now twisted around my mother's bony frame. I shuddered and felt impossibly miserable again.

*

That evening, in search of garlic toads, we cycled with the other volunteers to the Schöneberger Südgelände, where trees and plants grow over the abandoned Tempelhof Railway Yard, creating an elongated oasis by the train tracks to Lichtenrade and the sprawling Steglitz allotments. The morning at Langes Luch had tired us out, though, and we kicked about haphazardly, failing to find a single amphibian. As the sky darkened, we deserted the others and climbed the hill at Park der Insulaner to lie among the observatories on sleeping bags, listening to the field crickets chirping among the tall dry grasses and staring at the hazy blanket of stars above us.

I talked about the European Plain that we lay in, about the eastern edge, where Kazakhstania had crashed into Pangaea, forcing the Ural Mountains high into the primordial air and making the youngest supercontinent whole. When we camped out, it was always someone's turn to talk about what they'd been reading, but my geological stories were the most sought-after, because they were the most sedative. It wasn't that they were dull – or so my friends promised me – but rather the soporific effect of all that time and all that physical mass, the sense of extreme smallness it gave them.

By the time I had got onto the subject of post-orogenic collapse, they were all asleep. I rolled over and looked at Maike. Her mouth was open and her arm was thrown out on the bare ground as if raised in protest.

'I think my mum's having an affair,' I said, testing it out on her unconscious body. No one moved. 'She's having an affair with someone I was in love with,' I said. 'Or I'm still in love with.'

I lay on my front and listened to my heartbeat and thought about Oz in his bookshop, imagining him beside me, his fingers laced through the hair at the back of my head. I fantasised about his green Mercedes parked at the bottom of the hill, the engine turning over, waiting to take me away from Berlin and from ever having to hurt anyone or ever having to have an awkward conversation again.

*

I woke because of the silence, or perhaps because of a change in the light. The crickets had stopped singing and the stars above us had been bleached by the risen moon.

'Ralf?' It was Maike. She was standing over me.

'You OK?' I whispered.

She put her finger to her lips to shush me and held out her hand. I took it and she led me through the pale observatory buildings, round and rendered like dreamt-of adobe houses in a Mexican village. We walked in jumpy movements as the flinty stones in the mud dug into our bare feet.

'Where are we going?' I said.

'To find a place,' she whispered.

The place was the moon shadow of the furthermost observatory, where she pushed me against the rough wall and kissed me. When I pulled her close and she let out a little moan, I whispered, 'Here?'

She nodded and kissed my neck as I slipped my fingers into her shorts. She gripped the hair at the back of my neck, then pulled away, squatted down leaving my fingers cold and patted the ground. I could feel the damp beneath my feet and said, 'We can do it sitting up.'

'No,' she said, feeling around her wildly like a seer, 'I want to be in the dark. I want to be covered in you.'

She let out a sharp intake of breath and put her finger in her mouth.

'What?'

'Nettle.'

'We can go back if you want,' I said, but half-heartedly, because I was already hard.

She crawled forward to the dry ground of the path and pulled down her shorts, rolling over, so that her buttocks were exposed, pale and round in the dark. 'Here,' she said. 'But cover me.'

'Can they see us?'

'No,' she said, but she hadn't looked. She slipped her hand

between her legs. 'Ralf,' she said, and I pulled down my shorts and we had sex on the bare ground, my face full of her hair and her mouth, my elbows and knees digging painfully into the hard stones.

*

'Hey,' someone said. 'I don't think you can sleep here.'

I rolled over and saw that it was light and a nervous-looking pimpled student in an orange windcheater was standing over me. Maike was back between Stefan and Petra, fast asleep.

Bleary-eyed, we rolled up our sleeping bags and stuffed them into our rucksacks, then coasted down the hill on our bikes, winding down the wooded paths half conscious. In Berlin, we were almost never allowed to camp out where we actually did camp out, and so expected this kind of awakening. It didn't worry or annoy us. We just cycled to the main road, then split up and cycled back to our various homes. It was only when Stefan left me at Kolonnenstraße and I was alone that I realised how terrified I was of going back to Charlottenburg.

Ten

A walled-in exclave surrounded by a hostile country with sweltering summers and glacial winters did not make West Berlin an attractive destination for many Germans in the Bundesrepublik. The city's special status, however, afforded us a few advantages, as West Germany and the occupying powers pumped in huge quantities of money to keep the shopfront of democracy looking as shipshape as possible. One such advantage was the West Berlin flat rate – a fixed price for a phone call within West Berlin no matter how long that call lasted. We treated our telephones like intercoms, ringing friends and chatting idly, staying on the line while the caller went to the toilet, took something out of the oven, got dressed. People watched TV together at opposite ends of the city, smoking a cigarette in silence with the receiver under their chin, only speaking sporadically to comment on Dagmar Berghoff's ugly blouse on the *Tagesschau*. It was not uncommon to find our phone lying on the kitchen floor, hanging from its spiral cord. You would pick it up and say, 'Hello?' to see who was there. Sometimes Beate was at the other end, sometimes Stefan, sometimes the caller had long since hung up.

The flat rate meant that I was able to avoid my mother that

Monday by talking to Maike for three hours when Mum got home from work. I then skipped dinner and went and watched *Aguirre, The Wrath of God* with Stefan at his flat. Petra and I worked at the beer garden on Tuesday evenings, and when I came through the door, my skin and hair smelling of fried *Leberwurst*, the lights were off and everybody was already in bed. On Wednesday mornings my mother did paperwork and so slept in an extra hour, so I got up at seven to get out of the house before she woke up.

When I came into the kitchen from the shower my father was already at the table taking apart *Die Zeit*, and the room smelt of coffee. He frowned and said, 'You all right, Ralfi? Couldn't you sleep?'

'I'm fine,' I said. 'We're doing a nature thing in the woods.' The vagueness was intentional – I'd watched an episode of *Tatort* in which one of the detectives had said that you could tell if someone was lying if their story was too elaborate.

'Bit early, isn't it?'

'A bit.'

I opened the fridge and took out a yoghurt. The day was already so hot that I lingered in front of the cool fridge for longer than I needed to, feeling the cold air on my bare chest, still damp from the shower.

'Do you want a boiled egg or something? You'll need more than yoghurt if you're going to be out all day.'

I shook my head. I had barely eaten anything since I'd bumped into Tobias and seen the watch in his fingers and the smile on his lips. 'Stefan's bringing *Franzbrötchen*.' It was awful how easy it was to lie to my father and terrible how he just accepted it. He was too good, betrayed by everyone around him. It made me sick, thinking of him climbing into

81

their bed, not knowing that Tobias's body had been pressed into it a few hours earlier.

I tried to imagine him losing his temper, finding out about Tobias and flying into a rage, but it was unimaginable; my father was pathologically calm. It frustrated my mother. I had seen her driven into rages so passionate in the face of his impossible serenity that she had broken cups, plates and glasses, dashing them to pieces in the sink when he calmly ended an argument by saying, 'Well, yes, of course I'm sorry. I'm sorry that it's made you so upset.'

I watched him carefully remove the fliers from the newspaper and stack them up for the recycling bin. He ordered the important parts of the paper to read first, and made a second pile with the football section, the cultural sections and the magazine that he would carry through to the living room and place on the coffee table, to be read slowly over the week. His attentive movements, the perfect trim of his moustache, his neatly clipped fingernails and his lemon-yellow polo shirt, creased where it had been ironed, made me hate my mother for betraying him.

I peeled off the yoghurt lid and sat opposite him at the table, licking the thickened yoghurt off the silvered underside. My dad pulled over a cup from the group gathered in the middle of the table and poured me coffee from the thermos jug. The cup was decorated with offensively bright birds and flowers, a ubiquitous 1970s Villeroy & Boch pattern called 'Acapulco' that I often see nowadays in trendy bars in Prenzlauer Berg, because it was ugly enough to become ironic.

'Do you want milk?'

I shook my head. 'Do you get up this early every Wednesday?' I said.

'Where do you think the bread rolls come from?'

'I don't know,' I said. 'I never really thought about it.'

'You know where the food in the fridge comes from, don't you? And your pocket money?'

'I think we all know the money comes from Mum.'

He laughed and opened *Die Zeit* to a page containing a picture of happy people in summer clothes running through a field, with the headline 'A Chink of Freedom: A Break in the Iron Curtain'.

'What are they doing?' I said.

'Running. The Austrians and Hungarians opened the border for a few hours.'

'Why?'

'Ostensibly, to celebrate freedom.'

'And not ostensibly?'

'Because thousands of East German holidaymakers in Hungary have decided not to go home, because they think there's a chance that Hungary will open their borders after these democracy talks. They sell it all under the banner of freedom, but they just don't want a load of East German refugees freezing to death in tents when winter hits. So they advertised a picnic to celebrate freedom and left the gate open for a few hours. Of course, hundreds just ran for it.'

His moustache twitched.

'You annoyed?' I asked.

'Me?' He laughed and shook his head. 'No, not annoyed, just worried. In the Sixties the Russians put down a lot of things like this.'

I looked at the black-and-white men and women fleeing into a grey meadow. 'Did anyone ever get through when you were little?' Dad had grown up in Hessen in the West, but near the East German border.

'Oh yes,' he said. 'Once or twice someone appeared at the farm.'

'How did they manage it?'

'It wasn't impossible, just dangerous. They have automatic guns, mines, all sorts. Someone was always losing their dog in the death strip.'

'Because it got blown up?'

'Or shot.'

'That's horrible.'

'Once someone's toddler wandered in.'

'Did he get shot?'

'No, but the mother did. Lived though. She was rescued by …' He spun his finger around, inviting the inevitable response.

'Opa the Great.'

He laughed.

I had never met my father's father, nor his mother. My German grandfather had become a family joke, because of his relentless heroism. An enthusiastic socialist before the war, he had been persecuted and then tortured by the Nazis, losing an ear and all of his toenails. Despite this, he had briefly been a member of the regional parliament in Wiesbaden, had rescued a collection of rare manuscripts from the burning village library, and saved from drowning a woman, two children and a border collie, though, as my father was always careful to point out, all on different occasions.

He had died, to everyone's shock, from a heart attack two days before I was born. His wife, my grandmother, had never got over the death and died herself six months later, superficially of pneumonia, but really, we all knew, from a broken heart. There was a beautiful black-and-white photograph of them that hung in the hall, both of them handsome in the way that everyone is handsome in wedding pictures taken before the mid-Sixties. 'I'm never going to live up to that,' my dad would say whenever Opa's name was uttered, and we would hug him and say we didn't mind if he didn't.

'Thank God for Opa,' I said. 'Would've ruined my day if she'd died.'

Dad smiled, his moustache flaring out like the wings of a pigeon. 'I'm sad you didn't meet him.' He reached out and touched my hand. 'He would have loved my boys. And you're the spit of him.'

'Dad, I don't look anything like him. He was two metres tall.'

'The eyes though.'

I smiled and adjusted my towel so that it clung to my waist more securely. 'Dad?' I said.

'Yes, *mein Lieber?*'

'If you thought you knew something bad about someone's boyfriend – if it was a friend of yours, I mean – something that your friend would be really upset about, would you tell her? Even if you weren't completely sure.' I considered this approach very subtle; I'd been thinking about the wording of the question for some time. I tried to read his face, but it was impenetrable. Did he ever cry? I thought. Beate liked to joke that my dad was the only real 'new man' in West Berlin, but that was only because he earned less than Mum and sometimes filled the dishwasher. He was very affectionate, but I'd never even seen him wet-eyed in front of a sad film. The idea of him screaming, weeping uncontrollably – it was incomprehensible.

'Is this Petra by any chance?' he said. He liked all of my friends and enjoyed seeming knowledgeable about them.

'I can't tell you, but . . . ' I shrugged as if to imply 'maybe'.

85

'Well,' he said, 'I think if it was someone else's relationship and I wasn't sure I probably wouldn't say anything.'

I felt both relieved and disappointed. 'Why not?' I asked.

'Well, I don't know what you think you know about this boyfriend, but unless you're a hundred per cent sure I think you could really hurt your friend and potentially your friendship.'

I murmured in agreement. I wanted him to give me permission to tell him. I wanted to rat my mother out, not for my father's sake – he would be destroyed – but for simple old-fashioned revenge. She had betrayed us. All the supposedly happy family moments, all the dinners and holidays and nights in front of the TV when I felt safe and loved had all been a lie. When Dad was teasing her about her crush on Peter Weck in *Ich heirate eine Familie*, rubbing her thickly socked feet as he reached over for a pretzel stick, she laughed in the blue glow of the television, having fucked Tobias perhaps an hour or two earlier, perhaps on that sofa where she now sipped *Grauburgunder* and complained about the British poll tax.

'Everything all right, Ralf?' Dad said.

'Yeah, I'm fine. It's not about me. It's not really my problem, but . . . ' I trailed off.

'Your mum mentioned you still weren't sure about where you were going to study. And you've been in and out this week at funny times. You weren't here for Sunday lunch. We picked the food for your mum's birthday and Martin had to pick for you.'

'That's in like two weeks' time,' I said. 'And we always eat the same thing.'

'It's just a bit erratic, for you.'

'Erratic? I just left school. I'm still doing my Wildlife Trust things. I'm still working at the beer garden. And I will decide about university, but I just want to be free to think about it. Otherwise what's the point of living in the West?'

Dad laughed.

'Don't laugh at me.'

'I'm sorry,' he said. 'You just usually tell us if you're going to be out all night. You're usually very considerate.'

'I haven't become inconsiderate. But maybe ... I don't know. Maybe I feel like I've been behaving a certain way for too long and I haven't been very honest with myself. And that everyone else just does what they want and doesn't care what the consequences are.'

He put both hands on my arm. 'Well, that sounds *kacke*.' *Kacke* was the second-worst swear word my father used. *Scheiße* was reserved for slicing a finger or stubbing a toe.

I got up, threw my yoghurt pot into the bin and rinsed the teaspoon under the tap.

'Ralfi?' he said.

'What?'

'D'you want to do the coffee before you go?'

He retrieved a new packet from the sideboard, vacuum-packed into a hard brick. I wavered, but then went to the table and gripped it, trying to concentrate on its hardness as he snipped the edge of the golden foil with a pair of scissors. I felt the packet instantly soften and collapse beneath my fingers. I took the open packet and inhaled a noseful of the thick aroma, so rich and chocolatey it was almost savoury.

'I wish coffee tasted as nice as it smells.'

'I'm glad you asked me about your friend,' said Dad, taking the packet back.

'Oh,' I said, adjusting my towel again and feeling ashamed of myself for even thinking about telling him. 'That's OK.'

In my room, I pulled on a T-shirt and shorts, put on my

battered trainers over high white socks and, hearing my mother stirring in the bedroom, ran out of the house. I wheeled my bike onto the street and sat on the crossbar with my hands draped over the handlebars. I had planned to cycle to Kreuzberg, to lie on the grass in Volkspark Friedrichshain until ten or so and then call on Maike, but suddenly felt indecisive. It was so early that I calculated I couldn't call on Maike for another two hours, and I'd forgotten to pack a book. I certainly wasn't going to go upstairs again. Cautiously, I turned and looked up the street. Close enough to make out that there was a driver, but too far away to make out their face, I saw a green car parked beneath a lime tree alive with sunlight.

I turned my bike towards it, lifted myself onto the saddle and lazily kicked down on the pedals of my bike. I was aware, in my peripheral vision, of the Tweetie Pie bell on my handlebars, an ironic gift from Maike when I'd turned fifteen. But my gaze was fixed on the driver of the green Mercedes, that resolved into Oz, his hand hanging over the steering wheel holding a smoking cigarette, his other hand at his mouth and his eyes locked onto my face.

Eleven

We sat side by side. The car smelt of old leather and cigarettes, the smell of every second car in those days. Oz was wearing a pale pink T-shirt tucked into white shorts. I stared at his knees, like smooth, brown fists. After I'd locked my bike to a lamppost and got into the car I was silent for a while. At some point I managed, 'You probably need to go to work.'

'Ralf,' he said, which I read as meaning, 'Calm down and pull yourself together and you came to me, which is fine, but you don't need to pretend you didn't.'

I caught sight of Frau von Hildendorf tottering out of the front door of our apartment block and ducked my head, covering my face with my hand. I scratched at my hairline, as if that was the purpose of the gesture, embarrassed that Oz had seen me embarrassed. Oz watched Frau von Hildendorf go into the bakery. 'Shall we drive somewhere?'

'Where, though?' I said, the tone more desperate than I'd intended.

'Out of town.'

I looked at his face for the first time. He was frowning and smiling, patiently waiting for me.

'Out out?'

'Why not?' he said.

My assent was a muddle of shrugging, nodding and the mouthing of unsounded OKs.

*

As we turned into Kanstraße, Oz pressed down the button for the cigarette lighter. Automatically, I drew my hands into my lap. I'd stuck my finger onto the glowing rings of the lighter in my parents' car as a child and could still remember the ghastly sizzle and bone-white pain. When the button popped, Oz steered with his bare knees and lit a Gitane. 'Want one?' he said.

I nodded and lit a cigarette from his. The wind from the open windows battered my face and the sun fluttered across my legs, turning the hairs amber. The smoke from our cigarettes disappeared to nothing over our shoulders and the car roared beneath us to the edge of the city, to the border.

'I always loved these cars. Dad drives Opels,' I said, my lips loosened by the cigarette.

'I've had it for ever. I love it, but it's a nightmare in winter.'

The queue at the Dreilinden checkpoint was shorter than normal. We'd been waiting for two hours and I guessed we'd wait another thirty minutes at least. We were all very good at guessing the waiting time based on the length of the queues, but the vagaries of the East German border guards were impossible to fathom, and sometimes they stripped down car after car.

'What if I'd left my ID at home?' I said, listening to the chugging engine.

'I don't think you're the sort of person who leaves their ID at home.'

I rubbed my index finger along my chapped lips. 'I think my mum's having an affair.'

'*Ach*, I er . . . ' Oz stuttered. '*Scheiße*. Sorry. That was . . . That was unexpected.'

I leant against the door and felt the sun on my neck and the heat tumbling up from the concrete beneath us. I felt panicked; I felt like opening the door and running.

'I'm sorry,' I said. 'It's been on my mind.'

'No, I'm sorry. For you, I mean.'

'Don't be sorry for me. You should feel sorry for my dad.'

'He doesn't know?'

'Why would he know?'

Oz put his hand on his chest and said, 'I don't know him, so . . . But, maybe it's one of those kinds of marriages where those things are allowed.'

'What kind of marriages are those?'

'I don't know. As I said, I don't know him.'

I stared out of the window at the cars in the neighbouring queue. There was a canary-yellow VW Beetle with a red setter hanging its head out of the window, filmy bubbles of spit clinging to its panting pink tongue. It turned its head, looking down towards the East German checkpoint, where a Russian tank – the first tank to reach Berlin in 1945 – was parked with its gun pointed at the queues of West Berliners.

'Sorry,' I said. 'It was stupid just saying it like that. I don't normally tell people things like that. Just this one's driving me . . . It's made me sick and with you . . . '

'What about me?'

I turned. He looked so worried. 'Nothing. It's just . . . I don't know. I feel like I left school, was finally excited to start, you know, life, and everything's just falling to pieces.'

The red and white barrier lifted and the cars moved forward. 'Tell me about it then,' Oz said.

'I can't even explain it to myself,' I said, as the East German guard waved us to the first window.

*

When I was a student in Britain I discovered that many people believed that Berlin sat exactly on the border between East and West Germany. In fact, when the occupying powers carved up the country after the war, they divided both Germany and Berlin into four zones. Berlin sat in the middle of the Russian zone, so when the Allies turned into Cold War enemies, West Berlin was left stranded, a semicircular island in the middle of enemy territory. Eventually transit routes through East Germany were negotiated, including three roads, the most popular of which ran from West Berlin to Helmstedt-Marienborn. It was this road that we joined, when the final barrier lifted to let us through.

As we juddered over the joins between the concrete slabs at the mandatory 100 kilometres an hour, the interminable banks of pine trees dropped away revealing East German fields filled with wheat turning a pale yellow. I reached out my hand to feel the jellyish substance of air at speed and looked over at Oz's mouth, at his lips slightly parted, the edges of his front teeth visible. I had to turn away again. I felt as though his face would turn me to ash if I stared at it for too long.

'What?' he said.

'I don't know. I keep thinking how ridiculous this is.'

'What? Me?'

I laughed. 'No. I don't mean you're ridiculous. I just mean this situation. Getting in a car with a stranger and driving to West Germany.'

'I'm hardly a stranger.'

'I don't know anything about you!'

'There's not that much to know; I'm not that interesting.'

'Yeah, yeah,' I said.

'It's true,' he said. He smiled at me. 'Ask me whatever you like. I'm going to turn out to be a massive disappointment. You'll see.'

'OK,' I said. 'What do you do when you're not spying?'

He laughed. 'I'm not a spy. Not in the way you're thinking about it.'

'How do you know how I'm thinking about it?'

He looked at me. 'I don't want to disappoint you,' he said seriously.

I didn't know what to say to this. 'I don't care,' was the best I could come up with.

'No?' he said.

'No.'

He shifted in his seat. 'I'm a paid informant.'

'Which means?'

'Which means I'm not technically employed by the Federal Intelligence Agency – the BND – but I get paid for helping out.'

'Why can you be helpful?'

'Well, Dad's businesses are pretty diverse, so I take the deliveries at the shop, look after his flats – like the ones in your block – sort out bulk sales, things like that. I get around a lot in Berlin and meet a lot of people. Also, there's the Turkish thing. That gets me into some places that other people can't, makes me more invisible.'

'Why?'

'Well, if you were looking out for a spy in your building, what kind of person would you be looking for?' I thought of Tobias eating his bowl of soup. 'It would be some white guy in a raincoat, probably. If I'm sniffing about and asking

93

questions people just think I'm some nosy brown person. If they see me at all. And if they tried to describe me, they would just say I was an *Ausländer*. They wouldn't be able to describe me after they'd met me. I'm twenty-two – even better, right? A Turkish youth. People actively try not to look me in the eye. It's perfect. If people get suspicious, at worst they're going to think I'm part of some sort of Turkish mafia. Either way, they don't think I'm working for the West German government. I'm not married, so I'm hard to blackmail.'

'Why aren't you married?'

He looked at me and frowned. 'Ralf, you know why I'm not married.'

I blushed and stared at the cigarette butts sprouting from his ashtray. 'What do you do though when you're not working?'

He shrugged. 'I don't know. I, er ... I read. I read a lot. Go to the cinema. Listen to music. Go out and eat.'

'What do you eat when you go out and eat?'

He smiled. 'What everyone else eats. Turkish, of course. German, Italian.'

'What's your favourite pasta shape?' I said.

He laughed, flashing his white teeth back to the molars. 'Now that's a good question,' he said, grinning and wagging his finger in the air. 'Now you're going to get some real insight. My favourite pasta shape is ... penne.'

'Which one's that?'

'Like little flutes.'

'Oh, OK,' I said. 'My favourite's bow-tie shape.'

'Good choice,' he said. 'Although it's sometimes still hard in the middle bit, where the sides meet.'

'True,' I said.

'You know, penne's actually pronounced "pen-ne" with a

stress on the "n" and if you don't stress the "n" then it means "penis" in Italian.'

I laughed. 'So you could accidentally end up with a big bowl of dick.'

'Covered in tomato sauce.'

We both laughed at this.

'And what about friends?' I said.

He shrugged again. 'Not so many friends.'

'Why not?'

'I mean, I had school friends. And I see my family, but I ... I don't know. I'm on my own in the shop or in the car most days. My only colleague's my dad.' He looked embarrassed. 'Also, I'm shy.'

'You're not!'

He laughed. 'I am a bit. Really. And I'm not sure I'm some-one people just like.'

'What are you talking about? That's dumb.'

'I don't know,' he said. 'My family aren't that into all my books and films and music. They think it's all a bit ... I don't know, poncey.'

'What would they rather you were into?'

'I think they'd rather I had a big group of mates, like my brother. I was the clever one, which meant I was going to be an accountant or a solicitor, or something like that, but I did cultural studies, and then dropped out of university after a year. It wasn't for me.'

'Why?'

'I thought the other students were dicks, to be honest. Now I'm helping my dad out and, you know, saving the Western world. But I'm not going to do that for ever – you can't, I don't think. West Berlin's too small and at some point people are even going to start noticing me. I still need to try and work out what the fuck I'm going to with my life. This is a process that's been in motion for some time. Bit of a disappointment to my poor dad.'

'I'm sure you're not a disappointment,' I said. We were overtaken by a red VW Beetle with Cologne number plates. 'What about swotty school friends?'

'I used to hang around with a group of guys at school, but they all ended up working at Siemens and Bayer and places like that – one's at the Sparkasse. His mum's happy. We left school like four years ago now; I don't really see them. Turned out we didn't have much in common. Not like you and your friends. You're lucky.'

'I am,' I said.

I stared across the flat fields of Bezirk Potsdam at the farm-houses with their high tiled roofs and the grey-brown render on their walls. 'It all looks so bucolic,' I said. 'Do you think they think they're oppressed?'

Oz looked at me, then back at the road. I could see behind his sunglasses; his eyelashes were so long that they touched the lenses. 'I don't suppose so. Certainly not most of the time. Maybe once in a while, when they can't get something. No one can think about something like that all the time.'

'Did you read about those people in Hungary?'

'Going through the gate?'

I nodded.

'Yeah,' he said.

'Can you imagine things being so bad that you'd camp out by the border just in case? What if they're there in winter? With kids.'

'I can imagine it,' he said. 'If life was awful enough, I'd probably do the same. If the offer was good enough . . . '

'Dad thinks the Russians are going to send in tanks.'

Oz laughed. 'They're not sending any tanks. You need to tell your dad it's not the Sixties any more.'

'You think it's going to collapse? East Germany?'

'Oh yeah,' Oz said. 'I mean, at some point. Doesn't mean things are going to get any better. Might turn violent. But it won't stay the same.'

I looked down at his hand resting on the gear stick. There was a ragged white scar that ran from his wrist to the knuckle of his thumb.

'What's that from?' I said.

'The scar?' he said, flexing his fingers. 'SodaStream.'

'Really? How?'

'I got my thumb caught between the handle and the machine. I wasn't meant to be using it. I pulled the lever down and it trapped my thumb and I panicked and pulled the whole thing off the countertop. Ripped a great gash in my hand. It was gross. Hands really bleed. I'm still terrified of them.'

'Hands?'

'SodaStreams. It's like Pavlov's dog.'

'Did he get his thumb caught in a SodaStream?'

Oz laughed drolly.

He held up the hand and said, 'Touch it. It's lumpy where one of the stitches got infected.'

I reached out and touched his skin, stroking the white scar, forgetting that I was meant to be searching for a lump. The air filled with the wail of a truck horn and we looked up to see a lorry surging past, the passenger looking down into the car, laughing silently behind the glass of his cabin and using his middle and index finger to mime fucking. I pulled my hand away, and Oz's hand drifted back down to the gearstick. 'Bon voyage,' he said and waved at them with ironic enthusiasm.

97

I turned away from him, my ears burning with shame, and stared concentratedly at the hot countryside, listening to cars and lorries and – when we slowed at the final checkpoint to cross the border into West Germany – the shrill cry of grass-hoppers in the dry grass by the side of the road.

After Helmstedt, Oz pulled off the main road to Brunswick. We drove down a narrow country lane that turned into a trail, then wound up into high woodland. The canopy closed around us, the hot breeze brushing the leaves together like silk dragged across silk.

Oz turned off into a clearing where he stopped the car and cut the engine. The ensuing silence slowly filled with the sounds of birds and the tick of the hot engine as it cooled. I could hear running water and smell sap, hot earth and hot dead leaves.

'Where are we?' I said.

'It's like this little wood on a hill,' said Oz, pulling his keys out of the ignition. He reached over me, pulled open the glove compartment and tossed his sunglasses inside. They'd made a maroon ridge on the bridge of his nose. 'Just some-where to go for a walk. Unless you want to go into Hanover. Or Brunswick.'

I shook my head. 'No, this is great.'

I opened the door and climbed out. My T-shirt was stuck to my back and my underpants were uncomfortably bunched up beneath my shorts.

'It's just a wood. I stopped here once to have a wander – you can get really lost in there. I love woods.'

'It's the Lappwald,' I said.

'Is it?' he said. 'How do you know?'

'I read about it. There are some old watchtowers and the border passes through it.'

'Yeah, that's it. Sounds like you know more about it than I do.'

'Have you got a route?'

'No. I thought we could just wander.'

'Fine by me,' I said.

We walked along forest paths, with steep banks covered in a stippled blanket of brown and ochre leaves. The foliage above formed a gauzy tunnel and the path below was unyielding, peppered with rocks and the perfect indentations of horses' hooves set hard in the baked clay. The air was filled with buzzing insects that brushed our faces and the high whine and itch of mosquitoes, real and imagined.

I saw some stone steps leading steeply up a bank and away from the path.

'Let's go up here,' I said.

'Oh,' said Oz, out of breath. 'OK. I don't know what's up there though.'

'If we get high enough we'll be able to look down over the Weser-Aller-Flachland; we'll be able to see the slope.'

'The what?' he said, as I clambered up. The stone steps disappeared, were replaced with a yellow carpet of dying leaves and resinous pine needles. 'I'll show you,' I said, my face to the slope, so that it came out echoless and close. Brambles snagged my T-shirt and shorts and whipped at my legs like switches. The tiny cuts became hot and itchy.

We reached a clearing with a broken view east where, among the woods and fields, we could see patches of the barbed-wire barrier and a concrete watchtower peeping out of the green canopy.

'This is great,' I said, stopping, out of breath from the climb.

'Yeah,' said Oz, panting, unconvinced. 'Sorry, what are we looking at?'

'So this is all the Weser-Aller-Flachland,' I said, stretching out my hand to mime its flatness. 'We're at the highest point on this hill, which is why it's full of old watchtowers.'

'And new ones,' Oz said, nodding towards the East German border.

'Yeah, so this whole plain is tilted,' I said, showing him with my forearm. 'Starting up here at Bremen at like seventy or eighty metres above sea level, and then it slopes down all the way to Magdeburg in East Germany, dropping slowly, slowly, like a tipped plate. You can even see it in the flora.' I grabbed his shoulder and pointed it out, aware of the bone and muscle moving beneath the pink cotton. 'We're not quite high enough, but you can see a bit here at the tree line, and over there where the poplars are.'

'I wouldn't know what a poplar looked like.'

'The tall skinny ones. Can you see? And this bit we're standing on used to be a hollow too, but all of this land around us was flooded and washed away and then flooded and washed away again, leaving this bit sticking out. That's called a horst – it's the same word in English. That's why there's so much coal here – because of the flooding. This would've all been tropical. Can you imagine? Giant dragonflies and huge plants. Like the Bahamas with dinosaurs. It's great for fossils.'

Oz laughed.

'What?' I felt myself going red and on my pale, freckled skin it spread in an expansive wash over my cheeks and out of my collar.

'No, it's amazing,' said Oz. 'It's … you're so enthusiastic about it.'

'But it is amazing. To me. And we get so bored with all the same spots in West Berlin. It's amazing just to have that vista, you know.'

Oz's smile faded. Sweat was beading his forehead and

had formed dark circles under the armpits of his T-shirt. His breathing had calmed, the whites of his eyes widened. A woodpecker thrummed at a tree trunk deep in the forest and my nose filled with the smell of hot dead foliage and the green breath of the trees. He took a step towards me. His shoe was very loud on the dry bed of twigs and leaves. I swallowed drily.

He grabbed my T-shirt. I looked down at the material bunched in his fist as he put his other hand on the back of my head, and found his way to my mouth.

My heart beat so loudly that I was afraid he could hear it. But then we were kissing and nothing happened, nothing but the kiss. The woodpecker continued to thrum and then the forest was still. There was just the noise of our kissing, and my heart, and the creak of the cotton of my T-shirt gathered up in his hand.

Twelve

We joined the queue of cars leading to the checkpoint into the East, past the hitchhikers holding up their thumbs and cardboard signs with areas of Berlin in wild biro letters: Friedenau, Wedding, Neukölln. I felt cut loose from the world, floating dangerously free. I thought of the East German refugee who, that spring, had built a balloon out of polythene and Sellotape in his East Berlin apartment, filled it with gas and floated over the Wall. He must have felt free, he must have felt elated for a few minutes in the cold night air before the makeshift balloon climbed and climbed and finally crumpled in the thin air, falling 2,000 metres, thumping into the manicured lawn of a Zehlendorf villa.

'It seems funny to have a sign, when they could only be going to West Berlin,' I said.

'There are so many, it's good to know if they're going to exactly your part of town. And sometimes they're going to Warsaw, or somewhere like that. Do you want to take someone?'

I loved him asking me, as if I had a say in what he did in his own car. 'No,' I said.

On the transit road, I watched the purple sky darkening over the fields and read the road signs for the exits that the

East Germans were allowed to take into Bezirk Magdeburg. 'What's it famous for, Magdeburg?' I said, not because I cared, but because I wanted to hear his voice.

Oz looked up at the sign. 'There's a cathedral. And the Elbe runs through it. There's a famous statue – the Magdeburg Rider.'

'Why is it famous?'

'Because of the poem.'

'What poem?'

'You know. "The auburn spray of hair entwined, the horse's head appealing".'

I shook my head. 'Never heard of it.'

'Where the hell did you go to school?'

'The British School. In Charlottenburg.'

'Oh!' he said. 'That explains it. We all had to do it in German.'

'Why?'

'It's one of those ones that's easy to study. It's about women and patriarchy and German history. Dream combination, if you're a German teacher.'

I yawned and stretched in my seat, pleasantly warm and tired. 'Who's it by?'

'Ingrid Mandelbaum. My sister was very into her. Lots of female friendship, duty, pregnancy, that sort of thing. I think she was the first person to refer to menstruation in print.'

'Really? That's funny.'

'She also translated lots of English poems. If you read anything Victorian and English, she's almost always translated it.'

'And she's from Magdeburg?'

'No. Berlin I think. But she died years ago; her husband was Jewish. They were all shipped off to Sachsenhausen or Auschwitz; one of the two. I can't remember.' He looked behind him and pulled out to overtake a lorry. 'He had a sister too who was in parliament before the war, but I think she was gassed as well. There was an article about it in *Die Zeit* a few months back.'

'That's really sad.'

'I know,' said Oz. 'The daughter was on the Kindertransport, though. She writes children's books in London.'

I smiled.

'What?' said Oz.

'Just you and your books and your women's poetry.'

'As I said, we all had to do it. And my sister was the fan.'

'How many brothers and sisters do you have?'

'Five sisters, one brother.'

'Really? No wonder you know a lot about menstruation.'

Oz chuckled.

'Are they all . . . ' I paused, unsure if I was phrasing it wrong, 'Muslims?'

He looked amused. 'Of course. We're Turkish. Did you not . . . ? You noticed, right?'

I hit him on the shoulder and he laughed.

'But I mean, do you all do the praying and the headscarves?'

'Well, I don't wear a headscarf,' said Oz.

I rolled my eyes. 'You know what I mean.'

'Yeah, I mean, one sister is married to a man called Cem, who no one likes. He's from quite a devout family – that's not why we don't like him, by the way – he's just a dick. And she wears a headscarf. But the others don't and my mum only did when we had Dad's family over from Turkey.'

'Isn't it weird never seeing your sister's hair?'

'Well, first, my sister's hair isn't that exciting, and, second, I do, because I'm her brother. She only wears the headscarf in front of strangers. Strangers who are men. You, though, are gonna miss out.'

'Just my luck,' I said.

We passed the sign that read 'Welcome to Berlin, the Internationally Recognised Capital of the German Democratic Republic'. The car slowed down to queue for the checkpoint and I thought about the men and women in the newspaper fleeing across the Hungarian border. As we passed into Berlin and were released from East German restrictions on speed and distance, Oz kicked down on the accelerator and the Mercedes sped over the baked tarmac of the AVUS motorway. I touched the luminous dials on the car radio. 'I want to stay in here for ever.'

'I know,' said Oz. 'Me too.'

When we parked back on my street I didn't move.

'I'm sorry about your mum,' Oz said. 'Maybe you should just ask her about this guy.'

I lay back in the seat and looked at him. In the dark of the car, his eyes were mahogany and flecked with the bluish light of the dying day. 'That's what I wanted to tell you,' I said.

'What?'

'The affair. It's Tobias Rode. The neighbour you asked me about.'

'Shit,' he said. 'So you *have* seen him doing something suspicious?'

I shrugged.

'Ralf,' Oz said. 'We're already watching him. We've been watching him for a while. Anything you tell me, it's not going to change anything. It just might speed things up.'

'Can you tell me what's he done?'

'He may've done nothing, in which case you'll be helping him.'

I laughed. 'I don't want to help him.'

Oz turned so that he was facing me and settled his shoulder into the seat. I could tell that the intrigue of the story was starting to overcome his anxiety about sharing it with me. He did odd jobs playing second fiddle to a father he felt he was disappointing, and then someone had asked him to help out with something real, something about life and death and nations at war. 'This is like . . . '

'Top secret,' I said. 'I know. I won't tell anyone.'

'OK,' he said. 'So, for about ten years, the BND have been after an undercover Stasi agent in West Berlin called "Axel" who deals in *kompromat*. It's like compromising information about someone that you can use to blackmail them. The stuff that "Axel" gets hold of is really good-quality, and he's never been caught out passing it back East. A few months ago, the BND turned a Stasi agent who was able to link "Axel" back to Windscheidstraße 53 – your apartment block.'

'And you think it's Tobias?'

'Yes. No one's seen "Axel", but we know that he was in a sanatorium in East Germany for kids with polio – and Tobias limps – and the description in the register said he had red hair, which, of course, fits. The timing also fits – "Axel" started delivering the *kompromat* soon after Tobias "fled" to the West.' He added the quotation marks around 'fled' with his index and middle fingers.

I stared at the spotted bark of a young lime tree newly planted to replace one that had blown down in a thunderstorm the summer before. I thought about what Oz had said, but still wasn't convinced. 'Have you actually met Tobias? Or talked to him?'

Oz shook his head. 'I've just watched him.'

'He's nice. I mean he's an arsehole, it turns out, but not like a Stasi blackmailer.'

Oz smiled. 'I'm sure he's nice,' he said. 'And we don't think he's using the material, we just think he's collecting it.'

A woman rattled by on high heels. We waited in silence until she'd passed.

'Why don't they just arrest him?'

'They want to catch him in the act, so that they can work out who his sources are. That's why they asked me to watch him. The information he's passing on is about important people in West Berlin from a lot of different walks of life and a lot of different places. That means lots of leaks that need to be found and stoppered.'

I touched the steel keyhole of the glove compartment.

'So what did you want me to do?'

'Just keep an eye on him. Your flat looks directly into his.'

I was well aware of this.

'Did you know who I was and where I lived when you bumped into me at the pool?'

He nodded. 'But I wasn't expecting ... I mean, I was just going to try and befriend you, ask you a few questions. I wasn't expecting ... this.'

I did believe him. Or rather, I believed that he believed that what he was telling me was true. But I still wasn't convinced that Tobias was an agent for the East German government. I couldn't tell Oz that I'd been watching Tobias for years and he'd never done anything to suggest that he was anything other than a charming, bumbling bachelor. He was affection-ate and scatty, and that could lead to adultery, I supposed, but not to espionage.

I did agree to help Oz, though. Because of the answer to my next question. 'If it turned out he was this agent, would they still arrest him at some point? Once they'd worked out what his sources were?'

'Of course.'

'But they wouldn't hurt him?'

'What do you mean?'

'I don't know,' I said.

'No,' said Oz. 'He'd just go to jail. If he's lucky, he'd be swapped back East after a year or two.'

I nodded. 'I'll see what I can do.'

A fox trotted across the street. It stopped in Oz's headlights and stared at us. I felt there had to be a consequence for what I'd done. People didn't just take trips out of the city with strangers, didn't just grass up their mothers, grass up people they'd once adored, men didn't just kiss men without paying for it.

'Good,' said Oz. 'If you didn't want to, though … I mean, I'd still like to see you. If you didn't want to help, or felt like you couldn't.'

We had left the known world too far behind and I didn't understand the language in this new space we existed in. I could only make a gesture: I touched his scar, luminous in the dark, and got out of the car. The sound of him pulling away and the plaintive bleep of the horn made me feel desperate and alone.

Thirteen

Maike's mother opened the door and I was shocked by how old she looked. A narrow flap of skin joined her chin to her neck and the shape of her skull was perceptible beneath her waxy, freckled forehead. Knowing about the cancer, I had expected her to be bald or at least be wearing a wig or a headscarf, but she had white hair permed into tight curls, clinging to her head like the wispy seed head of a dandelion.

'Hello,' I said. 'I'm Ralf.'

This didn't seem to spark any kind of recognition.

'I'm here to see Maike.'

'This late?' she said. 'Well, I'm not sure she's here.'

'She's in her room,' came a weary female voice from the kitchen.

'Oh,' her mother said. Her eyes passed over my face. 'Lena and Maike's room's on the left.' She grabbed my arm – her grip was surprisingly powerful. 'Leave the door open when you're in there.' And in response to a 'Jesus Mum!' from the voice in the kitchen, she said pleadingly, 'Ajar at least!'

I nodded, smiling as comfortingly as I could, and watched her make her slow progress back to the dark living room, where a ceiling fan rotated above her husband's sleeping form.

I pushed the door open to Maike's room, feeling nauseous and light, my bare legs cold. It was dark and there were two single beds – one pushed against each wall. She'd never told me that she shared her bedroom with one of her sisters.

The room smelled sweet, the artificial smell of bright, fruit-scented erasers. Although the heavy curtains were drawn, I could make out a desk separating the beds, strewn with stationery and neat piles of books and magazines. The sister's side of the room was papered with posters and pages torn from *Bravo* and *Mädchen*, depicting famous young men from American bands, with teeth as white as the T-shirts they wore beneath their loose denim shirts. The images of these boys stopped in an almost perfect line where Maike's half of the room began. Here hung only a large map of the world specked with a few coloured flag-pins.

Maike lay on her side facing the wall. I knew that she had bad periods, and when she did she stayed at home. She always called me and told me it was coming on and then I didn't hear from her for a few days. I'd never considered this odd. I put my hand on her bare arm and, without any movement to suggest consciousness, I heard her say, 'Ralf? You all right?'

In the dim room, with my hand on her arm, there was nothing I could say except for, 'Me? I'm fine. What about you?'

'It's just my period. I called, but your mum said she hadn't seen you in a few days.'

'No,' I said.

The air outside was so warm that I didn't notice the windows were open behind the curtains until a ripple ran down the length of them like a wave, releasing a pleasant breath of wind that cooled the sweat on my arms.

'Is it really bad?' I said.

'No worse than it always is,' she said. 'You should go. I'm not going to be any fun for a day or two.'

'You don't have to be fun,' I said, trying out on her the line that Oz had used on me in the bookshop.

She didn't answer.

'Can I get you something?' I said.

'No, it just hurts. I just have to wait for the pain to go away.'

The pain, we would discover fifteen years later, was endometriosis. The lining of her womb had migrated onto her other organs, her fallopian tubes, her ovaries. When the same ovaries pumped out oestrogen each month, the tissue responded, leaching blood into her innards. Once she had been diagnosed, she had to be medicated with opiates. That was what was going on beneath her still fingers as she lay there on the bed – excruciating pain, like a monthly dose of appendicitis.

'I was in the Lappwald today,' I said.

I waited for something to happen, for the question that would lance the boil and spill out the whole mess, infecting everything. '*Schön*,' she said. I stared at the side of her body, trying to see if she was breathing, but she was as still as a dropped puppet. 'You should really go,' came her voice again. 'But I do love you.'

'I love you too,' I said, and I did. In leaving the room, though, I recognised that I'd failed to reconcile the world that contained Oz and the real world that I lived in. I'd failed because it was impossible.

*

When I got home, I shut the front door very gently and slid over the parquet, the streetlight from the living-room windows reflecting in amber stripes on the polished wood. In my bedroom, I dropped my rucksack onto the floor and pulled open the wooden double windows. When I turned back to the room and my eyes adjusted to the darkness, the panes of the wardrobe mirror glowed blue grey and my bed sheet was picked up by the wind, lifted and then resolved into a human figure.

I inhaled in terror.

'Ralf?' the figure said.

'Jesus Christ!' I said, my hand clamped to my mouth.

'It's just Mum.'

The fear burst, creeping away into my extremities.

'What the fuck are you doing?' I said.

'I was waiting for you to come home. I fell asleep.'

'Fuck.'

I switched on my table lamp and she turned her face from the light, closing her eyes and shielding them with her hand. She was wearing a satin nightgown the purply silver of river water, from which her shoulders emerged, hard and freckled. She smiled, squinting. Without make-up, she looked puffy and lipless.

'Why the fuck were you waiting for me in the dark?'

'It wasn't dark when I started waiting.'

'Why were you waiting at all?'

Her hand smoothed the cotton of my bed sheets. 'I changed your bed.'

'Why?'

'You haven't been home. I haven't seen you in a week.'

'So?'

'You weren't here for dinner on Sunday. Stefan wasn't even sure where you were.'

'I've been with Maike.'

'She called. She was ill. A bad period.'

Maike had just told me that. I was frustrated at being

112

caught out in a lie and terrified that Mum might somehow have found out about Oz, so I desperately threw out, 'What, you've been spying on me?'

'I haven't been spying on you, Ralf. Why are you being so arsey?'

'Because you just scared the shit out of me.'

'I said sorry.'

'No you didn't.'

'Oh,' she said, and blinked. 'Well, I'm sorry.'

In her nightdress, on the edge of the single bed, in the low light from the desk lamp that threw her shadow giant and brown onto the wall behind her, she looked like a fallen woman from a Walter Sickert painting.

'Is everything all right with Maike?' she said.

'Yes. Why wouldn't it be?'

'You're upset about something.'

'Well, it's got nothing to do with her.'

She considered this. 'You know,' she said, 'these early friendships and relationships seem terribly important when you're your age, but it'll be a different world at university.'

'What's that supposed to mean?'

'Just that they'll make new friends too. And you'll meet new people, fall in love—'

'I am in love. You just don't like her.'

'Did she say that?'

'No, you make it completely obvious.'

She wrinkled her nose. 'I do like Maike. She doesn't like me. She doesn't say a word to me.'

'You said she was cold.'

'She is cold, Ralf. She's very cold with me. And I don't think she's all that warm with you. You're never over there. We've never met her parents.'

'You wouldn't like them. They're poor.'

She jolted upright. 'What do you mean? What on earth do you mean? "They're poor." That's your judgement. I've never even met them. Your grandfather was from Hull. We're not snobs.'

'You don't know anything about it,' I said.

'No, clearly I don't.' She screwed up her face as if she'd eaten something disgusting. 'And you're being very unpleasant.'

'Fine,' I said. 'I'm a terrible person. Can I go to bed now?'

'Of course,' she said, defeated.

She stood, put her hand on my shoulder and kissed my cheek. Her face was hot from sleep, like a child's. I found it hard to bear.

'Night then,' she said.

'Yes, night.'

Once she was gone, I undressed, turned off the light and fell onto my bed, feeling like I'd already let Oz down by losing my temper. My pillow smelt of her perfume. I threw it to the floor and tried to sleep face down on the bare sheets, but then my eyes opened in the dark. Was she going to leave us? It was the first time the thought had occurred to me. I pictured my father, Martin and me abandoned, watching our mother and Tobias home-making in the flat across the courtyard.

Do we all believe that our mothers are powerful, loving and infallible, interested only in us and our needs? This is how my mother had always seemed to me. In her wit, in her small, wiry frame, she seemed to embody a brisk vigour whose sole focus was the protection and care of our family. Even her job I understood as a way to keep us fed and safe and to stay near us as she did it.

And now? Now she had become human. Her fallibility had been exposed in an instant, like the lights going on in a club, revealing the shabbiness of all the dark forms that had a second earlier seemed so solid and so exquisite. Lying on the fresh sheets that she had changed for me I realised that this mortal form of my mother was able to make mistakes, to make selfish decisions, to leave us because it suited her, and that new possibility terrified me.

I closed my eyes and forced myself to think about Oz, seeing snatches of him in the woods, still feeling the burn of his stubble on my chin. With him on my mind, I was able to drift off, but woke up a few hours later needing to pee. When I crossed the hall to the bathroom, I could hear Mum crying and my father's soft, comforting voice emanating from their bedroom. Sitting on the toilet listening to the diminutive scream of a mosquito from the ceiling, I rubbed the palms of my hands into my eyes and smiled a little because although my life was coming to pieces, I was at least in love.

Fourteen

I felt like the kiss with Oz in the Lappwald had changed everything. I held on to the feeling throughout the stilted breakfast with my family, which I spent avoiding my mother's gaze, until she addressed me directly to remind me it was Beate's private view that evening and that I had to be ready by seven. I spent the morning lying on the sofa, while Martin lay on the floor, watching the beginning of the US Open in a stupor broken only when a wasp flew through the window and had to be urgently batted out because Martin was allergic.

As I pulled the window shut, I saw the tall man with neat hair that Stefan, Martin and I had seen in the dusk on the day I'd met Oz. He was walking out of the courtyard, away from our side of the building where he must've been seeing Mum again. Was he suspicious? I thought. It was odd that he didn't use the front entrance. But taking the back entrance only led him past Tobias's windows, not to his front door.

I looked up to see if Tobias was there, thinking perhaps that they were able to signal to each other, but Tobias's flat was empty and the man was walking unhurriedly with his head down. In the daylight, his hair was very white, but still full, and he was wearing pale trousers and a white shirt, all beautifully cut and expensive-looking, but oddly unfashionable. It meant that he was probably someone important in the British Army – Mum had a few of those patients.

The man stopped; was this the moment? But instead of turning to Tobias's apartment he turned to me and squinted, and I saw for a second his pale blue eyes and the large raised mole caught between the deep frown lines on his forehead. I pretended to be looking about for something in the courtyard, then turned and fell back down onto the sofa. He was probably just some old Army officer who was in love with one of his privates, I thought. It all seemed possible now.

It was during the breaks in play, as I stared at the cloudless sky thinking about Oz, that I began to understand that, seen from any distance, the kiss was nothing, that everything in my life wasn't dramatically collapsing, but was completely unchanged. Oz wasn't a part of it. He was an adult gay man, I realised, with a sinking sense of disappointment. I had read an article in *Stern* in which a gay man, blacked out to hide his shame, talked openly about his sexual partners, how he met them in the woods around the Aachener Weiher in Cologne. When the interviewer asked the man how many sexual partners he'd had, he couldn't even count. Hundreds, he supposed. That was Oz, I realised with a heavy heart: a gay man who'd eyed me up and I'd got into his car. The kiss must have been a huge disappointment. He was probably in a bar on Motzstraße now regaling his friends with the story of the ginger Englishman from the traffic lights who talked about horsts and hills and just kissed him.

Once Boris Becker was ahead in the match, I fell asleep. I woke up to find my dad clicking through the three channels, his thumb on the thick chrome buttons of the veneered set.

'Did he win?' I said.

'Becker?' Dad said. 'Of course.'

117

He turned over to the news and stayed standing with his arms crossed as he listened to the headlines. They talked about the build-up of East German refugees in Hungary and the story of Kurt-Dörsam Schulz from Weimar, who shared half of our surname and had been shot in front of his mother and six-year-old child trying to cross the Hungarian border into Austria. They showed the border, rolling curls of barbed wire laid along rolling green hills, what the presenter described as a 'bucolic landscape of meadows and buttercups', though I could see from the close-up of the site of the man's death that the flowers were yellow field mustard, dandelions and showy goat's-beard.

My father nodded at the TV. 'See,' he said. 'Always ends in violence. This is what I was talking about.'

'They're not sending in any tanks though.'

'Who told you that?'

'Read it somewhere,' I said.

Dad sat on the edge of the coffee table to watch and Dagmar Berghoff's voice lulled me back to sleep. I was woken by Mum pulling on my big toe. The TV had been turned off and the windows were closed. The room was hot and airless.

'Are you ready?' she said.

Miserable about Oz and furious with her, I grunted and rolled off the sofa.

'You need to get changed.'

'I'm wearing this,' I said.

Mum had on a white silk dress with a soft bow at the neck. She fussed with the white leather belt at her waist, then agitated the large pearls in her ears. I wondered if she'd seen Tobias since she'd returned the watch. Perhaps he'd said something about the conversation we'd had in the hall.

'Can't you put something nice on?' she said.

'What's wrong with what I'm wearing?'

I had on shorts, grubby white socks and an old white T-shirt with a cartoon orange on it that Dad had brought back from a business trip to Valencia. The orange had a plaster on its head and was saying '*¡34° Congreso Nacional de la Sociedad Española de Farmacia Hospitalaria!*'

'It's a private view,' Mum said.

'It's Beate. She doesn't care what I wear. She wore her dead dad's old suit last time.'

'That was art.'

'OK,' I said. 'This is art.'

'You know,' Mum said, 'you're very prickly at the moment.' She looked small and angry, like a bird.

'I don't know what "prickly" means,' I said, wandering to my room, her following. I pulled on my beaten-up Puma trainers, still caked in dry grey mud from the garlic-toad count. I had actually planned to wear a yellow polyester shirt that I saved for special occasions, but I wanted Mum to know how angry I was with her without actually having to talk about why.

'You know exactly what "prickly" means,' she said. 'You always pretend not to know English words to win arguments. It's very petty.'

'If you say so.'

Mum folded her arms, and touched her throat with her fingertips. 'What's up with you at the moment, Ralf? Is something wrong? Dad said you were up at six for some nature project this week. Do you want me to speak to someone at the Wildlife Trust? Dr What's-His-Face?'

'It's not that,' I said, pushing past her to go to the bathroom.

'Well, what is it then?'

'Nothing,' I said. I had always been so convinced about my

abilities to hold in my feelings, but I saw now that I'd been mistaken. Oz had asked me to act normally around my mother and I was failing. 'I'm just tired,' I said.

'Do you want a tea? Or I could make us all coffee.'

I waved the comment away and kicked the bathroom door shut behind me.

*

We could see the crowd as we turned into Schlüterstraße. In front of Galerie Schmelling a group of men and women in beautiful pale clothes were laughing and drinking *Sekt*. Now I wished I had changed. Mum had put on white broderie anglaise gloves to match her dress and looked like Daisy in *The Great Gatsby*. Dad was wearing a light blue suit, and even my brother was wearing chinos. I felt like somebody they'd bumped into on the street and had convinced to tag along.

Beate greeted us effusively, covering me and Martin in kisses scented with sparkling wine and red lipstick. Mum became teary in her friend's arms. 'I'm so proud,' she said, stroking her face. 'I'm so proud of you, darling Beate.'

Stefan appeared in white jeans and a white shirt, red leather slip-on shoes and a skinny red leather tie.

'That's an outfit,' I said.

'Oh, Mum found the tie. The shoes were my dad's.' This was a running joke, since Beate claimed not to be completely sure who Stefan's father was. There were a few candidates, all vanished. Stefan maintained that he didn't mind and that it was his mother's right to throw off the chains of the dominant patriarchy.

'Well, you look lovely,' Mum said, kissing him, leaving apricot-coloured smudges on his cheek. 'Like you're in Depeche Mode, or something.'

I locked up my bike and stood with Stefan beneath a tall

plane tree at the edge of the kerbside crowd. We watched the artists, dealers and local buyers mill in and out. Among the suits and sheer dresses were a few punks and pierced youths with black hair, some students of Beate's from the Akademie der Künste.

'All OK, Ralfi?' Stefan said.

'Fine,' I said. 'Why?'

'Your mum was looking for you yesterday. Said you weren't at Maike's.'

'I was cycling about.'

Petra tripped out of the gallery in an electric blue dress and gold high heels, carrying three glasses of *Sekt*.

'Well you made an effort,' she said, kissing me on the cheek and handing out the drinks. We clinked glasses and emptied them in one.

Petra put a fist to her chest and burped. 'Ooh, it burns,' she said. 'Maike not coming?'

'She's still ill,' I said. 'Period pains.'

'She really bleeds.'

Stefan nodded reverentially. He was, he liked to say, 'very down' with menstruation.

We watched Beate kissing a new partner, a tall man with a beaten-up old rocker's face, a leather jacket and hair too long for his age.

'What's this one called?' I said.

'Rainer.'

'Is it a six-weeker or a six-monther?'

'Six-weeker, I think,' Stefan said. 'He's an artist and those ones never last very long. He's already taken over a little corner of her studio, which she hates, and she's started critiquing his woodcuts. Once she starts picking apart the work, they're done for. It means she's embarrassed by them.'

Rainer licked Beate's lips with a long, pink tongue and she roared with laughter.

'Your mum doesn't seem like someone who's easily embarrassed,' said Petra.

Beate took out her lipstick and painted Rainer's lips and the laughter of the crowd around her rose up to engulf her own. A tall man in jeans and a white T-shirt rolled up at the arms like a rock-a-billy strode across the street and joined the crowd around us. He looked about him, double-took and came over to us.

'Hey, you're Beate's son!' he said. His hair was straight and fair and he had a big friendly face, with a large knobbly nose.

'Yeah,' said Stefan.

'I remember you from when you were this high,' the man said, holding out a big hand.

'I don't remember you,' said Stefan.

The man laughed. 'Joachim.' He shook hands with Stefan, and then Petra and me, but he only glanced at us two. 'I was your mum's assistant for about a week back in eighty-three, but then got a place in Düsseldorf, so ran off West. God, you look really well.'

'Oh, thanks,' said Stefan. 'Joachim, was it? Yeah maybe I remember. Vaguely.'

'What are you up to now?'

'Camping and masturbating,' said Petra.

Joachim acknowledged Petra's joke with a brief smile, then fixed his eyes on Stefan again.

'I am camping,' said Stefan. 'We've all just finished school and are off to university at the end of summer. Ralf's doing geology in England somewhere, Petra's off to Hohenheim to do biology, I'm doing biology too, but in Hanover.'

'What about your military service?'

'This is Berlin,' I said. 'No one does military service here.'

'Oh yeah,' Joachim said, laughing at Stefan as if it was a joke and as if he'd said it. 'Lucky. I did the social year and had to work in an old people's home for eighteen months. Saw some sights there,' he said, raising his eyebrows. 'A lot of adult nappies.'

Beate screamed, 'Joachim!' from the door.

'Beate!' Joachim said. 'I haven't seen a thing yet, but I'm sure it's amazing.'

He left us, squeezing Stefan's shoulder as he went. We watched as Beate enveloped him, covering him in kisses.

'I think Joachim was flirting with you,' I said.

'You think, Jessica Fletcher?' Petra said.

'Bit inappropriate.'

'Jesus, Ralf,' said Stefan, 'don't be such a prude.'

'I'm not being a prude. It's just ... You just might've confused him. Why didn't you drop in you were straight?'

'It wasn't particularly relevant to the ten-second conversation we were having.'

'No, I know,' I said, embarrassed by myself, 'but he might have got the wrong impression.'

'Why would it matter what kind of sex someone may or may not be having?' Stefan said.

'He's not going to prise Stefan's bum open because he briefly didn't know whether he was gay or not,' Petra said.

'No, I know,' I said again.

'Poor Ralf,' said Petra, patting my cheek. 'He lives a very sheltered life. The English can barely talk about vaginal sex.'

'Fuck off,' I said.

Petra and Stefan laughed and I got cross and said, 'I'm going to look at the sculptures now, otherwise it'll never happen.'

'Careful of the gays,' Petra called out behind me. 'They will bum on sight.'

Galerie Schmelling was housed in the large ground-floor space of an old supermarket. The architect had stripped away all of the fixtures and fittings. The floor was polished concrete, still stained with beige patches where the old lino tiles had been torn up. The walls had been taken back to the brick, scarred with deep holes where shelving had been removed. It was stifling and the people wandering among the works were fanning themselves with the photocopied price list.

Scattered around the floor stood Beate's sculptures, like frozen shoppers. I had seen some of her new work through the windows of the studio. They were highly expressive, and for the last five years, since Beate's father had died, had been made of bent iron and white plaster. She used a blowtorch to soften the rebars sourced from building sites, which she bent into shapes, always the height of a human being and always supporting themselves on the floor. The sculptures were finished with white plaster, which she dripped onto the rusting iron, so that the final expressionistic creations might have resembled creatures emerging from a swamp. Except that Beate exhibited the figures upside down, so that they seemed to be dripping backwards, pulled up into the air by a reverse gravity. In places, where the rebars still poked out, the plaster picked up the iron colouring, staining it orange and adding a sense of desolation to the objects that were, elsewhere, almost unbearably white, like shop-bought meringue.

One sculpture seemed to be reaching an arm out, its skin pouring away to the ceiling, and beneath it I saw Tobias in a linen shirt squinting at the label.

He noticed me and smiled. 'Hey Ralf!' he said. 'What do you think of all this? It's really good, isn't it? I've never seen her stuff before.'

'What are you doing here?' I said coldly.

'Your mum invited me.'

I laughed in disbelief. 'Oh right. Nice.'

He smiled at me again, mistaking my tone. My mother shouted, 'Tobias! Oh, I'm so glad you could come.' She had the nerve to shake his hand as if they barely knew each other and they fell into an awkward hug. She blushed and gestured to him, saying, 'Tobias's brother is a sculptor back East. I thought he might like to see what Beate was up to.' So this was why she'd dressed up so smartly, I thought, disgusted by her thin shoulders beneath the silk dress and her thin lips smothered in coral lipstick.

'Well, now he's seen it.'

My mother frowned. 'Are you all right, Ralf? Do you need to get some air? It's so hot in here.'

Tobias seemed to sense that something was up. He lifted his wine glass and said, 'I'm going to have a browse.'

'You do that,' I said to his retreating back.

'Ralf!' my mum hissed. 'What's got into you?'

I walked away from her to get another drink from the paint-spattered trestle table in the corner of the room.

'Ralf!' she said, coming after me. 'Why are you being so rude? Tobias is our friend.'

'Why did you invite him?'

'I thought you liked him.'

'No, I think he's a dick. Doesn't he have anyone else to hang out with?'

'Ralf!' she said, and laughed in exasperation. 'You do know he had to leave his whole family behind when he fled East Germany? He doesn't have any contact with them at all. He doesn't have anyone. Can you imagine that?'

'He has you.'

Her smile wavered. 'He has us.'

'Whatever,' I said, fishing out a dripping bottle of *Sekt* from a plastic washing-up bowl. The ice had long since melted, and the slippery labels that had come loose from the cooling bottles brushed against my hands like trout in a stream.

I filled up my glass, and when I turned back I saw that her expression had changed. She looked tearful and her chin had wrinkled and was jutting forward, which meant she was holding back angry tears. 'Ralf!' she said. 'You are being absolutely horrible to me at the moment. And I think it's very cruel.'

Tobias was an amber blur behind her, leaning on his good leg, casually staring at a sculpture. I heard my dad laughing outside. For a moment I didn't care what Oz had said to me about acting normally, I just wanted to hurt her. A moment later the feeling was gone, but by then I'd already said, 'Cruel, like fucking your crippled neighbour?'

She drew her chin back and her mouth opened a little. Her eyes relaxed too and the first large tear that escaped from them was a tear of genuine misery. The anger had dissipated the moment I offered her a salient explanation.

'Has it been going on for years?' I said.

She looked so heartbroken.

'You're going to leave us, I suppose?'

She frowned. 'What are you talking about?' she whispered.

'Are you going to leave us? It's a simple question. Are you going to leave us for your new lover?'

She shook her head, dazed. 'Ralf, I'd never . . . '

We heard a smash and turned. Rainer, Beate's rocker, had drunkenly kicked a glass over and was apologetically dabbing at a young woman's leg with a tissue.

'What kind of rocker carries tissues with them?' my mother

said absently. It was the sort of joke that would have made us laugh a month ago, but she didn't laugh and neither did I.

I turned away, but she gripped my arm just long enough that I had to pull it to release it, touching the spot where her fingers had been as if she'd hurt me. I knew this would upset her. I heard her high heels snapping on the concrete floor as she ran to find a toilet to weep in.

I found Petra and Stefan beneath the tree. Joachim had returned, guffawing at a story Stefan liked to tell about falling into salt pans in the marshes on Juist and soiling himself. Petra looked bored and was draining another glass of *Sekt*.

'Do you wanna get out of here?' I said to them.

'Where too?' Petra said.

'Der Gammler?'

'Sure,' she said.

'I'm going to stay and make sure Mum's all right,' said Stefan. Joachim smiled.

Petra and I unlocked our bikes and Petra tucked the skirt of her dress up under her bum as she sat on the saddle. 'Tell me if my *Muschi*'s showing, yeah?' she said as we cycled off, loud enough for my father to turn and raise an eyebrow as we passed.

Fifteen

Petra and I sat at the bar at Der Gammler. We'd been drinking bottles of Jever for some time. Peter locked up and washed and dried the last of the glasses. 'How was the exhibition?' he asked.

'Good,' I said. All I could recall was my mother's face and all I could think about was how impossible life had become.

'Do you think, though,' Petra said drunkenly, 'without Stefan here to worry about, do you actually think they're good? Because I think they might be shit.'

'No,' I said. 'I think they're genuinely good.'

'Anywhere else in Germany people would think they were shit. She's just got a captive audience of Berlin weirdos.'

'You're a Berlin weirdo.'

'You think?' she said.

'Of course. I don't know what you're going to do when you get to Stuttgart. They're going to chase you out of town with forks.'

'Forks?' she said, looking confused.

'Like pitchforks. Like in villages in films.'

'I thought you meant dinner forks,' she said. 'Like I was a sausage.'

This non-joke sent us into fits of giggles, causing Petra's

mascara to run down her cheeks and me to lay my head on the sticky bar and honk like a seal.

After a few more swigs of beer, and once our tears had dried, she said, 'There's got to be some weirdos in Stuttgart. I'll find them.'

'Weirder than you, though?' I said, as Peter lined up three shot glasses and poured us a round of Fernet Branca. We knocked it back and grimaced.

'Aren't you going to miss Berlin?' Peter said.

Petra shrugged. 'Shouldn't think so.'

'But you've never lived anywhere else.'

'That's why I won't miss it. And what's there to miss?'

'Us,' I said. 'Your family.'

'Well, none of you guys are going to be here, and my family – those fuckers are never around anyway.'

'Yeah, but then you've got the run of a villa in Wannsee, not some grubby shared room in some crappy part of Stuttgart.'

'I'd rather have the company. I hate being on my own. Anyway,' she said, lighting a cigarette, 'there aren't crappy parts of Stuttgart. Down south, it's the land of milk and honey.'

'Can't understand a word they're saying though.'

'Probably for the best,' she said and we laughed again.

I stared at the last inch of beer in my bottle and felt sad for an imagined Petra alone in Stuttgart, and the rest of us awkwardly trying to make new friends. She and everyone else would make a success of it, I thought. It was only me who would really be alone, abandoned by my friends, abandoned by my mother.

We said goodbye to Peter and knew we were very drunk because we hugged him and then we hugged each other.

On the dark street, I pointed my bike towards Schöneberg and Petra said, 'Why are you going that way?'

'I'm taking the scenic route,' I said.

She frowned. 'You would tell us if you were doing something stupid,' she said seriously. 'Just so we knew.'

'What do you mean "stupid"?'

'I don't know. Heroin, prostitutes, gambling.'

'I'm not doing any of those things.'

'But you're doing something.'

My ears burned and I looked down at the cobbles on the pavement, belching and trying to think of the most evasive way of answering, already feeling tired of having to. When I looked up though she was already cycling away, impressively steady, her back straight.

'Bye Petra,' I shouted.

I thought she hadn't heard me until she took her hands off the handlebars and raised both middle fingers in salute.

When I got to Oz's bookshop, the shutters were down. It was too early; the sky had only just begun to blue. I didn't even know if the shop opened on a Sunday. I was almost sure it wouldn't, but decided to wait until morning anyway. It seemed very important to me that I see Oz before he saw me, so I locked up my bike further down the road, on the corner of Hohenstaufen Straße, and sat on the pavement diagonally across from the bookshop, behind a Saab, over the boot of which I could still see the shop's shutters.

I woke twice. The first time, to a dog licking my bare leg. I grumbled and kicked at it, thinking that I needed to open my eyes, but I was already gone again. The second time was to my name being called gently but insistently – 'Ralf. Ralf. Ralf.'

I looked up and saw Oz squatting in front of me. He was wearing chinos and a white polo shirt and was carrying a little paper bag from the bakery. Behind him, the Saab was gone.

'Ralf, are you awake?'

'I'm awake,' I said, taking a deep breath, and rubbing my face with my arm. I stood, steadying myself against the crumbling plaster on the wall of the building behind me, and said, 'Oh fuck, I'm sorry. I fucked up, I'm sorry. I was really angry and I ruined everything. I was drunk too, I think.'

'I think you're still drunk,' said Oz, getting his arm round me.

'No,' I said, 'I don't want you seeing me like this. I'm going to go home and sleep it off, but first I wanted to tell you about all the terrible things I've done.'

'Don't be dramatic,' he said. 'I'm sure it's not that bad. Just come and drink something and lie down for a bit.'

'Where?' I said.

'At the shop. You can lie down in the stockroom.'

'I can't,' I said, stumbling beside him, letting my head swing blissfully onto his shoulder, so that the skin of my face touched the skin of his neck.

'Someone's going to come and see me, though,' he said. 'So you'll need to stay quiet.'

'Yes,' I said. 'Yes.'

Sixteen

I could hear the chirrup of an industrial fridge and a grumbling, ancient boiler. Oz had laid me down on a pile of cardboard boxes opened out flat for recycling. I could feel the corrugations beneath my fingertips and could smell the wood pulp mixed in with a scent that reminded me of my grandparents' kitchen in Bournemouth: ancient foodstuffs in an unheated room.

Oz was squatting beside me and stroking my cheek with the back of his hand. 'What time is it?' I mumbled.

'Seven. How're you feeling?'

'Bit rough,' I said, sitting up cross-legged and pushing the heels of my hands into my eyes. 'Fuck,' I said.

'Listen,' he said, standing and picking up an envelope from the chest freezer. 'My dad's arriving soon, so we should head off. You think you can handle a car ride?'

'Where to?'

He guided an ancient kick stool along the floor with his foot and stood on it, reaching up to a high shelf and moving aside two large stoneware jugs. He hid the envelope behind them. 'I'll drive you home.'

I shook my head, thinking of my mother's crying eyes, and said, 'I can't go home.'

'You want to sleep it off back at mine?'

'At your parents'?'

'No, my flat.'

'Oh,' I said, my terror somewhat subsumed beneath my dizziness. 'OK.'

He moved the jugs back and stepped down from the stool, brushing his hands on his trousers.

'What are you hiding up there?'

'Nothing. I keep stuff up here that I don't want Dad to find.' He kicked the stool skitting across the floor to the other side of the room.

'In his shop?'

'They're *Bembel*, the jugs. We lived in Frankfurt when we first came over and Dad thought that all Germans drank apple wine from these jugs. He got some deal on a job lot of them when we moved to Berlin, but no one here had ever heard of them. He didn't sell one, so they're all still up here. And he can't throw anything away. For years, he used to send them back to Turkey as presents. There's a whole corner of İzmir where all the flower vases, water jugs and pen pots are Frankfurter apple wine jugs.'

I laughed. It made my head hurt.

'So anything I want to keep safe I put up here. He'll never sell the jugs and he's run out of people to palm them off on.'

'Why doesn't he just sell them to someone back in Frankfurt?' I said.

'Too proud,' said Oz. 'In his mind, he's never made a mistake in his life.'

*

Oz parked on a square centred on a deserted playground that was shaded by tall acacia trees. I followed him across a

133

courtyard, into the back of one of the old buildings and up to the third floor. As Oz unlocked the door of his flat, there was a creak in the apartment opposite.

'Frau Riemann at her spyhole,' Oz whispered. 'She's been expecting the Soviets for forty years.'

Oz's apartment consisted of a small hallway, a living room, a tiny bedroom with a Juliet balcony, a kitchen with a yellow-melamine-covered table and chairs, and a long Berlin bathroom, with the sink, toilet and shower arrayed in a long line, one after the other. Everything was spare and painted white, except for the tiles in the kitchen and the bathroom which were a light mandarin orange, a colour I couldn't believe had ever been fashionable or ever would be again.

It smelt of all the scents I had smelt on him, but didn't know for sure were his: the bonfire smell of his old coal heater, cigarettes, lemony aftershave, an indescribable male scent – not sweat, but something like clean scalp and clothes left for a long time in a dry closet.

He took the can and wrapper from my hands and said, 'Do you want to lie down? I've got some reading to do.'

I nodded, pulled off my trainers and lay on his bed. The pillow was cold and smelt of his hair. He leant against the door and we stared at each other and smiled.

*

I slept for an hour or two and woke to gulp down a glass of water that Oz had put by my bed. Then, half awake, I pulled off my socks, knowing that they were the hardest garment to remove erotically, and waited for him. I heard him click a fan on and felt its oscillating breeze buffeting my bare feet. I heard him turning the pages of a book and him filling a glass with water from the tap in the kitchen. I heard him using the toilet, heard that he put the seat up to pee, but didn't put it back down again. I heard him boil a kettle, light a cigarette and stub it out.

Eventually I climbed off the bed and walked into the kitchen, the floorboards pleasantly cool beneath my feet. He turned in his chair and stubbed out the cigarette he'd just lit.

'How do you feel?' he asked, waving the smoke away from his face.

'Yeah, all right,' I said, my heart thudding. 'I thought . . . '

'What?' he said.

'I thought you were going to come.'

'Oh,' he said. 'I thought you needed the sleep.'

He seemed uncertain and I was worried that there'd been some misunderstanding. But I'd come so far and I was standing in his flat; the idea of leaving again without trying was more awful than walking away and feeling the emptiness I'd felt since the kiss in the woods. I touched his cheek. I felt like my heart had dropped into my stomach. He smiled and looked up at me, his eyes impossibly golden, his thick eyebrows black, pulled together in a sweet frown.

'Is it going to hurt?' he said.

'What?' I said. I thought I'd misheard him.

'Sex.'

'Oz,' I said, stunned, 'I don't have a fucking clue what I'm doing.'

His face softened instantly. 'Fuck, Ralf,' he said. 'Me neither.'

And we began to laugh.

*

What surprised me most about sex that first time was how like sex with Maike it felt, how alike two people in bed become. And also how completely unlike my blurred fantasies of sex with Tobias it was, which all involved someone

135

face down in bed enduring penetration. Instead, my memory is of two bodies in a process of awkward but gleeful discovery. Stripped of my assumptions, a vast field of possibilities opened up in front of me, licking and touching, laughing, trying to ascertain from groans and mumbled 'yeses' what he and what I wanted. I came with my head pushed uncomfortably against the wall with my balls in his mouth, and when Oz came sweat bloomed across his skin, making him slick beneath my fingers.

I lay panting on his chest, the grey plastic fan rotating at the end of the bed, the buffeting breeze drying the sweat on my back. I looked at my fingers in his black chest hair and the colour of his nipples, a dark liver-brown, his gold chain a blurred string of sparkling light far, far away at his neck. In that pre-digital age, his body was fascinating to me. Like all of my friends, I'd seen the ubiquitous soft-core pornography on late-night German television that our English relatives found scandalous. Police interviews, maths lessons, doctors' visits turning unexpectedly sexual and ending with grunting dry humping. But I'd never seen an erect penis that wasn't my own, I'd never seen a pale pink circumcision scar, I'd never seen, piece by piece, how a man's body joins up, how the landscape of skin and hair changes in texture and tone, from the folds of the lips to the folds of the testicles, the tufts of black on his toes to the perfect triangle of hair above his buttocks on his otherwise hairless back.

I lifted my head to kiss his other nipple, the one beneath my cheek, and touched his belly, rough where his semen or my semen had dried. I stared at his face. There was a speck of white dust stuck to the end of one of his long eyelashes. By his eyes, I saw a few very fine lines that would one day become crow's feet, and between his thick eyebrows two lines that deepened when he frowned. I could see the tiny spots of his blue-black stubble already pushing through his skin, burrowing out from the surface. I touched his lips and pulled his bottom lip down, so that I could see his teeth and the inside of his mouth. He shot out his tongue like a snake.

I laughed and snatched my hand away, sitting up in bed cross-legged. The breath of the fan swept past and cooled the sweat on my back and set the black hair on his body in violent motion.

I looked about me. The walls of his bedroom were bare, except for a postcard in the centre of one white wall: a drawing on green paper of a man or a woman – I couldn't tell – covering their eye with their hand, their head tilted back.

'Who is it?'

'I don't know,' said Oz.

'Why do you have it?'

'It's a postcard. It's by Käthe Kollwitz; I got it at the Gemäldegalerie.'

'I like it,' I said.

Along the floor, beneath the postcard, was a single row of books that circumnavigated the whole room. Thumbed and battered, I saw novels in German and French, books on economics and philosophy, books of poetry in German and Turkish. I picked out a slim Turkish volume. 'Read me something from this.'

He looked at the cover. 'You won't be able to understand it.'

'No, but I want to hear you read it.'

He pushed himself up on his pillow and opened the book in the middle. He started reading and I put my head on his chest, listening to the humming depth of it as he spoke.

The old double window was open, but covered in a floor-length voile curtain, through which the sun beat, painting an elongated rectangle of bright light across the foot of the bed. Outside, beyond the courtyard, a lorry rattled over a junction. The air tasted dry and metallic. I put my hand into the sunlight, felt the heat of it and saw the skin of my palm become translucent, the blue veins threaded beneath, and listened to the booming poetry spoken in a foreign tongue.

Seventeen

Beyond the bedroom, Oz's small kitchen contained a gas stove, the yellow table, two mismatched chairs and a large window, surrounded by ivy, that looked over the leaf-spotted earth and rusting bicycles of the back courtyard. In the bathroom, the window had been replaced with stacked and ribbed glass blocks softly misted with limescale, the grout between the blocks speckled with mildew. One block swung open – a rudimentary window – but the hinge was broken and the block had been strung to the shower head to keep it permanently ajar. When I showered, I could peep out of the gap there and see the swaying branches of an acacia tree filled with large magpies that screeched, fought and coupled in the branches.

Like the bedroom, the high windows of the living room were swathed in thin voile curtains that moved languidly in the warm wind, rolling and parting. Almost all his furniture – a divan made of stacked Arabic-looking mattresses, a scratchy Turkish rug on the wooden floor, a brass rice tray on folding wooden feet – was made up of damaged cast-offs from a shop that his dad ran selling orientalist furnishings to West Germans. The only item Oz had bought himself was the hi-fi, which was surrounded by his cassettes stacked in tumbling

139

plastic ziggurats. He played me Echo and the Bunnymen and Kraftwerk, and when I asked him to play me something Turkish he put on Müzeyyen Senar, a folk singer. Her deep voice seemed more full of feeling and despair than anything I'd ever heard before.

It was in this landscape that we made love for what seemed to me like years, but could only have been a day or two. Never dressing, we wandered the rooms like two Adams, every kiss, every tenderness leading to sex, until I felt too hot and too full up and didn't want it any more. But then he touched my leg, then the skin of my inner thigh, then he raised my hand and put my fingers in his mouth and it would begin again.

When he left to get food I begged him to go to the Turkish supermarket and buy us something 'authentic'. The oven was never turned on. Instead we sat naked on the floor eating sticky baklava, stuffed vine leaves cold from the tin, oranges, pears, dates, wrinkled olives and salty strings of dil peyniri cheese. He introduced me to flaky börek pastries and rings of sesame-encrusted simit bread, foods that I still love and eat when I have a night to myself, thinking of his fingers stained red with paprika. We drank tea from tiny glasses, strong powdery coffee, and in the evening got drunk on Efes beer and rakı made cloudy with water.

As August rolled to a close, the storms arrived. The weightless curtains of the bedroom flicked open and we felt rain on our skin, but we didn't close the windows to the courtyard. Oz said that on the Turkish coast storms sweep away summer's dusty mugginess, but not in Berlin. I told him that the difference was the climates: Mediterranean versus continental. I talked about Wladimir Köppen in Hamburg establishing weather forecasts and mapping out the climatic regions of the world, I told him about Glenn

Thomas Trewartha reclassifying the middle latitudes. He listened, never looking bored, asking questions, asking me to pause when he had to go to the toilet or boil the kettle for more tea.

I could imagine no end to it. But the end did come. I knew that Mum would be calling round my friends, so I phoned when I knew no one would be home and left a message on the answering machine saying that I was staying at Maike's. Connecting with the outside world made me feel nervous and uttering Maike's name made me think of her lying on her side in pain in that bedroom. But her fuzzy shape in the darkening room was like the memory of a film I'd once seen. It felt like another life with different rules to this island apartment in Berlin-Schönenburg.

Oz and I sat on the living-room floor, our legs entwined. It was dark outside and the room was lit with a single candle stuck to a broken saucer. *Graceland* was playing on the hi-fi and I was reading a few pages of *On Photography* by Susan Sontag that I'd found lying on the dusty brass side table in the corner of the room.

Oz was smoking with a grey glass ashtray on his naked belly. He had just told me that he had to be at the shop that afternoon while his dad was at the wholesaler's. I had murmured to acknowledge I'd heard him.

'Ralf?' he said.

I looked up. He was frowning and looking down at his knees.

'You're going to ask me about Tobias, aren't you?'

'I feel dumb asking,' he said. 'It feels like I'm spoiling something.'

I put the book down on the floor.

'I've only seen him once since you asked me about it. It was at this private view and my mum was there. And I got cross with her again. I told her I knew about the affair.'

'Oh,' said Oz.

'I'm sorry. I just got really angry.'

He nodded. 'Did you say anything about me? Or about what I told you?'

'Of course not,' I said. 'I wouldn't do that.'

'OK,' he said. 'And he wasn't doing anything suspicious at this private view?'

I shook my head. I felt terrible and Oz was right; talking about Tobias did spoil something.

'What about you?' I said. 'Are you still following him?'

Oz nodded.

'Also nothing?'

'Also nothing.'

I wanted to be able to give him something. I thought about Mum's patient in the courtyard, with his long limbs and blue eyes and his white hair, pressed and parted like an ironed napkin. But Tobias hadn't been there the last time I'd seen him.

'Ralf?' Oz said. 'Is there something else you're not telling me?'

'I think it's nothing.'

'What's nothing?'

I pulled up a knee and rested my chin on it. 'I saw this guy again. This patient of Mum's. I saw him the day before I came to the shop. It's only odd because Mum's patients normally come in the front entrance, so we'd never see them. And the first time I saw him walking across the courtyard Tobias was there. But then he wasn't there the second time and he didn't actually go anywhere near Tobias's flat. There's also no way they're working together anyway.'

'Why not?'

'He's in the British Army. The patient. I mean, I think he is.'

'Why?'

'Just the way he looked. There's a type. Mum has a few British Army patients.'

Oz thought about this. The untapped ash at the end of his cigarette fell to the floor, exploding silently beside his bare leg. 'Your mum's a psychiatrist, *oder?*'

'No,' I said. 'A psychologist. A therapist.'

'What's that got to do with the Army?'

'Well, she used to work there.'

'The Army?'

'Yeah. My grandad was an army doctor. She used to work at the military hospital when she was a student and then when she was doing her psychotherapy training. Just admin stuff. But because of that and because of Grandad she often gets referred Army people if they're having relationship crises. I mean, to be fair, it's usually the wives that get in touch, I think. But she's the kind of go-to counsellor if you're a British expat with a relationship problem or sex problems – that's her speciality. I mean, the British are pretty reticent about getting any kind of counselling, but she once had this *capitaine* who—'

'This what?' he said. He sat up and the ashtray clattered to the floor and rolled along on its side like a detached wheel, shedding its dust and knocking against the skirting board. It fell flat and came to a whirling stop like a spun coin.

'*Capitaine,*' I muttered. 'It's just French for captain. It was this French captain who—'

'She treats French people too?'

'Yes,' I said. 'Gran's French. Mum grew up bilingual.'

'And she treats Germans? She speaks German?'

'Of course,' I said. 'She . . .'

Oz got onto his knees and gripped my outstretched foot. His eyes were darting about the floor in between us. 'So she talks about her patients with you?'

'No,' I said. 'I mean, not who they are, but she talks about them in broad strokes. Like if something funny happens.'

'So you couldn't identify any of them?'

'No,' I said. 'But why is that . . . ? What's going on?'

'Diamonds on the Soles of her Shoes' had been playing. Oz's hi-fi didn't have auto-reverse and once Ladysmith Black Mambazo's voices faded out we listened to the hiss of the magnetic tape tense and the cassette crunch to a stop, then fall silent.

'Tobias doesn't need to go anywhere to get his *kompromat* information. That's why we haven't caught him out by following him. He's getting it all from your mum.'

'No,' I said automatically. 'She wouldn't do that.'

'Wouldn't she?'

'No,' I said, unsure now. 'No. I don't think so.'

'Have you ever heard of Romeo spies?'

I shook my head slowly.

'They're agents, men usually, who target women who have access to important information. They become the men of their dreams – read the same books, like the same music, dress just the right way. All of that. The women they go for are usually secretaries working for someone important, but your mum's files would be absolute gold. It would be irresistible.'

'You think Tobias is having an affair with my mum so she'll pass over files about her patients?'

'It can't be a coincidence.'

I thought about my mum carefully recording someone's

144

sexual problems and then handing them over to Tobias, his upper lip still sweaty from sex. It was horrible, but also impossible. I couldn't believe it. And then I realised: 'She doesn't need to pass them over.'

'What do you mean?'

'Mum's consulting rooms are attached to our flat. If he's in the flat then he can get to her files. He has a key to our flat and we have a key to his – he waters our plants when we're away.'

Oz nodded slowly, entranced by his breakthrough. 'But surely your mum's consulting room is locked.'

'Yeah, but it's a bolt,' I said. 'It's locked from inside our flat. You can't get to our flat from Mum's consulting rooms, but you can always get into her rooms from our flat. And the keys for the filing cabinet are next to this African mask. I mean, it wouldn't take a genius to find them.'

He was grinning. 'Ralf,' he said and put a hand on my bare knee.

'This is awful,' I said. 'I don't think Tobias is ... I mean, I hate him. I do hate him. But stealing people's files and blackmailing people?'

'But if he is "Axel" then he believes that what he's doing is going to save the world. Save people's lives.'

I looked at him, unconvinced. 'So what do we do now?'

'Well,' Oz said, considering, 'if we could get a look at your mum's files or find out who this Army person is, for instance, then we could find out if the information from her patients matched anything that "Axel" has delivered.'

'So, what, we just let ourselves into Mum's office and take a few files?'

Oz frowned and scrutinised my face, checking that he'd understood my meaning. 'Yeah,' he said, 'absolutely. If you and I could get hold of a copy of a file or two, then potentially that'd be it. We might be done.'

But he hadn't understood me at all. My 'we' was a vague 'we'. I meant we West Germans, not me and Oz. His frown was unknitting, though, and he was touching my cheek with his thumb. 'Is that really something you'd be up for?'

'I mean, I suppose,' I said, not really understanding what I was agreeing to.

He sighed a little and sank back, sitting on the balls of his feet.

'What?' I said.

'No, it's just … I was just thinking, if you could get your hands on a few files and they really did incriminate Tobias, then we'd be done with him.'

'OK,' I said. 'But that's good, right?'

'Yeah. And it just means this,' he said, indicating me, 'would just be about this, if you know what I mean.'

He opened his mouth to rephrase what he'd said, but I touched it and said, 'No, I understand,' and he laughed with pleasure. Then he gripped my neck and kissed me.

*

He lay beside me, his head resting on my chest. His hair smelt good and I didn't want him to move away, but eventually he pecked at my cheek and said, 'I'm going to make some coffee.'

I sat where I was for a moment, thinking that I should stay until he returned, but the long discussion about life outside, about Tobias, about my mum and her files, had made my nakedness feel odd for the first time, and I went to Oz's bed-room to pull on my pants. I'd been naked for so long that I struggled to find them, uncovering first a sock, then my shorts, kicked under the bed, and then finally my pants by the window.

I heard a hiss and a gentle woof from the kitchen and found Oz at the gas hob, shaking out a blackened match. I sat at the table and he smiled at me, passing out of the room without comment and returning wearing sky-blue Y-fronts. He filled the little Turkish coffee pot from the tap, added grounds and sugar, stirred it and put it on the flame, then leant against the wall, clearly aware of the subtle change in my mood. I had started to think about my own bedroom, realising that I would be going back to it, back to my mother and to my friends who were about to leave for university. I realised it would all have to be dealt with, that it was foolish to believe that I could escape my life. I looked at Oz, beautiful against the cracked plaster of his bare kitchen walls, and imagined going into my mother's office and stealing someone's file, a solemn military man with sexual health problems.

The coffee pot jumped and crackled.

'Why do you do it?' I asked.

'Do what?'

'Spy on people.'

He folded his arms. 'I mean, it's not really spying,' he said. 'It's not the main thing I do.'

'It's literally spying. You sit in your car and spy on people.'

He looked at me and licked his lips. 'Really, I only do things that relate to Dad's apartments, to the shop, to things like that. I'm not on a retainer – they just pay me when I can be useful, but I don't plan anything.'

'They just use you, then?'

His head twitched as if someone had blown dust in his face. 'I mean, I wouldn't put it like that, Ralf. The money's good for not doing very much. And because it's all unofficial, I get paid in cash, so I can save up.'

'So it's about the money?'

'Well, yes and no. I mean, if the Stasi came knocking I wouldn't do it for them. I do it because I believe it's the right thing to do. But I wouldn't just do it out of the goodness of my heart.'

For a moment he looked attacked.

'It's not dangerous, is it?' I said. 'Doesn't it make you a target for the Stasi?'

He softened and his arms dropped to his sides. He touched the wall behind him. 'Honestly, Ralf, Berlin is full of informants. I'm just keeping an eye on a couple of people, maybe getting hold of some information, and then I report back to this Bavarian that comes to the shop. He'll have a hundred Ozes all over Berlin and, yeah, there'll probably be a few of them involved in pretty serious military stuff. But no one cares about some brown-skinned newsagent's son from Schöneberg.'

He pushed himself off the wall and ruffled my hair, then rinsed a small cup in the sink and held up a second cup to say, 'You too?' I shook my head. The coffee foamed and he poured off a layer of black lather, put it back on the heat, then repeated the process when it foamed up again.

'Why do you do it like that?' I said. 'Why don't you just pour it all out?' I'd watched him do it many times over those past few days, but had never asked, afraid that it would confirm in his eyes my naivety. But I'd broken the magic now and felt like it didn't really matter what he thought.

'That's just how you do it,' Oz said. 'How Mum did it.'

He poured off a last layer and turned the gas off.

'What are you saving up money for?' I said.

He smiled, holding the steaming coffee pot in one hand.

'What?' I said. 'Is it something weird?'

'No,' he said, shaking his head. 'Just a bookshop.' He put the coffee pot on the draining board and sipped at the small stoneware cup, its grainy brown glaze the colour of glossy peanut butter.

'You already work in a bookshop.'

The coffee clung to his upper lip like a pencil moustache. 'That's a newsagent with a couple of books. And I want my own one. I want to do it properly.' He put the cup down and stood there in his pants, offering up his sweetest smile.

Eighteen

I arrived back home at midnight. When I shut the door behind me I saw the light under the door of my parents' bedroom click off, but no one emerged. I crept across the cool parquet to my room, fell into bed, slept and woke to hear my family going about their morning routine without me. I waited for the inevitable knock on the door, my mother's tearful face, but it didn't come. Me confronting my mum had opened up a chasm too wide to cross, and I was both terrified and glad that she hadn't tried to.

I snoozed through the morning and finally emerged into the gentle silence of the empty flat long after they had all left. I showered and pulled on the checked red shirt and lederhosen that we had to wear for work at the beer garden. The shirt had been freshly washed and pressed.

At the kitchen table, I ate a large bowl of cereal and watched Tobias's flat across the courtyard, but it was empty. If he knew what I'd said to Mum, I supposed, he might've seen me first and retired to his bedroom, which was on the other side of the building. I felt like I was hiding from the world and the world was hiding from me.

A hush of wind through the leaves of the horse chestnut moved the adjoining door to my mother's practice. It was open. The door was never left open when she was seeing patients: the aerodynamics of the flat meant that opening Mum's consulting-room door would push open the adjoining door to our flat, revealing to her patients the hidden family behind the waiting-room wall. If a patient had cancelled and she had used the opportunity to go out, then I was two unlocked doors away from her files.

I stood, my heart thumping, and reached out to the door. It swung towards me and hit me hard on the arm.

'Shit!' I said, as my mother bustled through holding her keys, then screamed when she found me behind it. 'Jesus, Ralf!'

'Fuck!' I said, and scampered back to my bowl of soggy cereal.

'You all right?' she said. 'Did I hurt you?'

'It's fine,' I said, nursing my arm.

'What were you doing behind the door?'

'I wasn't behind the door,' I barked. 'I was going past the door and you opened it into my arm.'

She looked at the door and then back at me. I glared at the spots of milk on the plastic tablecloth.

'I thought you'd already gone to work,' she said, appealing to me.

'At one.'

'Oh.' She looked at her watch and then at my cereals on the table. 'Then ...' she said, unsure of herself, 'then, I might pop out for lunch.'

I think she was hoping I would say 'You don't have to', but the prospect of sitting with her as we silently ate was unbearable. She moved towards me, as if she was going to touch me, but then stopped herself. 'You're obviously welcome to come, but ...'

'No,' I said.

'No,' she said.

She waited. I stirred the milk in my bowl.

'Ralf, is there anything you want to ask me?'

I looked up at her in surprise. 'Er, I think I asked you already.'

She nodded.

'*Are* you going to leave us?' I said, and felt ashamed of myself, because my voice faltered at 'us'. I swallowed to stop myself from crying, but Mum didn't swallow. Her chin reddened and puckered like an old peach and tears began to run down her face.

'I'd never leave you,' she choked out. 'I'd never do anything . . .'

'What, to hurt us? And if Dad finds out and leaves us anyway? Is that better?'

She covered her face with her hand. 'Oh God, Ralf,' came her muffled voice. 'I've never felt so wretched.'

'And what am I meant to do about that?' I said. 'It's not my fault.'

'No,' she said quietly, rubbing her bare arm across her eyes. 'No.' She sniffed hard and picked up her keys. 'I'm sorry, Ralf,' she said. 'I'm sorry for you. And I'll make it right.'

'I think it's too late for that.'

She nodded, composing herself. 'I can see how you would feel that.'

She looked at the phone and I was suddenly afraid that 'making it right' meant telling my dad and leaving. So I said, 'I think you should keep away from Tobias, by the way. I think he's a pretty dangerous person.'

She turned to me frowning, her face still red. 'What do you mean?'

'I mean you should keep away from him.'

'I understand,' she said, though of course she didn't. She picked up her keys. 'I'll make it right,' she said again, and fled out through the front door.

I stared into my cereal bowl – the few sodden Choco Krispies that remained turned the same lilacky brown as the pool of milk – and thought that this would be our relationship now until I moved out. It seemed impossible to think it would ever be any different. Would Oz let me stay with him? I wondered. The idea of inviting myself to live with him seemed ridiculous, but perhaps if I was there often enough I could engineer it. I imagined him stopping as he brushed his teeth and saying, 'Hey, Ralf. Why don't you just bring your stuff over? You're here all the time anyway.' And I would feign deliberation before shrugging an OK.

I heard the front door to our building boom as Mum left. I stood and peered into her waiting room and, beyond, through the open door of her consulting room. I had assumed I would have to take the files at night when everyone was asleep, but I saw now that that was stupid, and much more suspicious than just wandering through in my lederhosen and taking them when I had the chance.

I rinsed out my cereal bowl in the sink and went and stood at the door, afraid of touching the door jamb in case I left fingerprints, and then realising that the whole house was covered in my fingerprints and it didn't matter. I took a deep breath and walked straight through the waiting room and into her consulting room. On the right was a mahogany desk, on the left my mother's green leather armchair facing a small two-seater sofa for the patient or patients, covered with a hardy mustard velour. I thought about all the people who must have sat there weeping.

I heard the distant thud of a car door being slammed and

realised that Mum might be picking up something to eat from the baker's and coming straight back to the practice, so I grabbed the key from beside the African mask on her bookshelf, unlocked the filing cabinet and pulled it open. It emitted a gasp of ancient paper. I looked through the patients' names on the plastic tabs attached to each mud-green hanging file – Becker, Butler, Lambert, Leicester, McLaughlin, Mayerbach, Michel. Most of Mum's patients were women or couples, so it was easy to pick out the important-sounding men. I looked for official-sounding titles and ranks in the descriptions. The files were dated from the start of their treatment to the end, and I took the summary notes from three completed therapies with men, reasoning that she wouldn't look at these any time soon. The only current file I took something from was a Major-General Hillary Purser, who I guessed was the man I had seen in the courtyard, since he was in the British Army and the dates of his treatment matched. From his file, I took Mum's notes from his first session, assuming that Oz could copy them and I could get them back into the file before Mum noticed.

I scanned the typed pages and guiltily read snippets from her summation of the Major-General's problems:

The patient is forty-eight, male, and a high-ranking officer in the British Army. He is a smoker. Three years ago, he was diagnosed with Peyronie's disease, a connective tissue disorder that leads to abnormal curvature of the penis when erect, making penetration difficult. The patient was referred by a German urologist Dr Gelbhaare, who is treating the disease with vitamin E, though the treatment has not yet been effective and the prognosis is unclear ...

154

... The patient has been married for twenty years and has two children, 18 and 16, both girls. He has not had sexual intercourse with his wife for five years. He masturbates regularly. He has never been unfaithful ...

... The patient shows clear signs of depression. He suffers from fatigue and insomnia, waking early in the morning and being unable to fall back to sleep again. During the day, he has a lack of energy and struggles in social situations. He also suffers from digestive problems and a loss of appetite ...

... The patient sometimes self-medicates with alcohol, regularly drinking more than a bottle-and-a-half of red wine in an evening ...

My prurient interest in the details of the man's sex life flickered and died in the cold wind of his misery. I returned the file, put the notes in a hard-backed envelope from Mum's desk and crept through the house to my room, where I stuffed the envelope into my rucksack. 'I am a spy,' I thought. I wanted these words to resonate, to make me feel something, but they didn't. As my heart stopped thumping, I realised that my overriding emotion was sadness for a middle-aged Army officer and his patient wife.

Nineteen

At the Bavarian beer garden, it was my turn on the flat grill, turning the bratwurst and pork steaks, and pushing the curling squares of *Leberkäse* down with a spatula so that they browned on the edges. I did most of my shifts with Petra and a tall, overweight boy called Dirk, who had a repaired harelip. On him, the lederhosen that we all had to wear were so tight at the crotch that they parted his testicles in the middle, creating a puffy vulva beneath the suedette shorts. They only provided one size, and on me the same outfit was baggy, making me look like a five-year-old Alpine child.

Every hour we rotated stations – the grill, the till, the beer – until we'd done each job twice. In the first few minutes at the grill, as the savoury smoke wafted over my face in hot waves, I always thought I wouldn't be able to bear it for the full hour, but at some point the process hypnotised me and I only real- ised how hot I'd been when I moved on to the relative cool of the beer tap, the smell of frying meat emanating from my hair and chequered short-sleeved shirt.

From the till, Petra shouted over her shoulder, 'So where've you been for the last two days?'

I'd been expecting the question, but still didn't have an answer for it. 'Just cycling about, avoiding my parents.'

'Someone was asking after you.'

'Who?' I said.

'Oh yeah,' said Dirk from the beer taps. 'Woman with curly hair. She came and asked for you on Friday too.'

'No,' said Petra. 'This was a man. A bit older with blond hair.'

'What did they want?' I asked.

'She just asked whether you were around.'

'Yeah, the man too,' said Petra.

'That's weird,' I said.

She shouted out the next order. I used the palette knife to flick the sausages onto the grill, pulled the plastic lid off the five-kilo tub of potato salad and dropped the basket of chips into the shimmering fat, where they bloomed in a frenzy of frantic bubbles.

'What about you?' I said, watching a wasp bounce along the roof of the wooden cabin. 'What've you been up to?'

'Saw Stefan actually, when we couldn't find you. Haven't been to his flat in years. His mum was being extra weird.'

'Don't call Beate weird.'

'She walked through the living room naked, Ralf. Stefan didn't bat an eyelid. And then he made me watch this pirate copy of a film called *Andre Roubel* . . . '

'*Andrei Rublev*,' I suggested.

'Oh my God. It was a stone-cold Stefan classic. Black-and-white, Russian, naked peasants, mental people. It seemed to mostly be about a giant bell.'

'He's made me watch it. He says it's the greatest film ever made.'

'I'm not being funny,' Petra said, 'but how can he even judge that? He only watches those kinds of films. I tried to make him watch *Working Girl* and he wouldn't even give it a chance. He makes me watch a film where they set cows on fire and he won't watch ten minutes of *Working Girl*?'

'Shift change!' shouted Dirk, holding out one hand for the spatula and pulling at the crotch of his lederhosen with the other.

'Hey, *Arschloch*,' said Petra, over the sound of the gurgling beer tap, 'why do you always kill the barrel just before changeover?'

She pushed the blue-and-white chequered curtain aside and retapped the metal barrel of *Weizen*, pulling off the plastic pipe with a hiss.

'I didn't know it was empty,' Dirk said.

'What, it's just a coincidence, is it?'

'It's not a coincidence that you always moan about it.'

'Is it a coincidence that you're a cunt?'

I greeted the next customer, a stone-faced-looking couple, both in beige trench coats and hats despite the warmth of the evening.

Towards the end of our shift, Herr Kniff, who ran the beer garden, shoved open the flimsy wooden door. He was very thin and over two metres tall, having to crane his neck in the little shed. With his goggly eyes and protruding upper lip, he reminded me of tall bony birds – ostriches and rheas. 'Someone's complained,' he said, his reddish moustache twitching, which it did when he was cross. He was often cross.

'What about?' said Petra, now at the grill and holding the palette knife in the air like a sceptre.

'Swearing. Foul language in front of children.'

'I haven't seen any children,' Petra said.

'The worst possible language.'

'I burnt my finger,' I said.

158

'Badly?'

'No,' I said, 'but it hurt. And I swore.'

Herr Kniff pursed his lips. 'What did you say?'

'Oh bloody shit.'

Petra covered up a snort of laughter with a cough, putting her forearm to her mouth.

Herr Kniff looked at Petra, his wrists pushed into his hips, his large eyes quivering. 'Just be more careful,' he said.

When I turned back to the open hatch Maike was standing in front of me. She looked better, but tired. The sun was dying and behind her, pink washes streaked the sky, filling the garden of drinkers and diners with a golden light that stained her skin satsuma orange.

'It's good to see you alive,' I said, leaning across the counter and kissing her. Her lips felt cool and familiar and I felt a throb of pleasure deep in my stomach, but also fear.

'Isn't that your neighbour?' Maike said, nodding behind her.

It was Tobias, sitting at a long table near the entrance to the beer garden, his wood and green metal chair slightly turned so that he wasn't facing me.

'Yeah,' I said. He was chatting to two young women his age. 'That's weird.'

'Is it?' Maike said. 'It's a pretty big beer garden near your house. And it's sunny.'

'S'pose,' I said. Did Tobias know that I worked there? I'd never told him, but he must have seen me come and go in my lederhosen and made the connection. I had bumped into him before with his friends. But with everything that had happened the sight of his broad back unnerved me.

'Maike!' Petra shouted from the back of the cabin. It was five minutes before closing and she'd started to clean the grill.

'Hi Petra.'

Petra stopped scraping and squinted into the sun, holding her hand above her face. 'You look better,' she said.

'I feel better,' said Maike.

'It really hit you hard this time, *oder*?' I said.

'It did,' said Maike, 'but Petra's talking about last night. I threw up outside Der Gammler.'

'She was fucked,' Petra shouted.

'A *Weizen*, please,' said a small woman with a tight perm. Behind her, I could see that Tobias and his friends had already left.

'Large or small?'

'Is there medium?'

'Yup,' I said, and called the order out to Dirk.

'Were you all out?' I said to Maike, taking the woman's money and shoving the till shut.

'Don't be grumpy about it, Ralf,' Petra shouted over my shoulder. 'No one could find you.'

'Where were you?' Maike said.

In the warm magic of the late-summer sun, I heard myself saying, 'I was with Oz.' I was desperate to uncork the terrible feeling that had been building up in me, part anxiety about another secret I had to keep, but part just missing him. Uttering his name seemed to be the only way to stop me from bursting.

'Who's Oz?' said Maike.

Petra appeared by my side, frowning. 'Who the fuck is Oz, Ralf?'

The woman with a perm muttered something about standards and wandered back to her table with her beer.

'A friend,' I said. 'A new friend.'

We saw Herr Kniff advancing across the gravel towards us. 'I'll explain later,' I said.

*

We sat in the middle of the Tiergarten smoking in the dusk. Through the arches of the trees the purple sky was broken with silhouettes of black branches, like church windows.

'Can you smell that?' said Maike, as the wind shifted the leaves above us.

'Like smoke,' I said.

'We're smoking,' said Petra.

'No, it's like wood smoke. Or coal fires. It smells like autumn coming.'

Petra lit a new cigarette from the stub of her old one, and flicked the dog-end into the bushes. I watched it turn in the air, smoking wispily as it spun like a tiny stick of dynamite.

'*Ihr Lieben!*' It was Stefan walking towards us through the dark holding a pearlescent bottle of *Küstennebel*, an aniseed liquor none of us liked, but drank because it was cheap and very alcoholic. He joined our circle and placed the bottle in the middle. We sipped from it reverently.

'Any sign of our Army officer, Ralfi?' Stefan said.

I shook my head, imagining the poor man's bent penis.

'You remember Joachim from the private view? He was telling me how the British Army . . . '

'Hey, you didn't tell him you'd seen him, did you?' I said. 'He's one of Mum's patients. You can't talk about it.'

'Oh no,' Stefan said, unconvincingly. 'We were just talking about it generally.'

'Fuck,' I said.

'I didn't say he was one of your mum's patients. I promise,' he said.

I took the *Küstennebel* from Maike and took a syrupy gulp

161

of it, wincing as I swallowed it down, then passed it to Petra and stared at the patchy grass by my bare legs.

We were quiet for a while. I thought I heard a nightingale, but then the song changed from a jug jug jug to a rising whistle – a blackbird mimicking a nightingale. Behind us, the scrubby woods crackled with branches broken underfoot and the skipping firefly dots of men's cigarettes as they waited for other men in the dark.

'Have you guys ever had sex in the woods?' Petra said.

Stefan shook his head. Maike and I nodded.

'You two?' said Petra. 'Really? I don't see the attraction, myself. I did it once. The feeling of sticks and wet leaves on your bare bum.' She shuddered dramatically. 'And I was terrified the whole time about getting a tick on my labia.'

'Who were you with?' asked Maike. Stefan leant back on the grass. He always tried to act particularly cool when Maike discussed her sex life. Jealousy, he liked to say, was a disease of the bourgeoisie.

Petra frowned and sucked at her cigarette, as if she was struggling to recall his name. She blew out a rolling cloud of indigo smoke and said, 'Doggle, I think. He was an exchange student.'

'Dougal?' I said.

'Maybe. Is that a name?'

'Seems more likely than Doggle.'

Petra nodded her assent. 'Come on then. Who's this Oz? And why have you deserted your friends for him? Is he rich and interesting?'

'Who's Oz?' Stefan said.

'Ralf's new best friend,' said Petra.

I pulled my face into an expression of nonchalant semi-boredom, as if I could barely remember. 'He's just a guy I

162

bumped into. I actually knew him already – his dad owns some of the flats in our building. I mean, I knew him to say hello to. I just bumped into him and got talking. He's cool. I'll bring him along to something.'

Maike picked at the grass by her legs, pale in the twilight, while Petra pondered what I'd said. 'And you spent two days with him?'

'No. Well, I got drunk with him and then ended up crashing out on his sofa. He lives in Schöneberg. He's Turkish,' I added, hoping somehow that that might help my case.

They looked confused. 'I don't understand why—' Maike began.

I broke in with, 'I was just trying to get out of the house.'

'Why though?' said Maike.

'I think my mum's having an affair.' It was my final card.

Petra sat up and Maike raised her eyes to mine. She took my hand. 'What?' she said.

'Fuck, Ralf,' said Petra.

Stefan just said, 'Ralf?' very quietly and very sadly.

'I didn't know what to do,' I said, on the verge of tears, not about my mother, but because for a second I thought it was all going to come out, everything dishonest that I'd ever said or done. 'I just wanted to get out, get away from her.'

'When did you find out?' said Petra.

'At the private view,' I lied, because I felt embarrassed I'd known for so long and not said anything.

'I knew there was something up,' said Petra triumphantly.

'Fuck,' said Maike. 'Who's she having an affair with?'

'Tobias,' I said.

'The guy at the beer garden?' said Petra.

'No wonder you went white when you saw him,' Maike said.

'Your neighbour, Tobias?' said Stefan. He looked furious.

I nodded.

'*Eh, du Scheiße,*' Stefan said under his breath. 'What did your dad say?'

'Nothing. I haven't told him.'

'Why not?'

'He'd be crushed.'

'*Fotze,*' Stefan said, sitting up. 'We always thought he was up to something.' He looked worried. 'You don't think our stupid spy game meant we missed the signs?'

I didn't think so, but before I could answer, Maike said, 'It's not your responsibility to spot the signs. It's no one's.'

'No,' Stefan said, 'I suppose not.'

'I'm really sorry, Ralf,' Maike said.

'Thanks.'

I told them about the watch and what Mum had said about not leaving. They called him names and asked me lots of questions I couldn't answer: How long had it been going on? Does your brother know? Was it the first time she'd done it?

A plane rose in the East and turned, avoiding the proscribed air space above us. Its jet roar softened to an insistent, pulsing murmur.

'I was the affair once,' Petra said. 'I dated one of my dad's friends. Very suave. But under all those lovely clothes he was just a middle-aged man, with a paunch and a hairy back. He even smelled like one, d'you know what I mean? They smell different, middle-aged men. Like dads. Something about the smell of the office in their shirts. Tobacco. Neat, unwashed hair.' She shook her head in disgust. 'I stuck it for long enough for Papa to find out and be furious, then I dropped him. I felt bad, because he kept crying. He had white hair; can you imagine? You don't imagine men with white hair crying.'

'That's awful,' I said.

'Awful,' echoed Maike. Stefan said nothing.

'Oh, it wasn't so awful. I wouldn't call it awful. Not like you and your mum.'

I swigged from the schnapps; it burned. The plane thundered distantly and faded.

Petra lay on her back on the grass and closed her eyes. Maike and I lay down too, but rolled over so we were facing each other.

'Are you OK?' she said.

'Yeah, I'm fine. Really.'

'I miss you,' Maike said, tears filling her eyes. 'I feel like we're barely seeing each other at the moment.'

I wiped away Maike's tear with my thumb. 'I know,' I said. 'We can do something together tomorrow.'

She nodded.

'Come on, misery guts,' Petra slurred, getting to her feet unsteadily like a newborn foal. 'I want to go and look at the Wall.'

'Why?' Maike said.

'I'm not going anywhere,' said Stefan, reaching for the schnapps.

'We'll go and pray to it and then go home. I have another shift tomorrow.'

'You didn't answer my question,' Maike said.

'Fuck off, Maike.' Petra held out her hands and pulled Maike to her feet.

I scrambled up after them, brushing the grass from my palms, taking the schnapps bottle from Stefan, who followed it and me reluctantly. I was drunker than I'd thought I was, but the air felt cool and good, and it felt good to hold Maike's hand.

We dipped beneath the black trees, heading across the

park to the Wall's floodlights, accompanied by the flying insects that believed the light was the light of the moon. It was unbearable, when you thought about it: their visceral joy and then the feverish disappointment as they rubbed their abdomens against the hot glass of the bulb, bathed in the light they sought and finding nothing but death.

Where the grass of the Tiergarten ended, streetlamps marked a strip of red-and-white metal barriers designed to stop people wandering onto Ebertstraße. Between us and the street stood the statue of Goethe staring out East over the sheer, graffitied wall, which looked low and meaningless. Behind we could see the lamplit tops of buildings and a few light industrial chimneys steaming straight and thin in the hot summer air. The jumping insects chirruped in the stumpy trees behind us and we could smell cut grass.

'It's ugly, isn't it?' I said.

'Mmm,' said Petra.

She moved one of the red-and-white barriers; I was afraid that we were going to get told off, but when I followed and looked down the length of Ebertstraße, down to the pitted Brandenburg Gate trapped between the two borders, we saw no one, only the fluttering shadows of bats.

Petra skipped across the road and put her hand on the concrete. We joined her, also pushing our palms against it, but I didn't feel anything. It was like a graffiti-covered concrete wall at the back of someone's allotment, smelling faintly of piss and spray paint, like the lift in Maike's building.

'Do you think there's someone behind there now?' I said.

'Hello!' shouted Petra. 'Border guards? Are you there? There are some teenage deviants back here waiting for you. Woods, beds, tents, you name it, we've fucked in it.' She slapped the Wall with her hand. 'We've fucked everywhere!

We're here waiting for you behind this wall. All you have to do is knock it down.'

'Knock it down!' shouted Maike drunkenly.

'Knock it down!' Stefan echoed.

I slapped the concrete too. 'Knock it down!' I shouted.

'Knock it down!' we chorused. 'Knock it down!'

When we fell silent, we heard cars in the city accelerating, braking, sounding their horns. We wandered back through the park to the beer garden where we'd left our bikes, not talking, holding hands in a line like paper dolls.

Twenty

Oz was waiting for me at the open door of his flat. His hands were tucked beneath his armpits, and when he closed the door behind me, we stood opposite each other in silence. It was strange to see him washed and shaved, strange to imagine that he had been leading his life without me there.

'Did you ...?' he said.

I nodded and took the envelope out of my bag. He moved towards me. I let him come. We held each other and he kissed my neck. We held each other for a long time.

At the kitchen table, we sat either side of the envelope.

'Was it difficult?'

I shook my head. 'She was out for lunch and the door was open.'

He pulled the onion-skin pages out of the envelope, frowned, and tipped them towards the light.

'I know,' I said, thinking he'd read the first lines of the officer's file. 'Depressing isn't it?'

'Are these the originals?' he asked.

'Of course,' I said.

'*Scheiße*,' he said, and sat back in his chair, as if being near them was dangerous.

I went cold. 'What?' I said. 'What've I done?'

'It's my fault,' he said.

'What?'

'I said a copy of the file. Not the actual file.'

I touched my face. 'I thought you meant a copy like *the* copy, not a photocopy.'

'I should've explained it better.'

'What've I done?'

He crossed his arms and then slowly reached up and covered his mouth as if he was trying to stop himself from saying something. 'If I photograph these now,' came his muffled voice, 'can you get them back tonight?'

'Mum'll be there tonight. And tomorrow's Sunday. She'll be there all day.'

'Fuck,' he said, gripping his head. 'When's this officer have his appointment?'

I counted back. 'Friday, I think.'

'OK,' Oz said, calming. 'Then let's get all of these back in place as soon as you can next week. Does she go for lunch every day?'

'No,' I said. 'But maybe if I'm there.'

Oz looked unconvinced.

'I'll sort it out,' I said. 'I'll fix it.'

'Great,' Oz said. 'OK.' His hands found their way back to the table.

'I'm really sorry,' I said. I was embarrassed to hear my voice trembling.

'Oh, shit, Ralf. I didn't mean to freak you out.' He moved his chair around the table. I let him pull me close. His thumb burrowed under my T-shirt and touched my back. He kissed my neck and lingered there. The shaved skin around his mouth brushed my skin and I shivered. 'I didn't mean to scare you,' he said, his breath wetting my skin.

169

'I don't want to fuck it up.'

'You didn't. I was only worried about you. I shouldn't've asked you to get the files.'

'I wanted to,' I said, as I undid the top button of his shorts and slipped my hand into his pants. 'I wanted to do it.'

*

The next morning I lay in his bed watching him pull on the pink T-shirt he'd been wearing the day we drove to the Lappwald. Thunderously loud in the courtyard outside, the bin men were rolling the huge metal containers out to the street to empty them into their rumbling truck.

'Will you come back this evening?' Oz said.

I shook my head. 'I have to go home. I'm getting my A-level results tomorrow morning.' It should have been the defining moment of the year, but I'd barely thought about it.

'What's that?'

'It's like an English *Abitur*. It'll decide whether I can go to university or not.'

'Oh, wow,' he said. 'Good luck.' He took socks out from the drawer under the bed and unrolled them. 'If you got in, when would you go?'

'End of September.'

'Fuck,' he said, sitting on the bed and pulling the socks on.

I felt nauseous and stupid. I hadn't yet connected leaving Berlin with leaving Oz. I sat up and gripped his back. The T-shirt was soft and creased, and after a brief moment I could feel the heat of him through it. 'I'll get like twenty weeks off a year, or something,' I said. 'I'll be here a lot. I'll definitely fly back for Christmas and for summer. Definitely for summer.'

'Yeah,' he said, encouragingly. 'That sounds like a lot.'

'Or I might defer for a year. You can do that. It's something I was thinking about anyway.'

'Why?' he said, turning and putting his hand into my hair.

I shrugged. 'I was just thinking about it.'

He smiled and kissed me.

'Did you read the stuff?' I said. 'About that Major-General's sex problems?'

He nodded. 'Bent dick. That's harsh.'

'Bad enough to get him blackmailed?'

'Dunno,' he said. 'I'd be pretty embarrassed about it.'

I stared sadly own at the sheets. 'So what about Tobias? What happens to him if these files match up with someone that "Axel" has blackmailed?'

'They'll check if all of the leaks are coming from your mum. If they are, then all they need to do is arrest him. There'll be no more leaks to be plugged.'

'And Mum?'

'Sounds like she needs to put a better lock on that adjoining door, but I'm sure everyone would rather keep all of this as quiet as possible. I'm sure she's going to be fine.'

I thought about Tobias, tried to imagine him leaving my mother's bed, hobbling into her office and going through her flat, then meeting his East German handlers in some park, Volkspark Wilmersdorf perhaps, beneath the golden deer. I hated him, but he still didn't seem like a traitor to me.

'Could someone else in the building be the Stasi agent?' I asked

'Ralf, this is all far more common than you think.'

'But, *do* you know why he does it?'

'As I said, we know he attended a children's home and that he had polio.'

'But how's that explain it?' I pictured Tobias as a child abandoned on the steps of an East German orphanage, his leg in calipers, and felt miserable. 'He's not the type.'

'Ralf, is there a reason you're defending him? You should hate him. You should be happy he's going to be put away.'

'No, I know,' I said, thinking of his sweet, gappy teeth. 'It's just, I've talked to him. I know him. He's clever. He knows how fucked up the East is. Everyone I've ever met from the East knows it was fucked up.'

'Yeah, but those are the people that escaped. There are loads of people over there who are completely convinced that communism is a great thing, however much *Schwarzwaldklinik* they're illegally watching.'

'But you're saying he's an actual spy, not just someone who's going along with things. Why would he become a spy?'

Frowning, he pulled on a pair of white Reeboks and did up the laces. He seemed to be wondering whether he should go on.

'What?' I said.

He kicked his heel on the floor to get his shoe on properly. 'Well, I can tell you exactly why. And, you know what, my handler let me read what they had on Tobias – sorry, on "Axel" – and I actually sort of got it.' Oz leant back on the bed. 'So, his mum has him when she's sixteen, there's a sister too. But Mum's not interested in either of them. She doesn't even tell them who the father is; maybe she doesn't know. The children are shipped off to her parents, who are both proper, committed communists – were communists before the war and really suffered. So that's all this boy hears – Nazis are terrible, West Germans are Nazis, et cetera, et cetera. Then, when they've had enough of them, the boy gets sent off to an East German children's home in Königshain. He's six, but this is a pretty nice children's home, as far as East German children's homes go. They do drills all the time and get visits from Walter Ulbricht. And for this kid, he's finally got a family. He's finally got someone to believe in.'

Oz got up and picked up a battered book of Stanisław Lem short stories. 'Here,' he said, and took a folded A4 sheet from its pages.

I opened it up. It was a photocopy of a diary page written in a young person's hand, with tight letters and conscientious loops. The dates had been redacted out with thick black strips.

'What is it?' I said.

'From his diary.'

'Why do you have it?'

'It was in his files. I copied it on the fax machine at the shop. I couldn't get it out of my head. It's not marked or anything. Out of context, if someone found it, it wouldn't mean anything.'

I read:

If I can't sleep, I think of two things and both make me feel guilty. I imagine being a really important official and living in Berlin, with my own bathtub in one of the new buildings on Karl-Marx-Allee with a television set and a sofa. I imagine a family, a boy and a girl. Maybe more. And a wife, also passionate about our state and work and our family. Someone who loves our family. The other thing I imagine is Papa coming. I imagine eating in the canteen here and the door being thrown open and a man, a strong man with kind eyes shouting my name and us running towards each other, embracing each other. Then we get in his car and drive away. Where are you Papa? Are you still alive? Is it impossible to think you're searching for me?

'Jesus,' I said. 'That's really sad.'

'Right?'

'So you think Stasi agents are just really damaged? That's why they do it?'

'No,' Oz said, taking the piece of paper and putting it back in the book. 'No way. Most of them are just arseholes. Loads get something practical out of it. Nice apartment, place at a good university, constant back-patting. And there are loads of people, especially the petty informants, who are just reporting on their neighbours because they hate them. But with this guy I really felt like I got it. The state really did look after him. I'm sure his dad never turned up, but he got a flat in the West in your nice block in Charlottenburg with a sofa and a TV.'

'Tobias doesn't have a TV.'

'OK,' he said, conceding the point with a smile. 'But he doesn't have to queue to buy bread and he can eat all the bananas he likes.'

'Still not sure that excuses him becoming a Stasi spy.'

'I didn't say it excuses it, but don't you think it makes you see how it's all just a human process? You've got to believe they're humans, otherwise you never dig any of them out.'

He bit his lip and looked worried.

'I'm not going to talk about it,' I said. 'Who am I going to tell?'

'No, I know,' he said and kissed me.

'And I don't think you should keep copies of this kind of stuff in your flat,' I said.

'Oh what? I should just take the originals?'

I responded with a sarcastic laugh.

'You'll put the notes straight back, the moment you have the chance, OK?' he said.

'Like a good boy.'

He slapped my foot. 'Hey, I almost forgot: I got you something.' He brought his holdall into the room and opened it up. 'I was in this antiquarian bookshop round the corner from yours and they had loads of English stuff.' He retrieved a brown paper bag and gave it to me. 'It might be really boring, but ... I don't know, I thought it looked cool.'

Inside the bag was a folded map that smelt of ancient, yellowing books. I opened out the foxed paper to reveal a large cross-section of a mountain, tinted in pastel shades and marked with the names of each rock stratum and drawings of the flora and fauna found at each level. On the other side was another cross-section, but of a volcanic landscape, with the title of the map, 'Ideal Section of a Portion of the Earth's Crust, Intended to Show the Order of Deposition of the Stratified Rocks with their Relations to the Unstratified Rocks'.

'Is this original?' I said.

'I don't know,' he said. 'I think so. Do you like it?'

'It's William Buckland's wall map.'

'Says "Thomas Webster",' Oz said, pointing.

'Yeah, but it went on the front of Buckland's *Bridgewater Treatise*. It's a really important book.'

'Well, they didn't have the book, just the map. I thought you could put it on your wall.'

'This is amazing,' I said, smiling at him in disbelief.

He chuckled and kissed me.

'It's perfect,' I said.

'Good,' he said, and kissed me again. 'I'm glad.'

From the bed, I listened to him descending the stairs and crossing the courtyard, then I showered, and wandered

dripping through the flat, flicking through his books and burying my face in the clothes he'd discarded on his bedroom floor.
In the bathroom, I touched the hairs caught in his comb and
in his safety razor, and carefully pored over the contents of the
cupboards, finding earplugs, deodorant, ancient toothbrushes
and battered boxes of aspirin, antacids and something called
Hypnorex retard – a name I would've laughed about with my
brother – that contained lithium. I didn't know what lithium
was back then, or what it did.

I put on a Joni Mitchell cassette, made myself coffee and
ate a breakfast of stale flatbread, tinned olives and slices of
smoked Circassian cheese. I ate it staring at the pages from
the officer's file on the kitchen table. In my mother's tight
hand was her little signature, 'Patricia Rees', full of neat
English loops and slanting consonants.

Twenty-One

When I arrived back at Windscheidstraße I felt like I'd been away for years. I was shocked at how unchanged the apartment looked, how homely it smelt. Did Tobias go straight to the files, photograph them and leave? Did he go through everything? Our drawers? My cassettes? Had he seen the logbook that Stefan and I had kept on him? Surely he didn't care about those things. I hoped he didn't.

I dropped my bag in my bedroom and followed the chatter of the television to the living room, where I found Martin watching Bundesliga.

'I'm home,' I said.

'Coo-ool,' he said slowly and unenthusiastically, without turning to look at me. He had his arms behind his head and the sunlight through the window lit the straggly blond hairs thickening in his armpits.

'Is Mum cross I've been away for a few days?'

He paused, waiting for Jochen Sprentzel to stop speaking, then turned to me and said, 'No. You left a message saying you were at Maike's, didn't you?'

'Yeah. But I never stay at Maike's, so . . . '

He looked over at me open-mouthed. 'It's Maike, Ralf. No

one's worried about you staying with her. No one's cross. No one talked about it.'

'Fine,' I said.

'OK,' he said. 'Great chat.'

I sat at the open window in the kitchen and read a few pages of *Midnight's Children*, but it felt like a completely different person had started reading it and I found it impossible to concentrate. I hoped that Martin would suddenly need to leave the flat so that I could put the notes back, but when had that ever happened? He was fourteen – he had nowhere to go.

Tobias began to play his viola. His music stand was always set up to the right of his living-room window, so that when he practised you couldn't see him, unless the music became particularly expressive. Then his bow would poke into view, shuddering at the summit of a mournful vibrato. Without the surrounding orchestra, the pieces he practised often sounded unfinished, oddly broken for gaps that would be filled by other instruments. It was very lonely music.

Did I really think that Tobias was a spy? The honest answer is that I didn't think he was 'Axel', I wasn't even sure that I believed 'Axel' existed at all. But when I was with Oz I believed what he was telling me about Tobias was true. I could say that this position was indefensible and inexplicable, but it isn't. We all live like this. We know we'll die, we believe it, but at the same time we don't really believe it. Not us. Before my first daughter was born, I knew that there would be a new human being arriving in our lives that we had to look after, but I didn't really believe it. It was incomprehensible. And then suddenly she was there and I couldn't believe she had ever not been there.

This is how I felt about Tobias and Oz. I believed in them

both. But as with death and birth, belief always fall foul of the truth in the end.

*

The envelope was waiting for me on the kitchen table propped up between the toast rack and a sticky jar of *Aachener Pflumli*. My parents and Martin were already up when I came into the kitchen, hugging their coffee cups, bug-eyed and anxious.

'Morning,' I said, opening the fridge.

I took out the milk and got the bright red box of Smacks from the cupboard.

'Ralf, come on,' Mum said desperately.

'Don't be a dick all your life,' said my brother.

I opened the envelope and read out the results: an A for Geography, an A for Biology and a B for English Literature. Mum cried and clung to me. Dad gave me a hug and kissed my forehead. Even Martin hugged me, slapping my back and then painfully twisting my nipple through my T-shirt, saying, 'Clever dick.'

'Are you pleased?' Dad said, when I filled my bowl with pinging cereal.

'Course,' I said.

'Opa would've been so proud of you.'

'I'm sure Opa wouldn't've been that bothered,' I said.

'Too busy saving a cat, or something,' Martin said, and laughed, but neither of us could spoil the mood. Mum and Dad were in each other's arms, rocking and giggling through their tears.

The celebration was at a Chinese restaurant called Plumhaus that we went to on the first Friday of every month. We listened attentively to the specials, but always ordered the same thing: spare ribs, chop suey, spring rolls and chicken with cashew nuts, which all had an identical salty brown sheen.

Maike, Petra and Stefan had been invited, Beate too. Maike kissed me and patted my cheeks, Petra hugged me and apologised for getting tearful. 'I don't really care,' she said, smearing her mascara with a white napkin.

'Well done, Ralfi,' Stefan said, patting the back of my head as he sat down. 'Though Maike got a 1.0 for English, so I guess she's better at English than you.'

'I guess,' I said, relieved they were there.

My standoff with Mum disturbed the usual flow of such evenings, and even Beate's chatter died without the support of Mum's constant encouraging laughter. Maike, Petra, Stefan and I talked across the table about Doro Kretchmann, a middle-aged woman in the Wildlife Trust who came on every research trip, every count, every talk. She had short grey hair and round, red-rimmed glasses and wore socks with her Birkenstocks, making her for us the archetype of the German nature lover, the person we were destined to become.

Beate, Martin and my parents didn't know her, and I was aware that the conversation was boring them. But divided up between us, they weren't able to talk to one another, especially because we talked loudly and enthusiastically and Petra's screaming laughter drowned out any chance of comment long after the punchline of the story had been delivered. Whenever the conversation threatened to move on, I would recall another moment when Doro had slipped into a ditch or enthusiastically corrected people, despite refusing to be corrected herself.

The break came when the main courses were served and our sight lines were broken by the bald waiter rearranging the glasses, teapots and cups of jasmine tea to make room for the steaming bowls of white rice, allowing Beate to say, 'Tell us all about Durham, Ralf.'

'Yes, tell us about Durham,' my mother echoed.

'I don't really know anything about it,' I said. 'I got the offer without an interview, so . . .'

'It's "Oop Narth",' said my mother in English, doing the accent, then translating into German, 'Up north, near the Scottish border. Tell them about the geology up there, Ralf.'

'What about it?'

'Well, it's just two hours from Siccar Point, isn't it? You know better than me.'

'What's Siccar Point?' said Beate.

'The birthplace of geology,' my mum said.

'Well, that's debatable,' I said.

'Is it?' said Mum.

Because Beate was looking at me with pained optimism, I conceded, 'It's one of the places that James Hutton used to show unconformity.'

'What's that?' said Beate.

'The fact that different kinds of rocks are laid on top of one another. It just proves that all of the rocks weren't created at the same time by God, which is what most people believed in the eighteenth century.'

'Sounds fascinating,' said Beate.

'It's just one of the places Hutton used, so . . .'

'But it's the most famous,' said my mum. 'Isn't it?'

I shrugged.

'And he's the father of geology.'

'Only British people think he's the father of geology,' I said, using my teeth to rip a strip of sticky meat from a spare rib. 'Nicolas Steno, Johann Gottlob Lehmann, Füchsel – loads

181

of people came first. Even the ancient Greeks were at it. Even Goethe.'

My mother, crestfallen, stared down at her empty plate.

My father served her some rice and said, 'Come on, Ralf. You'll have the Peak District and the Lake District nearby, the Highlands, after being stuck in West Berlin for eighteen years. Surely the saddest town in the world for a geologist.'

'It's going to be amazing,' said Petra. 'I don't think you're going to miss Barssee and Pechsee.'

My mother gave her a wounded smile, her shoulders sunk in injured disappointment, a pose I found particularly annoying.

'Yeah,' I said, my mouth full and my lips greasy, 'I mean, I'll probably go to London anyway. It's a good course and it's a bit more interesting – the city I mean. But actually I'm probably going to defer university for a year. I'm pretty sure.'

I wiped my mouth with the back of my hand and held out my hands for the bowl of rice. Maike passed it to me with trembling eyes. No one around the table spoke. I could hear shouted Cantonese from the kitchen and a man lecturing his wife on a nearby table about the differences between Chinese and Korean chopsticks.

'Why would you defer for a year?' My mum's voice sounded low and heavy with rage.

I spooned too much rice onto my plate. The sound of the spoon hitting china was sharp and seemed excessively loud.

I shrugged. 'Just thought I might.'

'And do what?'

'Same as now. Work somewhere and save up some money. Be a bit better prepared, I suppose.' I opened my napkin and laid it across my lap.

'And you think you can just stay at home for another year without talking with me or your father about it first?'

182

I laughed and took a mouthful of rice. 'What?' I said, looking up at her. 'Are you going to throw me out?'

Her lips were parted, her lower jaw pushed forward. She clutched her white napkin in one hand as if she was going to hit me in the face with it. I heard a series of muffled thumps and then a clang as a chair fell over and hit a radiator. By the time I looked over to where Maike had been sitting she was halfway to the door.

'What's . . . ? Where's she going?'

'She's in tears, you idiot,' Petra said.

I got up and wearily followed her outside, wishing that someone would be on my side for once. Maike was walking away down the road with her hands gripped behind her neck and her elbows pushed together in front of her, as if she was bracing herself for an emergency landing.

'Hey,' I said. 'Maike!'

She didn't turn until I'd reached her and spun her round. She shoved me back with surprising force and I stumbled.

'What the fuck?' I said. 'What's going on?'

'What's going on? You can't guess?'

'No!'

'Deferring university for a year?'

'It's good news, isn't it? If I defer, then I'm here in Germany. I'm closer. I can get the train to Heidelberg anytime I want.'

'Why didn't you tell me? Why do I find out with everyone else here in the middle of a fucking restaurant?'

'Jesus, Maike. I just decided.'

'What, just like that? While you were eating spring rolls, you just thought, I'm going to defer university for a year?'

'No, I've been thinking about it for a while, of course. But it only, like, crystallised over the last couple of days.'

'Which I didn't know anything about because you never see me any more.'

'Yeah, well it's pretty complicated. You don't like coming to mine, because you and Mum don't get on, and I'm not allowed round yours, because of your parent issues.'

'What are you talking about? What issues?'

'You know I'm not welcome there.'

'Of course you're welcome there. You just don't like it there, because it's not some pretty Charlottenburg flat with plaster ceilings and varnished floors and a fucking TV the size of a car.'

'What do you mean by that? That's nuts. I don't care where you live.'

'Then why do you never come over?'

'You made it pretty clear you don't want me there.'

'When?'

'Whenever I come.'

'You've been twice. Once you turned up out of the blue just after Mum had chemo . . .'

'Well, you didn't tell me that . . .'

'And the second time I was ill. That's it.'

'Oh, so I've just imagined it, have I? I've just imagined the weird atmosphere there. The fact your dad and your sisters have never said hello to me. The fact that your mum doesn't even seem to know who I am.'

'She's dying, Ralf!' Maike's nose and eyes squeezed together, reddening. Tears escaped down her cheeks.

'No, I know,' I said, trying to hold her. 'I'm sorry. I'm being a dick, I'm sorry. It's just the results and Mum.'

'You're being a cunt to your mum, by the way.'

'She's been fucking some other man!'

'Which has nothing to do with you!'

'It has everything to do with me!'

She tried to turn away again, but I got hold of her arm and pulled her into a hug. She fought me off half-heartedly, but I got her into my arms and she cried into my shoulder.

'I should've told you about deferring,' I said. 'I should've said something. I'm sorry.'

'You don't tell me anything,' she wailed, her voice muffled by the cotton of my shirt. 'You're making new friends, you're away for days, you don't talk to me about any of it. I don't know who the fuck you are.'

'Of course you do,' I said.

'This isn't a relationship, Ralf.'

'It is,' I said. 'Of course it is. There's just loads going on.'

She pushed herself off me and found some tissues in her handbag. I put my hand out and touched her arm, but she let the arm drop and my hand fell away.

'Look, I'll come over tomorrow, OK?'

'That's what you said at the Tiergarten, then you didn't come.'

'This time I'll be there.'

She shook her head and smiled sadly, dabbing at her eyes and sniffling. 'I don't want you doing it like a favour.'

'It's not a favour.'

'But that's how you make me feel,' she said, her tears abating into dry, shivering gasps. 'I don't need favours. It makes me feel horrible and needy.'

'We all get a bit needy sometimes.'

'No,' she said. 'I've had enough of it. I'm done with it.'

She kissed me on the lips. Her mouth was hot and wet. I watched her cross the road to where her bike was locked up on a lamppost, beneath a shredded campaign poster of the mayor, Eberhard Diepgen. Someone had drawn a Hitler moustache on him and given him swastikas as pupils.

'But we're good together,' I shouted. 'We work *because* we give each other distance. We don't try to understand every single thing that's going on with the other person. That's why it works.'

Holding the handlebars of her bike, she looked stunned. 'No, that's why it works so well for you. Because you don't have to get close to anyone. And you don't have to get close to me. I thought that was going to change when we got together. I thought it was going to be different, but it wasn't different. Why were we having a relationship, if you didn't want to talk to me about anything except rocks? For a bit of sex? I can get a bit of sex anywhere I like.'

'Well, that's classy.'

'Not classy enough for you, apparently,' she said, mounting her bike and cycling away.

'Don't run off!' I shouted. 'I'll call.'

'Please don't,' she shouted back.

In the restaurant, I walked straight past the table, feeling them all staring at me as I passed. I sat on the toilet with my face in my hands listening to the waiters outside in the courtyard the other side of the high barred windows, smoking and gossiping. I fantasised about tapping my teacup and announcing to the table that I was fucking a man, that I was fucking a West German informant, and that Mum was a whore who was revealing state secrets because she was fucking a Stasi spy. What would they do? Nothing probably. A few more people would leave in tears and it would be forgotten and in a month's time we would all be around the same table again, burning our mouths on the jasmine tea and reading fortunes from the cookies as we rubbed the tiny crumbs from our fingers.

The toilet door opened and high heels clattered on the tiles. 'Ralf?' Mum said. 'Are you OK?'

'Mum, this is the gents.'

She came to the cubicle door. I could see the patent-leather tips of her black shoes poking beneath the door like bats' ears.

'Are you OK, though?' she said.

'Yes,' I said. 'I'm just on the toilet.'

Mum didn't move. The waiters outside had fallen silent. I could hear dishes being washed and the sound of water trickling through pipes. The air smelt of pine disinfectant, urine and mildew.

'Of course you can stay with us if you defer. You can live at home with us for as long as you like.' She moved her hand and the golden bangles she was wearing jangled down her wrists. 'Was Maike very upset?'

'Can we talk about this later?' I said.

She sniffled as if she'd been crying. I could hear her swallowing. 'Ralf, the thing with Tobias. The thing you asked me about.' I remained frozen to the black plastic seat. 'You don't need to worry about that, OK? There's nothing happening now. I love your father very much. There's nothing happening.'

'OK,' I said. 'Whatever.'

'And I love you, Ralf. So much. And I know I'm not always a good mother, or wife, but I do love you all so much. I couldn't love you more. That's the truth.'

'OK,' I said. Mum's shadow moved and the door banged slightly as if she was leaning on it. I was afraid she'd started crying again. 'I love you too,' I said weakly.

I heard her move to the sink, the sequins on the hem of her dress rasping. The tap was run and then the dryer screamed, covering her retreating steps. When the door knocked shut, I knelt down on the cold red tiles in front of the toilet and threw up the spare ribs and rice, and four cups of jasmine tea.

Twenty-Two

What I'd said to my mother about James Hutton was true. In Britain, writers tend to overstate the primacy of Hutton, ignoring the long history of geological discoveries in France, Germany, Hungary and Russia, with their traditions of mining and mining academies, churning out incredible fossils for centuries. When Wordsworth bemoaned the explosion of amateur geologists hacking at the rocks of the Lake District in search of substances known 'by some barbarous name', those names – greywacke, schist, gneiss – were all German.

To give Mum her due, though, it's impossible not to be won over by the romance of Hutton, John Playfair and Sir James Hall bobbing in the sea at Siccar Point in Berwickshire, as Hutton's hunch solidified in their minds that the earth had not been created in a single moment by the hand of God some six millennia ago, but billions and billions of years before. 'The mind seemed to grow giddy,' Playfair said, 'by looking so far into the abyss of time.'

One of the most passionate groups of amateur geologists was vicars, like Reverend William Conybeare and Reverend William Buckland, trying desperately to find in geology proof of the great flood that God had once sent to engulf the earth. Instead, they had to watch as the waters ebbed further and further away. I can imagine the nauseating anxiety that these men felt, trying to fit their newly gained knowledge to their old worldview, confidently exclaiming how each discovery proved their thesis, but feeling the constant contradictions as a persistent anxious pain in the stomach.

It was a pain I also felt in the last weeks of that summer. Sitting at the dinner table with my family, turning sausages on the grill at the beer garden, sunk into a beanbag in Stefan's bedroom, I could pontificate passionately about how me staying in Berlin for one more year made complete sense, how I was too young anyway, and how I needed the money now I was going to study in London. I could even cycle to Oz's apartment, have sex with him on the rough rug of his living-room floor and tell the same stories to the crown of his head as he lay on top of me stroking my bare leg. But through all of this, I was plagued by a chronic anxiety, a sense that I was about to lose my grip on something. And it came out physically. An itchy rash appeared on the back of my hand and every week or so I would get a blistering headache. At night, I would suddenly wake up as if someone had called my name, and then wouldn't be able to fall asleep again for an hour or more.

I felt as if a void had opened up around me. I realised that up until that point I'd always felt as if my life was following a clear course, but Oz had revealed the giddy multiplicity of lives that I might live, of people that I might be. The whole world had become unstable, the things that I believed, however laughable it may seem, to be permanent – my girlfriend, my friends, my family, my understanding of myself – had begun to shift. And I had the uneasy feeling that I was just old enough to see these things shifting for the first time, a snapshot of a much longer cycle, a split second in the inestimable history of my own deep time.

Almost a week had passed by the time I managed to get my mum's notes back into her filing cabinet. I was sleeping at the flat again, so that I could exploit the first opportunity that it was empty to do so. Mum was happy, because she thought I was spending more time at home because of what she'd said to me at the Chinese restaurant. I would often catch her staring at me with dewy-eyed gratitude while we were all watching TV. It made me uncomfortable and I would lie on the sofa sandwiching my head between the arm and a cushion, or lie on the floor in front of the coffee table where she couldn't see my face.

Once, when I fell asleep on the sofa I woke to find her pulling at my toe.

'Ralf,' she said. 'Are you awake?'

'I am now,' I said.

She smiled down at me. 'What is it?' My mouth tasted foul and I was aware of the silence in the flat. 'Where's Dad and Martin?'

'Dad's taken Martin to the football. He's going to do the shopping and then pick up Martin on the way back. Beate wanted to go and look at an allotment in Westend, so I'm going to tag along. I wondered if you wanted to come too.'

'Not really,' I said, sensing my chance to put the notes back.

She nodded. It was the weekend and she was wearing an oversized grey T-shirt over black leggings. Her feet were bare. She splayed out her toes and stared down at them. 'Can we ever be friends again, Ralf?' she said.

'We're not friends,' I said. 'I'm your son.'

She looked at me and considered what I'd said. I saw that there had been a shift in the balance of power, that in a discussion about relationships, about friendship and love, her opinion no longer took automatic precedence over mine. She had revealed herself to be just as weak as any of us. So she appealed to me. 'Do you understand what I'm saying, though?'

I pushed myself up into a sitting position. 'I think what you did is horrible. We can't go back to how it was before, even if you stopped it.'

'I know,' she said. She let her feet drop and stared at the coffee table. She looked sad and lost, and I could suddenly picture her as a sullen teenager in front of a black-and-white TV in the 1960s. 'I love you so much and I don't know what to do. What should I do?'

I sighed heavily, because I was welling up. 'I don't think you can do anything,' I said. A tear escaped down my cheek. She saw. Her chin puckered and her mascara began to run.

'It didn't have anything to do with you and Martin,' she said in a choked voice, wiping away her tears with the sleeve of her jumper.

'I know,' I said.

She nodded. 'Do you want me to tell your dad?'

'Don't ask me that!' I shouted. 'Don't make me make that decision.'

'No, no,' she said, through her tears. 'You're right, I ... I suppose I'm asking ... No ... ' She took a deep, shuddering breath. 'I suppose I'm saying that I'm not going to tell your father. Because it's over with Tobias. And I don't want to tell him. I don't want to upset anyone else. You don't have to keep any secrets for me, but if you don't tell him, I won't. And if you do talk to him about it, that's OK too. But that's what I want to do.'

'OK,' I said, my face wet.

She nodded and sniffed. 'Can I have a hug?' she said.

'I don't know,' I said. 'I still feel so angry.'

She nodded and looked down at my feet on the sofa. 'Can I hold a foot?'

I laughed and she laughed. 'Sure,' I said. 'I haven't had a shower though, so they probably stink.'

'I don't mind,' she said, grabbing my foot. 'I don't mind your stinky feet.'

I lay on the sofa, listening to Mum's sandals snap against her soles as she left the flat and made her way downstairs. When the front door to the apartment block rumbled shut, I stood and took the files from my bag. I was surprised to find that my hands were trembling.

I walked silently into the kitchen, through the adjoining door and into Mum's consulting room, where I put my hand up to the shelf with the African mask on it. I felt a hot wave of terror when my fingers alighted on nothing. I looked about in panic, opened one of the desk drawers and then another and – thankfully – found the key on its lilac plastic fob among coloured rubber bands, pencils, stamps and various quasi-practical trinkets gathered from foreign holidays: an olive-wood letter opener, a Majorcan pencil sharpener, a pen with a flamenco woman whose clothes fell off when you turned it upside down.

Relieved, I squatted by my mother's metal filing cabinet and carefully replaced the notes. But the hanging file for Major-General Hillary Purser was missing.

'Fuck,' I muttered to myself.

I searched her desk and got on my knees to look about the floor for it.

I didn't know what to do. I thought about cycling over to Oz's, but our flat would only be empty for a couple of hours, and that would waste too much time. I went to our balcony in the hope that he might be parked on our street, but when

I leant over I couldn't see his green Mercedes, only swallows snapping up invisible insects.

The heat was everywhere, exuding from the plasterwork of our balustrade, from the painted metal table and chairs, from the cobbles on the street below that looked black as burnt loaves in the orange light. The open windows of the apartments filled the street with a song of radios, televisions and noisy meals, mixed with the hush of cars on Ku'damm and Kantstraße and the twitter of the sparrows in the acacia trees. The air smelled of lime blossom, exhaust and kebab meat. And I had waited too long to put my mother's notes back and now I'd ruined everything.

A wasp swung into view and I brushed it away, but the movement of my hand encouraged it into an abandoned glass of *Apfelschorle* on the metal table.

'*Mist*,' I said and took the glass to the kitchen, where I emptied the trickle of juice and the sticky wasp onto the ivy that fringed our window. It rolled free of the clinging droplets, then stood on the dusty green leaf for a few moments, cleaning its antennas and buzzing its wings experimentally. It turned and droned deeply as it flew across the courtyard to the windows opposite. It was there, behind Tobias's shut windows, that I saw a file on his kitchen table, the exact dirty moss green of the hanging files in my mother's cabinet.

I grabbed the binoculars from my room and ran back to the kitchen, but couldn't read the tab on the file, because the top of the file was obscured by the edge of a discarded newspaper. I knew that if I thought too hard about what I was doing I wouldn't do it, so snatched up the keys for Tobias's apartment from the bowl on the hall table and tried to look as relaxed as possible as I trotted over the courtyard in my bare feet. In the dim light of the cool back staircase, I knocked gently at his door and called his name. 'Tobias? Tobias? Are you there?'

There was no answer. I unlocked the door and went in.

The smell of him that filled the little entrance hall made me feel unbearably nostalgic for all the years I'd watched him longingly from our kitchen window. Automatically, I reached out and touched one of his jackets hanging from a hook in the wall. It was soft and cold.

In the kitchen, the table contained the paper I'd seen from the window, a plate dusted with a few breadcrumbs and the green file. I moved towards it, had my fingers on it, but saw no plastic name tab, no Major-General Hillary Purser. I opened it and found, beneath the dog-eared paper, a pile of sheet music.

'Herr Rode? Oh! Who are you?'

I turned.

'Oh, it's you!'

It was old Frau von Hildendorf from the ground-floor flat. She must've seen me come up the stairs from her spyhole and followed me up.

'Are you meant to be here? Herr Rode didn't tell me he was going to be away.'

'He called,' I said. 'I had to check on something. And I'm going to go now and call him back from our flat.'

She frowned, unconvinced.

I rushed past her, back to the door. Her eyes followed me. 'I should call him back straight away,' I said. She followed me out frowning.

When I got back to my apartment, I could see her at her window looking disdainfully up at our kitchen through ancient, hooded eyes. Terrified, I found the number for Oz's bookshop in the phonebook and rang it. A man answered.

'Is Herr Özemir in?' I said.

'Yes, speaking,' the man said.

'Oz?'

'Who?'

'Osman Özemir?'

There was a silence, and then the voice said, 'No, he's not here. Who's this?'

'Do you have a number for him? It's important.'

'I don't know,' the man said. 'Just . . . ' He put the receiver down and started talking to a woman in Turkish. 'Have you got a pen?' he said, loud again.

'Yes.' I wrote down the number on a receipt magnetised to the side of the fridge, thanked him, hung up and redialled immediately.

'Özemir.'

'It's me,' I said. 'There's a problem.'

Oz paused, then made a sound, like a soft whistle.

'What?' I said.

The sound came again and I realised he was shushing me. 'Where?' he whispered.

'Where am I?' I said. 'Home, but I—' He'd already hung up. I called back, but he didn't answer.

I walked around the house sweating, not knowing what to do. I stared at Tobias's windows, went to the toilet twice, stood on the balcony again peering down into the street, hoping to see Oz's car. It was there that I heard a gentle knocking. It came again and I realised it was the door to the apartment. When I put my eye to the spyhole I saw Oz's head distended by the convex glass, looking down at the floor.

I opened the door and he pushed me in, shutting the door silently behind him.

'Are you alone?' he whispered.

'Of course.'

195

'For how long?'

'Like, a couple of hours,' I said, looking at my watch.

'You're sure?'

'Yes.'

'OK,' he said. 'What is it?'

'I tried to put the notes back, but the Army officer's file was missing. Then I thought I saw it in Tobias's flat, so I went over with our key, but it wasn't the Army officer's file. It was just a green file with his music in it. And then someone caught me.'

'Who?'

'Frau von Hildendorf. The woman who lives on the ground floor in the back building.'

'Shit,' said Oz, touching his forehead. 'Who else has a key to his flat?'

'No one,' I said. 'Not that I know of.'

'Do you know where he is now?'

'At the Philharmonie, I suppose.'

'OK. Where's your phone?'

I pointed him to the kitchen, where he snatched up the *Gelbe Seiten* and dialled the number for the concert hall. 'Hello!' he said, enthusiastically. 'Yes, this is Müller from Berlin Water. I need to get hold of someone in the orchestra. A Herr Rode.'

From the receiver came a burst of buzzy chatter.

'Yes, it's rather an emergency, I'm afraid. There's been a water leak in the adjoining building and we need to make sure it hasn't come through to Herr Rode's flat, which backs onto it . . . Yes . . . I understand . . . Yes . . . Thank you.'

There was a pause and he peered out of the kitchen window, down to Tobias's apartment. A voice came on the line.

'Herr Rode? Oh, they found you. That's great. It's Herr Müller from Berlin Water. There's been a leak in the block adjacent to yours, the flat that backs onto your flat, as it were, and we urgently wanted to check whether there'd been any ingress into your apartment ... No, we're hopeful, but it is urgent. It was a broken washing machine ... How quickly can you get back? Oh I see ... No, that won't work. Is there anyone in your block that has a spare key – someone that could take a look for you? OK ... Duzm? Oh, Dörsam ... Can you spell it for me? Front building, second floor ... OK. Listen, Herr Rode, I don't want to disturb you again, so why don't I knock at the Dörsams' and send one of them over. If you don't hear back from me in the next half-hour, then you can assume that everything's all right. Is that OK? Super ... You too! *Auf Wiederhören!*'

He replaced the receiver and we were quiet for a moment. 'OK,' he said. 'That's sorted. When your neighbour tells him she saw you, it'll back up your alibi.' He was wearing a turquoise T-shirt and there were huge royal blue sweat rings radiating from the armpits. 'Now, show me the filing cabinet.'

I took him through to Mum's consulting room and gave him the key. He carefully slid open the cabinet and ran his fingers along the plastic name tabs. 'Fuck, Ralf, it's here,' he said, lifting it up. 'It was just out of alphabetical order.'

'Oh fuck,' I said. 'I'm sorry. I'm so sorry.'

We put the notes back in and locked everything up. When we were back in the cool hallway he clasped my head, shaking it gently. I was so hot and so ashamed of myself.

'Ralf. You can't phone me. I shouldn't be here, not when there's no one else around, OK? If you'd said anything over the phone about this ... Fuck,' he said.

'Do you think our phone's bugged?'

'Probably not, but it isn't worth the risk. Tell me again why you went into his apartment.'

'There was a file there. Like one of Mum's files. I thought it was the one missing from her filing cabinet. I thought you'd be pleased and that it would all be done and all be over.'

'Just leave that to me now,' he said. 'We just need to be patient.' He rubbed my cheeks with his thumbs and laughed, shaking his head. His face was lit orange by the sinking sun. 'Fuck,' he said. 'It's good to see you, though.'

*

We lay side by side on the hallway's slick parquet. The flat was filled with purple light and a hot breeze slunk through the rooms. I was watching my own stomach heaving up and down as I tried to get my breath back. My shorts lay discarded near the door, and I could smell Oz's breath and the sickly sweet jasmine that grew in pots on the balcony. He touched the hair sticking to my forehead and said my name.

My pants were still clinging to one of my ankles and I kicked them off and walked to the bathroom. When I emerged Oz was standing naked in the living room, the setting sun painting a thick russet shadow down his spine and between his buttocks.

'Snooping?' I said.

He turned and smiled. 'Maybe. Grandparents?' he said, pointing to a photograph of my German grandparents on skis in the Alps.

'Opa the Great,' I said, 'and Oma the Big-Hearted. They're legendary. Opa was tortured by the Nazis.'

'Fuck,' Oz said, crossing the room. In the shadow of the doorway he kissed my bare shoulder. 'Can I see your room?'

I shook my head. 'It's really embarrassing.'

'Please,' he said.

I watched him take in the desk, the stickered mirror, my

posters and pictures of insects, forests, volcanoes and cliffs. 'You weren't lying about the nature shit,' he said.

I laughed.

'Where are all the rock pictures?'

'There are some,' I said, pointing them out. 'Mostly volcanoes though, a few caves. You get more animal pictures in the magazines, obviously, and I like animals too.'

'But not as much as rocks.'

'Not as much as rocks.'

'Who's this?' he said, pointing to a sepia postcard of an old man with mutton-chops in a leather armchair. 'Is this my competition?'

'No,' I said, laughing. I held him from behind and rested my chin on his shoulder. 'This,' I said, touching the picture, 'is Charles Lyell. He wrote *Principles of Geology*, which is one of the most important books on geology ever written. Before him, it was all vicars and their wives stumbling around caves finding fossils of dinosaur turds.'

'Nice,' he said. 'And this?' He pointed to a painting of a rotund woman with a sack and a small border collie at her feet.

'She's just hot.'

Oz laughed.

'That really is your competition,' I said.

He turned his head and kissed my cheek. His back began to sweat where we were pressed together. 'No, that's Mary Anning,' I said. 'She was a famous fossil hunter on the Jurassic Coast. It's like an hour away from where my English grandparents retired to. She unearthed ichthyosaurs and plesiosaurs. She sold the fossils. She even had a visit from the King of Saxony.'

'It's so cute,' he said, putting his arms around my back, locking his hands together above my buttocks. 'It's massively geeky.'

I laughed. 'I know.'

'And now you're in your bedroom with a naked man.'

'That would've blown my mind about ... well, about six weeks ago.'

'And now it doesn't?'

'In a different way,' I said.

I looked across the hall to the open French windows in the living room and said, 'I'd love to watch the sunset with you on the balcony.'

'Why not?'

'Someone'll see us.'

'We'll go like this,' Oz said, dropping to his knees. He crawled naked across the hall, and I got down on my knees and followed him through the living room, stopping as he lay down on the balcony floor by the table.

'Can't the neighbours see you?' I said.

'Not from down here. If we stay lying flat.'

He beckoned me over and I crawled laughing into his arms. We lay side by side staring at the pink clouds in the powder-blue sky, our bodies orange beneath it. I rested my head on his shoulder. The sky was turning indigo at its apex and the first stars dotted the clouds.

'I wish you could stay,' I said.

'Shall I greet your parents like this?'

I smiled.

'They'd like you,' I said, 'but with clothes on.'

I put my ear to his chest and listened to his heart through the soft crinkle of his chest hair.

'Mum's files,' I said. 'Did you find anything in them?'

'We did,' he said.

'And?'

'Two matched people who'd been blackmailed by the Stasi.'

I listened to the watery pulsing inside his body.

'Ralf?' he said.

I lifted my head.

'This is good,' he said. 'It means we've got him.'

I couldn't believe it. Everything he'd said was true. 'What'll happen now?' I said, afraid.

'They'll come for him. They're just waiting for the right time. You've done great,' he said. 'It's all over now.' He wrapped his hot arms round me and kissed my head repeatedly.

'Can I come back with you?' I said.

'I want you to,' he said, 'but I have to go away for a couple of days.' The bass of his voice boomed in my ears.

'OK.' I pushed myself up on one elbow. 'Where?'

'Bonn.'

'For work?'

He pressed his lips together and nodded.

'Can you not talk about it?' I whispered into his ear.

He smiled and shook his head.

'It's OK,' I said. 'I've got tons of things to do.'

'Really?' he said.

'Oh yeah,' I said. 'I'm really busy.'

Twenty-Three

'I'm coming anyway,' I said to Stefan. I could hear the sound of Beate singing in the background as she cooked.

'You're just going to make it awkward,' Stefan said.

'So I'm never going to get to do any more Wildlife Trust stuff, because Maike's grumpy with me?'

'This Saturday it's all grass and moss and things like that,' said Stefan. 'It's her thing.'

I touched the rough poster paint on a childish picture of a bird-shaped plane that Martin had drawn at primary school. It was stuck to the side of the fridge with two magnets: a Berlin Zoo giraffe and a smiling ZDF Mainzelmännchen. Outside in the courtyard someone was playing 'Voyage' at full volume.

'But all the Wildlife Trust things are plants or animals. No one's trying to save any rocks, so I'm never going to get to go again.'

'Of course you will. Just wait until things have calmed down a bit with Maike.'

'Calmed down? She dumped me!'

'*Alter, hör mal*, you were being a completely shitty boyfriend.'

'Did she say that?'

'No, that's my own thesis based on empirical evidence.'

'But peer-reviewed, I bet.'

Stefan sighed. 'Look, why don't you come to this exhibition – *New Positions*? Joachim asked me to go ages ago and Petra's coming, but Maike can't.'

'Joachim? When did you speak to Joachim?'

'You're not the only one that can make new friends, Ralf.'

'Fine,' I said, the other option being sitting at home with my parents and Martin watching *Wetten Dass*. 'But I'm coming on the next nature thing. I'm not going to be shut out of everything now. It's not fair.'

'Yeah, yeah, I hear you,' said Stefan. 'See you at five.'

*

Joachim, wearing a white vest and jean shorts, greeted me enthusiastically, holding my forearm as he shook my hand. 'Everyone's always telling me stories about Ralf. It's good to finally meet you.'

'We met at Beate's private view.'

'Yeah, of course,' said Joachim, 'I just meant good to finally meet you again.'

I tried to roll my eyes at Stefan, but he turned away. Petra pushed me through the glass doors into the gallery and whispered, 'Stop being a dick, Ralf.' I shrugged her hand off my shoulder.

We wandered through the cool carpeted rooms of the Neue Nationalgalerie. I'd been a few times, mostly on school trips, and loved how buried the building was, like a sea volcano with its true mass hidden beneath the waves.

There were a few paintings I liked, but generally the pictures, with their emphatic lines, made me uncomfortable. Perhaps that was the point. I had a feeling that this kind of expressionism would be something I might like when I was older, developing a taste for it like for the bitterness of wine and beer. Up ahead, Joachim and Stefan barely seemed to be looking at the pictures at all. They just kept giggling at the labels.

'What's up with them?' I whispered to Petra.

'What do you mean?'

'When did they get all pally?'

Petra ignored me and moved into the next room. In front of a Cy Twombly canvas, covered in scratchy lines and scarlet splotches, a woman whispered, 'It's almost like a crazy person painted it.'

I smiled at her. She was tall with a beaky nose and brown clothes and shoes. 'He's not my favourite either,' I whispered back.

'It's like he did it for therapy,' the woman said, and we both laughed. As the woman moved away to the next painting, she muttered, 'Keep away from the Turk.'

'What?' I said too loudly.

The woman turned and looked at me shocked, as did a young couple that had just entered the room, the man in a baggy Keith Haring T-shirt.

'The talk,' the woman said, her face pale. 'I just said, keep away from the talk. The one this afternoon about Cy Twombly. It's ... it's ...'

'You said "Turk".'

'I didn't,' the woman said.

My face burned. 'I thought you said Turk.'

'But I didn't,' she said.

The woman scuttled on and I stared about the beige room unnerved.

*

When we came out of the exhibition, Stefan and Petra had to pee, so I stood in Mies van der Rohe's high glass hall with Joachim. I stared out at the grey square, watching the beaky woman escaping past the Staatsbibliothek and the Philharmonie where Tobias played and which emerged golden from the ground like a chunk of sulphur. I kept rerunning my brief conversation with the woman, feeling shame consuming my initial fear. The rash on my hand itched and I rubbed it against my shorts.

'Stefan takes a piss every ten minutes,' Joachim said, as if I didn't know.

'Yeah,' I said. 'He's always been like that. He drinks too much water.'

Joachim put his hands in his pockets and scuffed his sandals on the veined marble. Even with the limited emotional awareness I had at eighteen, I knew that I primarily disliked Joachim because he was a threat, hanging out with my friends when I wasn't there. But I also had a feeling about him then that I struggled to articulate. It was a sense that his unselfconscious openness was the real threat, promising to unseat me with his terrible honesty.

'So, Stefan said you were going to do geology. That like rocks?'

'Not just rocks, but, yeah, rocks, earth, glaciers.'

'What's this?' he said, nodding at his feet.

'What, the floor?'

'Yeah.'

'Marble,' I said. 'Some kind of greeny marble.'

'Where's it from?'

'I don't know.'

'Maybe you'll learn in your course.'

'Probably not,' I said.

'No, probably not. Sorry. I'm just blathering.'

Then I felt bad, so I asked him what he was working on.

'I'm doing a project at the Kunstgewerbemuseum just opposite.'

He told me about the work and invited me to come and look at the collection. Something metal was dropped, cracking like gunshot onto the marble floor, and the sound reverberated around the great hall. I looked about instinctively for Oz or the beaky woman in the brown clothes, but instead saw, with relief, Petra and Stefan emerging from the galleries below.

'What are you guys up to now?' Joachim said as we unlocked our bikes from the racks outside.

'Fuck all,' said Stefan.

'I thought we were going to Der Gammler,' I said. 'If I'm still allowed.'

'Why are you being so grumpy?' said Stefan.

'Have you got your period?' said Petra.

'A couple of friends of mine've put on an exhibition down in Neukölln by the canal,' said Joachim. 'It's in this squat above a pharmacy there and you can get up on the roof. It's pretty cool. And it's the night for it.'

'Sounds great,' said Stefan. 'Come on, Ralf. Stop being such a misery guts.'

'Fine,' I said. 'If that's what everyone wants to do.'

'It is,' said Petra.

'Fine,' I said.

Twenty-Four

W e cycled over the vast concrete square. Having been baked by the sun all day, it radiated a particularly oppressive heat, reminiscent of gridlocked freeways in American movies. We found the Landwehrkanal and followed it down through Kreuzberg to Neukölln and locked up our bikes by the canal railings, where the green vegetation hung over our heads in drowsy boughs, entwined with bindweed dotted with bell-shaped white flowers. The ground was covered in cigarette butts, drink-can ring-pulls and broken bottles and the air was full of clouds of insects and the smell of stagnant water.

The block Joachim led us to was noticeably rougher than the other Neukölln buildings, with peeling plaster and paint, bed sheets for curtains blooming out from the open windows of each of the five floors, and so much graffiti at street level that it was almost neat, the way it stopped just above head height. On the wide blank side of the building, someone had used a roller to paint 'Those who do not move do not notice their chains' in giant square letters. From the open windows, we could hear the thudding beat of electronic dance music and the muffled din of intoxicated voices.

'Welcome to the squat!' Joachim said. 'I lost my second virginity here.'

'What do you mean, "second virginity"?' I said.

'Bumming.'

Petra nodded approvingly.

As we crossed the street, two Turkish children sped past us on bikes shouting to each other in Berlin dialect. On one side of the pharmacy was a shop selling stockings, tights and socks, on the other a Turkish greengrocer with a green articulated awning. As we approached, the breeze skitted silver onion skins over the pavement towards our feet and I could smell traces of oranges, mint and cucumber. I suddenly pictured another me in Bonn, another in Frankfurt and Munich, Oz arriving at their doors and feigning innocence before bedding them. Was that what he was doing in his work for the West?

Joachim knocked on the door of the squat. It opened a few centimetres revealing the face of a woman made up like a Chinese opera singer, her face painted white, her eyes swathed in sweeping pink make-up, the same colour as her doll-like lips. She stared at us for a second and then the mask broke into a smile. She fell backwards and pulled the door open, revealing a tiny figure with thin arms sticking out of dungarees, under which she appeared to be wearing nothing. Her hair was crow-black and hair-sprayed up into a wild pile as high as her face was wide.

'Joachim, you came!' she said and threw herself at him, clinging to his neck. Her compactness made him look like a giant. She released him and grabbed my cheeks, her fingers smelling of cigarettes.

'Look at these babies you've brought us,' she said, and cackled. Her back molars were missing on both sides.

We climbed the stairs, following a constant trail of graffiti, dominated by crapping dogs who were saying, '*Schuldig!*' and

'*Keine Kneipen für Nazis*' and in English: 'Fucking is more important than Germany'.

Joachim led us into a large flat that had been emptied of furniture and painted white – the doors and window frames, but also the floor, the lampshades hanging from the ceiling, even the curtains, which were stiff and locked into their folds like asbestos roofing.

Paintings covered the walls, giant canvases showing women driving cars with a range of surreal passengers. They were painted in bright colours with expressive cartoon strokes and the perspective in each was either front-on or slightly diagonal to the car, cropped close, so that the woman driving was prominent and the cars seemed to be bearing down on you, driving homicidally into the room.

In one the passengers were all large men who seemed too tall for the car, and were hunched over with aggressive smiles, their faces cut off in the middle by the top edge of the windscreen. In another the passengers were vegetables – a cucumber, a carrot, a leek. In another children. In another the same woman who was driving was also all of the passengers, front and back.

'They're by this guy,' Joachim said, gesturing to a man in his thirties surrounded by a clutch of admirers. His white shirt clung to a beer-belly out of proportion with the rest of his body, as if he were pregnant.

'Joachim, you cunt,' the man said. He appeared to already be wildly drunk. The men embraced and the artist held Joachim at arm's length. 'Look at you, you beautiful shit.' He patted his cheek. 'You wonderful shit.'

'This is Stefan, Petra and Ralf,' said Joachim.

'Oh, you've brought children,' the artist said. Petra smiled witheringly at the repeated joke. He kissed all of us on the hand with his chapped lips. 'Kurt,' he said.

'I like the paintings,' said Petra.

'Oh, you're sweet,' Kurt said, peering about the room. 'The series is called "Women Driving Cars". It was a hard title to come up with.'

I laughed, but Kurt didn't smile and I realised too late that he wasn't being ironic.

Someone shouted, 'Kurt, you fuck!' from the door and Kurt pushed past us shouting, 'Alfred, you desperate cunt!'

'He's going to drink himself to death,' Joachim said, as we wandered around the rooms, looking at the woman in the car joined by Saudis in dark glasses, joined by Christ and Buddha and, finally, the woman alone. It was impossible to read from her expression whether the emptiness of the car was a relief or a tragedy.

'Do you like them?' I asked.

'I don't know,' said Joachim. 'I can't really judge Kurt. It's hard to separate it from him, if you know what I mean?'

I nodded, because Joachim seemed very sincere, but I didn't know what he meant at all.

I saw another man staring at the pictures who looked as confused as I felt; someone Kurt's age but alone and apparently bewildered, conspicuous in the dullness of his clothes – grey trousers, a white short-sleeved shirt, tinted glasses – and a combover that had shifted in the heat of the afternoon revealing a shaft of glossy scalp beneath the carefully greased hair.

'Who brought their accountant?' said Petra, and we sniggered.

The squatters used the second floor as their living room and kitchen and it was filled with mattresses, herbal cooking smells and marijuana smoke. In one corner, a series of large brown buckets were filled with water, and next to them were three gas camping stoves in various stages of rusted disrepair.

The third and fourth floors were filled with more mattresses and were hung with woollen blankets that separated different sleeping areas. As we passed the open doors, I heard, beneath the chatter of several transistor radios, the sound of people fucking.

The fourth floor led up to the attic and a door that opened straight onto the roof.

The sky was honey-coloured. Around a large brick and plaster chimney, men and women drank, danced, and lounged on sofas that had improbably found their way up onto the large flat roof. A black man in sunglasses sat in a folding chair by the record player, from which two long cables snaked away to two standing speakers pumping out the electronic dance music that I'd heard from the street. The bass was so commanding that the floor seemed to liquefy beneath our feet every time it reverberated.

Joachim guided us over to a group of friends on one of the sofas. He embraced them all, introducing them to us one by one. One girl was completely naked. She was chatting so seriously and unselfconsciously to another woman that I felt as if I was just imagining her nude.

We were given warm bottles of beer and sat with our backs to the chimney in front of the group, asking questions and discovering that they were all artists, filmmakers and photographers, except for the naked woman who worked at a Penny supermarket in Wedding. Then it emerged that one of the photographers worked in the same supermarket, and as the sun went down and they became more intoxicated we slowly understood that almost none of them just painted, made films or took photographs. They all also worked in galleries, in publishing, at petrol stations and in bookshops. That was why they admired Kurt so much; he had given his life to it. Even Joachim was doing a PhD and teaching in Düsseldorf.

As the sun burst into reds and pinks and the lights of the city shimmered, Joachim had to take Stefan to the other side of the roof to point out where, behind the planes landing at Tempelhof, you could almost see the block of concrete that Albert Speer had built to test the firmness of the Berlin soil, to find out whether it would take the weight of Hitler's giant domed Reichstag. I was relieved to see the naked woman pull on a large mustard-coloured jumper, though she continued to flash her bush every time she moved her arm to pick up her beer from the side of an empty rabbit hutch. I also spotted Petra drunkenly trying to talk to the man with the combover, who scampered away from her down the stairs.

'What did you say to him?' I asked as she walked past.

'If he wanted to fuck,' said Petra.

'And?'

'Apparently not.' She winked at me and danced backwards into a gathering crowd gyrating near the speakers.

I pushed myself to my feet. I had pins and needles, and felt drunker standing up than sitting down. At the edge of the roof, I looked out across the city, where West turned to East, and saw the death strip of the Wall, a bright highway cutting the city in two. On the Eastern side, the street lights were dimmer, a grubby orange, the colour of unsmoked tobacco.

In the street below, I saw the man with the combover from above. He crossed the road to a gold-coloured Ford Cortina, touched the door handle and then looked up at me. For a second we were staring at each other, his black eyes fixed on my face and then moving along the roof as if he were searching for someone else. He let go of the door handle, walked around the car looking at it as if he was admiring it, then walked off towards Kreuzberg.

A skinny man with straight black hair brushed into curtains leant against the low wall beside me. He lit a cigarette. 'Friend of yours?'

'No,' I said. 'I thought he was going to steal the car. He tried the door then wandered off.'

'Did you lock it?'

'Oh, it's not mine. We came on bikes.'

He held out the cigarette packet. 'Want one?'

'Sure.'

We smoked together staring out over the Wall into East Berlin.

'Do you think there are some communists right at this moment staring over the rooftops at us?' I said through the clearing smoke.

'Maybe,' he said. 'But I think in the East we're always more interested in ourselves than you think. Most East Germans care about East Germany, the politicians too. I don't think anyone's even that bothered about West Berlin. It's just there, you know. But most of the time you're not even thinking about it at all.'

'You're from the East?' I said.

He nodded.

'How did you get out?'

'Just applied.'

I laughed. 'Just applied?'

'Well, I'm an artist. And not the kind they like.'

'Political?'

'Not really,' he said. 'Not what you'd call political. Like sculptures of birds, but made out of iron. Kind of shitty Arte Povera.'

213

'I'm sure it's not shitty.'

He grimaced and scratched the skin above his eye with the long nail of his little finger.

'I thought you were Turkish,' I said.

He raised his eyebrows and nodded as he sucked on his cigarette. 'I get that a lot. My family's actually from Yugoslavia. Pristina.'

I shrugged; it wasn't a city people had heard of back then.

'It's a small town,' he said. 'We visited a few times, but actually I barely remember it. Maybe I'll have a chance soon.'

'Why?'

'It's all coming to pieces, I think. Tiananmen Square, Gorbachev in Bonn, Solidarność, the Love Parade. That Wall's not going to last.'

'You think?' I said.

He nodded. 'Yes, mon,' he said in English, imitating a Jamaican accent. 'Were you at the Love Parade?'

I shook my head.

'It was beautiful. We're going to change the world, you know.'

'Who?'

'You and me,' he said. 'All of us. When we kill the pigs.'

'Which pigs?'

'The capitalist pigs.'

I thought about my dad behind the counter of his pharmacy in his neatly pressed shirt. 'I thought you left East Germany because of the communists.'

'Yeah, but they're not real communists. They're just dry old men in suits. What's going on here, man. Braunmühl, Beckurts, you know? That's action. That's changing things. Because there are fascists, right? Everywhere. You know they didn't find any fingerprints on the guns in Baader and Raspe's cell?' He was talking about the deaths of the Baader-Meinhof Gang in '77. 'And Ensslin's chair was too far away from her body for her to have hanged herself. They were assassinated by the BND. By the West Germans. In a fucking "democracy", excuse me.'

'The West doesn't kill people,' I said, repeating what Oz had told me.

He laughed. '*Alter*,' he said, 'you need to get informed. Uwe Barschel. CDU prime minister in Schleswig-Holstein who'd been found dead in a hotel bath. You think that was a suicide?'

'I . . . I don't know. I know it was weird, but wasn't it meant to be the Israelis or something?'

'It was a West German Intelligence hit – trust me. All about oil, of course.'

I felt afraid for Tobias. But then Barschel was an important politician. And the Baader-Meinhof Gang were actually killing people. Tobias wasn't that important; I was sure he wasn't.

Joachim barged in between us and got his arm around me. I could feel the hair of his armpit damp on my shoulder. 'You met Mo!' He turned to Mo. 'Ralf here's got a new Turkish friend, called Oz.'

Mo nodded with scant interest; his gaze wandered back to the amber lights of East Berlin.

'How do you know about Oz?' I said.

'Stefan told me,' Joachim said drunkenly. 'You know your friends love you, right?' he said, putting his hand flat to my chest. 'You're all they ever talk about, even since you dumped your girlfriend.'

'She dumped me.'

'Are you listening to me?' Joachim said. 'They really love you.'

215

I looked at the brick lip of the roof and sucked at my cigarette. 'Yeah,' I said, embarrassed. 'Well, thank you for saying.'

'*Sicher*,' said Joachim, earnestly. 'I'm going to get beer. Everyone wants more beer, right?' he said, dancing off, his sandals scuffing on the worn bitumen.

Mo told me about a project he was working on about movement and history. I didn't really understand if that meant he was an artist or a dancer, and the look he gave me when I asked implied that it was stupid to ask. The conversation died after that and the girl in dungarees appeared on the roof and dragged Mo and me to the DJ and his speakers, which were blasting out Talking Heads.

I danced for what felt like hours. Stefan, Joachim, Mo, Petra, the naked girl, the girl in the dungarees, Kurt – they all passed by, their hands raised in the air, holding cigarettes and bottles of beer. When Petra and I sang all the words to 'Irgendwie, Irgendwo, Irgendwann' and danced like Kate Bush, Joachim laughed so hard that he had to sit in the middle of the dancers, who continued to move around him as he shrieked.

I smoked marijuana for the first time, taking a stinging gulp of it from a tall Dutchman called Pieter, who started crying when they played 'Every Day is Like Sunday' and told me and Petra that his mother had been killed in a gliding accident when he was ten. It made me and Petra cry too, but the naked girl was painting my nails with apricot-coloured varnish, so I couldn't reach over and hug him.

Stefan hugged me though. He gripped me from behind and said, 'Don't be cross about Maike. She'll come round, but you were a dick about things.'

'Was I?' I said.

Petra danced past and Stefan shouted, 'Hey Petra, was Ralf a dick with Maike?'

She nodded. 'Absolute cunt.' She raised her hands above her head and moved them like a snake as she swung her hips to The Bangles. 'Why were you such a cunt, Ralf?'

'You don't really think I'm a cunt,' I said drunkenly.

Petra hugged me from the other side so that I was sandwiched between them, and Joachim joined in enthusiastically. 'We're all cunts, Ralf,' Petra said hotly into my ear. 'It was just your time to come into the fold.'

We fell over and rolled laughing together across the roof and our faces and hands were covered with cigarette ash and spots of melted tar, so that we were flecked and stained like chimney sweeps by the time we stumbled apart.

We danced and danced. I noticed the sun rising when the skin of my arms, high above my head, turned purple.

I wandered through the heaps of drunk and sleeping people on the sofas, on the floor, propped up against the chimney looking for Petra and Stefan, but I couldn't find them. Blue cigarette smoke trickled into the sky and I felt like I was stumbling through a burnt-out village the morning after it had been pillaged by Vikings.

I wandered onto the staircase; it felt strange to be inside. I called their names, but the only answer came from the dungaree girl, whose cackle deep in the belly of the building rattled up the bare plaster walls.

At the door to the bedroom floor, I heard snoring, but also giggling and the creaking of old springs in damp old mattresses. I wandered through the large rooms, smelling of smoke, stale beer and sleep, looking through the gaps in the hanging sheets to see if I could spot Petra or Stefan. The sleepers and lovers unfolded themselves as I passed, but I didn't find either of my friends, just two amber eyes.

I stopped, startled. I reached out and slowly lifted the

hanging blanket and there was Oz standing by an empty mattress, the sheets kicked into a dirty pile in one corner.

'Oz!' I said, dazed. 'What the fuck are you doing here?'

Someone shushed me.

Oz pulled me into the pale space. I stumbled on the mattress and it gave off a stink of human hair and patchouli oil.

'Ralf,' Oz whispered. 'Don't worry. I've been here the whole time.'

'Don't worry?' I said. 'What the fuck are you talking about? Why are you here at all? How did you . . . ? Were you following me around all day?'

We were shushed again and from the far side of the room someone let out a deep orgasmic groan.

'Listen,' he whispered. 'I know this seems weird, but I think someone's on to us.'

'What? Why?'

'When I got back yesterday, all of the bulbs in my flat had blown. And someone had swapped round all of my cutlery in the cutlery tray.'

I stared at him astonished. 'Why does that matter?' I hissed.

'It's gaslighting. It's what the Stasi do. They try and make you think you've gone crazy.'

'This seems pretty crazy to me at the moment,' I said.

'I know, I know,' he said. 'I shouldn't've come. But I was scared. I was scared that they'd somehow find out about you and follow you. I wanted to be nearby in case anything happened.'

His eyes were large and beautiful and he looked incredibly sad. It was hard not to touch him, and I put my hand on his chest. 'You really freaked me out.'

'I know,' he said. 'I'm sorry. It was dumb.'

I sighed. 'Do you want to get out of here? Go back to yours?'

'I think we should keep away from the flat for the next twenty-four hours. And I think it'd be best if we stuck together.'

'What do you mean?'

'I want to make sure you're safe. If you've got stuff to do, I can just keep an eye on you, like tonight. You won't notice me.'

'You can't follow me around, Oz. It's creepy. And it's my mum's birthday tomorrow.'

'I could come.'

'What, and disguise yourself as a waiter?'

He looked put out. 'You don't want me to meet your family?'

Someone shifted behind the hanging blanket and five grubby toes appeared by my foot. 'Of course. I mean, yes, at some point. I just wasn't expecting it to be like this.'

'It won't be weird. I'll be on best behaviour. I just want to be close to you. We'll just say I'm a new friend.'

'OK,' I said unenthusiastically.

'Can I see you home?'

'I've got my bike.'

'I'll follow in the car.'

'That's also really weird, Oz,' I said.

'I don't want to take any chances,' he said. He kissed me and pulled me out through the blankets.

I crossed the road gingerly and unlocked my bike, sensing that Oz's appearance was going to seem much more odd to me once I was sober. Someone had parked very close to the gold-coloured Ford that the man with the combover had looked at, and with gritted teeth I unsteadily pushed my bike through the gap, the pedal scratching along the car's corner, above the bumper. With my face pulled into a guilty grimace, I touched the scratched paint and some of the gold flakes came off on

219

my fingertips. I looked up and down the street and, seeing no one, cycled swayingly back home through the waking city, the sound of Oz's ancient green Mercedes grumbling along behind me.

The streets were almost completely devoid of vehicles, except for delivery trucks and an empty yellow bus that overtook us at Kottbusser Tor. Otherwise, the city belonged to me and my escort and a smattering of drunks and revellers sloping back home in their high-waisted jeans, cigarettes hanging from their lips.

On Windscheidstraße, I heard him pull in and lifted my hand in a wave. He beeped his horn. In my room, I opened the window and lay on my bed and from the bakery that backed onto the courtyard I could smell Sunday rolls being baked. The day was already too warm for sheets, and I fell anxiously asleep on top of them, still wearing my clothes.

Twenty-Five

Oz had gone back to his dad's to get changed, and I purposefully took too long to get showered and dressed so that Mum, Dad and Martin would go on ahead without me to the party and I could meet Oz back at his car and drive over with him. I'd mentioned that he was coming as casually as possible, and Mum and Dad seemed pleased that I'd made a friend outside of the nature group.

When I found Oz leaning against the car, he was wearing chinos and a sky-blue shirt and looked very handsome. I still felt disturbed about him following me to the party the night before, but when I got into the passenger seat, he got in beside me and held my hand. 'Ralf,' he said. 'I'm really sorry about last night. It was really weird. This lightbulb thing got me really paranoid, but I didn't want to spoil your evening. And then when you came down the stairs at the squat, I just thought the best thing to do was to hide, which I can see now was really odd.'

'It was really odd,' I said. 'How did you even know I was there?'

'I'd followed you all day. I know,' he said. 'It's really weird. I'm sorry. Honestly.'

'It's so weird,' I said.

He laughed his big laugh. 'You know,' he said, 'I've been thinking about this "Axel" thing, and when it's all over, I'm going to stop doing it.'

'The spying?'

'Yeah. It's making me mental. I've been thinking about doing this booksellers' training. I can get a loan for it. And it'll make Dad happy.'

I smiled, picturing Oz's bookshop and me pushing open a glass door with his name on it.

'Are we OK?' he said.

'Of course,' I said.

'Good,' he said, letting go of my hand to start the engine, 'Now, let's go to a middle-aged woman's birthday party.'

We both whooped and he pulled away.

As we drove towards the restaurant, I refined my introduction to Oz that would evoke the heterosexual brotherliness of our relationship and how unsurprising it was that we were friends. The approach I had landed upon was to briefly imply I had forgotten he was there, to greet my mother, father, Martin or my friends, and then to say, 'Oh yeah, this is Osman, by the way.' Then I was going to turn to Oz and say, 'Or Oz?' implying that I wasn't completely sure what he liked to go by, and thus that we weren't all that close. Then, as Oz shook their hands, I was going to slap both of his shoulders in a way that showed that I was physically, but not sexually, comfortable with him.

All of this came to naught when my dad spotted us coming down the street and waited smiling by the door. 'You must be Ralf's new friend,' he called out as we drew near, before I'd had time to start my practised routine.

Oz pushed ahead, gave him his hand and said, 'Nice to meet you, Herr Dörsam.'

'Call me Dietmar,' my dad said, 'please.'

'Osman,' Oz said.

'Wonderful to meet you. Come in, come in. Pat's going to be so happy you came.'

Mum had booked out the whole of Fellini's for the evening. They had changed the lighting for the party, dimming the spotlights so that the candles glimmered in the sheen of the shiny brick walls, making unfamiliar shadows of the dusty baskets, pots and fishing nets hung from the ceiling.

'Who's this?' Mum said, emerging from a gaggle of friends and colleagues. She was swaying, clutching a small glass of red wine that had already drawn a blue line on the inside edge of her lips.

I made a face of slight confusion, as if I didn't know who she was talking about, but she didn't look at me and my dad slapped Oz on the back and said, 'This is Osman.'

'Oh, how nice you came,' said Mum, blushing with genuine pleasure and offering up her little hand.

Oz took it and said, 'I'm so sorry to gatecrash, but Ralf insisted.'

'He's very persistent,' she said, stumbling on her high heels and putting her hand on Dad's arm to steady herself. He smiled and touched the hand. 'How do you know Ralf again?' she said.

'He comes to my bookshop sometimes.'

'You have a bookshop!' said Mum. 'How nice. I love reading. Ralf loves reading.'

'I know,' said Oz. He put his hands in his pockets. 'It's really just a newsagent, my dad's.'

'But you like to read!' Mum said with too much enthusiasm.

'Yes,' Oz said. 'I read a lot. And you're a psychiatrist, is that right?'

'Psychologist.'

Oz offered her the perfect expression: smiling, self-critical amusement at his own lack of knowledge. 'I'm afraid I don't really know the difference.'

'Oh, no one does,' Mum said, waving away the comment. 'I'm more talking, the other one's more pills.'

'And you're English?'

'Yes,' she said.

'Your German's incredible.'

'And yours too.'

'He is German, Mum,' I said.

Mum's smile wavered and she offered a stuttering apology.

'Don't, please,' he said.

I looked at my mother's wounded expression and felt terrible.

'My mother actually came across when she was pregnant, so technically I started off in Turkey.'

Mum laughed. 'I thought Ralf said you were Greek.'

'Greek! *Mein Gott!*' Oz said with faux rage. 'Ralf, how could you?'

'I didn't say that.'

My parents laughed and I rolled my eyes. 'I'll educate him yet, Frau Dörsam.'

'Pat,' Mum said, 'Please. I'm English. I can't be doing with all of this "*Sie und du*" anyway.'

'Who can?' he said.

My mum's eyes sparkled. I seemed intent on upsetting her in front of Oz, and he had saved the situation for me. I sighed at my own petulance, grateful for his easy confidence, for his physical weight, for his beauty. I was so in love with him, and in that moment I imagined reaching out my hand and taking his arm, becoming a couple in front of my parents. I looked at his hand, beautiful, his nails neat, the half-moons on them large, his fingers shapely and the fine black hair reaching his knuckles then dissipating, but it was so far away, it would have been impossible to touch him there in public under anyone else's gaze.

'Are you all right, Ralf?' Mum said. 'You look tired.'

They all turned to me. 'I'm fine,' I said, pushing out a smile. 'I'm going to get a drink.'

I looked up at Oz, encouraging him to escape with me, but Dad said, 'Tell me about Turkey,' and Oz started answering the question with thoughtful assurance, as if he knew all about it. I imagined saying, 'He's not even Turkish, don't you get it? He was born in Berlin! He's a spy! For fuck's sake, he's a spy!' Instead I made my way through the crowd to the high, tiled bar and asked for an Orangina.

I spotted Stefan at the other side of the room. He was talking to Tobias, who was dressed in the suit he wore when he was playing with the orchestra. I couldn't believe Mum had invited him and I couldn't believe that Stefan was talking to him. I waved at Stefan, but he didn't see me; Tobias raised his hand instead, thinking I was waving at him. I nodded a greeting, then felt stupid for doing it. He smiled at me and I hated him.

I looked about to see where Martin was. Instead I found Beate sitting alone at one of the little square tables covered in a red-chequered tablecloth, picking at a bowl of apple-green olives stuffed with almonds. She wore a lilac kaftan and her straw-blonde hair was held back by a matching Alice band. She looked tired too, as if it was the end not the beginning of the evening. When she saw me she smiled wisely and reached out her hand, inviting me to sit. I sat the other side of the table and picked up an olive, nibbling out the waxy nut before eating the salty flesh around it.

Beate nodded at Mum and Dad talking to Oz and smiled sleepily. 'He's very handsome. If I were ten years younger...' She trailed off and ate another olive.

'You all right?' I said, out of politeness rather than genuine concern, because my parents and Beate were still proper adults and, despite everything that had happened that summer, I didn't really think that proper adults ever weren't all right, especially not Beate, who was always happy.

'Oh, I don't know,' Beate said, drying her fingers on a red paper serviette. 'No.'

'Why not?'

'Birthdays make me sad sometimes. Getting older.'

'Stefan told me you always say your current age is your favourite age.'

Beate nodded. 'That's true. But no age comes without its sadness. And its nostalgia.'

'For the Swinging Sixties?'

Beate laughed a little. 'No, I was still in the East in the Sixties. Very little swinging in Zwickau.' She swirled the red wine around in her glass, then lifted her chin and said grandly, 'No, Stefan is making me nostalgic today.'

He was at the door now, laughing with Frau Klemens, Dad's assistant at the pharmacy.

'But he's still here,' I said.

'You can be nostalgic about things you already have, when you know they're going to disappear.'

'Where's he going?'

'University.'

'Oh that,' I said, thinking that going to university didn't really count as moving out. 'But he'll be back during the holidays.'

'But when you've had him in your house for two decades,'

she said. There were tears in her eyes. 'And he'll make new friends, he'll go abroad, he probably won't live in West Berlin again.'

'Why not?'

'Because it's a silly little island near Poland filled with miserable people and terrible weather.'

'I thought you liked it here.'

Beate smiled. 'Oh, I like it. But I don't think it's going to be enough for you and Stefan and your friends. Not for ever. No, I'll see him in the summer, but he'll start to drift away. Then I'll just be a crazy little old lady in a garden I can't keep up. I'll probably get some cats and call them my children.'

'You'll never be a little old lady.'

'We're all going to end up being little old people, Ralf. If we're lucky.' She took a gulp of wine. 'Stefan told me about Maike.'

'Yeah,' I said. 'I don't think I've behaved very well.' Confessing gave me a pleasant feeling that there might one day be absolution.

'There's no point behaving well when you're eighteen,' Beate said. 'There's plenty of time for that later, when you really have some regrets.'

'Do you have regrets?'

Beate considered this and I was afraid I'd been too forward. 'You know,' she said, 'the only things I regret are the things I didn't do and decisions I didn't make. When you decide to do something and it turns out to be a terrible mistake, well at least you did it. You know it was wrong. If you don't do something then you'll always be wondering what if. What if I'd slept with him? What if I'd kept the baby? What if they really did love me? Those are the ones that gnaw at you.'

I looked over at Oz laughing brightly at something my

mother was saying. I didn't know if he represented a decision I was making or not making.

Someone started clapping and a loud Italian voice said, '*Signore e signori*, dinner is served.'

The room came alive with chatter and movement, honking wood against terracotta tiles, as chairs shifted and the guests swarmed around the dinner table, arrayed in one long line, with carafes of water, green wine-bottle candle-holders streaked with red wax, straw baskets filled with sliced baguettes and straw cupping the Chianti bottles' bottoms. As I pulled my chair in and Oz found his way to me, I saw that Stefan was stranded at the far end of the table.

'Tobias is here,' I whispered as we sat down.

'I know,' he whispered back. 'Forget about him. He doesn't matter any more.'

I sat opposite Martin and Mrs Walters, my old maths teacher. I tried to concentrate on a story she was telling me about her adopted daughter, Rita, but was distracted by a string of bright pink Parma ham caught between her yellowing teeth and Oz pressing his leg into mine beneath the table.

Frau Klemens was the other side of Oz and giggling loudly, a spotlight above the table turning her frizzy blonde hair into a mist of gauzy gold. Martin, who was sitting next to Brian Foster, a surgeon and an old colleague of my English grandfather's, was excluded from conversations on both sides, until Oz asked him to pass the Parmesan cheese shaker and said, 'You're Martin, right?'

Martin nodded, surprised at being recognised.

'Oz,' Oz said, reaching out his hand, which Martin shook enthusiastically. 'And you're into football, Ralf said.'

'Yeah,' said Martin. 'But everyone's into football.'

Oz laughed as if this was funny. 'What else?'

'Reading.'

'Reading?' I said, laughing.

Martin looked crestfallen.

'What d'you read?' said Oz.

Martin shrugged, red-faced.

'Ignore Ralf,' Oz said. 'Always ignore older brothers.'

Martin pulled apart a slice of bread and muttered, 'Like, detective novels.'

'What like?'

'I dunno. The Kayankaya books.'

'Jakob Arjouni,' Oz said.

Martin brightened and nodded. 'I just read the second one. It's really good.'

'I've literally never seen you read a book in my life,' I said.

'Well, you're never around,' Martin said, squashing the middle of the bread into a hard grey ball.

'Have you read any Maigret?'

Martin shook his head. 'Is it English?'

'French,' said Oz.

'My French isn't good enough.'

'It's translated. Into English too, I'm sure, if you prefer reading in English.'

'I don't really mind either way,' Martin said. 'What are you reading at the moment?'

'Farewell Sidonia.'

'About the gypsy!' said Martin, thrilled.

'Yeah, have you read it?'

'I literally just took it out the library.'

'That's crazy,' said Oz. 'It's great. Heartbreaking, but ... You'll really like it.'

I knew it was stupid to feel jealous about this exchange, so I excused myself, feeling cross and ashamed in turn all the way to the toilet. Stefan was already there and I joined him at the urinals.

'That the famous Oz?' he said.

'It is.'

I usually struggled to pee next to people I knew, but Stefan was an exception after years of pissing competitions as children and having to relieve ourselves together in any number of German forests.

'Seems friendly.'

'He is friendly.'

'Loads of people were asking after you at the Wildlife Trust. We were checking the elm seedlings we planted two years ago. They're huge. Shame you weren't there.'

'It is a shame,' I said. It came out colder than I'd intended.

He finished, shook and began washing his hands behind me. 'Come over soon, OK?' Stefan said. 'I know it's still weird with Maike, but you can still come over to ours, Petra's too. We're all going to be off in a few weeks, and then we're not going to see you until Christmas.'

I shook and washed my hands while he was drying his on a sea-green paper towel. 'OK,' I said. 'I will.'

'Bring Oz, if you like.'

'We're not that close,' I said automatically.

'Oh, OK,' said Stefan, apparently confused. 'Well, whatever you want.' He held the door open for me.

We ate tiramisu and were served neon-yellow limoncello in frosted glasses. Stefan and I, separated by four tables, silently toasted each other and knocked it back in one. On his way back from the toilets, Oz managed to fall into conversation with Stefan, and soon they were both roaring with laughter. I felt sick from the limoncello and from thinking that I shouldn't have invited Oz. He had been too much of a success, and now my family and friends were going to start inviting him to things. I didn't want them to, I realised, because I didn't want them to have any part of him. He was mine.

The chair beside Stefan became free as the party began to loosen and new groups formed around the room. I stood to go round and join him and Oz, but as I turned I found Tobias standing in my way. He was smiling tightly.

'Hi,' I mumbled, and pushed past him.

'Hey, Ralf,' Tobias said, touching my shoulder.

'What?'

'Thanks for checking about the water leak last week. Frau von Hildendorf said it was you that went over.'

'Oh,' I said, paling and hoping he didn't notice that I was paling. 'That's OK.'

He smiled

Behind me, Oz laughed loudly. Tobias looked up over my shoulder. 'Who's your friend?' he said.

'Just a friend.'

He sighed. 'Ralf, I don't want to speak out of turn—'

'Then don't,' I said, trying to head him off. If he mentioned my mother I would've shoved him, I would've pushed him to the floor and screamed in his face.

He folded his arms. 'Ralf, that friend of yours has been harassing me.'

I laughed. 'Harassing you?'

'Haven't you seen him parked on our street? You must've seen him.'

'He was there to see me.'

'Ralf, he's been there for months, watching the apartment block. And he keeps turning up at the Philharmonie. He followed me in once and hung around in the lobby. It was really creepy.'

'Well, I don't think you're going to have to worry about him any more.'

'Why not?'

'I don't think you'll be seeing much of him soon.'

He looked bewildered. 'OK,' he said softly. 'Well, I hope so.'

'Yeah, I hope so too,' I said.

He looked down at his feet and said, 'OK then. Well, thanks about the leak anyway.'

'Sure,' I said, and then added petulantly, 'Any time.'

I watched Tobias limp off down the table and help himself to red wine from a carafe. He took a sip and looked around the room with a squinting stare, as if he was trying to work out where he was. I did want him gone, but for the first time since I'd seen him take his watch from an envelope with my mother's handwriting on it, I felt sorry for him. He had been abandoned and betrayed as a child, and now he had been abandoned by my mother and betrayed by me.

Oz came up behind me and whispered that he had to leave, filling my ear with his hot breath, his lips brushing my earlobes. While he was saying goodbye to the coterie of new friends he'd already made, Mum gripped my hand and said drunkenly, 'He's very nice, your Oz friend.'

'Thanks. It's nice of you to say.'

She smiled and squeezed my hand.

When Oz said goodbye to my mum, she embraced him. Oz laughed with surprise. And when we tried to leave the restaurant, my dad emerged from the drunken crowd holding up a wallet, saying, 'Is this yours?'

Oz patted his pockets. 'Jesus! Yes! Where was it?'

'On the floor under your chair.'

'*Danke*,' Oz said. The men shook hands and my fantasy of a future with Oz was sparked again, flamed briefly and then died. I followed him outside and, looking about to check that the dark street was empty, stole a kiss. I smiled at him, but he met it with suspicion.

'That went all right, didn't it?' he said.

'I know,' I said, touching his neck.

'Your parents are really nice.'

'They're OK,' I said. 'Did Dad crack out his Opa stories?'

'A few,' he said, and laughed. 'Apparently you look just like him.'

'I don't look anything like him.'

I touched the buttons on his shirt, my lower lip jutting out childishly. 'Tobias recognised you. He said you'd been harassing him. Following him around.'

'Oh,' he said. 'Sounds like I wasn't as subtle as I thought I was being.'

'What if he calls the police?'

'That's not going to be a problem,' Oz said. 'Not for us.'

I heard high heels on cobbles and sprang away from him. Oz made a show of taking out his cigarettes and we crossed the road metres apart to get into his car and drive back to his flat.

Twenty-Six

Oz laid his hand on my leg between gear changes. We didn't talk. I felt sleepy after the food and wine and rolled down the window, letting the warm evening air thunder against my cheek. Oz was right, I realised. The evening had not been a vision of how life might be, it was life.

My parents were open-minded enough that I wasn't going to be driven from the house for having a relationship with a man. Telling them I was in love with Oz would be crushingly awkward, especially with my mum, who would try so hard to pretend it didn't matter. My dad's reaction I couldn't fathom, but it certainly wouldn't be rage. Martin wouldn't care; it would just confirm to him what a weirdo I was. I felt horrible about telling my friends, but only because they might guess I'd been seeing Oz and Maike at the same time, and because of all the other times I'd lied to them. It was a lifetime of lies that would be hardest to own up to.

We pulled into Oz's square. The Berlin streetlamps, flecked with dead insects and veiled by the leaves of the acacia trees, filled the car with a dim orange glow. Oz turned off the engine and we listened to it ticking as it cooled. We held hands and stared at one another.

'Osman.'

It was muffled as if spoken behind a door. I heard impassioned voices imploring in Turkish, and I thought that a conker or an acorn had dropped on the car from the tree above. There was a face at the window on Oz's side. Staring eyes, a thick moustache, the shoulders of a black coat. Oz opened his door, but his hand was still on the wheel and I realised that the door had been opened from the outside. Hands came in, grabbed his shirt and hauled him out.

I shouted Oz's name and grabbed at his trousers, but he slithered away and I heard the grunts of a scuffle, the voices imploring, 'Osman! Osman!'

In my panic, I opened the car door hard into the tree trunk and saw a young man coming around the car to help. 'No, he's there!' I said. 'He's there.' The young man punched me in the face, a thud that flashed white like an electric shock. He grabbed a handful of my shirt and pushed me hard against the car. His glowering face pulled away from mine and I realised he was going to hit me again, so I struck out, pain erupting in my knuckles as he disappeared from view.

I scrambled around the car and found Oz grappling with the man whose face had appeared at the window, the man who kept repeating 'Osman!' so sadly, mixed with sorrowful foreign words. Terrified and confused, but not knowing what else I could do, I hit him too, the pain in my hand shocking as it met his cheek, sending him rolling to the ground.

He cried out and tried to scramble up so I kicked him back down, but Oz grabbed at my shoulder and said, 'Ralf, don't.'

The man looked up at me and I saw behind the moustache Oz's face, but older and fatter, with the same beautiful amber eyes.

Oz pulled me back and we stood panting as the man got to his feet again. The younger man I'd punched stumbled out from the other side of the car, gripping his cheek. He shouted something at Oz and the father cried his name again, tearing at his hair, snot and blood running from his nose. Above us a window clattered open and someone shouted, 'Get out of here! Fucking foreigners!'

Oz held his hand out and released a cascade of sorrowful Turkish, begging and gesturing. The older man covered his head and the younger man shouted as he led him away to a parked car at the other side of the square.

'Are you all right?' I said, searching Oz's face, but he was uninjured.

'Yeah,' he said. 'Close the car doors. Let's get in. Let's get inside. Quick.'

As we came up the stairs, my face and fist throbbing, Oz's neighbour was standing at her open door opposite his flat.

'Frau Riemann,' Oz said, 'it's fine. You haven't called the police, have you? You don't need to call the police.'

She threw a torn envelope on the ground in front of us and spat on the floor. 'Filthy Turk,' she said and slammed the door shut.

Oz snatched up the envelope, unlocked his door and ran into the living room.

'What the fuck's going on?' I said.

He had taken a set of large photographs from the envelope and was flicking through them. He cried out in anguish and let them fall to the floor, rolling onto the sofa and gripping his head in the same gesture of despair as the man on the street.

I picked up one of the pictures. They were colour images taken through the lens of a telephoto camera, the telescopic enlargement making the forms grainy and unsharp. You could see the blurred suggestion of two bodies entwined with one another, legs, arms and heads in the murky darkness of

236

an unlit room, the suggestion of curtains at the edge of the picture. I thought, my heart thudding in my ears, that they were pictures of Oz having sex with another man in his flat, but then I shuffled through to the most incriminating picture, which was not a picture of sex at all. It showed Oz crawling across the floor of my hallway in Windscheidstraße – I recognised the pattern of the parquet floor – and me kneeling behind him, about to come after him, the top of my head in shadow, our bodies lit by the warm summer light. But in the foreshortened gaze of the camera, and the eye prepped with image after hazy image of us actually having sex, I appeared to be fucking him from behind, my laughter and his smile reframed as sexual glee.

'Who took these?' I said. My voice was husky. All of the saliva had left my throat.

Oz fell back on the sofa, his head propped up against the wall. 'They did,' he said.

'Who's they?'

'The Stasi.'

'Why?'

'To discredit me.'

'They know about the file?' I said.

'Yes! I mean, I don't know. Not necessarily,' he said. 'They definitely know about me, though. Fuck!' he shouted.

'What do we do?' I said.

'You need to go home.'

'I don't want to.'

'Give me a week,' he said.

'To do what?'

'Sort things out.'

'How?'

He got up and went into the kitchen. I followed him and

found him searching about with a handful of his black hair gripped into a fist. He shoved his hand into an onion-shaped brass pot and shouted, 'Where the fuck are my cigarettes? Fuck!'

'They're in your pocket,' I said. 'In your top pocket.'

'No, I had some here,' he shouted. 'They've been in here. They've been fucking hiding things, fucking with the bulbs, and fucking hiding things.'

I tried to touch him, but he knocked my hand away and said, 'Just give me a minute, Ralf. Sorry. Just a minute.'

He slumped down onto one of the kitchen chairs and lit a cigarette, drawing a long lungful that caused the tip to crackle and flash. He leant his elbow on the table and put his hand over his face. The smoke rolled out through his fingers, like smoke through the barred basement grate of a burning building.

'Who were they?' I said. 'The men on the street?' Though I knew. I only wanted confirmation.

He let his hand drop to the tabletop, where it stood on its fingertips like a spider. He stared at the rising smoke and said, 'My father. And my brother.'

'They'd been sent the photographs too?'

He nodded. 'I'm sure anyone I've ever met has a copy.'

'What about . . . ?' I wanted to say, 'What about my family, my friends?' but it suddenly seemed incredibly selfish. He understood though.

'I don't think so,' he said. 'They could have picked photos where you were identifiable. Your face is cropped out in all of them.'

From the kitchen door I could still see the photographs spilled on the living-room floor, still make out the two bodies in the beautiful tangerine sunlight. 'Why didn't they just blackmail you with them?'

'That's not how they work. They don't want any information from me. I'm not important enough for them to have any interest in turning me. The little people, they just destroy. They make it clear that they have access to you – that's what the lightbulbs were about, the cutlery, all of that – then they start to discredit you, with your family and your friends.'

'Is that it, then?'

'I doubt it.'

He looked at my face. He looked furious, but then his mouth widened into a sad smile. 'You OK? Is your eye OK?'

'I'm fine,' I said. 'What about you?'

'I didn't get hit.'

'I thought your dad was attacking you.'

'He wasn't hurting me. Not really.' The cigarette was already spent and he stubbed it out in a used espresso cup. 'You gave my brother a run for his money, though,' he said, and chuckled. But his laughter died away almost instantly and his eyes became sad again. 'I'm so sorry, Ralf. I've been really stupid. I didn't think something like this would happen,' he said, shaking his head. 'What a massive fuck-up.'

I sat opposite him and took his hand. 'It's OK,' I said.

'Go home,' he said. 'Go and be with your parents. Give me a week to sort things out. I'll probably have to move out, find a new flat. You can't come back here.'

'Can I help?'

'No,' he said. 'You can help by keeping away, staying safe, OK. If anyone asks you about anything, just play dumb.'

'OK,' I said.

'I will sort this out.'

'I know,' I said. 'I know you will.'

Twenty-Seven

The Havel, a tributary of the Elbe, forms a large loop through Brandenburg, flowing into Berlin from the north and joining the Spree at Spandau, where genteel apartment blocks give way to brick mills, concrete factories and steel cranes. On its journey from Lake Müritz to Werben, the Havel flowed in and out of lakes that kept it eternally fed, slipping over the border into West Berlin at Heiligensee, sweeping past Spandau and Charlottenburg to pool extravagantly at Wannsee, where West Berliners swam and sailed and where the city's finest villas were reflected in the river's waters, before the river slid around the barbed wire at Babelsberg and pleasured the East Germans at Potsdam and Werder.

Petra lived in one of those villas at Wannsee, an icing-white building with a huge, steeply sloped roof and historicist columns, loggias and towers, and it was there that I went that night, catching sight of the Havel behind the fine houses as I cycled the empty roads to Zehlendorf.

I had to ring a buzzer at the gate of Petra's villa and the dog started barking inside the house. When I said who it was, I heard Petra's scratchy voice on the intercom saying, 'Oh. Ralf. Fuck.'

There was a screech and the gates swung open at an eerily

slow pace. I squeezed through the widening gap and made my way up the gravel path between floodlit topiaried box trees to the colonnaded portico lit by a large hanging lamp with a bright yellow bulb.

Petra opened the door, holding Katja, her large English sheepdog, by the collar. It barked, lifting its head to watch me from beneath its long white fringe.

'Ralf,' Petra began, 'it's half fucking eleven, are you . . . ?' but then she squinted as the light from the hanging lamp shone full on my face and my throbbing eye. 'Oh fuck, Ralf. What happened?'

'I got hit in the face,' I said from the bottom of the steps.

'Who by?'

'Oz's brother.'

'Why the fuck did Oz's brother hit you?'

'Because he found out about me and Oz.'

I wondered if this was too vague, but Petra said, 'You mean, about you and Oz fucking?'

I nodded.

'Wow,' she said. 'You better come in then.'

I had only been to Petra's house once, for her sixteenth birthday. Maike, Stefan and I and a girl called Bärbel from Petra's primary school were the only friends of Petra's who went. Every other guest was a colleague of her father's; he did something important at Bayer. I'd never been inside a house so grand before. It had a hallway with black and white marble tiles like a chessboard, and at the foot of the stairs a life-size bronze of a plump-breasted woman with her arms raised over her head, as if she were fighting off a bird.

'If you ask Klemens who it's by,' Petra had said, in her pink tulle, 'he says he found it in a reclamation yard.' Petra always referred to her parents by their Christian names.

'Didn't he?' I remember asking, sipping sweet punch ladled into a red glass from a huge silver bowl on the hall table.

'No, he bought it. For thousands. It's Arno Breker.' She waited for a spark of recognition and when it didn't come, added, 'Hitler's favourite sculptor.'

I frowned, trying to pick shredded mint out of my teeth. 'Why did he buy it then?'

'Oh, people love Breker. Certain people. Klemens isn't a Nazi, but he doesn't mind people thinking he is.'

'That's mental,' I said.

'I know,' said Petra. 'He's the worst.' She held her punch glass with both hands like a little girl and stared at the sculpture's pneumatic breasts. Petra had powdered her face so that the line between her skin and her straw-coloured hair, scraped back like Grace Kelly, was almost indistinguishable. 'If work people recognise it they think he might be a Fascist. And if they aren't interested in all of that then they just think it's a sculpture of a woman with big tits. Either way it works.'

I stared at the woman's face. She looked like she was sniffing the air, trying to trace a scent caught in the wind.

'You know that Bayer made the gas for the concentration camps?'

'No,' I said.

She nodded.

It was only towards the end of the evening, when I was standing on the jetty with Stefan in a haze of midges, that I realised that the concrete wall behind a line of trees on the opposite bank of the lake was not a private security measure, but marked the edge of East Germany. The villa on the other side of the river was boarded up, the tower at the end of its garden was a watchtower, and sitting in it, staring out of scratched glass windows at the summer party opposite, were two East German border guards dressed in green, the tips of their rifles just visible above the windowsill.

Three years later, as the first black eye of my life swelled into a hot lump, Petra and I sat on deckchairs with our bare feet on the villa's wooden balustrade, the lawn sloping away below us to the water. In the dark, the grass was sea-green and the rhododendron bushes around it were drenched with chirruping crickets and white and cerise flowers, pale and luminescent like moons among the indigo leaves. The border at the other side of the lake was lit floodlight-white; it reflected in the water in waving lines, its gloss dulled by dead insects and fallen pollen. In the watchtower sat different men to those who I'd seen before, but they were wearing the same uniforms, had the same dead gaze.

'So how long's this sordid affair been going on?' Petra said. She was wearing a white bikini top and shorts, a chipped ceramic ashtray in the shape of an open hand balanced on her outstretched legs. I'd cycled to Wannsee because I knew she would enjoy the confession more than she would judge it, and she would be thrilled to be told first.

'Since the beginning of summer,' I said.

'Fuck,' she said. 'Dirty birdy.' She took a drag of her cigarette. 'And Maike?'

'She doesn't know anything about it.'

'But it started before you two . . . ?'

'Yes,' I said. I picked up the citronella candle from the balustrade edge and lit my cigarette from it. The dimpled yellow glass was hot. 'What a cunt, right?' I said, blowing out a cloud of blue smoke.

'Bit,' said Petra. 'Who isn't a bit of a cunt though? Maike got fingered by some Swede when she went on that fjord cruise last year, so . . . '

'Are you joking?' I said.

'Oh, what? You're going to judge her for that after this?' she said, gesturing to the black eye.

I sat forward and gripped my knees. 'She's always talking about that trip.'

'Well, now you know why.'

'Fuck,' I said. 'Who the fuck are we?'

'Oh grow up, Ralf. It was only a finger.' She flicked the ash off her cigarette. 'A couple at most. She wasn't mounting Turkish booksellers.'

I slumped back in the deckchair.

'How did Oz's brother find out?'

'Dunno,' I lied.

I could hear laughter coming from someone's garden. Despite it being almost midnight, I caught a trace of grilled meat in the air.

Petra shook her head. 'I knew something was up. I thought it was crack.' She took a drag on her cigarette. 'In a way I was right.'

We laughed, but then I thought about Oz alone in his flat with the photos. It made me nauseous.

I stared at the garden morosely, at the lawn where a child had abandoned their bike. Petra had a much younger brother born when she was ten.

'When are your parents back from Spain?' I said.

Petra blew out a long stream of smoke and shrugged. 'No fixed date.' She fed the dog a pretzel stick. It munched it into an ochre dust that clung to its wavy beard. 'The contract's only for a couple of years, I think.'

'A couple of years? I thought they were on holiday.'

'No, Klemens is setting up a new factory there. They really like it, I think.'

'Why didn't you go with them?'

'I had to finish my exams.'

'How long have you been here on your own?'

'Oh, eight months or so.' The dog scrabbled to its feet and put its paw on Petra's leg. She gave it another pretzel stick.

'Jesus, Petra. I wish you'd said.'

'Why?'

'I would've come over more.'

'What, and looked after me?'

'Why not?'

Petra sucked thoughtfully at her cigarette. The tobacco crackled and the crickets lifted their chorus. The stars glittered in the black sky. 'It's all right,' she said eventually. 'At night, I sometimes get scared that someone's going to break in. Katja sleeps upstairs with me, though she's not meant to. And I keep a kitchen knife under the bed.'

'You do not.'

'Of course I do,' said Petra. 'The house next door's owned by Americans and there's never anyone there. And Frau Landau on the other side hates me, so no one's going to hear me being raped, or care.'

A frog croaked near the house. 'Do people get raped in their beds? Outside of films?'

'I'm sure some people do,' said Petra. 'I met this guy at the beer garden once – before you started – whose wife had rape fantasies. That was her thing.'

'That's awful.'

'I know. And you thought being a bum boy was bad.'

'I should've gone to Stefan's,' I said.

'Oh no,' said Petra, touching my arm. 'He'd've got really deep about it. Really into it.' We started giggling and Petra frowned and impersonated him. 'Ralf. *Alter.* Boning guys is cool.'

245

'Ralf, *Alter*,' I said, 'my friend Joachim's a bummer. It's so cool.'

'Ralf, *Alter*. Vaginal sex is so bourgeois.'

We laughed until our stomachs hurt.

Petra lit another cigarette and wiped her eyes with the tip of her middle finger. 'It's more common than you think,' she said.

'Bum boys?'

'No, rape fantasies.'

'Oh,' I said.

'This guy, the beer garden one – he had to pretend to break in and then, like, fuck her really roughly. She was a primary school teacher.'

'That's terrible,' I said. 'Makes my sex fantasies seem so dull.'

'Like what?' said Petra.

'Oh, like, having sex with a man. Honestly.'

Petra laughed. 'I bet it's more fucked up than that.'

'It isn't!' I said. 'It really isn't.'

'You should read Nancy Friday. The things that women are into. Do you want to know what my sex fantasy is?'

'I'm scared.'

Petra smiled and stubbed her cigarette out. 'That one of the border guards has always been in love with me. Is sitting up there with a boner the whole time. An aching boner. And that one night he's so desperate that he shoots the other guard and swims over to fuck me. Not in a rapey way, though.'

'Still, you wouldn't know it was him breaking in. So you'd probably just stab him to death with your kitchen knife.'

'That's true,' Petra said, frowning. 'Maybe I'll get some pepper spray.' She leant forward and slapped a mosquito dead on her leg.

I turned to her, lying on my side on the deck chair, curled up like a foetus. 'Why don't you have a boyfriend, Petra?'

'I hate that question. As if I'd know.'

'But you're so pretty.'

'Oh, am I the next stop on the Ralf Dörsam fuck bus?'

'No,' I said. 'Of course not, but ... But don't you miss having sex?'

'Oh, I have a lot of sex.'

'Yeah, with Stefan.'

'Stefan? Hardly ever. There was that artist Mo at the squat party. Herr Kniff from the beer garden.'

I burst into laughter. 'I'm being serious.'

'I am too,' said Petra.

'You're not,' I said, beginning to doubt myself. I sat up cross-legged and frowned. 'Are you, Petra? Herr Kniff? He looks like a pelican.'

'He has his moments.'

'But ... '

'But what?'

'I don't know,' I said. 'He's old, isn't he?'

'He's twenty-seven,' said Petra. 'He runs that whole beer garden by himself. It was about to go bust before he took it over.'

'Is it like a power thing then?' I said, imagining all those desperate limbs, like a swatted daddy longlegs.

'Not really. He just really wanted to fuck me. And he didn't think he'd be allowed to. So when I let him, he just ... ' She mimed his head exploding.

'That sounds like a power thing.'

Petra laughed. 'Maybe,' she said. 'He's got a BMW too. He bought me a Chopard.' She held out her hand. On her wrist was a slim cocktail watch with a tiny oval face.

'I didn't think you'd care about that sort of stuff,' I said.

'What do you know about what I care about?'

Katja barked and got the last *Salzstange*.

We watched a repeat of the news – the *Tagesschau* – in Petra's living room, sitting on a huge suite made of bent cane and a tropical blue fabric, covered in palm trees and parrots. We drank huge glasses of *Apfelschorle* chilled with wedges of ice that plunked out of the door of her giant fridge. I sank into one corner of the sofa and watched crowds of East Germans running over the Hungarian border into Austria. My face was hot and tight where Oz's brother had hit me.

'Do you think it's all going to come down?' I said.

'Not in Germany,' Petra said. 'Not in Hungary for long either. And anyway, no one really wants reunification, do they? I don't think Kohl does.'

I watched a family and a very blond, red-faced child weeping in his mother's arms as they fled across a field carrying clothes in plastic bags and bin liners. I heard Lech Wałęsa's voice briefly, before it was drowned out by the German interpreter. By the time they were reading the weather, I was dozing off, the skin around my bruised eye pleasantly cooled by the barest of breezes coming through the open French windows.

I woke deep in the night. The French windows had been closed and the room was empty. The light in the hallway was on. I pulled myself off the sofa and made my way through the hall and up the marble staircase, my bare feet slapping wetly on the cold stone.

I tried a few doors until I found Petra asleep with Katja. Her room had a pastel-pink carpet and glossy white furniture, but one wall was filled with ancient boxed insect specimens, the browns and beiges of moths specked with jade, ruby and agate butterflies that caught the light of the coming dawn through the old glass of the villa's double windows. Beneath Petra's bed I saw the glint of the kitchen knife.

I climbed in beside the dog and pulled the edge of the sheets over my leg. I imagined Oz's frowning face in the car as he drove West. Was he thinking of me? I hoped he was thinking of me. I recalled our smiles in the grainy Stasi photos and felt afraid. Through Petra's open window I could hear the trees rustle. The crickets had stopped and had been replaced by another sound, a lilting song, gasping and melancholy, peppering my thoughts and then my dreams as I fell back to sleep.

Twenty-Eight

When I returned home the next evening the flat was silent. A toilet flushed and Martin appeared from the bathroom, then froze in front of me as if I'd been brought back from the dead.

'What's going on?' he whispered.

'What do you mean?'

'There are people here to see you. And your face.'

It had stopped throbbing, but around a small red cut a colourful aura of purples, maroons and yellows had bloomed.

'Who's here to see me?'

'I don't know. Some old man and some not-so-old man.'

I put my hand on the door handle and turned to leave, but heard my father call, 'Ralf! Is that you?'

'I'll be there in a sec,' I said.

'Don't run off again, Ralf,' Martin said. He looked afraid.

'I wouldn't,' I whispered, dropping my rucksack and going into the kitchen.

At the table sat my mother, my father and, I was horrified to see, Oz's father and brother. In the harsh light of the kitchen, I could see that Oz's father dyed his thinning hair – it was a monotone matt black – and that his face was even more like Oz's than I had first thought, his eyes the same ochre brown, his skin more worn, but his nose easing into his cheeks in the same elegant way, his eyebrows joined by the same spray of black hairs. The brother looked younger sitting embarrassed by his father and, I was ashamed to see, had a blooming indigo and yellow bruise linking his ear to his eye.

'Jesus Christ!' said my mother in English, standing and reverting to German to cry, 'What have you done to your face?'

I put my hand up to my eye. 'I fell over.'

'Did he hit you?' Mum said tearfully.

'Who?'

'Oz.'

I frowned. 'No, of course not.'

I looked at Oz's brother. She turned to him and understood, letting out a sorrowful little yelp. She touched the skin on my face with her trembling fingers.

'Mum, don't.'

'Can you sit down with us, Ralfi?' my dad said.

Oz's father stared down at an empty coffee cup. His hands were clasped together in a ball of rough fingers, the brother's were hidden beneath the table. My mum gestured towards a chair that had been pulled out for me.

'Please,' Mum said, touching the chair.

I sat down reluctantly and looked at the empty cup that had been placed in front me. I felt ashamed and afraid.

'This is Herr Özemir and his son Yusuf,' my father said.

'Yes,' I said.

'Herr Özemir has something he'd like to say to you.'

I forced myself to look up at him out of politeness and because my father had asked me to. Herr Özemir looked as embarrassed as I did. He swallowed hard and said, 'Yusuf.'

'I'm sorry I hit you,' Yusuf said.

'We don't hit,' Oz's father said forcefully.

My mother nodded reverently and my father smiled as if everything was now resolved. But nothing was resolved – I had no idea why they had come. I didn't believe they were there to apologise for hitting me.

'Is that it?' I said.

'Ralf!' my mother muttered. 'Manners.'

'What?' I said loudly. 'This is weird. I don't know what's going on.'

My mum stared at me furiously. Rudeness was never acceptable, even if it was aimed at someone who'd punched you in the face.

Oz's father unclasped his hands and touched the handle of the coffee cup. 'Osman,' he said, speaking German with a Turkish accent, but in a gentle, fatherly cadence that made it hard to be angry with him, 'is not a well boy.'

'Why? What's wrong with him?' I thought they were going to tell me he had cancer.

'He doesn't have AIDS,' my mother said.

'What?' I said, turning on her. 'I didn't think he meant AIDS!'

'Ralf,' my dad said. He raised his hand to calm us both. 'Herr Özemir has come all the way over from Schöneberg to speak to you, because he's concerned about you. Could you just listen to what he has to say and then we can discuss … whatever this is,' he said, gesturing to the corner of the table where Mum and I sat.

I slumped red-faced in the chair. 'Fine,' I said, and stared at the man's anxious fingers.

'Osman has had a lot of troubles. He works in my shop on Eisenacher Straße, but only receiving papers and magazines in the morning and stocking up. He hasn't been in proper work for a long time. He has problems.'

'He's manic-depressive,' my mother said.

'Right,' I said, not looking at her.

'Ralf, we know he's a really close friend of yours,' Dad said, 'but it sounds like he's repeating a pattern, something that's happened before.'

'Sometimes they get psychotic symptoms. It's very common,' Mum said. 'It doesn't have anything to do with you.'

'I know what manic depression is, Mum.'

'He has these phases,' the man said, 'when he's very up and he stops taking his medication. He becomes very, er ...' he searched for the word, 'spontaneous, behaves quite erratically and forms these ...' his hands moved side to side, 'these very intense friendships. And he can be very convincing.'

All four of them looked at me, apparently waiting for a response.

'OK,' I said and stood. I felt that Oz's father was trying to do what he thought was the right thing, but I didn't believe a word of it. 'Well, thanks for letting me know.'

The man sat up and touched his side as if it hurt. 'He tells very tall tales and he gets very paranoid. About FBI agents and the government and espionage.'

I looked at Dad to try to glean how serious he thought he was being. He looked very nervous.

'Is that what's been happening, Ralf?' Mum said. 'Has he talked about the government, about people being after him?'

'There are people after him,' I said. My mum let out a cry of distress. She looked tearful. 'It's true, Mum,' I said. 'I've seen it myself.'

'Was it the lightbulbs?' his father said.

I didn't answer.

'He unscrewed all the lightbulbs in our flat and replaced them with dead ones,' Yusuf said, speaking for the first time.

He sounded just like Oz. 'He said the Stasi had done it so they could hide little wires in them to listen in to us.'

Oz's father had tears in his eyes. 'He's a good boy,' he said, his voice breaking. 'He's a good boy, but he gets very afraid. He needs to go back to the clinic.'

'What clinic?' I said.

'He needs to start his treatment again.'

Mum stared at me pleadingly.

'But all his bulbs had blown. And you saw the photographs,' I said to his father.

'Oh God,' Mum said.

My father held out a calming hand towards her again, but turned to me seriously and said, 'So you'd left the flat with him and came back with him and all the bulbs were blown? Or did he just tell you about it.'

I felt hot and confused. 'Well, no, but ... Look, I don't know what this is,' I said. 'But you seem like nice people and like you're really worried about him. So thank you for coming over.'

'We need to find him,' my mum said, standing and touching my shoulder. 'He's been missing since yesterday.'

'I don't know where he is,' I said. 'And I'm sorry, but he's not crazy.'

I went to my room and shut the door. I lay on the bed without turning the lights on. I heard the mumble of the Özemirs leaving and then the inevitable knock. I got up and pushed my chest of drawers against the door. It opened a crack and stopped abruptly. My mum said, 'Ralf! Can you open the door, love.'

'I'm going to bed,' I said. 'I don't want to talk about this.'

'I love you, darling, and I want to talk to you.'

'Yeah, I love you too, Mum, but I don't want to talk about this. This is crazy. I can't talk about this.'

I lay back down and wrapped my pillow around my ears, so that the feathers drowned out the knocking and my mother's voice. I listened to the feathers creaking and forced myself to think about Stefan telling us about the common eider plucking the feathers from its breast to build a soft grey nest for its eggs. I imagined winter-hardened Norwegians and Scots gathering up the sea-ducks' down after the birds had flown south with their young, the heat it would provide already palpable on their calloused fingers. I listened to the drakes' 'an-hoo' and dived with them into the shallow water, nibbling at the rocks for molluscs, until the imagined sound of the waves above calmed me down enough to take the pillow off my head and hear that the house had gone quiet, that I'd finally been left alone.

Twenty-Nine

While I waited for Oz to make contact, I tried to avoid talking to Mum and Dad, though they were both gentle and sweet with me, not asking any questions, not asking about Oz again.

Our evening meals were subdued. Conversation was only sparked by my mother if Tobias played his viola. Then she would talk loudly over the pleading strings, asking Martin about football or saying how worried she was about a friend who was having a hard time at work.

I cycled past the bookshop on Eisenacher Straße early in the morning, but the shutters were always down. In the late afternoon the shop was open, but I only saw Herr Özemir through the open door filling in a puzzle in a magazine, a soap opera playing unwatched on a small television above his head.

I cycled around the square in front of Oz's flat, but the lights were always off and the ripples in the curtains never shifted. Whenever anyone turned to look for their bus, handed me a receipt in a shop, knocked into me on the street, my stomach would clench, in anticipation of a message. But there were no messages, no files, no threats.

I accepted extra shifts at the beer garden so that I had something to do, but also so that I could cycle back and forth on roads that Oz had driven me down. As I filled large glass steins with *Pils* and *Helles* I looked across the crowd wishing his face would appear at the open hatch, but it never did.

'Have you heard from the Turk?' Petra said from the grill.

I shook my head and told her about the visit from Herr Özemir and Yusuf. I'd already begun to doubt myself.

'Fuck,' Petra said. 'That's some messy shit.'

I nodded. She put down the spatula to put her arm around me and her soft breasts pressed into my elbow. She had never been so tender.

*

For the first time in weeks, I was home for our Friday dinner with Beate and Stefan. When I heard Beate's laughter, I didn't move from my bed, where I lay staring at a crack that ran from the cable of my lamp to the window frame. I was thinking about the imperceptible movement of our apartment block, thinking how even buildings were in constant, sluggish motion. I thought about bergschrunds, the long crevasses that form when the glacier pulls away from the stagnant ice at its sides. There were so many stories of climbers falling down these crevasses, stories that had once terrified me, but I now imagined lying at the bottom of one, the snow beneath me soft, ice crisp in my nostrils, the high walls around me a perfect powder blue, the rough surface extracting every sound, so that all I would be able to hear would be my heartbeat in my ears, the creak of my clothing, my breath. As the cold turned to warmth I would grow sleepy and the white of the sky at the top of the crevasse would widen until it enveloped me and became everything. That would be a way to go, I thought, dissolved in glacial whiteness.

Stefan knocked on my door and opened it. From the bed I gave him the Vulcan salute.

'*Na, Alter!*' he said. 'Hey, I caught you doing nothing. You're usually so productive.'

'That's just for show,' I said.

'Pretty convincing.' He fell onto my red beanbag. 'Petra told me you had some freaky meeting with some Turks about your *friend*. And that your *friend*'s brother punched you in the face.'

'Yeah,' I said.

'She said this *friend* of yours has disappeared. Sounds like you were really close.'

He said the word 'friend' – *Freund* – very carefully, which in gendered German means both friend and boyfriend, depending on the context. I felt he was inviting me to explain myself. I had imagined that telling Petra would have a powerful effect on my ability to talk about Oz, but years of silence had left the connection between my mouth and my heart atrophied, like a vestigial organ – the withered legs of a whale or a mole rat's sightless eyes. The language to say to my childhood friend, 'Yes, I love him,' didn't exist. When I looked for the words, I found nothing. I just stared at Stefan's trembling eyes, so full of good intentions that they seemed to hum like a machine.

'I'll live,' I managed.

His body sank in relief and disappointment. 'Yeah,' he said. 'You'll live.'

There was prosecco left over from Mum's birthday and Dad doled it out generously. Even Martin was allowed a mouthful, though he grimaced when he swallowed it. Mum had cooked a version of shepherd's pie with lentils, which was one of the less disgusting things she made.

Beate and Mum came up with a story we'd never heard

before about Mum in the Seventies successfully smuggling tights into East Berlin before Beate had fled for the last time. Mum had got a day pass and gone over wearing ten pairs at the same time under her jeans, but was so hot that she fainted on the escalator at Friedrichstraße Station. The description of my mum slumping down and rolling to the bottom left us in hysterics.

'How did you get East?' Martin said to Mum.

'Well, they'd started letting people through back then if you had the right papers, and I was British, which helped a little bit, but not much.'

'And Beate couldn't come the other way?'

'No,' Beate said. 'Old people can, because they aren't going to be working any more. And you can apply to come over, but I was an artist and had left before, so they always rejected my application.'

'Then how did you come over the last time? When you fled?'

'Swam,' said Beate, forking mash into her mouth.

'Aren't the canals full of barbed wire and things?' I said.

'Beate swam the sea route,' said Mum.

'Fuck,' I said. Dad frowned at me for swearing and I corrected myself, saying, 'Wow. Sorry. I can't believe I didn't know that. I didn't realise that was even possible. Where did you go over?'

'Stralsund.'

'And you can just swim round to the next-door beach?'

'Sadly not. If you try, they just fish you out.'

'Where did you swim to then?'

'Denmark.'

Martin and I frowned. 'How is that . . . ? I don't understand how . . . ? How long did it take?'

Beate put down her fork and leant back in her chair. 'It's hard to say exactly.'

'You must have worked it out. Beforehand, you must have checked,' said Martin.

She shook her head. 'No, I just had to get away.'

'You hadn't planned it at all?'

'I'd thought often about escaping again. The idea of swimming only came to me when I was on holiday in Stralsund for a few days. Before I went, I didn't go near the water, because I was terrified that I would try and go, that I wouldn't be able to resist it. Then one summer evening when the beaches were empty I just got in the water and swam.'

'In the dark?' Martin said.

'Not when I set off.'

'It must have been terrifying,' I said.

She fingered the stem of her prosecco glass. 'Yes. But I wasn't sure whether the terror was the swim or knowing that I was leaving. It was like suicide, the hopelessness of it. I mean, it's what I imagine suicide would be like.'

We had all stopped eating.

'It must have got dark, though,' Martin said.

'Yes,' said Beate, 'though by then I was far out enough to see the lights at Gedser. But the current changes the further out you go, and I got disoriented. I was mostly terrified that I was going to climb out onto the beach and hear surprised East German voices; that I was just going to swim in a circle.'

'Weren't you exhausted?' I said.

'I'm a very good swimmer, but . . . Yes. I tried to take breaks by floating on my back, as best I could. The sea's not very salty there, so it's hard to stay afloat. Then I would just keep on swimming. I've never felt more exhausted or more alone. And then,' she said, frowning, 'I was overcome with this

260

wonderful peace. I was on my back, listening to the sea, black and vast all around me. It was calm and bobbing me up and down and all I could see were stars. Stars like I'd never seen before, a carpet of them, like a meadow of flowers, filling my vision. Everywhere stars and water. And I thought, if I just give in to it I'll dematerialise, I'll just turn into nothing and everything and I'll be free.'

Her lips were parted and she looked lost in thought.

'Then what happened?' said Martin.

'Then I slipped under the water and choked, and of course came up coughing and panicking.'

We chuckled.

'I kept swimming and just as dawn was coming and I thought I really was about to sink, a Danish fishing boat spotted me and hauled me out of the water.'

'What an incredible story,' I said. 'I can't believe I've never heard it.'

Mum and Stefan sitting either side of her looked on proudly; proud too that they knew all about it when others didn't.

The buzzer went and we all looked at the door. Martin ran and picked up the receiver of the intercom, but came back disappointed.

'Who was it?' Mum said.

'No one there,' he said. He turned back to Beate. 'You must've been so relieved,' he said. 'To make it, I mean.'

Beate smiled. 'I just sat there wrapped in a blanket that stank of fish, listening to them chatting in a language I didn't understand, and watched the sun rise over the Baltic Sea. Then I cried and it was like . . . ' she shook her head. 'It was like vomiting. I've never cried like that in my life. I thought I was going to die.'

'But you didn't,' Mum said, touching her hand.

'No, I didn't.'

It was Stefan who heard the clicking.

My brother ran back to the door and opened it. 'Hello?' he said.

From the kitchen we could see Martin, but not who was waiting in the stairwell.

'Light's here,' Martin said. He reached out and turned it on. 'Oh, it's you,' he said. 'Come in. Ralf's here.'

Through the door came Oz, wide-eyed and stooped, with a length of wire in his hand. His hair was greasy and his skin grey.

I pushed my chair back. 'Oz,' I said, standing, elated that he was alive, but terrified about the way he looked.

'Trying to pick the lock?' said my brother, laughing.

Oz threw the wire on the floor. 'Of course not,' he said, his voice hoarse. He smiled and my brother laughed. 'It's a joke,' Oz said. 'Click, click, click.'

'Oz,' said my mother, standing too. 'How lovely. Come in. We're eating. But join us. Will you eat something?'

'Oh, it's the friend,' said Beate. 'Come in, come in. Thank God you arrived. We'd just run out of good stories.'

Oz crossed the room to me, carefully watching his feet as he went as if the floor was made of ice. He looked so helpless as he reached out and gripped my arm. 'I'll explain it all later. For now, let's just be normal, like everyone else,' he said, lowering his voice, but still speaking loud enough that everyone could hear him.

Mum brought him a stool and a plate and Martin got him a knife and fork.

'Can I have something to drink?' Oz said, adjusting the cutlery with his fingertips so that it was lined up perfectly. His jaw was working, as if he was grinding his teeth. Everyone was watching us. Stefan whispered something to Beate and Oz shot him a glance.

'Of course,' my dad said. 'What would you like?'

'What are you all drinking?' he said, eyeing the glasses on the table.

'We're on prosecco, but we've got some red.'

'Or Fanta,' said Mum.

'I want whatever's open,' Oz said. 'I want it from the bottle you're all drinking from.'

'OK,' Dad said.

'This one here,' Oz said, leaning over and taking the open prosecco bottle in the middle of the table. He clutched it to his chest protectively like a child with a doll, only releasing it when Dad placed a glass in front of him. He sniffed the glass and eyed my father, then poured the prosecco into it until it reached the rim.

'I'll keep the bottle here,' he said, carefully placing it in front of his plate.

'You know,' Dad said, 'my father – Ralf and Martin's grandad – did the same. He once drank a bottle of champagne to himself, and—'

Oz laughed loudly. My dad stopped, alarmed. 'You know, your grandad stories are a joke,' Oz said, and smiled at me. 'Ralf said it was a joke. Everyone just laughs about it.'

Ashen-faced, my dad sat down, trying to maintain his smile. Stefan held up the large spoon in the serving dish, offering to serve. Oz nodded his assent, keeping track of the spoon as it went to the dish, to his plate and back again.

'Keep talking,' he said to the table. 'Don't mind me.'

There was a brief silence as everyone around the table tried to think of something to say.

'Finished your university packing, Stefan?' my dad managed.

'Not even started,' said Stefan.

Oz forked a large lump of potato and lentils into his mouth, watching my father and Stefan back and forth like a tennis enthusiast following a match. He turned to me as he chewed, mashed potato on his chin, and began smiling. He swallowed and touched my face, stroking my cheek with his thumb. 'This food is terrible,' he said, and giggled. I took his hand from my face and put it into his lap. 'What the fuck is this?'

'It's like a bake,' I said, 'but with lentils.'

'They're like lead shot,' he said, giggling huskily, like Muttley.

I stared down at the table.

'There's pudding,' said my mum officiously.

Oz turned to me and said, 'We need to get out of here. They're drugging me.' His breath smelt sour, of old booze and cigarettes.

'OK,' I whispered. 'Do you want to lie down first?'

'Very much so,' he said carefully. 'But I have to stay awake. And you'll need to come and watch the door. One of these ones may well be involved,' he said, gesturing to the table. 'But we know what they're doing now, so they can't hurt us any more.'

'OK,' I said, standing. 'Let's go and lie down then.'

'Yes,' he said, standing up and following me. 'I'm sorry about the food,' he said to my mother. 'It turned out horrible.'

I didn't look at the faces of my family as I guided Oz through the hall and into my bedroom.

I went to turn the light on, but he stopped my hand and said, 'No. They're outside too. This is just a trick. We're going to make your parents believe we're asleep and then we're going to leave in the night.'

'OK,' I said. 'Will you lie down for a bit though.'

'Only if you lie with me,' he said.

'Yeah,' I said, 'of course.'

He walked to the bed, but stumbled, falling to his knees. 'They gave me these drugs. It's like being very drunk. But I still know what's happening. I know it seems bad, but it's the drugs. Have they told you things about me? Don't believe them. They'll tell you lies to try and make you hate me.'

'I'm never going to hate you, Oz,' I said, helping him up. 'Are you OK?' I said, getting him onto the bed. 'Your knee, I mean.'

'Yes,' he said, but he put his hand to it as if it hurt. 'Lie with me.'

I lay behind him, spooned up against him. His body relaxed. I kissed his neck and said, 'It's going to be OK. Can we try and sleep?'

'They kept me awake for days,' he said. 'It makes you crazy. They drugged me.'

'But you're here now,' I said, stroking the back of his hand. 'Now you can sleep. I'll stay awake and look after you.'

'You're the most wonderful thing that ever happened to me,' he said. 'Do you know that?'

'That's nice to hear,' I said.

'You'll think it's the drugs and the not sleeping, but that isn't it. Life was so grey before you, Ralf. I was lonely. You're a remarkable person. Kind, loyal, beautiful. You're so beautiful, Ralf. I knew the moment you talked to me at Prinzenbad. I thought, that's it Oz, you're lost. That's you done now. You know what, it actually hurts when I'm not with you, physically. Sometimes I can't bear it.'

I squeezed him. 'But you're with me now.'

'Yes,' he said drowsily. 'I'm with you now.' He jerked and said, 'Can I see your eye? Is it OK again? I wanted to kill my brother, but . . . ' His voice became weak again. His body relaxed and tensed. He muttered my name.

When he eventually began to snore lightly, I got off the bed and went out into the hallway, shutting the door gently behind me. My mum was waiting for me, everyone else was standing at the kitchen door. There were two other men in the hall, young men wearing brown trousers and white shirts.

'I called the Park Klinik,' Mum said.

I looked at the men. They seemed friendly. One of them smiled at me.

'What will they do?' I said.

'It's a nice clinic. You'll be able to visit him.'

'They won't hurt him?'

'We won't hurt him,' one of the men said. 'We'll just talk to him.'

'What if he won't go with you?'

'That's rare,' the smiling man said. 'But we can deal with that. We won't hurt him.'

'Can I come with him?' I said. 'To the clinic.'

'You can meet us there if you want, but only family will be able to visit him until he's been assessed.'

'That won't take long,' said my mum. 'Then we'll go and visit.'

'Ralf!' Oz called, awake. 'Are you there?'

'Yes,' I shouted, 'I'm here. I'm coming. Just a moment.'

My mum held out her arms for me. 'They won't hurt him. He'll be happier. You'll see. They'll get him back on his medication and he can get some rest.'

She kissed the side of my head, as the men went into my room and started to talk gently to Oz, who kept calling my name, frightened because I wasn't there.

Thirty

The next morning, I went down to our section of the cellar and retrieved the ladder. I'd planned to go and buy paint, but found four half-used tins of white paint stacked in front of the caretaker's room. Upstairs, I bent the tip of a butter knife prising the speckled lids open to find that half the paint had separated into opaque white circles sunk into amber grease. I stirred it all vigorously with the knife, which I threw into the bin in the bathroom when I couldn't wash off the paint, glued to it like sticky double cream.

I stripped all of the posters and pictures off the walls, took down the lampshade and peeled the stickers off my wardrobe mirrors. Kneeling on a mosaic of ripped magazines, torn caves and stalagmites, ragged volcanoes and Stromboli sprays, halved bullet ants, goliath frogs and titan beetles, I used Mum's nail-varnish remover and a fifty-pfennig piece to scrape the last of the papery remains off the mirror. I pulled my mattress out of the room, along with my boxes and books and all of my furniture, except the bed frame and wardrobe. Then I painted everything white.

I got paint on my jeans, on my face and hair, on the glass of the wardrobe. I dug out one of my watercolour brushes and painted a wild white zigzag border to cover the mark on the glass, then did the same on the glass of the window.

'Jesus,' Martin shouted from the door. 'The flat fucking stinks, Ralf. What the fuck are you doing?'

'What's it look like I'm doing?'

'Moving out?'

I gave him the finger.

He peered about the room and said, 'You know that half of this is gloss and the other half's emulsion.'

Holding the paintbrush, I wiped the sweat off my forehead with the back of my wrist and looked at the shining paint covering two walls. I'd thought that the paint near the window was just drying slower, but of course that made no sense. 'Sure,' I said. 'That's the point.'

'Mum's visiting a client in hospital,' he said. 'She'll be back in the flat at two.'

'So what?'

'So she'll probably be pissed off about this.'

'Why?'

'Ralf, darling,' he said, mimicking her voice, 'all your lovely old things are gone. You're still my baby. Oh, but you made that lamp yourself, my darling Ralf.'

I laughed despite myself. 'It's only paint,' I said.

'Looks like a sanatorium.' His eyes widened. 'Oh,' he said. 'Sorry, Ralf, I didn't mean . . .'

'No, I know,' I said.

He forced a tight-lipped smile and left the room.

The wall I'd painted in emulsion was dry enough in a couple of hours for me to put up Buckland's large geological cross-section that Oz had given me. I didn't want anything else on my walls.

By the time my mother came home, I had packed away my

old posters and left them in an old apple box in the cellar, not quite able to throw them away. I was lying on my mattress on the floor, waiting for the paint on the furniture to dry, reading the end of *Homo Faber*. Mum stood at the door, with her huge blue leather handbag still slung over her shoulder and a postcard in her hand. She looked about the room open-mouthed like someone who'd returned home to discover the ceiling had fallen in.

'You've been busy,' she said.

'I just repainted,' I said nonchalantly.

'I can see that,' she said. 'You know you've mixed up gloss and emulsion?'

'That's the point,' I said.

My mother nodded, unconvinced. 'Are you just going to have the bare bulb like that? It's a bit . . . oppressive.'

I looked up at it hanging prison-like above me. I hadn't really thought about the bulb.

'And what about the curtains?' Mum said.

I'd considered painting those, like the curtains at the squat that Joachim had taken us to, but had lost my nerve after the emulsion–gloss mix-up.

'I was going to make new ones,' I lied.

'Right,' Mum said.

She walked over to the mattress and squatted down beside me, her knees clicking beneath her black tights. I stared at a ladder rising up from the rim of her electric-blue high heels.

'Look,' Mum said, 'I've got to run some errands at KaDeWe. Then I'm going to watch *When Harry Met Sally* with Beate at the Zoo Palast. Why don't you come along?' She stroked my hair, tucking a strand behind my ear. 'A little respite?'

'I don't know what that is.'

'A bit of relief.'

269

'No, the film.'

'Oh, it's a comedy. Meg Ryan.'

I closed my eyes and turned my face to the mattress, saying in a muffled voice, 'Is it the one where she has an orgasm in a restaurant?'

'Beate said it's very good.'

'Why would I want to go and sit in a cinema with you watching a film about a woman coming?'

'It's not a film about a woman coming. It's a funny American film.'

'I told you, I hate dubbed films.'

'It's original. With subtitles. You can ignore them.'

'It's boiling. Why would we go to the cinema?'

'Beate's asking Stefan too. Us four used to love going to the cinema together.' When I didn't answer, she added, 'What are you going to do instead? You can't sit in here all day; you'll get sick with all these fumes. And that gloss won't dry for twenty-four hours.'

I didn't answer. I pushed my face into the mattress and covered my head with my arms.

'I like the map,' she said.

'It's from Oz,' I said, because I wanted to hear his name.

'How good he was to you,' Mum said.

Something hot covered my arms and my face. The mattress shook beneath me and I realised that I was crying. I was appalled, but I couldn't stop it, and she stroked my hair as I wailed into the pinging springs.

Thirty-One

I cycled past the graveyard on Monumentenstraße where the Brothers Grimm are buried then over the bridge between Schöneberg and Kreuzberg. I looked up towards Potsdamer Platz as I crossed, over the ruined railway that used to lead up to Anhalter Bahnhof, but now led to its ruins and, beyond that, the Wall. Bathed in pink light, it was an insignificant strip between pastel-coloured foliage, the old train tracks a beautiful burgundy in the dusk.

I turned back to the road that led to the hill of Viktoria Park, which I rounded, hearing the blustery fountain and screams of playing children and the thick beats of hi-fis accompanying break dancers. I cycled on to Arndtstraße, where Beate and Stefan lived in a rundown street by the park, the high buildings covered in peeling brown plaster and the balconies filled with green potted plants and drying clothes.

I pushed open the shuddering door to the block, always unlocked, filled with wired glass and covered in battered claret paint the colour of raw liver. I could already hear Beate's high laughter from the courtyard, from which the smell of garlic, grilled vegetables and the sound of pleasant chatter emanated.

Beate rented a first-floor flat in the back part of the building and used another in a side building for her studio. She had filled the edges of the courtyard with plants, and once it became apparent that the neighbours didn't care, she had annexed the rest.

The courtyard's two original acacias towered above a garden of verdant leaves and blossoming flowers, planted into any kind of container that would hold them: wooden crates and terracotta pots, but also discarded drawers, metal and plastic bins, jute bags, any number of cups, teapots, jugs, jars and pans, as well as an upturned urinal that Beate had signed 'R. Mutt' in honour of Marcel Duchamp. These containers burst with lilies, roses, forget-me-nots and pansies, clematis, rustling bamboo, fragrant mock orange blossom, pampas grass, prehistoric gunnera, Japanese maple, ivy and two tall banana trees with glossy, shredded leaves that Beate moved into her studio in winter.

In the heart of her garden sat Beate in her kaftan, the same peacock blue as her eyeshadow, with a glass of red wine in her hand. Beside her, a bearded hippy with matted hair was grilling skewers filled with red peppers, aubergine, onion and courgettes, and peeping through the leaves were the hands, legs and faces of her guests, young and old. A child ran towards me waving a smoking joss stick in his hand. He stopped in front of me and said, 'It's my cigarette,' and puffed at it like Liza Minnelli in *Cabaret*.

'It's lovely,' I said.

'Ralf!' cried Beate, lifting her wine glass into the air, like a toast.

I waved. 'Is Stefan in?'

'He's skulking about in the kitchen,' said Beate, standing and covering my face in kisses. 'I'm sorry about your friend. Have you seen him?'

'No,' I said. 'You have to wait two weeks before they allow visitors.'

'He'll be well again. I know he will.'

'Of course,' I said. 'Thanks.'

Their kitchen was long and cool. In the middle was a huge wooden table with benches and a rocking chair at one end, where Beate sat when she was holding court in winter and couldn't sit outside.

Near the windows, filled with green summer air and barbecue smoke, stood Stefan with a steaming bowl of potatoes, chopping them one at a time and throwing them into a large handmade ceramic bowl, shimmering with a thick blue glaze. 'Ralfi! *Alter!*' he shouted and gave me the Vulcan salute, then went back to his work, slicing each potato two or three times, letting the pieces drop into the bowl. 'How the fuck are you?'

'OK,' I said, saluting him back.

'That was fucked up, with your friend.'

'It was,' I said.

'So he really was nuts, eh?'

I mounted the bench and held on to the varnished wood, like I was vaulting a pommel horse.

'Seems so,' I said.

Stefan inspected a potato, chopped out a black eye with the knife and flicked it into the sink.

'So the dad was telling the truth?'

I nodded. 'Yup.'

'*Scheiße, eh?*'

Outside someone smashed a glass. 'Just kick it into the flowerbed,' I heard Beate saying.

'What's the occasion?' I asked.

'No occasion. It was meant to be a faculty meeting of colleagues from the Kunstakademie but it's turned into a party.

They always do. Once Günter Brus turned up and puked all over the jasmine.'

'I don't know who that is.'

'Brus? He's an artist,' said Stefan, throwing another sliced potato into the bowl and looking out of the window, the light reflecting in his black eyes. 'He makes videos where he cuts his leg open and pisses on himself.'

'Well, let's hope he turns up tonight,' I said.

Stefan smiled, but it collapsed into a frown and he put down his knife and leant on the counter.

'Ralf. Can I ask you something?'

I felt dry and nauseous.

'Were you and this guy Oz, like, dating?'

My face flashed cold; the air between us was glacially clear. 'Yes,' I said.

He nodded. One of the children outside started crying.

Stefan began to chop the potatoes again. Their earthy smell reached me and I realised how hungry I was. 'I wish you'd told me,' he said.

'I know. I owed you that.'

'Fuck, Ralf, you don't owe me anything. But I might've been able to help. You've been fucking about with some Turkish nut job and we didn't know anything about it.'

'He's not a nut job,' I said.

'He's been committed to a nut house, Ralf, and he hit you in the face.'

'He didn't hit me. That was his brother. He'd seen photos of us having sex.'

'Right, but who sent the photos?'

'The Stasi.'

'OK. But we've since established that the Stasi aren't after him. That he's actually just crazy. Which means—'

'I don't want to think about what it means.'

'It means that he had those photos taken. He sent them to his own family. That's right, isn't it?'

This I had worked out while I was holding Oz in the dark. It meant that he was very sick, and this gave me a little solace when he stared at me desperately, tears pouring out of his tired eyes, as the men marched him past me out of the apartment and down the stairs to the street. And, as strange as it sounds, the fact that he had made sure, even in his fevered delusions, that my face was obscured in those pictures felt like a kindness, and I was grateful to him for it.

'He's ill,' I said to Stefan, 'but he's a good guy.'

'Sounds like a fucking dream.' He threw the last sliced potato into the bowl. 'Can you go and get some chives from the garden,' he said. 'They're in a pot by Mum's feet.'

*

We sat at the table eating the potato salad with our fingers. We hadn't turned the lights on and the darkening kitchen was lit in the circus colours of Beate's tinted bulbs strung across the courtyard outside.

'This is good potato salad.'

'It's my father's recipe,' Stefan said.

'I like it better with oil and vinegar like this.'

'What's the other way?'

'Mayonnaise. That's the English way. How Mum makes it.'

Stefan nodded and licked the oil from his fingers. 'But she's, like, the worst cook in the world. You know that, right?'

I laughed. 'It's true.'

'And when Oz said the shepherd's pie was disgusting . . .'

We started to giggle.

'*Alter*,' Stefan said. 'It was incredible. Your mum's face.'

'Poor Mum.'

I looked into Stefan's eyes. The bulbs outside were reflected in tiny coloured spots in his irises.

'Don't you mind about your dad? Not knowing who he is.'

Stefan pushed himself back, resting his arms on the arms of the rocking chair. 'Of course,' he said. 'It makes me really angry.'

'I'm sorry.'

He shrugged. 'Do we have to talk about all our problems now you're a gayer?'

I smiled and shook my head.

'Good,' he said, leaning forward again and picking out more potato. 'Hey, I talked to Maike. She said it'd be fine for you to come back on the Wildlife Trust things.'

'What did you tell her?'

'Just that this friend of yours had gone off the rails.'

'Isn't there only one count left, before you all leave for university?'

'Yeah, but you'll still be around after that. You can do them on your own.'

'Fuck,' I said, gripping my hair like Oz used to. 'I know. Fuck.' I had called Durham the day that Oz had returned from Bonn. 'I deferred for a year. What the fuck was I thinking? He's locked up, you guys are all gone ...'

'You can hang out with Joachim.'

'Great,' I said.

'He's actually nice, and you should make an effort with him. He can be like your gay godfather. Show you the ropes.'

I threw a potato slice at him, which he batted off. It smacked onto the tiles in a dim corner of the kitchen.

'You know, your mum won't mind about you being gay,' Stefan said. 'If you want to tell her.'

'She'll love it. It'll be awful.'

'My mum's sensed your "gayness" already,' Stefan said. 'Fuck, they're both going to love it. It's going to be so embarrassing.'

We laughed.

'My dad though,' I said.

'Yeah,' said Stefan. 'I don't think your dad's moved on from missionary.'

'*Eh, Manno!*' I shouted, kicking his chair.

Stefan laughed.

He leant over and touched the side of my head. 'You've got a spider in your hair.' He held out his hand. A tiny golden spider descended from his finger on a shimmering thread.

'They're called money spiders in England,' I said. 'Means you're about to come into some cash.'

'*Herrlich*,' said Stefan, watching it crawl up to his fingers. 'We'll buy your mum some cookbooks.'

We started laughing again. He turned his hand over and the spider scampered across his arm and up the pale hairless skin of his underarm. Cigarette smoke floated in from the courtyard on the hot air and a dog's bark echoed in the street.

Thirty-Two

M aike called me the next day; I was touched and surprised. It was good to hear her voice. She said she'd heard a bit about what had been going on and that we should meet up before we all did the last Wildlife Trust count. I agreed to meet her that afternoon after I'd visited a friend in hospital. The friend was Oz. They had just called to say I could come.

The hospital was nicer than I'd imagined. The reception area had large parlour palms and pale yellow curtains. There were silver-framed prints of ferns on the walls, and on the desk a grey glass vase filled with yellow dahlias and roses.

The visiting room was wide and bright and opened out onto a garden. At the far end in a grey tracksuit sat Oz, squinting into the afternoon sun. It illuminated a glass in front of him, criss-crossed with a diamond pattern, containing a sparkling soft drink the pale yellow of primroses. In my memory, he looked aged, but of course he was only twenty-two. To many of the other patients we must have both looked extremely young.

He smiled at me as I came close and stood up shakily. He seemed uncertain how to greet me. I embraced him and buried my face in his neck. 'It's good to see you,' I said. He smelt institutional, of scentless soap and too much sleep.

'Oh, you too,' he said, patting me weakly. 'You too.'

We sat in the garden on a bench watching a thin man digging up a plant and splitting it with a trowel. The man seemed content and undisturbed, as did the patient kneeling beside him with a white bucket filled with fibrous compost. There was no one dribbling, no one screaming. Maybe those patients were kept somewhere else, I thought.

Oz lit a cigarette. The flame trembled. I was surprised he was allowed to smoke. He sucked at the cigarette gravely. The tracksuit he was wearing was too big for him and made him look small. He stared at his drink. The glass was balanced on the wooden arm of the bench. The sun revealed a semicircle at the lip, where his chapped mouth had left a trace of saliva.

'I'm sorry,' he said. 'About everything.'

'Everything?'

'No, not you and me, but ... You know.'

I nodded. In a room somewhere someone started thumping out an inexpressive tune on a piano.

'Have your parents said anything?'

'Not really,' I said. 'I mean, Mum wants me to talk about it, of course, but I don't want to. I think they *get* what's been going on. I mean, between you and me, but ... I don't know. I don't really want to talk about it. Not yet.'

'Have they said anything about "Axel"?'

'What do you mean?' I said.

'Anything that's going to help us link "Axel" with Tobias?' He looked out across the garden. 'I've been thinking it over, wondering whether we couldn't set up some sort of trap. Bit unorthodox, maybe.'

I felt tears welling up in my eyes. He still believed it all.

He noticed the change in my expression and said, 'They really got to you, didn't they? They've ruined me for you.'

'No one's ruined you,' I said.

'But you think I lied to you.'

'Have you?'

He looked heartbroken. 'No,' he murmured.

'You've always been completely honest, completely yourself?'

'I mean, no one's completely themselves,' he said.

'How were you not completely yourself?' I asked, hoping he was creating an opening to tell me the truth.

'I don't know,' he said. 'Like Turkish stuff.'

'What do you mean Turkish stuff?'

'I mean, I suppose I tried to be more "Turkish" for you. A bit. You seemed to really want me to read you Turkish poetry and buy you Turkish food. I don't eat that much white cheese. And I don't make Turkish coffee at home – it's a massive effort. Even when we were kids we just had filter coffee.'

'I'd've drunk filter coffee,' I said.

'I know, I just thought it would feel a bit more' – he shrugged – 'authentic, or something.'

I laughed and he laughed lightly, shaking his head. He offered me a cigarette, but I said no.

'Were there other people?' I said. 'People like me?' I had been planning to get the question in somehow, and now that I had uttered it I waited for the answer with my mouth strained and my eyes half closed, as if waiting for a humane bullet to the head.

'No,' said Oz, sitting up excitably. I sighed audibly. 'No, not at all. It was just you.' I saw how bloodshot his eyes were. He looked afraid. 'You have to understand that every word I said to you, everything we did, it was true.'

'In your head,' I said.

'No,' he said.

'But you were taking medication. Lithium, or something. And then you stopped taking it.'

'Did my dad tell you that?'

'I saw the packet at your flat.'

He looked at his hands. The skin on them was dry. 'Yeah, I did take medication. I got really depressed in my first year at university before I dropped out. It's why I dropped out. I didn't know what I was doing with my life. So I took lithium for a while and it helped. And then after I'd been back in Berlin for a bit I felt better and I stopped.'

'But Mum said that people with depression sometimes lose touch with reality. They have like a psychosis.'

'Well, I'm sure that happens. And I was a bit depressed, like I said. But I wasn't psychotic.' He looked up at me. His golden irises were undimmed. 'I really think I wasn't.'

A nurse with short, bottle-blonde hair leant out of the French windows and said, 'Another ten minutes, OK?' The patients looked up at her with automatic, gentle smiles, Oz too. A girl in a headscarf was crying, and I felt relieved that someone else was sad, not just numb and exhausted.

'They're always warning you like that,' Oz said. 'You can't concentrate on what you . . . Why do they have to keep saying twenty minutes, ten minutes? I hate it.'

'I'll come back on Monday,' I said.

Oz seemed upset and frustrated. 'Ralf, I'm going to be here for a while. You do understand that? They've made sure of that.'

'That's OK,' I said. 'It's really close to our flat. It's like a ten-minute bike ride.'

'No,' he said. 'You need to go to England. Call the university. Change it. Your friends are leaving, I'm in here. What are you going to do in Berlin?'

'I'll earn money. See you.'

'I can't . . . ' He closed his eyes, and rubbed at his creased forehead with his middle finger. 'I can't be responsible for you being in Berlin. It's not fair. And it's not safe for you with "Axel" still out there.'

'I'm fine. And I don't mind being in Berlin. I'll visit you,' I said. 'Maybe they'll let you out a bit earlier if they know I'm around to look after you when you get out. I can check your medication, things like that.'

'Look after me?' he said. He seemed exasperated. 'I don't think you thought that was what you were getting yourself into.'

'No,' I said. 'But no one ever really knows what they're getting themselves into.'

He laughed.

'What?'

'You and your wise words.'

The nurse leant out of the door again and said, 'Can visitors start to say their goodbyes and patients make their way back to their rooms or to the social room.'

Throughout the garden and the visitor room, parents, partners and children separated themselves from patients, who moved towards the building like ghosts called back to the grave at the break of day.

'That wasn't even ten minutes,' he said. He was on the verge of tears.

'Hey, it's fine,' I said. 'I'll come back on Monday.'

He nodded. We stood and I hugged him.

'Ralf,' he said into my ear. 'You mustn't come any more.'

'I can't keep away,' I said. 'I'm sorry. I love you.'

'It's too dangerous for you. Please.'

'It's all right,' I said. 'I'm always going to be around.' But he clung on to me as if it was the last time.

I sat in the clinic's garden for a while, alone on the bench. Oz had forgotten the glass, and I poured the contents into the flowerbed, careful not to wash away the film from his lips. As I was leaving, the woman at the reception desk said, 'Excuse me, but you can't take anything away with you.'

'I brought it with me,' I said.

She frowned, but I saw that she had a plastic cup on her desk, and said, 'Look, it's not even from here. Look at your cup – it's plastic.' I held up Oz's glass as proof.

She waved me away, unconvinced, and I carefully tucked the glass into my rucksack.

*

Maike met me outside the clinic and we cycled to Grunewald. I was silent the whole way, thinking about Oz, thinking about his smallness in comparison to the powerful man I had met at Prinzenbad in his red swimming trunks.

We locked up our bikes at Grunewald station, walked through the woods and sat beneath swaying moor birches looking out over the quagmire at Barssee and Pechsee, two kettle-hole lakes surrounded by a rich peat bog. It was an unassuming strip of treeless land that was special to us, because it combined all of our passions.

Barsee and Pechsee are two perfectly round lakes that were formed when Berlin's retreating glacier left behind balls of ice pressed into the ground that melted over centuries, long after the glacier had gone. I knew it was rare not to find them choked with sphagnum. For Maike, it was one of West Berlin's few real wetlands, the landscape that would make her famous, speckled with the tiny unassuming plants she loved: white beak sedge and sea pink, elegant Kievan nettles. They in turn were home to Petra's insects, and the swelling water had brought back the white-faced darter dragonfly and diving-bell spiders that lived in web-walled air bubbles under water. When Stefan was with us, his binoculars followed cormorants, black kites and Eurasian jays, which we call 'acorn jays' in Germany, because they hoard them like squirrels. And he'd tell us about the bitterlings, small silver fish that were once used to test if women were pregnant, their ovipositors shooting out when injected with hormone-rich urine.

Maike thought that she was pregnant once. If she had been, it was lost within a week in a crushingly painful period. I sometimes wondered about the child. She wouldn't have had it, I supposed back then, though I didn't feel sure about anything any more.

'This Oz,' Maike said. 'Stefan said there was some kind of fight?'

The bruise around my eye had faded, leaving a bluish hue, like badly applied make-up.

'The fight wasn't with him,' I said. 'But he's not very well. Mentally.'

'It's hard,' she said, 'loving people who are ill.'

I took her hand. She let me hold it for a few seconds, but then took it away, rubbing it as if it was sore. A breeze, which had a bite of autumn in it, tugged at the long strands of her brown hair and set the delicate leaves of the birches above us into shimmering, festive motion.

'I really loved you,' she said. 'That's why I couldn't see you for a while.'

'I know,' I said. 'I loved you too. I still love you.'

'Ralf,' she said.

'It's true.'

She tucked her hair behind her ear. 'Like a sister?'

'No, like a girlfriend. I'm not saying I didn't ... I don't know, massively fuck up, but I loved you. I do love you.'

'But now you love someone else more,' she said.

It wasn't that I didn't think she'd be hurt by what I'd done, it was just that the inevitable revelation had seemed so distant, as if it belonged to another age.

'Did Petra tell you?'

Her eyes were fixed on the toes of her trainers, where a line of grey-blue mud was gathered in the flap between the rubber sole and the nylon toe. On her wrist against her brown summer skin was a green and black friendship band that I'd never seen before. 'She implied that ... I'm assuming that Oz ...'

Two dragonflies hovered iridescent blue in front of us, as if awaiting instruction, then swept off sideways.

'You can love more than one person,' I said.

All this truth, I thought, seems so inconsequential now that it's finally been aired. But then she started crying. She cried into her closed fist and hit it against her forehead. She wouldn't let me stop her, but she let me leave a hand on her back, as beetles popped from the mossy ground and her wailing echoed off the exposed trunks where the wood ended and the bog began.

Eventually she turned her head and looked at me, touching the back of her neck. A strip of red had formed from ear to ear across her eyes like a mask. 'Be careful, Ralf.'

'I think it's too late for that.'

'In life, I mean,' she said. 'Be careful.'

'OK,' I said. 'Yeah, of course,' and she started to cry again, her shoulders pulsating in desperate sobs.

Thirty-Three

Maike and I separated at Sophie-Charlotte-Platz and I cycled down Windscheidstraße unable to keep my eyes off the cars, thinking about Oz in his green Mercedes at the start of summer. When I wheeled my bike into the court-yard I found Tobias under the horse chestnut inspecting his shirt, his viola case lying abandoned on the ground by his foot. I had been so caught up in Oz that I'd barely thought about him, and realised now that the revelation of Oz's lies meant that Tobias was going nowhere. He wasn't a spy. He was never going to be arrested. We were going to live opposite Mum's one-time lover until the day I moved out.

'Oh, Ralf,' he said mournfully, oblivious of the extent of the true role he had played in my short life. 'A pigeon shat on me.' When I didn't respond, he added, 'I don't know whether to go back and change the shirt.'

The shirt was white linen and had only been caught by the dropping. The greyish mark was barely noticeable, but it was shit after all. I would've gone and changed it, but I still didn't want to offer him any help, however banal.

He smiled. I tried to push the bike past him, but he said, 'Ralf, is your mum OK?'

For a second the question numbed me, and I stared at the

concrete floor at his feet, which was studded with split, spiked conker shells and their mahogany seeds.

'Why did you do it? The affair.'

'Ralf, I didn't mean to ...' He trailed off, and when I looked up at him he was staring at the stain on his shirt, fingering it like a child.

'What does that mean?' I said. 'We were your friends. At least, I thought we were.'

'Of course,' he said quietly but insistently. 'But it's over now. We should all just ... It's time we all forgot about it.'

I shook my head. 'No,' I said. 'I'll never forget about it.'

'Ralf,' he began to say.

'Excuse me, do you know if Frau von Hildendorf's in? I've tried her bell, but ...' We turned to find a blonde woman standing in the courtyard. She was older than Mum, but her curling hair was so perfectly set, her blouse and pleated skirt so white and so perfectly pressed, that she seemed ageless.

'If she didn't answer her bell, she's probably not in. She always answers,' I said, feeling Tobias's presence beside me like a pain.

'Oh,' the woman said, disappointed. She took off her large orange sunglasses, revealing huge blue eyes.

'You're not ...?' Tobias said.

She smiled patiently; she was the sort of woman who was used to this question.

'You're not Eve Harris, are you?'

She nodded shyly.

He laughed in disbelief. 'She always said you were coming.'

'And now she's not here,' Eve said. She looked up to the top floor where the smallest flat was. 'I always promised to come. But I used to know someone who lived here, a good friend who died recently, and I just couldn't bear it. But now I'm

287

here ... It's funny with places, isn't it? They don't quite hold their sentimental promise. You always think you'll feel more.'

Her German was idiomatic, but there was something awkward about it, as if she hadn't spoken it in a long time.

'I always thought you were American,' Tobias said, 'because of your name.'

'No, I was born Eva Hirsch,' she said, 'but I had to change it. German names weren't terribly popular back then. And there was Eva Braun of course.'

'Of course,' Tobias said.

She looked back up at the top-floor flat again. 'Now I'm here, I wouldn't mind taking a look at it.'

'I'd take you up, if it wasn't for my leg,' Tobias said. He limped forward to expose his awkward gait.

'My father had polio,' she said, but corrected herself. 'You're probably too young for that.'

Tobias nodded. 'I fell off a balcony when I was a child and broke my hip.'

'How awful for you.'

I stared down at his leg. Poor Tobias. 'I thought it was polio too,' I said weakly, thinking of Oz's red-haired agent, feeling the last vestiges of his lies crumbling away. I could never forgive Tobias for the affair, but it was awful imagining all the terrible things that Oz and I might have instigated with our witch-hunt.

'Most people do,' Tobias said. 'But they'd wiped it out in East Germany by sixty-one. Mass vaccinations are one of the few advantages of communism. My older brother had it, and my mum, but they were fine.'

'Daddy had a bad hand,' said Eve. 'But his brother had it and he was fine.'

I smiled as pleasantly as I could, being too young to add to these reminiscences. I locked up my bike and headed for the front building, hoping that the conversation with the actress would stop Tobias from following me. But he shouted, 'Ralf!'

I looked back. His face looked pale and afraid. Eve Harris stood behind him, a peach-coloured clutch held between her fingers. I knew that he was stuck with her, too polite to desert her and come after me, so I turned and ran up the stairs.

*

The call came on Sunday evening during *Tatort*, which was a strange time for someone to be phoning. It was Duisburg *Tatort*, and I was the only person in the family who didn't like Commissar Schimanski, so I pushed myself off the sofa when the phone started to ring, wandered to the kitchen and picked it up.

'Dörsam,' I said.

'Ralf Dörsam?' It was a woman's voice.

'Yes,' I said, surprised that the caller was asking for me.

'My name is Topal – Aslı Topal.'

The mention of a Turkish name frightened me.

'OK,' I said.

'I'm calling about Osman Özemir. His father said I should call. That I might . . . ' She sighed and said, 'Listen – Osman and I are engaged. I've heard he's a friend of yours and I thought . . . I don't know, I thought maybe I could answer some questions you might have. About how he's behaved. I heard you got caught up in things.'

I didn't answer. What would I have said? Instead, I rested my forehead against the cold wall and closed my eyes.

'I don't know if he talked about me.'

'No,' I said, 'he didn't. But he's not been very well.'

'No,' she said. 'He's looking better though.'

I opened my eyes. 'You've visited him?'

She paused. 'Of course.'

'Right,' I said.

'He's a good man—'

'So everyone tells me.'

'He is telling the truth when he talks about his feelings. But other things are a bit . . .'

'Did he send you the photographs too?' I said.

She hung up the phone.

I dialled the Park Klinik and, taking a chance on their ignorance about the gender of Turkish names, said, 'Hi, it's Aslı Topal. You couldn't help, could you? It's so dumb, but I've lost my wallet and I'm trying to retrace my steps. The last time I remember having it was at the clinic when I visited Osman Özemir, but I can't for the life of me remember which day it was. You couldn't just check what day it was I came in last week?'

I thought that the trick hadn't worked. The pause was too long, but then I heard the sound of pages being turned. 'We have Aslı Topal down every day. And the week before. Is that wrong?'

I crossed my arm over my eyes to stop my tears and said, 'No, that's right. I thought I'd missed a day. Well, thanks.'

I cried into a dishcloth for as long as it took to calm down. Then I washed my face in the sink and went back to the living room.

'Everything all right?' my father said, reaching out for my hand, but luckily not turning his eyes from the television to see my face streaked red. I took his and made a vague noise of agreement – 'Mm.' I waited a second so that he didn't think I was pulling away, then sat on the floor and watched the rest of the drama from the rug.

*

The next day, instead of cycling to the clinic, I cycled to Stefan's. When he answered the door I was shaking as if I were cold. 'It's over, I think.'

Stefan held the door open for me to come in.

'It's all fucked up,' I said. 'And now you're all going, and I've got nothing.'

Stefan's big brown eyes looked sad, but not surprised. 'That's pretty dramatic, Ralfi.'

'I've fucked up my life and everyone else's.'

'Ralf, you're eighteen. You haven't fucked up your life. You haven't had a life.'

I heard male laughter coming from the kitchen. 'A fresh catch,' Stefan said, and steered me towards his bedroom.

*

We lay side by side on Stefan's floor staring up at a ceiling filled with papier-mâché insects that we had crafted in Beate's studio when we were twelve. That summer, goaded on by Beate, we became wildly excited by the project, creating plump bees, leggy grasshoppers, cruel-looking wasps, ungainly spiders and daddy longlegs, fleas, flies, mosquitoes and midges. Their brightly painted tissue skins over coathanger frames gave them a rough angular charm, but six years gathering dust and the meagre glow of Stefan's nightlight made them look like the lumpen residents of an amateur haunted house.

'They're pretty creepy.'

'The insects?' said Stefan.

I nodded.

'I don't even notice them any more. If the window's open and Mum goes out into the courtyard they knock about as if they're alive, and cover everything in dust.'

'That's horrible,' I said.

The largest insect was the flea, its great springing legs, made from tights stuffed with balled newspaper, hanging down below it.

'What time is it?'

Stefan turned to the boxy Braun alarm clock on his bedside table. 'Five,' he said. It was visiting time.

'Then I've abandoned him,' I said, closing my eyes and picturing Oz alone on the bench in his dressing gown.

'I'm sorry, Ralf. What a shitty summer.'

'It wasn't shit,' I said.

We heard the high whine of a reversing car out on the street.

'Look,' Stefan said. 'I'm meeting up with Petra and Maike tomorrow night. We're going to have a barbecue at Schlachtensee. Come along.'

'Why didn't anyone invite me?'

'I didn't know how the rapprochement with Maike was going to go. And, anyway, I'm inviting you now.'

'She didn't say anything to me about it when I saw her. I think she still hates me.'

'She doesn't hate you. And she's leaving for university next week, me and Petra too. It'll be the last time we're all together until Christmas.'

'Maybe,' I said. I pushed myself up on one elbow. 'Do you think I'm being an arsehole not visiting Oz?'

'No,' Stefan said.

'I think I am,' I said, my eyes stinging. 'I think I'm an arsehole.'

'I think maybe we're all arseholes.'

'Not you. Not Maike and Petra.'

'Petra? Are you kidding me? And Maike got fingered on a boat in Sweden while you were dating, so she's as big a dick as anyone.'

'Does everyone know about that?' I said.

'Only because Petra told me.'

'Fuck,' I said.

He sat up. 'Do you want to get wasted on schnapps?'

I nodded.

'Come on then,' he said, slapping my cheek. 'We've only got pear and it's surprisingly disgusting.'

Thirty-Four

I sat at my desk. I'd written to Durham to ask if I could start university that academic year after all, but a few weeks later than everyone else. In anticipation of a yes I'd started reading a few texts mentioned on the geology page in the prospectus. I was pleased to have work to do, but my head had found its way to my folded arms and I was staring at Oz's lip mark on the glass I'd stolen from the clinic, filled with brushes and pens, so that no one would clear it away and wash off the last trace I had of him.

'It's Dörsam, sir,' Dad said, pretending to be a butler, a running joke whenever he came into our rooms to gather up discarded clothes from the floor for the washing. 'May I offer you a coffee, sir?'

'No, Dörsam,' I said smiling, playing along. 'No coffee today.'

He mimed tipping his hat to me, one arm filled with pants and socks and the chequered polyester shirt I had to wear at the beer garden. He looked unusually exhausted and I was worried he'd found out about Mum and Tobias. 'You all right?' I said. 'You look tired.'

'Oh, fine,' he said. 'Bit of back ache. And I ended up watching *Tagesthemen*, so was in bed late. If I don't get my eight hours . . . ' He yawned.

'Anything exciting?'

'Protests in Leipzig. I don't think it'll really lead to anything.' He seemed sad, his eyes red-rimmed, but then they landed on Oz's glass and he smiled. 'Where did you dig that out from?'

I shrugged; I didn't want to say.

He laughed to himself.

'What?' I said.

'Well, it's an apple-wine glass. From Hessen.'

'How d'you know?' I said.

'The diamonds. Makes me feel all nostalgic. Splash of sweet or sour?'

'What?'

'That's what they ask you in Frankfurt apple-wine pubs. You get your *Bembel* jug of apple wine with either lemonade or fizzy water – "splash of sweet or sour". And it comes in those glasses with the diamonds on. It probably found its way out of the back of the cupboard or the cellar. Your Opa had hundreds of them.' He looked proud.

'I didn't realise,' I said.

'We should all go back to Frankfurt sometime. With Opa and Oma dead, there never seemed to be a good reason, but we should go. It's your history too.'

I imagined Dad as a young man, sitting with his friends in a smoky pub, the table filled with diamond glasses and stout stoneware jugs.

'Dad?' I said. 'Were you ever in love with someone before Mum?'

He looked shocked and frowned with amused disapproval. But then he seemed to understand and said, 'Everyone's had their heart broken, Ralfi.' He picked up a last white sock, the toe and heel grey. 'You keep your chin up,' he said, and kissed the top of my head. 'You know what Opa always used to say?'

'They can lick my arse.'

'Exactly,' Dad said, gripping my ear and kissing me again. 'Exactly.'

This was the closest I ever came to a coming out with my parents: a suggestion that they knew what was going on with Oz and a suggestion that I knew they knew. In the light of their many faults, I've always been grateful for that quiet acceptance. If they'd asked then for any kind of explanation, I couldn't have offered them more.

*

At Schlachtensee, we wheeled our bikes to the edge of the lake and set up the barbecue on a small sandy cove in the woods where the clear water lapped the silt. Stefan lit the barbecue as Petra, Maike and I waded into the water to where the sand became velvety with rotting black leaves before dropping away completely.

We swam aimlessly, our heads above the water, our hair slick to our heads like seals. The setting sun turned the sky pink and the water reflected it, so that we appeared to be swimming in liquid light. The forest rose up around us, hiding the other bathers in their own coves. On our beach, Stefan squatted in front of the barbecue, the smoke of it stained blue by the dusk, rising straight up into the air like a signal. The smell of smoke mixed with the smell of lake water and we could hear the delayed crack and snap of the burning charcoal.

Maike swam back to tend the barbecue so that Stefan could swim. Then slowly, as the pink of the setting sun became purple and then blue, we returned to the water's edge where a crowd of midges jangled in a golden cloud above our heads.

The bratwurst hissed when they hit the barbecue and we ate them hungrily with crusty rolls and a blue tube of Thomy mustard. Stefan just ate the rolls with butter and Petra took out a joint.

'Where'd you get that?' said Stefan, as she lit the end and blew out the flaming threads of tobacco.

'Sven from work.'

'Have to fuck him for it?'

'I didn't *have* to fuck him for it,' she said, and took the first drag, passing it on to Stefan as she held in the smoke.

I lay back against the fallen tree beside Petra, Maike lay on her back, her head propped up on her rolled-up towel. Stefan lay against the thick stump of a felled ash, his hair still flattened to his head in damp curls.

'I wonder what we'll all be up to this time next year,' said Stefan.

'I wonder what we'll be up to this time in ten years,' said Maike.

'Ooh, that's a good game,' said Petra. 'Ralf, you start. Do everyone except yourself. Start with me.'

'Well,' I said, receiving the joint from Maike and taking a drag, 'I think you're all going to be biology and geography professors. You, Petra, are going to be the youngest recipient of the Nobel Prize. Stefan—'

'No, no, no,' interrupted Petra. '*Was für'n Scheiß*, Ralf. Jesus. Let's say what we really think; completely honestly. None of this Nobel Prize horseshit.'

'I do think you could all be professors!'

'Yes, but you know I'm not going to make it. You know I'm not going to sail through it without a crisis. Say what you really think, otherwise it's no fun. You don't have to say I'm going to be a crack addict. Just say what you really think.'

The dying coals of the barbecue clinked and the tinny sounds of someone's hi-fi drifted across the water from the bank at the other side of the lake. I stared at the embers of our fire, humped and orange like soft apricots.

'I think you'll be married,' I said.

'OK,' said Petra. 'To whom?'

'Someone rich.'

'Like my dad?'

I nodded.

'Where will I live?'

'Munich. You'll be a professor there.'

'Will I have children?'

'No. Your husband will think you want them, but actually you don't and you won't tell him. You'll keep taking the pill and just pretend it isn't happening.'

Petra smiled. 'Yes,' she said, pleased. 'You see? You knew I wasn't going to be winning any fucking Nobel Prize. Now what about Stefan?'

'He's going to fall in love at university,' I said, looking at him. 'She'll be studying biology, but'll become a teacher. She'll hate it and give up when they have kids.'

'So Stefan's having kids?'

'Yeah, four,' I said. 'They'll just keep coming.'

Stefan laughed.

'And the wife?' said Petra.

'She'll find it all too hard, because Stefan will pretend he's considering sharing the childcare, but really he won't and she'll have to give up her job so that he can keep working full-time. She'll never really forgive him for it and they'll get divorced.'

Stefan leant forward to take the joint off me.

'We'll stay friends though,' said Stefan. 'Me and my ex.'

'Of course,' I said. 'The best.'

He smiled.

'And Maike?' Petra said.

Fire danced in the lenses of Maike's glasses, obscuring her eyes, so that I didn't know if she was looking back at me, whether her eyes were open or closed.

'She's going to be a big deal. Important books, prizes, head of department.'

'Be honest, Ralf,' Petra cried.

'I am,' I said. 'Maike's the one that's going to really make it. She'll live in Düsseldorf and have dachshunds, a husband, also an academic, and one very bright child called something old-fashioned, like Gisela, who'll be tall and pale and play the piano very well.'

Maike laughed.

'Now you, Maike – you start with Ralf.'

I watched the twin flames where her eyes should have been.

'Ralf will go to university next year in England. He'll hate it, but he'll get through it and do well. He'll keep thinking that he's not really English any more, but also not really German, and it'll make him miserable. Because he'll have to face it. He'll have to face the complexity of it and he won't be able to hide from it there.'

'Fuck,' said Petra.

I smiled, but I felt that she was right and I was afraid.

'He'll meet someone later.'

'Who?' said Petra.

'A man, I suppose.'

The smoky air cracked with the sound of burning branches that Stefan had thrown on the barbecue to make a fire and the high whine of water escaping from the wood.

'He'll do something more important than Ralf, or he'll be older. Ralf would like that – someone to look up to. Sometimes he'll stray.'

'Ralf?' said Petra.

'No,' said Maike, 'the lover. But they'll never leave each other. They won't know how.'

I didn't want to believe it, but it wasn't impossible, I supposed. I pictured myself awake in an upstairs room in early-morning London light hearing the door below open and close, hearing my boyfriend coming up the stairs after a night out without me. But when I turned to him I only saw Oz. Perhaps that would pass. Perhaps there would be other faces after all.

We listened to music coming from the other side of the lake. Petra hummed along to it. I pulled on my jumper and pushed my bare knees together. The night air was cold now and smelt of smoke and minerals, the lake water lapped at the shore and, in the insistent breeze, the first dead leaves rattled above us among the green.

Thirty-Five

As Hutton and his friends discovered, the engine of geology is time. With enough time, anything can be metamorphosed even with the lightest pressure. If you put your hands against a wall and started pushing and kept the pressure up for hundreds of thousands of years, eventually it would become fluid beneath your fingers, and you could part it and walk right through.

There are also cataclysms, though. Sudden shifts that change everything, when all the hands are pushing in the other direction and the wall suddenly gives. The 1556 Shaanxi earthquake that destroyed every single building in Huaxian and killed 830,000 people living in cave dwellings carved out of soft loess, for instance. The Lake Toba eruption, pumping six billion tonnes of sulphur dioxide into the atmosphere, its glassy dust still found in the earth on the banks of Lake Malawi.

Oz's incarceration, me abandoning him and then my friends leaving in the autumn of 1989 were of course not catastrophic changes. But their sudden disappearances transformed West Berlin for me overnight. The feeling in the apartment changed too. While I waited to hear if Durham would let me start in January, I got a job in an outdoor clothing shop in

301

Steglitz and, like Mum and Dad, worked five days a week. When Martin sloped into the kitchen in the morning, Mum, Dad and I were already dressed and drinking coffee, our black bread and cheese packed and stacked in Tupperware, ready for our departure.

I thought about Oz constantly. Like a fan of some historical figure, I cycled about the city passing the sites that held some trace of him: his old flat, the bookshop, Checkpoint Alpha, Fellini's. Every evening I cycled home via the clinic and stopped there at dusk, in the brief period when the lights were on, but the blinds hadn't yet been drawn. From the road, I studied the faces that passed the windows, but never saw him, not once. I imagined his fiancée at his side, holding his hand. I hoped he was good to her.

I didn't hear much from Maike, but Petra phoned surprisingly often and Stefan hitchhiked back from Hanover every few weeks, because so many of the students still lived with their parents and his university halls were dead at the weekends. While Joachim didn't become my gay godfather, we often met up with him when Stefan was back in town and drank in Der Gammler, listening to Peter reminisce about the golden era of the West Berlin Wildlife Trust and Stefan complain about a Dutch anthropology student he was dating called Femke who didn't believe in monogamy. 'It's very challenging,' said Stefan.

'For you?'

He shook his head. 'For society.'

One evening it began raining heavily while we were drinking. After Peter closed up the bar, Stefan decided he didn't want to cycle all the way back to Kreuzberg and invited himself back to mine. He made a fuss about having to sleep on the floor and told me to stop being an old maid when I questioned whether it wasn't weird for us to share a bed. Since Oz, Stefan had become even more brotherly and explicitly unbothered by any show of intimacy; he was constantly pinching my cheeks and embracing me at the end of drunken evenings.

I slept uncomfortably sandwiched between him and the wall. The heat in the city was dying, but it was still warm at night, and every time his leg or arm touched mine a slick of sweat sprang from my skin like tears.

I woke in the night to find a void behind me, which I rolled into, enjoying for a moment the blissful semi-coolness of Stefan's absence. But the reasons for the absence turned over in my mind and I opened my eyes to find him standing at my window.

In the half-light his body was as pale as his white underpants, the limbs long and thin, his curling black hair a felt-tip cloud scribbled above it. The moon was high and threw a shaft of blue light that lit up his face. He looked ethereal, like the pale boatmen punting across the river to the Isle of the Dead.

'Stefan?' I croaked, sitting up. My mouth was hot and sour.

He didn't move, and for a second I thought he was sleepwalking. Then he said, 'Ralf. Do you think someone's watching you?'

I climbed out of bed and, still full of sleep, stumbled to the window, half slipping on a discarded packet of Chio Chips.

'Look at that car.'

Automatically I searched for Oz's green Mercedes.

'The low car, kind of golden brown.'

I saw it. A wide flat Ford, but it was in a part of the street too dark for me to be able to see into the unlit interior. 'Did you see someone in there?' I said.

'They're there now.'

I stared but saw nothing except for the barest glow of the car's phosphorescent dials. 'I can't see anyone.'

'There's something green and glowing.'

'It's the speedometer or something, isn't it?'

'No, it's a watch. If you wait long enough it'll move.'

Indeed, after a few seconds the glowing dial shifted.

I was hot and confused from sleep. My pulse throbbed in my neck and in my wrists.

'It's just a man in a car,' I said.

'Yeah, except why can't you see into the car?'

'It's dark.'

'But look, he's parked exactly in between two streetlamps and underneath a tree. It just happens to be the darkest spot in the street.'

'How could he have been sure of getting that spot?' I said.

'He was already there when we arrived. I mean, the car was. He wasn't in it. Or she.'

I left the window and fell back onto my bed. 'Why does that mean he's watching me? Why are you trying to make me paranoid? I've had enough of paranoid people.'

'But I saw the same car parked outside the squat when we went to that party with Joachim.' He looked up at me with his black eyes. 'I mean, what if Oz was right?'

I recalled picking up my bike and drunkenly scratching the golden car, but I couldn't remember if it was that car. 'Stefan! Please don't freak me out,' I said. 'My head's fucked enough as it is.'

'Fine,' he said. 'But if my boyfriend kept telling me the Stasi were after him and then it turned out I really was being followed, I'd want to know. I'd want to check it out, at least.'

But it was too much. It was all too much.

He lay down next to me and I shifted back into my spot against the wall, thinking about Oz in the car smoking his Gitanes as I fell anxiously back to sleep.

*

The next morning Beate rang early to tell Stefan to buy light bulbs and cigarettes on the way home. We ate Toppas at the kitchen table, then sat on the living-room floor with Martin watching *Alf*. Stefan hugged me before he left.

'Is Stefan a bender now as well?' said Martin, yawning and walking through the hall.

'Yes,' I said, 'we're all benders now.'

'Bums ahoy!' Martin said and farted.

At my bedroom window, I watched Stefan push his bike past the gold car and peer in through the window. He looked up at me, pointed to the car and shrugged, then cycled off towards Kantstraße.

I ignored Stefan's appeal for as long as I could. I cut my toenails and argued with Martin about using my razor for the peach fuzz on his upper lip. I had a bath, lying deep in it so that the water filled my ears. I blew bubbles into the milky water, thinking about Oz and the apple-wine glass he had left me at the clinic.

Down by the car, I held my hands over my eyes like binoculars and peered in. The interior was cracked toffee-coloured leather. The seats and brown plastic dashboard were worn and scratched, but otherwise the car was devoid of mess, except for the ashtray, which was overflowing. The stubs were all Camels. I looked gingerly around the side of the car and saw, above the bumper, the bright white scratches I had made with my bike pedals in front of the squat. I recalled the man with the combover trying the door, and looked up and down the road, expecting to see him dipping into the doorway of an apartment, but the street was empty.

I cycled to the Park Klinik, taking all of the main roads that I usually avoided. Behind the reception desk, the nurse who'd told me off about the glass was there and recognised me, over the rim of the plastic cup of Coca-Cola that she was draining. She wiped her mouth with her thumb and forefinger and forced her face into an expression of patient affability.

'Hello,' I said. 'It's Ralf Dörsam. I wanted to visit Herr Özemir today. Osman Özemir.'

'He's no longer in our care,' she said, without having to look up his name.

'He's been released?' This is what I'd come to find out, and yet hearing it made me well up at the idea of him free in Berlin without me.

'I can't give you any details about patients, I'm afraid, Herr Dörsam.'

'OK,' I said.

*

I waited for her on the junction of Sophie-Charlotten-Straße. Approaching in casual clothes, she looked older, the September light making the blonde in her hair look grey.

She recognised me and tried to walk past, but I said, 'I'm sorry. I don't want to get you into any trouble, but I'm just worried about my friend.'

'I can't tell you where he is,' she said.

The sound of her jeans was audible as she strode past – swish swish, swish swish.

'Could you just tell me if he was better when he left.'

She stopped and stared at me. I tried to make my face look as pathetic as possible. 'Please,' I said.

'He was fine. He was always fine.'

'What do you mean?'

She adjusted her handbag strap and shifted her weight. 'Usually the depressed ones try not to be involved at all when they're having their lows. They don't want to do anything they don't have to. But he did everything, he went along with everything, but he seemed ... ' She frowned. She was having trouble defining it. 'It was like he was on his best behaviour, agreeing to all his mistakes and going to all of his groups.'

I didn't know what to say. It just made me very sad, the idea of him boyishly behaving himself.

'Have a lot of people been coming and asking about him?'

She shook her head.

'His fiancée?'

'The woman? Ashley, or something? Foreign surname?'

'Yes,' I said.

She shrugged. 'I mean, her name was always in the visitor book when I started my shift, but I never saw her. And I cover visiting times, so I don't think she could've got in to see him.'

I began to feel excited.

She took a cigarette from her handbag. The flame from her lighter added a tinge of orange to the skin of her face, which was powder-blue in the late September afternoon.

'Did a bald man ever ask after him?' I said, thinking of the crumbs of gold on my fingertips by the car's bumper. 'With a combover. Black hair – what was left of it.'

She sucked at her cigarette and shrugged an acknowledgement. 'That's all you're getting, though. I shouldn't've said anything at all.'

'I know,' I said. 'Thank you.'

I thought about her behind her desk and felt jealous of her. Jealous that she had seen Oz more recently than me and knew things about him that I didn't know. And then it occurred to me. 'Why weren't you drinking from a can?'

'What?' she said.

'When I came in. You were drinking Coke from a plastic cup.'

'We're not allowed cans – the patients can bend them into something sharp.'

'What about glasses?'

'The patients don't have glasses. For the same reason.'

'They wouldn't have glasses at all?'

'No,' she said. There was a roar on the main road up ahead. 'My bus,' she said. She threw the cigarette on the ground and ran for it, clamping her handbag beneath her arm to stop it flapping. Above me, the streetlights came on, the fluorescent tubes blinking orange and then settling with a gentle buzz.

Thirty-Six

I waited under a balcony on the other side of the street for the shop to open, watching from a distance as Herr Özemir unlocked the shutters and pulled them up. I waited all day in the hope that he would take a lunch break or leave the shop for long enough to let me slip in, but at midday a young woman arrived – a sister of Oz's, I guessed – with a stack of battered plastic boxes, and they ate together, using the corner of the counter as a table.

The following day when the routine began again, I realised that my only hope was to appeal to Herr Özemir, so I entered the shop and stood in the stuffy room waiting for him to notice me. He continued smoking, staring down at a crossword. From a radio beneath the counter, some sort of sports contest was being commentated in Turkish.

He looked up. He sighed when he recognised me, blowing out his cigarette smoke as he shook his head from side to side.

'Herr Dörsam,' he said. I was touched that he remembered my name, though of course he hadn't recalled it out of affection.

'Herr Özemir,' I said.

He stubbed out his cigarette in the same glass ashtray I had watched Oz fill on that July morning. 'He isn't here.'

'I know. I was here yesterday.'

'I know.'

I nodded, no longer ashamed. It had all gone on too long to feel much shame about anything any more. 'Do you know where he is?'

'He told me Bonn, but . . . ' He shrugged.

The high twittering of the fridge containing the soft drinks suddenly cut out and the shop fell silent.

'I think he left something for me here,' I said. I took the Hessen apple-wine glass Oz had left for me out of my rucksack.

'Behind the jugs,' he said.

I let out a little puff of laughter. 'You know everything.'

'Osman is clever, but he's not always the genius he thinks he is.' He climbed down from the stool and walked heavily into the back room. From there he shouted, 'Well, come on then.'

Herr Özemir expertly flicked the kick stool across the floor towards me, where it skidded to a halt beneath the *Bembel*. I stepped up and parted the jugs where I'd seen Oz hide the envelope. The envelope was gone and in its place was a shoe box, taped up once round with silver duct tape. I took it down. It was heavy with papers that drummed against the side when I tipped it.

I looked over at Herr Özemir, and lifted the box. 'Shall we look in it together?'

'It is definitely not for me.'

I climbed down and stuffed the box into my bag. 'Thank you,' I said.

He flicked his hand towards the door, gesturing for me to leave.

'Herr Dörsam,' he said, when I was at the open door to the shop. I turned. He was climbing back onto his torn stool, putting on a thick pair of reading glasses. 'Osman is a complicated man, but not a difficult man.'

I waited for him to go on, but he settled himself, lit a cigarette and went back to his crossword. I thought he was just looking down at it so as not to look at me, but he fished out a biro from his shirt pocket and carefully filled out a clue.

*

I cycled home so fast that my legs were shaking when I went down the steps into the municipal cellar and shut myself into our section, walled off with high wooden slats. I wiped the sweat off my face with my T-shirt and sat down among the cardboard boxes, broken furniture, paint tins and oil tins that my dad had carefully sorted and stacked down there. The air was cold and moist and smelt of wet black things: coal dust and mildew.

I picked open the duct tape and pulled off the lid of the shoe box. On the underside was written: 'For RD'. Inside the box were papers, photographs, letters and postcards. The first scrap was a receipt for petrol from the station near Helmstedt where we'd filled up the car before taking the transit road back to West Berlin. There were other things I recognised: a discarded green-and-white Wrigley's Spearmint packet, a blue button that had pinged off my polo shirt while I was trying to get it over my head, an old parking ticket that I'd folded into the shape of a rhinoceros at Oz's kitchen table while he sat in his yellow Y-fronts telling me about paintings he loved, his hands clasped around the back of his head, the hot summer air filled with the smell of coffee and cigarettes and the good smell of him.

Beneath this stratum tracing our brief time together, I uncovered a letter with Oz's real name and an address in

Frankfurt. It was from the Goethe University confirming that he had abandoned his course of study. There was an ID card as well, with a colour picture of Oz. He was wearing a crumpled white shirt and was looking just above the camera. There was a smile on his lips and his hair was fluffy and uncombed, bulging out in ungainly black clouds. Beneath were the three photos taken in the same booth, but rejected; his eyes were closed in two and in one he was smiling, laughing at something someone was saying on the other side of the curtain.

There was a swimming certificate for twenty-five metres from the Waldschwimmbad Rosenhöhe in Offenbach, another for fifty metres, a certificate for proficiency in Spanish guitar, a geography exercise book with carefully drawn volcanoes, and in the white rectangle on the orange sugar-paper cover was written 'Osman Özemir, Geography, Class B, 1979' in carefully joined up letters. An oak leaf was pressed into the back page.

Beneath the book, winding itself around the box, was a red, reticulated plastic python, its orange pattern worn to smudges beneath an insistent child's fingers. I held it up and watched it sway from side to side.

The next layer revealed small colour photos with rounded edges, their surfaces textured like old wallpaper. Oz as a child in a German apartment sitting in the lap of his mother, a beautiful Turkish woman with a mass of black hair. She was wearing a forest-green polo neck, sitting in front of a table laid for dinner with a white saucepan decorated with brown and orange flowers. She was laughing like he laughed, her teeth a blur of white in the old picture. There was a photo of him as a toddler surrounded by sisters, the eldest, a girl with plaited pigtails and corduroy dungarees, kissing him on his fat cheek. Another photo showed him taking a flaky morsel of pastry from the hands of an old woman, in another he and his brother sat in a boat made of sand on a Mediterranean beach, their terrycloth nappies heavy with salt water.

A padded, red leather case popped open like a purse to reveal facing black-and-white portraits of his mother and his father, the whites of their eyes retouched, the name of an Istanbul photo studio stamped elegantly in the corner of each. Tucked between the pictures was a yellowed funeral notice in Turkish with his mother's name, Ela Özemir, and her dates: 1943–1978. Oz, I worked out, would have been ten, she thirty-five.

I lay back against the old top-loading washing machine that had once rattled about in our bathroom, and thought about how lucky I'd been to know him. Each fragment of his real life had been physically painful to open, to weigh in my fingers. I wished I'd known him for all of those years and I despaired for all the time in the past and all the time in the future that I would be without him. It was unbearable. And yet the box didn't reveal anything new to me. It just showed me that other people had loved him, and that made me feel less alone.

I held up the only paper that didn't fit. It was an olive-green library card for the East German Military Library for someone called Eckhardt Pietsch. It had been issued in Neuenhagen in 1965, before Oz was born. I put the library card in my pocket, and the rest I carefully packed back into the box and took up to my room to hide beneath my bed. Outside my open window a blackbird sang, unheard of so late in the year, and in the courtyard I heard Frau von Hildendorf laughing with her famous friend, a warm nostalgic cackle.

Thirty-Seven

The box didn't help me find Oz. I had no way of getting in touch with him. I took the train to Bonn that October hoping that he or someone who knew him would find me. I knew how absurd it was, but I had to do something. I told my parents I was visiting Petra and spent two days sitting on benches near government buildings as golden leaves rattled past me on the loam-black footpaths. In the evening, I wandered past restaurants and cafés, starting whenever I saw someone with black hair, terrified of finding Oz with another man, imagining a clone of myself, but more attractive, funnier, a better spy.

At night I slept on a bench by the Rhine, shivering and waking every time a drunk passed or a police siren screamed, but I never saw him. I caught a cold and hitchhiked home, snivelling and staring out at the autumnal East German trees on the transit road, realising that the shoe box was a revelation, but also a farewell, and that I had no idea what I was going to do next. I was frightened and heartbroken.

I spent a long time thinking about the library ticket. I kept it on me at all times, taking it out of my trouser pocket when I was in my bedroom or on the toilet, scanning it for meaning. Neuenhagen, I discovered at the library, was a small

314

town near Berlin in East Germany. There was a military base there, as the ticket suggested, but there didn't seem to be any obvious link to Oz. I found a few famous Pietsches in the *Brockhaus Enzyklopädie* – a newspaper publisher, a resistance fighter, a racing driver – but no Eckhardt Pietsch. It could have been something from Oz's work that had got caught up in the other ephemera, but it had all been so carefully sorted. Then I thought about the story he had told me about 'Axel', the red-headed Stasi officer with polio who'd been abandoned by his parents and who we had thought was Tobias. When the card was issued, Tobias would've been no older than five and far too young to be using a military library – I guessed that this was why Oz had included it. A final admission that in this he was wrong. Maybe in his guilt Oz felt it important to do Tobias a good turn. In a way, it was the perfect outcome: 'Axel' was real, Oz had worked for the BND, but Tobias wasn't the man they were looking for. I was glad that I'd been right about Tobias, but also miserable precisely because it did relate to my and Oz's story, was part of our shared history, and wasn't a key to his whereabouts.

Durham wrote to say that I could start university in January and I threw myself into the reading, enjoying having something to occupy my mind, but also feeling that this was fair punishment for what I'd done to my family and Maike over the summer holidays.

Things with Mum couldn't go back to the way they were, but they had improved a lot. Mum and Dad seemed close and happy and she was very conscientious with me, tactfully asking about the things that she knew were important to me: my friends and my reading for university. She didn't mention Tobias and neither did I, and she only mentioned Oz once, when I found her sitting in the living room with her legs pulled up, a battered copy of *Our Mutual Friend* on the arm of the chair. She was biting her knuckle and staring at the floor.

'You OK?' I said.

She smiled. It was the first time in a long time that I'd invited intimacy rather than tolerated it.

'I was thinking about your friend, actually.'

'Which one?' I said, though I knew by the microscopic pause before the word 'friend' which friend she was talking about.

'Osman,' she said. 'I think about him sometimes. I hope he's OK.'

'Me too,' I managed.

*

At the beginning of November we were invited to the Guy Fawkes Night dance at the British Military Base. I'd been reluctant to go, but had been won over by Dad's pleading on behalf of my mum, both of them knowing that I rarely had any other plans now my friends were gone.

In her excitement at the prospect of us going out together as a family, Mum made dinner early and then shooed us into our rooms to get changed. When we re-emerged dressed and gelled, there was still an hour before we had to leave.

'Can I watch telly?' Martin said.

'No, don't, Martin,' Mum said, distressed. 'We'll just talk. Let's have a drink.'

She took a bottle of *Sekt* from the fridge, and said, 'Let's have a glass. Why don't we all have a glass? Martin's fourteen – that's old enough for a glass.'

We shrugged our approval and Dad gathered the *Sekt* glasses from the cabinet. 'When we were in France I saw five-year-olds drinking wine with dinner,' he said.

'We also saw a man with a smoking monkey,' said Martin,

and we all laughed. Mum popped the cork, poured it frothing into our glasses, and we clinked them together.

'Let's listen to some music,' Mum said, and turned on the hi-fi. A thudding beat started to throb out of the speakers, a song that I'd heard countless times over the summer on roofs, in bars, in clubs and at the lakes.

'What's this?' Mum said.

'I don't know. It's not mine,' said Martin.

'It's the radio,' I said.

'Is this what the kids are listening to now?' Mum said.

'Not me,' said Martin.

'Ralf?'

I shrugged. 'I've heard it, but . . .'

'At the disco?'

I smiled and nodded. 'At the disco.'

Mum started to dance, biting her bottom lip and throwing out her arms in awkward staccato movements.

'Mum, don't,' said Martin.

But Mum frowned and started to wave her hips, saying, 'Come on, guys. If this is what's "cool" now, let's get down to it, like a family.'

We started laughing and she pulled Dad to his feet and he began to move too in jerking, flicking rhythms. Martin and I laughed so much that our bellies hurt. In his uncontrollable giggling, Martin farted, and this sent us all into howling paroxysms.

The drive to the party was spent recalling the dancing and the fart, and was accompanied by new outbursts of laughter.

'Your father was actually a very good dancer, back in the day,' Mum said. 'When he still had sideburns.'

We laughed at this. There was a black-and-white picture of them just after they'd met, my father's hair already greying at twenty, that made Martin and me particularly hysterical. I looked at my father and wondered if I would also start greying prematurely. My dad caught my eye in the rear-view mirror and winked.

The car slid onto the motorway and I watched Dad's eyes and nose in the rectangle of the rear-view mirror, watched the light of the streetlamps skim rhythmically across his head like the light of a photocopier – chin to forehead, chin to forehead – turning his white hair orange in rhythmic bursts.

My skin began to tingle.

There weren't any colour photographs of his childhood. The few pictures we had of him were all black-and-white.

My throat felt tight as I said, 'What colour were Dad's sideburns?'

Dad's eyes flicked back to mine in the mirror as my mother laughed and said, 'Oh, still squirrel-red back then. Grandad used to call us the ginger nuts.'

She misunderstood my silence and reached round to playfully slap my leg. 'Are you worried about your hair? Oh, Ralf! Doesn't greyness go down the mother's side? Or is that baldness?'

What did I really know about my father's youth, I thought, other than tall tales about my grandfather? I thought about the richness with which my mother and Beate talked about their past lives. Dad's childhood in Hessen was always re-created in repeated stories and cultural facts, like the apple-wine glass. Wasn't this just Dad, though? Wasn't this just the way he related to the world? A bit dry. A bit uptight.

The indicator stopped clicking.

What was I saying? That my father had invented his youth? Had lied to us about it? That he had been accessing Mum's files? What would that mean? That he was really East

German? That he was a spy? My ears burned. Dad reached across to Mum and took her hand in his. At the corners of his pale lips, the same colour as the skin on his face, there was the hint of a forced smile.

'Dad?'

His eyes locked onto mine again in the mirror.

'Do you know someone called Eckhardt Pietsch?' I said, repeating the name I'd read on the library card that Oz had left for me.

His eyes didn't change, but that was the giveaway. He didn't react at all, just stared at me, immobile.

'Who's Eckhardt Pietsch?' said Mum.

I waited, but Dad didn't answer. The red light of someone's brakes flashed and his eyes switched back to the road.

'I found his library card in an old box. I thought maybe it was someone Dad used to know,' I said, turning away to the road, my skin cold and clammy like a dead thing's. 'But maybe I got the name wrong.'

*

The dance was in a brick-built mess building, part of the British Army barracks behind our school. Because there was nowhere on the neat military lawns to build a proper bonfire, a brazier had been lit on the concrete terrace in front of the building, and it flickered like a fire at a medieval castle gate. The flames lit the edge of the surrounding lawn and the dark soil of the flowerbeds, stripped of their summer annuals, and our faces as we stood waiting to go in, making us look like conspirators lining up to be hanged in the night.

My old headmaster was standing in the low foyer with his wife to welcome the guests; a short queue of families had built up hoping to ingratiate themselves. I tried to hang back, planning to run home in the dark when I had the chance, but my father opened out his arm to guide me between him and my mother. Was he going to do something to me now that I knew? I was beset with a crushing panic as if I was being pulled towards a truth that I didn't want to acknowledge, like a dog dragged to look at its own mess. I watched my father's face bathed in the orange glow, looked at his neat moustache and large metal glasses, the pressed collar of his shirt. It was impossible to imagine him betraying anyone, but, I supposed, that would make him the perfect traitor. It was Oz that was the terrible spy, and me. It was we two who had failed.

As my mother reached the headmaster's wife and they said their hellos, my father, close to my ear, muttered, 'Ralf. You've got the wrong end of the stick.'

I pulled my hand into a fist to stop it trembling and didn't answer him, only opening it to shake my old headmaster's hand and talk vaguely about my good grades and Durham University for as briefly as was polite.

The moment I was clear of him, I pushed into the wide hall, which smelt faintly of canteen food, cigarettes and spilled beer. Inside, the partygoers hadn't yet filled the dancefloor and the battered lines marking the bounds of basketball, net-ball and badminton games were still visible on the parquet, which was peppered with the tiny dents of dropped cutlery and thrashed with spinning disco lights. On the strip of rough green carpet encircling the dancefloor, the guests, inured to the Stock, Aitken and Waterman hits pumping out of the tall speakers by the DJ's table, milled around paper-covered trestle tables strewn with rolled ham slices, curling sandwiches, and cheese-and-pineapple hedgehogs. I pushed through the crowds at the edge of the room towards the fire exit at the back, but as I reached it Dad stepped in front of me.

'Do you want to go outside and have a chat, Ralfi?' he said.

'I don't think we have anything to talk about,' I said, afraid of him, but also aware of a mounting rage. In that moment, it wasn't the spying or the communism or even the lying, really, that made me so furious, it was what a fool he'd made me feel.

'No,' he said, nodding meaningfully. 'We won't talk about any of this. Not ever.'

'That's not what I said.'

I abandoned the fire exit and turned to the buffet table. I ate a cocktail sausage, chewing on the stick that had been stuck through it, feeling sweat patches forming on my shirt beneath my coat. When Dad didn't come after me, I turned and saw that he had been caught by my mother's old boss, the head of the military hospital. He was chatting to him with his hands pushed casually into his chinos as if nothing had happened. He didn't look at me, but I could see that he had positioned himself in such a way as to keep me in his peripheral vision.

I looked towards the main door – I could definitely run faster than my dad once I got onto the drive that led down to the gates. But where was I going to go? And then I realised that if Dad was working for the Stasi, he probably knew where Oz was.

The DJ started playing 'Surfin' USA' by the Beach Boys and the floor filled with parents attracted by the easy-listening pop of their youth. A gummy woman with a crown of bright platinum hair and a pink-and-black polka-dot dress screamed with laughter, held her nose and shimmied to the floor, where she lost her footing and rolled drunkenly onto her side.

Mum had joined my dad and they were talking to her boss together. I ladled myself two plastic cups of punch and took them over to my parents. My mum smiled and waved the cup away, so I gave one to my dad and leant in to say, beneath the jangling pop music, 'Where is he?'

He put a hand on my waist and said, 'Ralfi, we're really sad about your friend.'

'Is he in jail?'

'Ralf,' he said. 'Do you want me to take you home?'

'What would happen to me then?'

'Happen to you? *Mein Gott!* Ralf!'

The disco lights spun across his face, turquoise, red, green, yellow, tumbling over one another. We heard a whoop. Mum had begun to dance with the woman in the polka-dot dress, a glass of Pimm's sloshing in her hand. Emboldened, more men and women began to edge onto the dancefloor.

My father started swaying to the music and began to stare at Mum, looking for a way into the circle of dancers she had gathered around herself, the tinned mixed fruit swaying in the plastic cup I'd handed him.

'I know about the children's home,' I said, recalling Axel's story. Mum looked over at us and winked, so I started to move in sync with my father so that she didn't worry about us and cut in. 'I know about your mother. That's why you did it, isn't it? Because she abandoned you?'

For the first time he seemed, if not angry, then at least confused.

'I don't know what bits and pieces you might have picked up from your friend, but—'

'You had polio. You don't know who your dad is. You have a sister. Where's she? I know that your mum gave you up because she didn't want you.'

He shook his head insistently. 'No,' he said.

'Where is he?' I said. 'Just tell me where Oz is and I'll drop it. I'll leave.'

322

'Why would I want that?' he said, bemused.

The DJ started playing 'Twist and Shout' and the British men and women who were too embarrassed to dance freestyle cheered and joined us on the floor, awkwardly mimicking the moves of the more proficient dancers.

Dad tried to twist away from me, but I followed him, saying, 'Did you make up Opa?' Someone bumped into me and fruit punch sloshed onto the back of my hand.

'He . . . ' I was desperate to make him scream at me, to make him burst into tears and tear at his hair, but I had to make do with him shaking his head and being lost for words. That was something, at least. I'd never seen him lost for words.

'You made him a war hero,' I said, thinking that if he lost his temper then he might reveal some nugget that would lead me back to Oz. 'It's so sad.' And although I said it to goad him, I suddenly felt wretched at the loss of my imaginary grandfather. I felt as if everything that had held me fast in the world was falling away like mooring ropes pinging from an airship.

'Don't,' my father said hoarsely as he twisted up and twisted down, looking at my mother for help. But she was too absorbed in the dance, dropping to the floor back-to-back with the polka-dot woman.

'Who are those photos of? The ones hanging all over the house? No wonder he looks nothing like me. Are we even your children?'

He stopped dancing and stood dumbly as the crowd moved around us. 'Of course you're my children!' he hissed.

'We won't be once I tell Mum who you really are.'

'You think your mother doesn't know?'

She bumped into us and cackled. I let my drink drop to the floor. It splashed against someone's trousers, but they didn't notice, and an overweight woman danced backwards and crushed the cup beneath a heavy heel.

I pushed through the crowd trying to get out of the building, but Dad caught me under the arm and led me into the empty foyer. The inner doors swung shut and muffled the music and a cold wind pushed at the wired safety glass and brown-stained wood of the outer doors. I stared at my father's grey leather shoes and the green carpet tiles beneath them.

'Who are you?' I said. The space was echoless.

'Who am I? Who are you? Who are any of us really?'

'You're going to defend yourself with philosophical platitudes?'

'Defend myself?' he said, apparently astonished. 'You of all people must understand what I've done. After Oz. After what you did.'

My mouth tasted sour and the air was filled with the smell of tropical fruit juice, in the cup still in my Dad's hand, splashed onto my skin and clothes. 'That's completely different,' I said.

'How?'

'I did it for the West.'

'That's not why you did it, Ralfi. You were in love.' I looked up at his face. He looked so boundlessly loving, his eyes glistening, his mouth stretched into a comforting, understanding smile. 'We're the only honest ones, Ralf, because we can see both sides, we live with the hypocrisy, we have to.'

'He loves me.'

'Of course he loves you. You're our wonderful Ralf,' he said with pride. 'You're easy to love. Like your mother. Don't doubt how much I love you. Don't doubt how much I love her. I was besotted with her, from the moment I saw her photograph in that file.'

'"In that file"? Fuck!' I said.

The music cut off and a heavy voice started speaking over the microphone. A cheer went up and people pulled on their coats and moved towards us. Martin pushed the door open. 'What are you two doing?' he said, wrapping his scarf round his neck. 'The fireworks are starting.'

Unlike a Berlin New Year's, where an unruly barrage of rockets is fired from the hands of drunks and children, filling the air with throbbing bangs and choking gunpowder smoke, the Guy Fawkes Night fireworks at the British barracks were lit in careful succession by soldiers and school teachers and exploded in a complementary display of pops and sparks. We stood on the grass in the middle of the expansive lawns and watched the black sky fill with electric sprays of blue and white, cascading down like the spokes of umbrellas, and listened to the dejected whines from a chorus of Roman candles. My father stood behind me holding my shoulders.

'How long were you following me?' I said over the bangs.

'We were following him.'

'Why didn't you stop it?'

'I did.'

The wind roared and the fire in the distant brazier flickered and bloomed as it drank up the gust. Three rockets thunked into the sky and exploded in lilac sparks followed by delayed bangs that thundered off the straight brick surfaces of the mess hall. I shivered as I gradually sewed my father into everything that had happened that summer. 'The photographs. How could you . . . ?' I muttered.

'I would do anything to protect my family. And my country. To protect you, Ralf.'

'How is taking . . . those sort of pictures of . . . of your son . . . How is that . . . ?'

325

A Catherine wheel began to spin, spraying out green and blue sparks like peacock feathers and emitting a high surging cry.

'It was very serious. Your friend was trying to expose us. Think of our family, Ralf. It had to be drastic. I made sure that you weren't identifiable. And it worked. Oz is gone, you're here. It worked perfectly.'

'The bulbs too,' I said. 'The clinic? He really was drugged when he came to ours, then.'

'As I said, it worked.'

'Where is he?'

As if he'd done me a favour, he said, 'This is West Berlin, Ralf. He's free to come and go as he pleases. We didn't need to put him anywhere, we just needed to make sure no one cared where he was.'

I turned and looked at him. A large chrysanthemum rocket burst behind his head.

'He loves me,' I said again.

'We all love you, Ralf.'

I broke away from the crowd. Dad called my name, but he didn't stop me. I walked to the gates, the grass beneath me flashing blue, green, pink and orange. As I neared the sentry boxes one of the soldiers frowned at me, surprised I suppose that I was leaving in the middle of the display. He opened his mouth to say something, but I couldn't bear to hear it. I ran past him and once I'd started running I couldn't stop. I ran through the black streets in my good yellow polyester shirt, through Charlottenburg, through the park and all the way home to Windscheidstraße.

Thirty-Eight

I ran up the stairs to our apartment and unlocked the door with shaking hands. The phone was ringing. I stopped in the black hallway. I had planned to grab some things and leave that night and I was afraid it was Dad calling to see if I'd come home. But it could also have been Oz, knowing somehow what had happened, coming to rescue me, so I ran to the kitchen and picked up the phone, putting the cold receiver to my ear.

'Hello,' came a voice. I fingered the loops of the cable like a rosary. 'Hello? It's Maike Willert, is anyone there?'

'Maike?' I said, unsure whether it was a ploy.

'Ralf? Is that you?'

'I'm here,' I said in a half-whisper, though there was no reason to whisper now. 'It's me.'

'Thank God,' she said. 'I was afraid I wasn't going to be able to get hold of you. I'm in Berlin.'

'Berlin? Is everything OK?'

'No,' she said. 'Mum's died.'

She moved her head and I heard the plastic creak of her handset. 'Shit,' I said. 'I'm so sorry, Maike.'

'I didn't know what to do before, when my sister called. The whole way down on the train I was a mess. I kept having

327

to go to the toilet to throw up. But now' – a police car passed nearby on Kantstraße and the objects in the kitchen took shape in the dim light – 'now I'm just tired.'

'What can I do?' I said.

'Come on Thursday. It's just small – not even a service, really. She wanted to be cremated. It'll be in Ruhleben. Petra and Stefan are coming.'

'They've come back for the funeral?'

'Stefan was already here, so he's staying an extra few days. But, yes, Petra came specially.'

'They're good friends.'

'Yes,' she said. 'Can you come though? I'd like it if you did.'

'Of course. Of course I'll come.'

I packed my things and the only smart clothes I had and cycled to Stefan's. At every junction I heard the car braking behind me and waited for the sound of the door opening and then the footsteps of the man with the combover or my father coming up from behind. But each time the lights changed to green and I cycled on.

I couldn't bear to tell Stefan what had happened that night. I said I was upset and exhausted because of Maike's mum. Whether he believed me or not, he let me go to bed straight away, and I slept fitfully through the night, waking at every creak and crack, expecting my father to come through the door at any moment and drag me out.

He didn't come though, and early on Thursday morning Stefan and I dressed in suits and pulled our denim jackets on over them – his blue, mine white. The only other jackets we owned were the bright Gore-tex ones we wore on field trips, and they didn't seem appropriate.

I shaved using Stefan's razor and wondered where I'd go once the funeral was over. I would hitchhike to Stuttgart with

Petra, I decided, and disappear for a while. I felt sad, thinking about leaving Martin with them, but I knew he would be happier in his ignorance. I would've been happier too.

Petra was waiting on the tarmac driveway that led up to the crematorium, a grey breeze-block building with a green copper roof, surrounded by autumn trees, still covered in a flurry of green, brown and yellow. She stood beneath a lollipop-shaped lamp wearing a beautifully cut skirt-suit, looking grown-up and elegant. I saw how she would look as an adult and it brought tears to my eyes.

'You look lovely,' I said.

'I stole it from Mum's cupboard. It's not mine.' She squeezed me.

We waited, unsure what to do next, but then Maike shouted from the building. She was already there, waving from the door.

We embraced her. Her cheeks were warm and wet with tears. She led us into a room laid out like a chapel, but with a terracotta floor, concrete walls and an inoffensive but inappropriate Sixties mural, showing factories with smoking chimney stacks and giant industrial wheels.

At the front of the room, by a wall of glass that looked out onto the grounds, was a simple coffin, light varnished pine like children's furniture, reflecting the white glare of the lights on the ceiling.

There were perhaps ten other mourners who smiled at us in a friendly way. A few dabbed at their eyes. Maike left us to sit with her father and sisters, all tall like her, their eyes red from crying.

A Catholic priest said some words about Maike's mother. I hadn't known she used to work as a teacher. I found it devastating hearing about her early life. As an invalid, she had always seemed to me to be a different species, not of this world, but she had been a young teacher with a family, had fallen in love and moved to West Berlin from Bochum to make a life for herself here. After the priest spoke, there were prayers. I only knew the words to the English prayers we'd been taught at school, but murmured along and said the Amens.

From films I'd seen, I expected the coffin to disappear into the floor, but it didn't. We just left it there, shuffling out into the foyer, where two pleasant-looking men with white hair were waiting to wheel it away again.

'You must be Ralf,' said Maike's father. He shook my hand warmly. He was tall and round, with Maike's wide brown eyes. His broad gap-toothed smile made him attractive, despite his pot belly and shining bald patch. 'I'm sad we never met,' he said. 'And sad about you and Maike. You made her very happy. I think you were good for each other.'

'Yes,' I tried to say. 'I'm sad too,' but the 'sad' died and I started crying. I felt so ashamed and gripped my face with one hand.

'There, there,' he said, putting his heavy hand on my back and rubbing it briskly. 'It's a sad day. There's no question about that. Sad for everyone.'

*

Maike, Stefan, Petra and I stood outside under the bright white November sky. Magpies cackled on the roof of the crematorium. One skittered down, flashing the iridescent blue of its black wings.

'We're going to Der Gammler for a few drinks. Dad too and my sisters,' Maike said. 'Come along.'

We all nodded our assent.

'Hey, Ralf,' said Stefan, 'is that your mum?'

We turned and saw her standing among the silver birches at the side of the car park, a bed of ochre leaves at her feet that made the red of her hair burn orange.

'I'll meet you at the bar,' I said.

Thirty-Nine

In the cemetery, we found an iron bench strung with glassy raindrops, which we wiped off with our bare hands, and sat down side by side, our cold fingers pushed into our coat pockets. Mum was wearing a long beige trench coat with wide shoulder pads, its hem reaching down to her ankles. The air smelt of pine needles and earth.

'I can't ever come back,' I said.

'That's very dramatic, Ralf.'

'Is it? I think my parents are committing treason. Or did I miss something?'

A crow cawed high up in a dark copper beech. A surge of wind brought a rush of ginkgo leaves with it, a cascade of pale gold keys turning over in the grey air.

'It's never that simple.'

'Isn't it frightening how simple it is?'

Mum stared across gravestones old and new, battered crosses and armless angels, their faces streaked green and black with lichen and smog.

'There are many small steps to the kinds of actions that seem most dramatic. No one gets up one morning and says, today I'm going to become a spy.'

'But he made you.'

'He didn't make me, Ralf.'

'He targeted you, because of your job.'

'No,' she said vehemently. Then after a pause: 'Well, yes to begin with. I was a student still and doing secretarial work for Daddy at Gatow. I suppose that's why he found me to begin with. But we fell in love very quickly and when he asked me to take a few files ... Well ... You know how it is.'

I didn't respond to this.

'So you're a communist?'

'Yes,' she said, 'in spirit, I suppose.'

I thought about Gran and Grandad and Bournemouth, his liver spots, his bungalow, the soft biscuits and spongy lawn where Martin and I played swingball. We had last visited two years before, when Grandad took us to the beach and we waded into the cold sea and ate ice cream with desiccated coconut sandwiched between brittle wafers shaped like oyster shells. Dad surprised us with his love of cheap attractions, riding carousels and waltzers at the pier, feeding twopenny coins into the coin pusher and beating Martin at round after round of *Street Fighter*, heat radiating from our burnt shoulders. When it started to rain, Grandad bought us matching hooded ponchos of thin yellow plastic, and we trudged home like a bright coven of witches, water dripping into our sandals. It wasn't how I imagined communists lived with the people they were betraying.

'So your practice – it's just a cover for getting compromising material to blackmail people?'

'No,' Mum said. 'Not at all. I love my work.'

'But you do leak what your patients tell you to the Stasi?'

'Well ...' she said, repositioning herself on the bench and tightening her coat. 'Your father has access to it. I don't get involved in any of that. He may not even use the files any more.'

'You don't believe that.'

She shivered and looked down at her knees. 'After I qualified, I worked in a clinic, but kept doing a bit of office work for Daddy, so still had access. But then someone at the Army base asked me if I'd privately see a major and his wife for couples' counselling. And of course your father was thrilled. And then that French ambassador got in touch and then ... Well, I got a bit of a name for myself. It's been very successful.'

'Not for all the people whose secrets you've been selling.'

'I haven't sold anything!' my mum cried. 'I don't get paid.'

'But Dad must get supported by the East.'

'I mean ...' She shrugged vaguely.

'The flat that apparently belonged to our non-existent grandparents. I assume they pay for that?'

'We own it. It's in our name.'

'But that's not even a real name, is it?'

'Legally,' she said weakly.

'And what about us?' I said. 'What about Martin and me?'

'What about you?'

'You put us in danger.'

'You've put us in more danger than we ever put you in.'

'Fuck you,' I said. 'That's different.'

Mum held up an appealing hand. 'Let's not ... I would never purposely put you in danger, Ralf, neither would your father. But we were already doing ... *it* when I got pregnant. The choice was that way round; did we keep you or not? And then once we had you, it didn't seem to make much difference having Martin.' The wind came again and three pigeons took flight, twisting in the air, and landing on the stout crematorium chimney. 'Anyway, I love being a mother, and if I'd had to whisk you all off to the East or hand in your father to save you, I'd have done it. I'd have made it work.'

'You would shop Dad for us?'

'For you two? Of course,' Mum said. 'Don't tell him, though.'

I smiled involuntarily, but shook it off. 'But how could you stay with him?' I said. 'After you found out he'd been lying to you?'

Mum released a short, contemplative sigh. 'It didn't come out like that. It wasn't like I suddenly found his gun.'

'Does he have a gun?'

'No, of course not. I mean, I don't think so.' She frowned. 'No, it came out in bits. First that he was a communist, or sympathetic. I found it a bit odd that he was so committed, but then he talked about it, explained the thinking, told me about all the fascists still in power here. I mean, it's not like at home. There are real Nazis running companies! Then at some point I knew he was attached to the Communist Party and that the pharmacy was a place where people met. Then he asked if he could take a look at one of the files at the hospital. That was odd, but by then I loved him. When it was all out on the table, well ...' She shrugged. 'I was sympathetic to socialism, he knew that, and he promised me it wasn't the sort of thing that was going to get anyone killed. Exactly the opposite, in fact; it was to ensure peace. And I barely have anything to do with it. I'm just turning a blind eye.' She squinted into the bright sky.

I shook my head; she was making it all sound so banal. 'Mum,' I said, 'Dad was pretending to be someone he wasn't.'

'No, he was just pretending to have a different name and identity.'

I laughed in disbelief. 'That's the same thing.'

'No it's not.'

'He pretended to be a West German pharmacist and he's an East German spy.'

'But he is a West German pharmacist.'

'You just said he was a spy.'

'He is, but he's also a qualified pharmacist who works in West Berlin.'

'I can't believe you're splitting hairs.'

'I'm not splitting hairs, Ralf. He does that job. He's done that job every day for the last twenty years. His customers like him, he helps support his family. All of those things really happened, they're not imaginary. Of course, there are layers to his life, but that's true of anyone. We don't know anyone completely. What's real is what people say and what they do. He's been a good husband, a good father to you and Martin. That's not changed. That's real.'

'But when you met him he was playing a part. He'd found out exactly what you liked, the sort of man you wanted, and he became it.'

'Well, I don't know about that.'

'Of course he did.'

Mum shook her head. 'But Ralf, he really is like that. He really does like cycling. He really does like separating out all the different bits of *Die Zeit*. He really does like Scrabble and books and ... We love each other. We always have.'

'You sound so naive,' I said.

'Don't tell me I'm being naive. Especially after what you've been up to for the last few months.'

I folded my arms across my chest. 'I can't believe you knew everything the whole time. All the lying ... ' I shook my head. 'It makes me feel sick.'

'We didn't know everything,' Mum said. 'Just the broad strokes.'

'Dad took pictures of me and Oz ... '

Mum sighed. 'He had them taken. Someone else did that.

And I didn't know anything about that. He's very upset about it. No one . . . saw anything. That was all done . . . ' She waved her hand, implying somewhere far away. She pulled her coat tighter and nudged along the bench so that our hips were touching. 'We all invent ourselves, Ralf. Whoever we are.'

'Do you?'

'Of course. I haven't always . . . you know I haven't been as good a wife as I could've been.'

I felt she was leaving a gap for me to chastise her. 'Why Tobias?' I said.

'Oh Ralf,' she said, her eyes glistening. 'He's a sweet man.'

'Sweet enough to destroy his neighbour's family.'

She let this comment go. 'I could list off the reasons,' she said. 'He made me feel desirable, he was very romantic . . . But really you don't think these things through in the moment. And when the advance comes, submitting is like . . . Well, like a kiss. A kiss is easy. And then once you've kissed someone . . . It's all very silly and meaningless. It shouldn't be as terrifying and destructive as it is.'

'Love?' I said.

She shook her head. 'That wasn't love.'

It still made me feel nauseous, this talk of romance and desire and submission. I wonder if the children of good parents retain the myth that their mothers and fathers are not hot-blooded creatures like themselves, do not form childish crushes, do not masturbate, are not easily flattered and afraid of dying.

'Why did you do it?' she said.

I imagined the information about the Army officer going to Oz, to his handler, to some faceless official, skipping through West Berlin like a dry leaf lifted by the wind.

'I was in love,' I said. 'I was angry. About you.'

Mum nodded.

'And I suppose I couldn't really believe that anything I did would actually matter that much. It's like smoking or having unprotected sex. You've been told what the consequences are, but they seem so ... I don't know, alien. So far away. They don't seem to have anything to do with you.'

Mum folded her hands in her lap. 'Have you been having sex without protection, Ralf? I mean, proper sex.'

'Mum, it was just a simile.'

'Well?' she said.

The tips of my ears burned.

'Ralf Dörsam, you've gone beetroot!'

'Mum, I'm not ... Jesus. Of course I ... I don't want to talk about it.'

'Have you heard of AIDS? It comes from gay men and Africa.'

'He's not African.'

'Where do you think Turkey is?'

'Asia. And Europe. And he's not even from Turkey. He's from Berlin. And I don't think he's riddled with AIDS.'

'Don't say "riddled". You know Rock Hudson died of AIDS.'

'I don't know who that is,' I said. 'And I don't know why we're talking about it.'

The bells of West Berlin's brick and concrete churches began to sound and a double-decker roared past behind a bank of oaks.

'Ralf, I want you to come back home with me,' she said.

'I don't want to come back home. I can't face him.'

'Where are you going to go?'

'I don't know. Stay with Stefan, then get away from Berlin. Then go to Durham in January. Then I'll be out of your hair.'

'Out of my hair! What's that going to achieve?'

'I don't know. There's just something … honest about it.'

Mum sat up and tucked her feet beneath the bench. 'Ralf, whether you go to university or India or wherever you go, soon you'll be gone for good. I'll never have you both around again. Do you know how awful that is for a mother? You're not going to be living with us for the rest of your life.'

'I can't see how—'

'And with Honecker gone in the East, and these protests in Leipzig, I don't know …' Her voice broke. She was crying. 'I don't know what's going to happen if …'

'Dad said it's not going to change anything.'

'Your dad's stubborn!' she shouted. 'I'm sorry.' She found my hand and held it. Hers was cold and dry like a pebble. 'I'm sorry. Your father's very stubborn, and he's often right, but it just feels like sixty-eight again, like things are in motion and we don't know what's going to happen next. And whatever that is, I want you to be home with us.'

'I don't know if I can do that.'

'Oh, Ralf,' Mum said, resting her chin on her chest, tears washing away her eyeliner. 'What about lunch tomorrow? Could you come back for that? Then we'll see.' She squeezed my hand.

'I doubt it,' I said. 'But I'll think about it.'

We sat a little longer holding hands, not speaking, until I leant in and hugged her. I left her on the bench and walked back to the bus stop, passing a section of new gravestones in shockingly glossy marble, jet-black, with gold lettering. The chimney of the crematorium, built stout so as not to be reminiscent of Auschwitz or Birkenau, began to smoke. Was there no other way of doing it, I thought, wondering if it was already Maike's mother being burnt beneath my feet and belched out black into the white sky. I supposed not.

Forty

Maike's family had drifted away one by one and left the four of us at the bar with Peter. 'It's like old times,' he said. We toasted Maike's mother and talked about what we thought of as our new lives, not understanding that the changes we were experiencing were small compared with the great shifts that would remake our lives over and over again.

I kept the events of the past week to myself, telling instead funny stories about the customers in the outdoor clothing shop where I still worked. It made me feel sad and alone that the few weeks we had all been apart had generated so many more secrets to keep. They didn't ask about Oz, but all gave me loaded, sympathetic glances and squeezes whenever sex and relationships came up. Maike said she loved university, the lectures, her new friends, all of it. It was clear that she was thriving away from us, and although it made me sad, I was also happy for her.

Petra was having a harder time, but had met a couple of 'weirdos' – 'Thank God,' she said – and 'an absolute non-starter from the maths department. He's sweet and forces me to talk about my work, but I'm days away from scaring him off.' Stefan said it was fine, it was all fine, but the Dutch girl had changed her mind about monogamy when she met a

Spanish exchange student called Jesus, and Stefan wondered whether he might not in fact have been in love with her after all.

'You never seemed that enthused,' said Petra.

'Yeah,' said Stefan. 'But now I think maybe she was really amazing.'

The door to Der Gammler was shoved open and the stuffed seagull on the ceiling swayed on its cord.

'Turn on the news,' came a woman's voice from the door.

There was a general moan, but the woman said, 'It's the border. It's important. Something's happening.'

'What's happening?' said Peter.

'I want to see it,' the woman said, pushing through to the back of the bar where the small television was balanced on a high plinth for football games. She turned on the TV and it flickered to life.

'Hey,' said Peter, emerging from behind the bar. 'You can't just come in here and ...' But he stopped short when he saw the newsreader and a crowd of tense Germans jostling around one of the border crossings.

'Which side's that?' Petra said, but no one answered. The bar fizzed with low chatter. The sound was on on the telly, but it was too tinny and distant for us to properly hear what was going on. There were shots of nervous East German border guards, then the red-and-white barrier went up and the crowd surged forward. In the room, there was an audible intake of breath.

'Is it open then?' Stefan said.

The bar erupted with chatter and people started paying up, pushing notes into Peter's hand with overgenerous tips so that they could get away.

'We've got to go and see,' said Stefan.

'Do we?' Petra said.

'Of course we do,' said Maike.

'Of course,' I said.

We followed a drift of Berliners up Potsdamer Straße to the Kulturforum, past dazed-looking prostitutes in high heels and leather jackets watching the exodus with folded arms. The night was cold and the road damp and our breath condensed into clouds as we talked.

'If it is open, it'll be shut again before the evening's out,' Maike said.

'But what if this is it?' said Stefan. 'What if it comes down tonight?'

We walked side by side silenced by the magic of what Stefan had said, but it was broken by the low growl of a car, its engine old and very loud. It spluttered towards us and, as it passed, we saw the driver astounded and half-smiling and the passenger, a woman, laughing hysterically.

'It's a Wartburg,' said Maike.

'What's that?' said Petra.

'It's from the East.'

As we made our way to the Wall more cars passed, coming in dribs and drabs: a Lada, a Trabi, a Skoda, more Wartburgs, their engines gurgling like old motorbikes, spitting out thick clouds of metallic-tasting exhaust, their horns tooting, their occupants laughing and waving.

When we reached the Wall, we saw that a crowd had started to gather. We were a little way down from the Brandenburg Gate, and people seemed unsure of what to do, standing in gossipy groups, swigging schnapps and beer and laughing nervously.

With the help of his friend, a man in a black bomber jacket jumped up and gripped the edge of the Wall. We watched him pull himself up and stick his head over.

'What's happening?' Petra shouted, but the man didn't answer. He dropped down and pushed his face to the concrete like he was eavesdropping. When he jumped up again, he kept his head over.

'Careful, Uwe!' someone shouted.

He swung his leg up and mounted the Wall side-on, as if he was riding a horse.

'They're not shooting,' said someone in the crowd. The air filled with camera flashes as the man got to his knees. A van pulled up and the door swung open. A news crew emptied out of it and they trained their bright lights on the man.

'Uwe,' cried his friend from below, reaching up to him. Uwe pulled him up. Other men and women ran to the Wall, shouting and jabbering, their shoes scraping at the graffitied concrete as they scrambled up. When they mounted the Wall they raised their hands in the air and howled like dogs. Below, others kicked at the Wall, someone produced a hammer and started to hit it, eliciting a high clink, clink, clink. The four of us stood gawping. We didn't know what to do.

I heard official voices talking through loudspeakers, but the sound was drowned out by the people on the Wall whistling so loudly that it sounded like the screaming whistles of fireworks at New Year's. Then a jet of water from a cannon on the Eastern side hit Uwe's friend from behind, and he tumbled off the Wall to the ground. A crowd surrounded him and he was helped up, dizzy but unhurt.

The jet of water moved along the Wall and others, now ready for it, jumped free, or dropped to their knees and gripped the Wall when the water hit. When it turned on Uwe, he stumbled but then regained his footing. Slowly he raised his arms, and in the white glare of the floodlights and camera lights, the water sprayed into the air as if it was emanating from him, and then fell down around us all like silver rain. He screamed and we responded by screaming back, whistling and singing, dancing in the falling water as it made puddles on the ground at our feet.

The water cut out and we ran at the Wall. Someone handed me schnapps; I swigged from it and passed it on.

'Let's go to the Gate,' I said. 'I want to see.'

Petra protested, but Stefan took her hand and I took Maike's and we ran together across the park. When we reached the part of the Wall by Brandenburger Tor we sprang up into the sea of hands waiting for us. Stefan was up first and on his feet, screaming. Then I found my footing and, holding on to the crowds either side of me, afraid to fall, I looked into the West at the crowds gathered there, at the cameras and flashes, and saw Oz. He was standing at the edge of the Tiergarten, beneath the bare trees, watching me. I slowly raised my hand to wave. He raised his in return, smiling, benevolent and ghostlike.

I bent my knees to climb down from the Wall, to run to him, but a little shove caused me to shift my foot and put my weight on nothing and I fell awkwardly backwards, hitting my coccyx on the concrete, sliding off the Wall into the East, where I was half caught by other men and women clamouring to get up.

'Ralf!' Stefan shouted.

'I'm fine,' I called back, but I'd landed badly on my ankle and when I tried to get up again, I fell. 'It's fine,' I shouted again when Stefan threatened to come down. 'Just get Oz!' I cried. 'Tell him I'm coming!'

From the top of the Wall, Stefan cupped a hand round his ear.

'Oz!' I shouted, but he shook his head.

'I can't hear you!' he mouthed.

I tried to stand and a pain shot up into my calf. I cried out. A middle-aged woman put her hand on my shoulder. 'Wait, wait. If it's broken, you'll make it worse.'

'It's not broken,' I said, trying to stand and falling again. 'Fuck!' I shouted.

'Just give it a second, *junger Mann*,' she said, holding me down.

I nodded, a tear wetting my face, and waited for the pain to subside, terrified that Oz was going to disappear, thinking I hadn't gone back for him.

Someone shouted, 'Monsters!'

I was in the death strip. I thought it would be a mess of deadly barbed wire and broken glass, but it was pristine. The ground was clear, like a car park, with inhumanly tall floodlights towering above. Beyond the flattened ground was a neat watchtower and beyond that curled barbed wire lit white, like crazed chalk-drawn loops, and then the second wall in the East. It was eerily quiet, the screams, whistles and song muffled by the high concrete, and the band of men and women standing on top of the Wall with their backs to me, shouting to the crowds in the West.

I looked at the back of the Wall that had encircled me my whole life and was shocked to see the concrete beautiful in its ungraffitied clarity. On top, the crowd, lit by film cameras and police lights, were silhouetted in front of the pale smoke of their own breath. Around me East German men and women silently clambered onto milk crates and were lifted or pulled up. A few stood triumphant on the Anti-Fascist Protection Barrier; most disappeared over it, not looking back.

'Monsters!' I heard again, and saw in the dark a middle-aged woman, with frizzled hair and gnomey features. 'You monsters!' A shifting barrier of border guards stood with their hands behind their backs and said nothing. 'Don't you understand what you've done? You'll never be forgiven,' she said. 'Never.'

I eased myself up; the pain had subsided a little. 'Lie down,' the middle-aged woman said.

'I can't,' I said. 'I've got to go. There's someone waiting for me.'

'Ralf!' I heard. It was Stefan draped over the Wall, holding out his hands. I limped over to him and scrambled up. The Wall smelt of wet concrete and I felt Stefan's arms on my arms, and strangers' hands helping me down to the ground on the Western side. Around me, East Germans slid down the Wall like raindrops, whole families, their children hastily dressed and sleepy, tearlessly going through the long-dreamed-of motions of escape.

I hobbled into the Tiergarten, to the place where I'd seen Oz, but he was gone and the park was full of revellers and lovers, drinking, crying and kissing.

I shouted his name into the dark – 'Oz!' – and people, thinking I was shouting 'Ost' – East – shouted it back to me in celebration. 'Ost!' they cried 'Ost!' I turned to look for my friends but we'd been separated, so I wandered into the Tiergarten calling Oz's name in the gathering dark until my voice was hoarse and the revellers were distant and forgotten.

Forty-One

At some point that night a bottle of prosecco was pushed into my hand and I wandered the city searching for Oz among the dizzy crowds thronging about the crumbling Wall. As the sky began to brighten, I headed back to our apartment, hoping that he had gone to Windscheidstraße to find me. I was also very drunk and tired and wanted to fall asleep in my own bed and, after everything, I still wanted to make my mother happy. I knew there would be a reckoning with my father, but watching East Berliners stream over the Wall I knew that nothing that he or I had done mattered any more. I knew that we had all been freed.

I unlocked the door to our apartment and went inside. A strip of pale morning sunlight slanted across the parquet and I stood staring at it, feeling the world open up around me.

'Hello?' I said. They must have heard the news, and if they hadn't it was important enough that I could wake them up and tell them. I walked through into the living room and was confronted by my family arranged as if for a society portrait. Dad sat forward in an armchair, his hands clasped together around his car keys, his trousers pulled up revealing his long red socks. Mum sat on the arm of the chair with one leg crossed over the other, wearing her trench coat over a long cornflower-blue skirt that I'd never seen before. She was staring out of the window, the pale light making her eyes impossibly green, like spring moss. Martin sat in front of them on the floor like a child, with his rucksack on, staring at his knees.

'What's going on?' I said. 'Did you see the news?'

'We have to leave,' Dad said.

These words grounded me. Martin and Mum stood up.

'What am I meant to do?' I said, my skin cold and my mouth dry.

'You're coming too, of course,' Mum said, and fished her arm around my head, pulling it into the crook of her neck so that she could kiss my forehead.

'Where are we going?' I said.

'East,' Dad said.

'The Wall's coming down,' I heard Martin saying.

'We've told Martin everything,' Mum said. 'They've broken into the Stasi's offices, Ralf, and it'll only be a matter of time before information starts leaking out.'

'We need to be bold, Ralf,' Dad said. 'Do you understand?'

'I've packed some things for you,' said Mum. 'You've got a couple of minutes to check it and then we'll head off. The car's packed.'

I felt suddenly very sober. 'I need to stay here,' I said. 'I saw Oz.'

'Ralf, you're drunk. He's gone. That's over,' said Dad.

Dizzy and confused, I went into my room, where I found a suitcase on my bed. Without looking inside I closed it and carried it out into the hall. I wanted to be with them for one last car journey, knowing that it would be the end of our old lives, the funeral procession for our eighteen years together in Windscheidstraße 53. I wasn't afraid. I knew that Dad was fooling himself about the resilience of the GDR. When I got out of the car just before the border I would soon see them again, crossing easily into East Berlin through an unmanned checkpoint.

Despite this I couldn't help trying to convince him to abandon our flight. 'Dad, this doesn't make sense,' I said as the car rumbled over the cobbles of our street, 'there isn't any East any more. Or there won't be soon. Why don't we just wait it out?'

'No,' he said. 'This is the end of the Wall, not the end of East Germany. It's a chance. There's a chance for a new more open socialism. It might be our best chance to really make a difference there. As a family.'

'But Dad, you—' I started, exasperated by his naivety, but my mother reached round the seat and squeezed my leg, telling me in that waxing and waning pressure to stop talking, that Dad needed to carry out his escape plan even if it would be rendered meaningless within a few months as East Germany slowly sank to its knees.

I sat back in my seat and stared at my father's desperate eyes as we immediately got tangled up in the crowds. I turned to the stunned faces passing the car's windows and Mum said, 'We shouldn't have come down Yorckstraße. God, how stupid.'

'Be quiet, Pat,' Dad snapped. 'It'll be fine.'

I stared at his red face. I'd never seen him this angry or afraid. Who was he? I thought. Who were we? Traitors, emigrants, West German, East German, British? We were all of these things and none of them, of course. And the trouble was that our history of lies was the only true and stable thing I'd known, however corrupt it was. But it was corrupt, and that was why I kept fingering the door handle, getting ready to leave the moment I felt our final journey had been fully played out.

The buzzing moan of the car's engine fan grew louder and louder as we crawled along in a snake of cars, the beeping horns fighting the cheers of the crowd. The pavement and the road were covered in food wrappers, the mashed orange paper of fireworks and the broken glass of *Sekt* bottles and beer bottles. People squeezed around us, East Germans streaming down the streets, standing in serpentine queues in front of banks, West Germans pushing towards the crumbling holes that appeared in the Wall. A drunk teenager in a leather jacket wearing a plastic red nose slapped the bonnet of the car and whooped.

The traffic loosened on Mehringdamm and we crossed the bridge at Hallesches Tor. I began to feel eerily calm. The last lies had been told. And however frightening the future might be, it would occur in that penetrating winter light that exposes every freckle of your face, picks out every grey hair and fleck of loose skin.

There was a small traffic jam at Checkpoint Charlie. I saw the half-kilometre of traffic in front of us and thought, this is the stretch of time I have to think about my old life and my new life, but I didn't know what to think about any of it. When I forced myself to consider my existence to date, all that emerged were odd snapshots: the bright playing field at my primary school, the synthetic feel of my grey school trousers, the smoothness of the knots in my pine headboard when I touched them in the dark feeling anxious about nuclear bombs as I fell asleep. My friends Petra, Stefan and Maike at the lakeside, the sound of them sleeping around me by the telescopes at the observatory on the hill. My family gathered around the television, the feeling of our grey carpet beneath my bare feet. Was that all I had of them? My family watching television, and this: four terrified people in an Opel Astra?

Someone knocked at Dad's window. The swathes of revellers

350

that had already bumped into the car meant that none of us looked up, until a second knock came, more officious, and a voice muffled by the glass said, 'Can you turn off here please?'

Dad wound down his window. 'What's going on?' he said.

The man bent down to make himself heard. He had greying hair greased into a side parting and when he said, 'Can you turn off here please and pull in behind my colleague?' I heard that he had a Bavarian accent. He fixed me with ice-blue eyes and gave me a brief nod.

We looked into Hedemannstraße and saw a police car with a policewoman standing beside its open door, signalling to them.

'We're going East,' Dad said. 'I thought we didn't need papers any more.'

'We just want to take a look,' Mum said, crouching to see the man's face. 'We just want to look around.'

'Just turn off here,' the man said. 'Just pull in behind my colleague, please.'

Dad wound up the window. His forehead was covered in sweat and I could smell the damp wool of his sports jacket. He looked at the police car and then at the border. The only way he could reach it without being stopped would be to mount the pavement, but it was filled with people. The car jolted forward and for a moment I went cold, thinking he was doing it, that we were going to bump over the kerb and ride over the bodies to freedom. But he jerked the wheel round and parked behind the police car just as he'd been told to.

He turned to Martin and me. His frown dissolved and he smiled at us. '*Jungs*,' he said, and his damp grey eyes searched our faces, trying to take in every detail.

The policewoman signalled to Mum and distantly we heard her say, 'Could you both step out of the car please.'

Martin and I watched them climb out. 'We'll just be a moment,' Mum said.

I clambered forward into the passenger seat, the leather still warm from where she'd been sitting. The policeman opened the rear doors of the police car and Mum and Dad got in. I watched the backs of their heads and listened to the ticking of the car's cooling engine. The Bavarian got into the passenger seat and turned to talk to them.

'Fuck,' I said.

'They're being arrested,' said Martin.

I turned round and held on to the back of the seat. Martin was grey, the colour he went when he was about to be carsick.

'It's going to be fine,' I lied. 'They're probably just doing random checks. I'm sure it'll be fine.'

He shook his head. 'They're being arrested.' Tears rolled down his cheeks. 'I called the police.' His shoulders shook and he looked down at his lap.

'What?' I said. 'When?'

'They were arguing about going. And they sat me down and explained why we had to go, what they'd been doing. What could I do, Ralf?' he said desperately. 'They were spies. They're East German spies.'

'They're our parents.'

'What about my GCSEs? And Cologne?'

'Cologne?'

'With the football team,' he said. 'The tournament. I can't just leave the team.'

'The school football team?'

'I was scared,' said Martin. 'I was scared I didn't know who they really were and you weren't there. And they were going to take us to Moscow.'

'Fuck,' I said, and pushed through the gap between the

seats to sit next to him. He put his head onto my shoulder and sobbed. I rocked him as his moans filled the car. He only stopped when the police came. Then we sat in the back of the police car, Martin taking shuddering breaths as the crowds parted in front of us, and were driven home without our parents.

Forty-Two

Auntie Linda didn't look like our mother, except for her skin, which had the same pattern of heavy freckles, surging up her neck and over her face. She wore leggings, lumpy polo necks in beiges and browns, and large red-framed glasses that gave her an owlish look. Her hair was brown too, and permed. She was calm and quiet with a girlish English voice, but had a habit, when she was thinking, of sticking her hand into the tight curls of her long hair and pushing it dramatically away from her face, as if she had suddenly remembered some terrible error she'd made: leaving the gas on at home or all of the windows open. It reminded me of Oz.

I sat on the kitchen windowsill watching my aunt in this pose, the fingers of one hand in her hair, a wooden spatula in the other.

'Are you OK?' I said.

'Oh, Ralf!' my aunt said. 'I don't know where it goes.'

'The second drawer down,' I said. 'By the dishwasher.'

'That's right. I don't want Pat to come back and find everything in the wrong place.'

I wasn't sure why she kept talking about Mum coming back. We hadn't been given any indication that she would be coming back any time soon. Perhaps it was meant to comfort us. It didn't comfort me.

Auntie Linda was a much better cook than Mum, and the house smelled of richly seasoned meat simmering in the oven. She seemed to do all her cooking in the oven, making pies and bakes and savoury tarts, giving them what appeared to me and Martin to be made-up names and being constantly surprised that we'd never heard of them.

'It's lovely,' Martin would say. 'What is it?'

'It's toad-in-the-hole, Martin,' she'd say, bemused. 'What else could it be?'

The phone rang. My aunt looked at it, the spatula still in her hand.

'It's fine,' I said. 'I'll get it.' I expected every phone call to be Oz, seeking me out again, despite me abandoning him twice over.

It was Stefan. 'I'm coming over,' he said.

'From Hanover?'

'I'm already back. For Christmas.'

'When did you get back?'

'Last night. You free now?'

'Yes,' I said. 'Yes, come over now.'

'You've got to be waiting for me in the street, though.'

'Why?'

'Just wait for me. I'll be half an hour.'

I didn't turn the light on in the staircase, and when I got to the hall I saw a figure standing in the gloom, silhouetted against the darkening blue of the afternoon sky.

'Hello?' I said uncertainly, stopping with my hand on the banister. I hadn't put a coat on and realised at that moment how cold it was.

'Ralf,' said the figure. It was Tobias.

'Oh,' I said, 'it's you. What are you doing there in the dark?'

'Nothing,' he said. 'I just got in.'

I didn't believe him.

'Any news about your parents?'

I supposed he couldn't say 'your mother'.

'No,' I said.

'They won't let you visit them?'

'Yes, we've visited them. At least I did. Martin's still a bit shaken up.'

I'd seen Dad first and then Mum. They were awful days, hours alone in waiting rooms and corridors, acres of polished green linoleum, distant frightening shouts, papers pushed under thick wired glass and high windows, unscalably high.

When I'd reached Mum, she was stoic and kind, turning back all the questions to me and Martin, citing tenuous positives in her incarceration: 'I'm reading so much, Ralf.' But Dad separated from Mum was tearful and ruffled, his hair crazy. There were patches of stubble on his neck that he had missed while shaving. He looked like a sick animal, too ill to care for its own fur.

'I'm sure you must all be shaken up,' Tobias said. 'Were they—?'

'She's fine.'

He nodded. My eyes had adjusted to the dark, and I could make out the glistening whites of his. He was smiling sadly but gratefully.

I didn't want to risk passing him again, so didn't go back for a coat. I waited outside, jumping about to keep warm with my hands in the pockets of my jeans. There was no snow on the ground, but a hard cold seeped out from every surface: the pavement, the lumpy render of the buildings, the black trunks of the trees. In the apartments opposite, coloured lights blinked at the windows, and a plastic Santa Claus climbed the crumbling plaster of one of the balconies.

The dying blue made me think about Mum brushing her hair in the mirror when I was a child. The lights were off and the sky made everything in the room blue: the wooden floor, the walls, the upholstered chair she sat on, the sparks that appeared between the brush and her hair, which was long then. 'Fireflies,' I had said, the pungent smell of static in the air, and Mum had touched her sparkling hair and laughed. In the weeks since she'd gone, I was often assaulted by these forgotten snatches: Mum covering my pillow with a scratchy towel when I was sick; the sound of emery boards on her nails; the softness of her warm abdomen when I pressed my face against it at the side of the pool.

The few times that both Auntie Linda and Martin were out at the same time, I'd sat at Mum's dressing table in my parents' room. It was cold and had begun to smell of dusty radiators and long-stored bed linen. I picked up Mum's make-up brushes and inhaled the smell of her face powder. The lipstick I touched once, but the scent brought her back too clearly, kneeling in front of me and Martin, licking a handkerchief to clean dirt off our faces before primary school.

An ancient silver Corsa rumbled over the cobbles and pulled into the empty space in front of me. Stefan climbed out, shouted '*Na, Alter!*' and embraced me. He smelt different, like oil-fired stoves, incense and someone else's washing powder. 'I can't believe you're back,' I said. 'It's been weeks.'

'But here I am,' he said. He released me and stepped aside to show me the car. 'What do you think?'

'It's nice,' I said. 'Is it your dad's?'

Stefan shook his head. 'No, this one's all mine.'

I smiled. 'How did you afford it?'

'I've been saving up a bit. Mum lent me a bit. It was really cheap. It's got like 180,000 kilometres on the clock.'

'Is that bad?'

'Pretty bad. You want to go somewhere?'

'Where?'

'Over the border, maybe?'

'OK,' I said. 'I'll have to tell my aunt.'

We followed the route I'd last travelled by car with my parents. Stefan asked me how I was and after I'd said, 'Fine,' I didn't know what else to add. There was too much to say. I looked at the dark water of the canal as we crossed it and imagined what a shock the coldness of it would be if you jumped in, so cold it would be almost like heat. I imagined Martin in the back seat of our family car in November, shivering, knowing what was coming but not when it would come.

'Mum said your aunt's really nice.'

'She's all right,' I said, touching the thick plastic strap on the car's ceiling.

I looked at him. His hair looked strange, shaved slightly shorter than normal around the back and sides by a new hairdresser.

'What?' he said.

'You look different. Like Hanover's changed you.'

'It hasn't changed me. Not really. It's a bit more fun now, though.'

'I'm sorry I haven't visited, but it's been . . . '

'I know,' he said. 'What has it been like here, since November?'

'Not that much different on our side,' I said. 'You still see a few stunned Ossis down Ku'damm and you hear the Trabis before you see them, but mostly life just goes on as if nothing's really happened.'

'I meant since your parents got arrested.'

'Oh,' I said. 'Same I suppose. In a way.'

I felt a pain in my chest. It was disappointment that all of my secrets had now been revealed and yet there was still an insurmountable distance between the feelings I wanted to express to my friends and my ability to do so. Was this what it meant to be an adult? I thought, and felt sad.

There was a small queue at Checkpoint Charlie, where the border guards still half-heartedly checked IDs, but never turned anyone back any more. We drove up through Mitte, and looked at the brown concrete buildings in the dim ochre light. Bar the odd candle, the windows of the East were devoid of Christmas decorations.

'Is there even anywhere to go?' I said.

'Joachim told me about this jazz bar on Schönhauser Allee.'

'*Herrlich*,' I said.

The band hadn't started playing, but nearly all of the tables were full. A grumpy woman with large breasts and a Saxon accent took our order and we sat drinking Köstritzer on a bench with a wood-panelled back. Around the room, beneath an undulating cloud of smoke, were East German regulars, recognisable by their stiff shoes, imitation jeans and imitation leather bags, by their numerous shades of grey. But dotted between I saw Levis, Marlboro cigarettes and Puma trainers on other Wessies or Ossies who had already spent all of their welcome money on a few novel luxuries.

'Have you heard from Maike or Petra?' Stefan said.

'Yeah. Petra's fine, I think. The maths guy didn't work out. Then she had some sort of American boyfriend, who wasn't really a boyfriend. And Maike's got a boyfriend. A geophysicist.'

'Completely different to a geologist,' Stefan said.

'It is,' I said, and we laughed.

'And Oz?'

I stroked a square window in the condensation of my beer glass.

'No sign?' said Stefan.

I shook my head. 'Why didn't he just wait for me?'

'Maybe he couldn't. Or maybe it wasn't him.'

'Maybe,' I said, but I knew it was. And really I knew why he hadn't waited: he thought I'd rejected him again. I suspected he'd been following me ever since he'd left the clinic. In the chaos of the ninth of November he'd thought it was a chance to reveal himself. But I looked at him and then disappeared over the Wall and didn't come back. He would have waited a minute or so after I'd seen him, while I lay flat on my back behind the Wall, and then he would have turned and disappeared into the park to make a new life in our new country.

In the bathroom, I discovered that the architecture of the building was exactly the same as in the West. It was more battered, but the windows and doors, the double wooden frames, were all familiar to me, the handles were the same ones we had in our apartment. Of course the building was as old as mine, so it shouldn't have been a surprise, but I found it astounding, as if I'd discovered the dark side of the moon.

'When are you going to go to England?' Stefan said when I came back.

'I don't know,' I said. 'They're still holding my place at Durham, but ... I don't know now.'

'You can come to Hanover, Ralfi,' he said and pinched my cheek. I smiled at him. 'You always can,' he said, and I believed him.

A drunk with a Wolf Biermann moustache and a white T-shirt stretched drum-tight over his distended belly stopped on his way to the toilet and said, 'You know you can fuck on your side too. You don't have to come over here to do it.'

'That's a lovely sentiment,' I said.

The man nodded humourlessly and walked on.

Stefan dropped me off in Windscheidstraße. We hugged in the car and I waved him off and saw, as he was turning into Kantstraße, that beneath the largest tree in the street there was a green Mercedes. I walked over to it, but it was empty and there were no Gitanes in the ashtray.

In the apartment, the lights were off, except in the kitchen. I found Martin at the table, his school books opened out around him.

'This looks serious,' I said.

He looked up and smiled. 'Just geography.'

'Where's Auntie Linda?'

'She's gone to bed. She said she had to go back to England after Christmas. Did you know that?'

'Yeah,' I said.

'Do I have to go with her?'

I shivered and leant against the oven, putting my hands flat on the door, but it was cold. 'Do you want to go with her?'

'Not really,' Martin said. 'But if you're going to be at university, then ... ' He shrugged. 'And I don't want to be here on my own.'

I nodded. 'Well,' I said, 'I was thinking ... ' But I hadn't been thinking, the thought was coming to me in that moment. 'I was thinking I could keep my job at the shop maybe just for the next year and we could see if we could stay here. At least until you've done your GCSEs.'

'Oh,' he said. 'You don't have to.'

'I know,' I said. 'But it's better to start at Durham at the beginning of the year with everyone else and, I don't know, maybe it'll help to be working for a bit. The flat's still in Mum and Dad's name, so there's only the maintenance charge to pay. I don't know how much it is, but I guess it's only a few hundred Marks. If Linda can help, or Grandad ...'

'I could get a Saturday job, or something,' Martin said, with an enthusiasm that made me well up. I blinked as if I'd got something in my eye and put the kettle on. 'Sure,' I said, with my back to him.

'I'm going to have some coffee,' I said. 'You?'

'I won't sleep.'

'OK.'

The coffee tin was empty, so I took a new pack from the cupboard.

'Do you want to do the packet with me?' I said.

He nodded, put down his biro and held his hands out to grip the golden brick. I stabbed the foil with a pair of scissors and we smiled as the hard block softened, emitting its thick roasted smell.

The bell for the apartment rang, meaning that someone was at our door, rather than down on the street where the intercom was. Martin frowned and got up. He opened the door, but all I could see from the kitchen was the dark stairwell.

'Oh, it's you,' Martin said. 'The light's just here,' and he reached out and turned it on.

Forty-Three

The arrival and the departure of a glacier is a permanent cycle of concealment and revelation. The glacier's prodigious appetite is blind to weight, mass and genus, swallowing boulders, plants and animals, caught and slowly engorged – like a snake with an egg – and shifted thousands of miles from their place of origin.

Having retreated, the glacier leaves a raw battlefield, the rocks deeply scratched, the ground strewn with grey, glacial till. Often this jumble of forgotten rocks contains fossil hoards: trilobites, giant ferns and dinosaurs that tell the story of the life that once thrived there, a world of giant molluscs two metres wide that propelled themselves in tropical waters where now the ground is cold and bare.

But there is sunshine and water. There is wind carrying seedlings to the rock face, curious deer, goats and bears feeding and drinking, excreting, birds with fish eggs glued to their feet landing in ice-blue kettle lakes, paternoster lakes and tarns. The scant plants that take root die, soil forms, new forests grow on old rocks and are felled again. Cities, like Berlin, are built on the banks of the old rivers that cut through the young forest, they are sacked and rebuilt, divided and reunited.

There are a few plants, though, that were here when the

ice came and returned when it left. The ginkgo, for one, its frilly fanned leaves present as fossils in the rocks beneath our feet, and also in the park opposite the Schöneberg Town Hall, where JFK declared that he was a Berliner some fifty years ago and where, an hour ago, I got married.

Our daughters run past the ginkgo, indifferent to its heritage, plumping instead for the autumnal magic of the conkers a few metres further down the path. They crouch down and show them to Stefan, with whom they are both earnestly in love. Maike, who flew back from Berkeley specially, passes them with Petra, who is trying to speak to her old friend as her own children paw at her skirt-suit jacket. A few metres ahead, their respective husbands and wives talk conspiratorially, having long since formed their own independent clan, which they call The Fringe.

It's called *Zersetzung* – disintegration – what my father did to Oz, harassing and framing enemies of the state until you break them psychologically. Once the details were laid bare, it made it very difficult for me to have a relationship with Dad after he was released, despite his constant declarations of love and regret, his trembling hands touching my face every time I saw him.

In a way, he didn't really survive prison. Like many of the hundreds of thousands of people who worked for the Stasi in the West, he was prosecuted but quickly released. He had lost the pharmacy though, and sat in the flat shocked by the new world he found himself in. He wouldn't travel East, he wouldn't even travel to East Berlin. Instead, he lived as if the Wall were still up, ignored by old acquaintances in the shops and restaurants he still insisted on frequenting, until he was found dead at fifty on the footpath that links Berlin Zoo Train Station and the Schleusenkrug beer garden, where the air smells of cake and coffee and the dung of exotic animals.

364

We wondered briefly if it was an old enemy taking their revenge, but the autopsy said it was a simple heart attack. When they opened up the Stasi archives and I was able to read about who he really was – the son of a mechanic from Chemnitz – I discovered that heart disease ran in our family.

My mother was in love with my father until the end; after he died, she never remarried. She continued to work in a newly unified Germany and is popular with her patients. She should have retired by now, but can't bear the thought of doing nothing, so still has her practice and works two days a week. Her greatest sadness is Beate, who couldn't keep up their friendship after she found my father's name in her own Stasi files. He had been reporting on her and her artist friends for decades. Since my father died, a loose contact has been reconstituted, but there is so much that can't be spoken of that the intimacy seems to have been lost for good.

Alone now, my mother stops beneath the ginkgo tree, giving Martin her stick to hold. Martin's wife, heavily pregnant, stops up ahead, shielding her eyes from the sun to see what's happening.

Mum was upset that I hadn't organised flowers, saying that some traditions matter. Flowers in buttonholes are only a thing at English weddings, I told her, and anyway, I said, the law that allowed us to get married only came into force this week; five days is not long enough to form traditions. But she wouldn't be placated. She bends down and gathers a few yellow ginkgo leaves. 'You must have buttonholes at least,' she says, and tucks a bunch of them into Oz's lapel and another bunch into mine. 'Otherwise it's like you're pretending.' Oz's brother and sisters crowd around us and his father pinches my cheek with his thick fingers, which is the limit of his physical affection, but a limit I can live with.

Acknowledgements

If, like me, you have a tendency to flick through to the back matter of a book while you're in the middle of reading it and in doing so ruin the plot, then be warned: the section of these acknowledgements that deals with my research contains potential plot spoilers, so, if you haven't finished the novel yet, read on at your peril.

As ever, I am hugely indebted to my agent Karolina Sutton at Curtis Brown for her invaluable feedback on early drafts of this novel and her championing of my writing from the word go. I also owe a huge debt of thanks to my publisher Little, Brown, particularly Clare Smith, whose in-depth editorial engagement with all of my novels is an increasingly rare gift in today's publishing landscape. Thanks are also due to Hayley Camis for her fine publicity work on this book, as well as Sophia Schoepfer for her editorial support. A special thank you also to Steve Cox for his invaluable proofreading skills.

I would like to thank all of the early readers of the book, particularly my mum, Loraine Fergusson. And I would especially like to thank my husband Tom for his thoughtful reading of countless drafts as well as for his constant encouragement.

The particular joy of researching this final book in a cycle of three novels set in Berlin's Windscheidstraße 53 was that

I was dealing with living history. Many German friends and family members offered countless small insights that I've incorporated into the book, with my friend Michael Ammann providing a particularly rich seam of 1980s snacks, TV programmes, songs and cultural touchstones. And I would also like to thank Naciye O'Reilly for helping me with the Turkish details in the novel.

I was also able to talk to many people who had lived in the city during the 1980s and who were generous enough to give up their time for in-depth interviews about their experience of East and West Berlin. When I set out to research the book, I was hoping to get small cultural details to bring the narrative to life, but in each interview I also heard incredible stories that showed me again how the strands of European twentieth-century history always lead back to this very special city. For sharing their time and their stories with me, I would particularly like to thank Carola Adam, Jimmy Adam, Dr Frank Getzuhn, Fanny Melle, Linda Greenwood and David Greenwood.

As mentioned in my previous two novels, I am generally disapproving of detailed research bibliographies in fictional books, but at the same time want to acknowledge a few sources that were either particularly useful or that come highly recommended. Among the books, TV programmes and films from 1980s West Berlin that I was able to lay my hands on, I found Peter Schneider's book *The Wall Jumper* particularly valuable and pilfered a number of sights, sounds and smells from its pages. Of the photographic books on West Berlin, Christian Schulz's *Die wilden Achtziger* (The Wild Eighties), Herbert Maschke's *Wirtschaftswunder West-Berlin* and Günther Wessel's *Leben in West-Berlin* (Life in West Berlin) all had a profound influence on my descriptions of the city at that time. I also got a wonderful sense of West Berlin's countercultural scene from Mark Reeder's *B-Movie: Lust & Sound in West-Berlin 1979–1989*, which is available to buy and stream in most territories.

Anna Funder's excellent *Stasiland* gave me a great grounding in the complex psychology of the hundreds of thousands of men and women who informed on their friends and families, and I would highly recommend it if you haven't yet read it. I am also indebted to Marianne Quoirin's *Agentinnen aus Liebe: Warum Frauen für den Osten Spionierten* (Agents of Love: Why Women Spied for the East) for her detailed account of the women in the West who wittingly married East German spies and colluded in their work. The book is sadly out of print and hasn't been translated into English, but can be found at research libraries. While finishing my book, I also serendipitously caught Peter Wensierski's excellent documentary on the Stasi informant Monika Haeger for Rundfunk Berlin-Brandenburg, and I used a number of details from her background in the German Democratic Republic for the background of my Stasi spy.

And finally, among the environmental and geological books and texts I read I feel particularly fortunate to have unearthed *Natürlich Berlin! Naturschutz- und NATURA 2000-Gebiete in Berlin* (Naturally Berlin: Nature and NATURA 2000 Reserves in Berlin), an unbelievably detailed summation of Berlin's nature reserves and the creatures that inhabit them. If you ever need to find a diving-bell spider in West Berlin, this is the book for you.

If you are visiting Berlin and are interested in finding out more about this period, there is a series of displays about the fall of the Wall in the German Historical Museum's permanent display. The Berlin Wall Memorial at Bernauer

Straße also has a very accessible new visitor centre and real sections of the Berlin Wall that you can visit. I would encourage you, however, to go a little further afield and visit the Tränenpalast (The Palace of Tears) at Friedrichstraße, the Berlin-Hohenschönhausen Prison for GDR political prisoners, and the Stasi Museum, both in Lichtenberg, as well as the Marienfelde Refugee Centre Museum. All offer excellent tours and displays and give you a real sense of the human impact of the Cold War in Berlin from both sides of the divide.

Much of my reading for the book was done at Berlin State Library on both Potsdamer Platz and Under den Linden, as well as the Jacob-und-Wilhelm-Grimm-Zentrum at Humboldt University, and I would like to thank the staff at both institutions for their help whenever I needed it.